P9-DBY-416

Praise for *COLD BETRAYAL*

"Incredible. . . . This is a gem by a winning author. . . . Yet another terrific book by Jance that fans and readers will absolutely cheer about."

—*Suspense Magazine*

"Lively. . . . Jance knows how to tell a story . . . series fans won't be disappointed."

—*Publishers Weekly*

"Ali's good heart and sense of justice combine with well-paced suspense to create a satisfying whole."

—*Kirkus Reviews*

"It's about time that Jance got props from literary as well as thriller readers. . . . Jance's plots are less about violence, more about family, problem solving, and individual character. They are always page turners."

—*Examiner.com*

MOVING TARGET

"Jance adroitly combines well-rounded characterizations and brisk storytelling with high-tech exploits, arson, kidnappings, and a shootout for an entertaining and suspenseful addition to this solid series."

—*Booklist*

"Crisp plotting, sharp characters, and realistic dialogue carry *Moving Target* through its many surprising twists."

—*South Florida Sun-Sentinel*

"Engrossing. . . . Jance provides enough backstory to orient readers new to the series, and longtime fans should enjoy insights into B.'s and Leland's pasts."

—*Publishers Weekly*

DEADLY STAKES

"Jance melds elements of the thriller and police procedural with a touch of romance to carry readers swiftly to an unexpected conclusion."

—*Kirkus Reviews*

"Jance's story is well-crafted and keeps one's interest to its final word. . . . The rapidly moving story makes it a fascinating mystery, full of multiple suspects and numerous possibilities."

—*Bookreporter*

LEFT FOR DEAD

"Jance at her best . . . engaging, exciting, and fast-paced."

—*Tucson Citizen*

"A truly thrilling case with red herrings, characters coming out of the woodwork, backstories that will make you gasp, and a conclusion that you will not see coming!"

—*Suspense Magazine*

"Entertaining on all counts."

—*Booklist*

"Loyal fans and newcomers alike will be glad to join feisty Ali in her latest adventure."

—*Kirkus Reviews*

FATAL ERROR

"The plot never stalls."

—*Publishers Weekly*

"An entertaining mix of sleuthing and human relationships."

—*Booklist*

"Jance continues to delight with her detail-filled suspense stories that capture so much of life."

—*Library Journal*

TRIAL BY FIRE

"Fast pacing, surprising plot twists, and a strong, principled heroine."

—*Booklist*

"Fans will not be disappointed with this new novel. It's a page turner."

—*Green Valley News and Sun*

CRUEL INTENT

"Compelling . . . satisfying."

—*USA Today*

"A fast-paced read with as many twists and turns as a county fair roller coaster."

—*Seattle Post-Intelligencer*

"Jance has honed her talent for writing entertaining, accessible mysteries that readers can zip through."

—*Booklist*

ALSO BY J.A. JANCE

J.A. JANCE

COLD BETRAYAL

Pocket Books

New York   London   Toronto   Sydney   New Delhi

Pocket Books
An Imprint of Simon & Schuster, Inc.
1230 Avenue of the Americas
New York, NY 10020

This book is a work of fiction. Any references to historical events, real people, or real places are used fictitiously. Other names, characters, places, and events are products of the author's imagination, and any resemblance to actual events or places or persons, living or dead, is entirely coincidental.

First Pocket Books paperback edition January 2016

POCKET and colophon are registered trademarks of Simon & Schuster, Inc.

For information about special discounts for bulk purchases, please contact Simon & Schuster Special Sales at 1-866-506-1949 or business@simonandschuster.com.

The Simon & Schuster Speakers Bureau can bring authors to your live event. For more information or to book an event contact the Simon & Schuster Speakers Bureau at 1-866-248-3049 or visit our website at www.simonspeakers.com.

Manufactured in the United States of America

10 9 8 7 6 5 4 3 2 1

ISBN 978-1-4767-4506-0
ISBN 978-1-4767-4507-7(ebook)

To J. B., perhaps you'll see yourself in this.

She threw that into the bag, along with
a scissors, needle and thread.

—FROM "MOLLY WHUPPIE" BY WALTER DE LA MARE

Prologue

As the snow started to fall in thick, feathery flakes, Betsy Peterson, seated in front, checked the tension in the seat belt against her collarbone, clutched her purse to her chest, and peered out through the headlights into the dark night. Marcia Lawson was a good driver, but a fast one. She seemed to be under the impression that just because she was driving a four-wheel-drive Kia, an older and decidedly dilapidated model, she didn't need to worry about road conditions.

It wasn't that Betsy was particularly concerned about the snow. Eighty-plus years of living through Minnesota winters had seen to that, but she had a healthy respect for ice, and that was the problem. A week of unseasonably warm temperatures had been followed by freezing rain, leaving a thick layer of ice coating the small country road that led to her farm. And she was right to be worried. As they approached the turnoff on Grange Road, Betsy knew Marcia was going far too fast. They skidded past the turnoff and came within inches of taking out a pair of mailboxes before finally coming to rest on the shoulder of the road.

"Sorry about that," Marcia muttered, slamming the gearshift into reverse and shooting back onto the narrow ribbon of iced-over pavement. "It's times like this when four-wheel drive comes in handy."

Betsy said nothing. Now that a combination of cataracts and macular degeneration made it impossible for her to drive anymore, Betsy had to count on the kindness of friends and relations to get her to and from wherever she needed to go. For decades Marcia had been Betsy's hairdresser. Once Marcia closed up shop and retired, she came to Betsy's home once a week to do her hair while also supplementing her meager retirement by ferrying people around and running errands as needed. In this case, she was driving Betsy home from Monday Night Bingo at the local VFW.

Monday Night Bingo, along with her lifetime membership at Bemidji's First Lutheran Church, were Betsy's main social outlets. She went to church on Sunday, Bible study on Tuesday, and Prayer Group on Wednesday. On Fridays she had Marcia come do her hair before the VFW's weekly evening fish fry. At bingo and at the fish fries, Betsy allowed herself a single sloe gin fizz. After all, those were her only purely social activities.

As far as bingo was concerned, it didn't hurt that her old high school beau, Howard Hansen—still Dr. Hansen, even though he no longer practiced, and now a widower twice over—came to both bingo and the fish fries, with a group bused in from the Sundowner's Assisted Living Center. He teased her about being too stubborn to give up living alone and dropped hints that it would be slick if she'd consent to taking up residence in his two-room "suite," always allowing as how he'd be willing to marry her if need be in order to keep her from living in sin. She liked the twinkle in his eye when he said those things.

Other people in the room might think he was just joshing her, but she knew there was more to it than that. Yes, he was teasing, but he also meant it. After their high school romance came undone, they had both gone on to love and marry other people, but the connection forged by young love remained a glowing ember in both their lives.

"I'm sick and tired of these Minnesota winters," Marcia was saying. "My one daughter keeps inviting me to come live with her in Florida, but I don't think I could handle all that heat and humidity. Besides, she takes care of her four grandkids when her daughter is at work. I definitely couldn't handle living in that kind of chaos."

Again Betsy said nothing. Her own son, Jimmy, was a dentist right here in Bemidji, but she wouldn't live with him on a bet, not ever, because living with him would also mean living with his wife, Sandra—never to be referred to as Sandy, by the way—who could charitably be referred to as a ring-tailed bitch. That was one reason Betsy didn't want to move into assisted living in town. Being in town meant that she would be living that much closer to Jimmy and Sandra, giving them that much more opportunity to stick their very unwelcome noses into her business.

Betsy's granddaughter, Athena, had made it clear that Betsy was welcome to come live with her family in Sedona. Betsy adored Athena, and her husband, Chris, was clearly a treasure. Their twins, Colin and Colleen, were cute as buttons, but when it came to living with little kids, Betsy was on the same page as Marcia. Having grandkids and great-grandkids come to visit was great—

twins were especially good when it came to bragging rights over bingo cards—but living under the same roof with them? Nope, that wasn't gonna happen.

"I'd hate it if you moved away," Betsy said. "If I didn't have you to take me back and forth to bingo, I wouldn't have any idea about what's really going on in town."

For Betsy, playing bingo was the least important part of going. Gossip was the central purpose of those Monday night gatherings: whose kid had been sent to jail or gotten out of jail; whose grandson had joined the Marines; whose granddaughter had staged a big church wedding even though her baby bump was clearly visible to all concerned; whose daughter had been picked up for dealing drugs in Minneapolis. All those little tidbits were grist for the bingo gossip mill.

"It's a shame about Tess Severson's older son," Marcia added. "This has to be the fourth or fifth time he's been through rehab. Maybe this time it'll take."

"I hope so," Betsy said. "It's got to be tough on his wife and kids."

"I'll say," Marcia agreed. "Why his wife sticks with him is more than I can understand."

With that, Marcia turned onto Last Road, the one that led to Betsy's farm. For a long time their road had been the last road, but the name had become official only a few years earlier when all the country lanes, most of which had been nameless before, were assigned names. Sometime after that, the intersecting road was extended as far as the new gravel pit. At that point, Last Road had stopped being last, but the name stuck.

Betsy's late husband, Alton, had loved having Last Road as part of their official mailing address, and it had certainly been the last road for him. Betsy suspected that despite Howard's sly invitation, Last Road would most likely be the last one for her, too. She had scattered Alton's ashes on the farm, and that was where Betsy had asked to have her own ashes scattered as well. At least that's what it said in the final directions part of her will, right along with her Do Not Resuscitate directive.

"Here we are," Marcia said, turning into the driveway and skidding to a stop in front of the house. The snow was already starting to stick. Betsy knew that beneath that thin crust of snow was a thick base coat of ice that would make for treacherous walking. She had meant to ask Harold, her next-door neighbor and general handyman, to come by and apply deicer to the walkway after that last bout of freezing rain, but she hadn't quite gotten around to it. Before she left for bingo, she had left the porch light switched on, and the lamps in the living room were lit as well. Leaving lights on when they were away for an evening was the kind of extravagance Alton never would have tolerated. Tonight, though, Betsy was glad the house looked warm and welcoming through the falling snow.

"Thank you for the ride," she said as she opened the car door and got out.

As Betsy tottered carefully around the vehicle, Marcia rolled down her window. "Want some help with those steps?"

"No, thanks. I'll be fine."

"I'll wait until you're inside all the same."

Marcia was good to her word. She waited patiently in the idling vehicle while Betsy carefully inched her way up the slippery sidewalk and then used the handrail to haul her protesting body up the front steps. She could have used the wheelchair ramp, but with the ice, the zigzag layout would have made for a longer and possibly even more hazardous walk. Crossing the front porch, she pushed the key into the lock. Then, before opening the door, she paused long enough to use the key-fob control to shut off the alarm.

Jimmy and Sandra had given her the alarm system and had it installed as a Christmas present two years ago. Betsy despised the annoying beeping sound it made—not unlike the obnoxious racket her hearing aids made whenever she turned them on or changed the batteries. As a consequence she always tried to turn the alarm off before she entered the house. Once inside, she turned back and waved at Marcia, then stood in the open doorway and watched until the Kia's departing taillights faded into the snowy darkness.

After closing and locking the door, Betsy dropped her keys into the bowl on the entryway table and put her purse on the shelf in the coat closet. Still wearing her coat, however, she went to the laundry room to rescue Princess.

Living alone in the country, especially now that she could no longer drive, was inconvenient. It would have been incredibly lonely had it not been for the presence of her beloved and very spoiled long-haired miniature dachshund. Princess was the other reason Betsy Peterson couldn't and wouldn't move into assisted living. Sundowner's Assisted Living in Bemidji didn't take dogs.

Princess suffered from what the vet called separation anxiety and wasn't entirely trustworthy if given the run of the house in Betsy's absence. Locking the dog in a laundry room equipped with food, water, and her favorite bed limited the amount of damage Princess could do. After picking the squirming little dog up and being given an ecstatic whimpered greeting, Betsy fastened the retractable leash on Princess's collar, and then stood in the doorway while the dog went to the far end of the leash to do her business.

Betsy had considered installing a doggie door but had given up on the idea. She had heard of too many instances where other critters, raccoons mostly, had let themselves inside houses and done plenty of damage. Due to Princess's tiny size and the many predators roaming the nearby woods, the dog was never allowed outside without being on a leash.

Once back inside, Betsy removed her coat and hung it in the entryway closet. Then she went through the house, turning down thermostats and shutting off lights. She kept the bedroom door closed and the thermostat in there turned off. Betsy and Princess both slept far better in a chilly bedroom than in a warm one.

By the time Betsy undressed and took out her hearing aids, Princess had already burrowed her way to the far end of Betsy's duvet, where she functioned as a living foot warmer. Snuggling under the covers, Betsy turned on her iPad and read a few pages in the most recent Mma Ramotswe story before turning off the device as well as her bedside lamp and falling asleep.

She was awakened sometime later by Princess, who was whining piteously and licking her ear. The glowing hands on the bedside clock said it was ten past one. Betsy was a little surprised that Princess would need to go back outside so soon. Usually she could make it through the night without a problem. Sighing, Betsy climbed out of bed, pulled on her robe, and headed for the door.

As soon as she opened the bedroom door, Betsy smelled gas. Gas? The whole house seemed to be full of it. How was that possible? Where was it coming from? With her heart pounding wildly inside her chest, Betsy raced toward the kitchen, limping as fast as her arthritic feet would allow. She entered the room and switched on the overhead light. Even without her hearing aids, she heard the ominous hissing of the unlit burners on her gas stove top.

Alton had insisted that pilot lights used too much of the LP gas kept stored in a tank outside the kitchen wall. Even though her husband was long gone, Betsy still had the same pilotless stove top he had bought for her and that necessitated the use of matches to light the gas ring burners.

Rushing to the stove top, Betsy twisted the knobs to shut off the gas. Then, coughing and choking on the foul-smelling stuff, she staggered through the laundry room to the back door and flung it wide open. The instant the door opened, Princess slipped between her legs and tore outside, into the yard and up to her belly in six inches of new-fallen snow.

"Princess, come here!" Betsy yelled.

Most of the time, Princess would have ignored her and gone in the opposite direction. This time, the desperation in Betsy's voice must have impacted the dog. She stopped where she was and waited. Terrified and heedless of the danger of slipping, Betsy limped down the steps, scooped up the dog, and then hurried, barefoot, to the far end of the yard. Standing with her bare feet ankle deep in freezing snow was nothing short of agony. Still, she stood there shivering for what seemed like forever, holding her equally shivering dog and waiting to see if the house would be blown to smithereens.

She may have been there for one minute or five, but

in the end nothing at all happened. By then the snow had quit. Around her the night was still and quiet. The sky had cleared and the moon was out, revealing a layer of unblemished snow as far as Betsy could see.

Her fingers strayed briefly to the Medical Alert medallion Jimmy and Sandra had given her for Christmas. "You can't be out there in the country all by yourself without some way of contacting help," her son had insisted. "What if you fell and couldn't get up?"

Betsy supposed he had been genuinely concerned about her. Unfortunately, Betsy regarded that remark as another stab at her independence. Ever since Christmas, however, Betsy had worn the medallion dutifully, if under protest, because she knew that if she ran into either her son or daughter-in-law while she was out and about and they discovered she wasn't wearing it, there would be hell to pay. Wearing it meant less trouble than not wearing it.

Now, touching the medallion with her chilled fingers, she considered hitting the Medical Alert button, but she hesitated. After all, thanks to Princess, this wasn't a medical problem. What Betsy really needed was her cell phone so she could dial 911. The trouble was, her phone was still in the bedroom on the nightstand next to her iPad and her clock.

Eventually Betsy's breathing steadied and her heart stopped pounding. If she was going to suffer a heart attack, it would have already happened. As her breathing calmed, so did her brain. Who had turned on the burners? How had someone come into her house without her hearing them? Yes, she wasn't wearing her hearing aids, but still. Why hadn't Princess alerted her? The bedroom door had been closed, but a closed door was not a deterrent to a dachshund's nose.

As for the burners? Betsy was sure they hadn't been on when she went to bed. Someone must have come into her house while she was asleep and turned them on. Looking down at the dog in her arms, Betsy realized gratefully that Princess had most likely saved both their lives.

"Treats for you, baby girl," Betsy promised, hugging the dog closer, "but only after we call the cops."

Her feet were freezing. Knowing she wouldn't be able to walk if she stayed outside any longer and hoping that the open door would have allowed some of the gas to dissipate, Betsy limped back into the house and placed the 911 call from the landline phone on the kitchen wall.

"Nine-one-one, what are you reporting?"

"Someone just tried to kill me," Betsy managed, speaking into the phone.

"Pardon me?" the operator asked.

Damn, Betsy thought. Had her teeth been in her mouth, they probably would have been chattering. As it was, they were still soaking in a dish on the bathroom counter. No wonder the emergency operator hadn't understood what she said.

"Just a minute," Betsy muttered.

"Wait," the operator was saying. "Come back."

By then Betsy had already dropped the phone. She left it hanging there, dangling on the cord, while she hobbled on pins-and-needle feet back to the bathroom. She retrieved her teeth, rinsed them, and shoved them into her mouth. When Alton had insisted on installing a telephone on the wall in the bathroom next to the toilet, Betsy had objected on the grounds of simple decency. Now, glad it was there, she grabbed the receiver.

"Ma'am," the operator said. "Are you injured?"

"No, I'm not," Betsy said, "but it's not for lack of trying. Somebody just tried to kill me. Whoever it was came into the house while I was asleep and turned on the gas burners on my kitchen stove. If Princess hadn't awakened me . . ."

"Is the assailant still in the house?"

"No, just me and my dog. No one else is here. Whoever did it left before I woke up."

"Are you all right? Do you require medical assistance?"

"Would I be talking to you on the phone if I wasn't all right?" Betsy snapped, growing impatient. She was still chilled to the bone, and she resented being asked the same question over and over. "Of course, I'm all right. I want you to send a deputy. This is an attempted murder, and I intend to report it as such."

"All right," the operator agreed. "I'm sending a deputy to your location right now."

Deputy Raymond Severson, who showed up half an hour later, was Tess Severson's other son—the one not currently in rehab. Raymond was nice enough, but very young. He looked like he was barely out of high school. Betsy couldn't help but wish they'd sent someone older and more experienced.

"What seems to be the problem, Mrs. Peterson?" Deputy Severson asked, stamping loose snow from his boots on the front porch while Princess danced circles around his feet, barking her head off. Betsy picked up the dog and tried, unsuccessfully, to quiet her.

"As I told the 911 operator, someone came into my house while I was asleep, turned on the gas burners on my stove, and left them running without lighting them,"

Betsy explained. "Whoever did it tried to kill me and would have succeeded if Princess here hadn't woken me up. When I opened the bedroom door, the whole house reeked of gas. If I'd had a gas hot water heater instead of an electric one, the whole house might have blown sky high."

"You're saying whoever did this broke in?" Deputy Severson asked.

Betsy wasn't feeling especially charitable about then. "How would I know how he got in?" she demanded. "Isn't that your job?"

For the next hour or so, Severson took his time examining the locks on the front and back doors and peering at the windows both inside and out. The locks on the doors appeared to be undamaged. None of the windows were broken, either.

Betsy had used the time before the deputy's arrival to give Princess a treat and towel her dry; then she put in her hearing aids and got dressed—complete with a pair of thick wool socks over her still tingling feet. In the time that was left, she, too, had checked for signs of a break-in and had found nothing amiss—not one thing.

"No sign of a break-in," Deputy Severson concluded at last after completing his outdoor inspection and coming back into the house. "You believe the doors were locked?" he asked.

Betsy nodded. "I know they were," she said.

"That means that if someone entered the house without your knowledge, they must have used a key. Does anyone besides you have a key to the residence?"

"My son has one, of course. At my age, there's always a chance of waking up dead and someone would have to come get me, but Jimmy wouldn't turn on the burners and risk burning the house down. That's utterly ridiculous."

"There's another problem here."

"What's that?"

"There's only one set of tire tracks in the driveway, Mrs. Peterson, and those belong to my patrol car. I can't see any sign that anyone else has been here, although there is one set of bare footprints coming and going from the back door."

"Those are mine," Betsy told him. "After I turned off the gas, Princess and I went outside."

"In your bare feet?" Deputy Severson asked, peering at her closely.

"Of course I went out in my bare feet. If the house was about to blow up, I wasn't going to waste time going back to the bedroom for my shoes. That would have been nuts."

"I suppose so, Mrs. Peterson, but unfortunately, that leaves us with only one other possibility."

"What's that?"

The deputy sighed. "Is there a chance you turned the burners on yourself and just don't remember doing it? Maybe you were going to make yourself a hot drink before you went to bed and then changed your mind."

Furious, Betsy leveled a withering look in his direction. "My dear boy," she said scathingly, "I do occasionally make myself a cup of cocoa before bed, but when I do so, I use only one burner at a time, never all four at once."

"It's been cold as hell all week," he suggested, perhaps still hoping to give her an ego-soothing way out. "You said you were in town earlier this evening. Maybe you turned the burners on after you came home in hopes of warming the place up."

"I'll have you know the house was already warm when I came home from bingo," she fumed. "And why on earth would I turn on the stove burners to warm up the kitchen when I have a perfectly functioning thermostat right there on the wall? If the room had been cold—which it wasn't—that would have been a completely inefficient way getting the job done. I may be old, Deputy Severson," she added, "but I'm certainly not stupid."

"Yes, ma'am," the deputy agreed. "Of course not. Is there anything else I can do for you?"

"Yes," she told him. "You can go straight out to your car, get your crime scene kit, and dust the kitchen for prints. I want to know who turned on those burners."

"I'm sorry, Mrs. Peterson," Deputy Severson replied. "That's not up to me. My job is to turn in a report. Once I do that, someone upstairs decides if any further investigation is warranted. If that happens, the CSI team wouldn't be here until much later this morning. As for the knobs on the stove? I wouldn't count on their finding anything. After all, you turned off the burners yourself."

"You let the sheriff know that I expect someone to show up here to go over the kitchen and the rest of the house as well," Betsy said, escorting him to the door. "And I expect them to be here bright and early."

She slammed the door shut behind him. And then, just for good measure, she turned the alarm back on before she went back to bed. She didn't sleep.

1

Would you care for coffee, madame?"

Ali Reynolds glanced up from her file-littered desk as the French doors between her library office and the living room swung open. Leland Brooks, her aging majordomo, entered the room carrying a rosewood tray laden with a coffeepot as well as cups and saucers for two. It had taken years for Ali to convince Leland that when it was just the two of them at home alone, their sharing a cup or two of midmorning coffee wasn't some terrible breach of employer/employee etiquette.

"Yes, please," Ali said, rising from the desk as he placed the tray on the coffee table set in front of the burning gas-log fireplace. Before she could settle into one of the room's two upholstered wingback chairs, she had to move her recently acquired miniature dachshund, Bella, to one side.

Bella, an unexpected wedding surprise, had been found abandoned in a hotel parking lot in Las Vegas. Ali and B. Simpson, her new husband, had taken time away from their wedding activities to locate the dog's owner, a woman named Harriet Reid. After suffering a debilitating stroke, Harriet had left her beloved dog in the care of her ne'er-do-well son, Martin, who not only had mistreated the dog—locking her in a closet by day and in his garage by night—but also had abandoned her, shoving the terrified creature out of a moving vehicle and speeding away in the midst of a busy parking lot. Only lightning-quick action on the part of Ali's grandson, Colin, had saved the dog from certain death.

At the time Bella was found, she'd had no collar or tag, but she had been chipped. Unfortunately, the phone number listed in the chip company's records led to a disconnected telephone line. Undaunted, B. had utilized the talents of his second in command at High Noon Enterprises, Stuart Ramey, to locate the dog's ailing owner. In the process, they discovered that not only had the son mistreated the dog left in his care, he also was systematically emptying his mother's bank accounts. An anonymous tip to an elder abuse hotline had put a stop to that.

Bella had been part of B. and Ali's family for just under three months. In the beginning, unused to having a short dog underfoot, they'd had to resort to putting a bell on her collar. With persistent effort, they had convinced her to spend at least part of the night sleeping on a chair positioned next to their bed rather than in the bed itself. During the day, Bella's preferred place to be was on a chair anywhere her people were. In this case, since Ali was working in the library, Bella was there, too.

With Bella's long body stretched out between Ali's thigh and the arm of the chair, Ali waited while Leland poured coffee. She noticed that his hand shook slightly as he passed the cup and saucer. The delicately shaped Limoges Beleme cup jiggled a bit, but not so much that any of the coffee spilled into the saucer.

Ali was glad Leland had seen fit to use her "good" dishes. Her mother's good china had been displayed but mostly untouched from the time her parents married until they moved into an active-retirement community. At that time the whole set, with only a single dinner plate missing, had been passed along to their grandson, Ali's son, Christopher. Chris and his wife, Athena, with two young twins in the house, didn't use their inherited dishes for everyday, either. Ali suspected the set would be passed on to yet another generation still mostly unbroken and unused.

Leland, seeming to notice the tremor, too, frowned as he set his own jittering cup and saucer down on the glass-topped table.

"Sorry about having the shakes like that," he muttered self-consciously. "Comes with age, I suppose."

"It does," Ali said with a smile as Leland settled into the matching chair opposite her own. "In that case, you've earned those tremors in spades."

In a very real way, eightysomething Leland had come with the house on Manzanita Hills Road in Sedona, Arizona. He had served in the same majordomo capacity for decades for the house's two previous owners, Anna Lee Ashcroft, and her troubled daughter, Arabella. When Ali had purchased the aging midcentury modern home with the intention of rehabbing it, Leland had stayed on to oversee the complicated task of bringing the place back to its original glory. That remodeling project was now years in the past. Once it was completed, Leland had also played a vital role in creating the lush English garden out front—a garden Anna Lee had once envisioned but never managed to bring to fruition.

Years past what should have been retirement age, Leland simply refused to be put out to pasture. Ali had seen to it that the heavy lifting of cleaning and gardening were now done by younger folks. Leland stayed on, making sure those jobs were done to his stringent standards, but he had yet to relinquish control of his personally custom-designed kitchen to anyone else. There Leland Brooks still reigned supreme.

"How's it going?" he asked.

Ali glanced over her shoulder at the scatter of files that littered her desk. They contained information on students from various Verde Valley high schools, all of whom had been nominated as possible recipients of that year's Amelia Dougherty Scholarship. The scholarship was named in honor of Anna Lee Ashcroft's mother, and students receiving those highly sought awards would have the benefit of a four-year full-ride scholarship to the in-state institution of higher learning of their choice. Years earlier Ali herself had been the first-ever recipient of an Amelia Dougherty Scholarship. Now, through a strange set of circumstances, she was in charge of administering the program from which she had once benefited.

The rules of the award stated that the recipient had to have graduated from a high school in the Verde Valley. At the time Ali had been granted her award, there had been only one of those—Mingus Mountain High in Cottonwood. Now there were three, all of them with scores of deserving students.

Knowing that she held the futures of some of those students in her hands, Ali took her selection responsibilities seriously. In the beginning, Amelia Dougherty scholarships had been awarded to female students only. Ali had widened the scope to include both boys and girls, making her selection task that much more complicated.

Teachers at the various schools were encouraged to nominate students for the award. Once the recipient was chosen, he or she would be invited to tea at Ali's home—usually toward the end of March or early in April—to receive the award in the same way Ali had been given hers, at a celebratory afternoon tea. Awarding the scholarships that early in the academic year gave recipients who might otherwise not have attempted to enroll in college a chance to do so. In the past several years Ali had expanded the tea attendees to include as many previous recipients as were able to attend.

This year a total of seventy-three nominations had come through the application pipeline. Leland, operating as Ali's boots-on-the-ground intel agent, had tracked down information on all the nominees and she had winnowed those down to the twenty-four files that were now on her desk. Ali had spent days conducting personal interviews with the last ten finalists. This morning she had been up for hours poring over the individual files. All the students were deserving. Much as she wanted to help all of them, there was a limited amount of money at her disposal. One by one she had moved most of the files into what she called the "almost but not quite" heap. At this point only two remained in the semifinal category.

"It's been slow going," she admitted, "but I'm almost there."

On the surface, Sedona was considered to be both a tourist mecca as well as an enclave of privilege, but the downturn in the economy had taken a huge bite out of the tourism industry in Sedona just as it had everywhere else. The people who had been hit hardest were the "locals"—the blue-collar workers who waited tables, cleaned hotel rooms, tended bars, manicured yards, and worked in kitchens. Many had lost their livelihoods, their homes, and, in some cases, all hopes for their children's futures. Ali had it within her power to make a huge difference in someone's life.

Leland nodded sympathetically. "I don't envy your having to choose," he said, "but results are the final judge. Your previous choices have been nothing short of remarkable."

That was true. Ali's very first scholarship recipient had graduated magna cum laude and was now a second-year teacher down in Phoenix. The next year's choice, due to graduate in May, had already been accepted into law school, having found additional scholarships to help pay for her graduate studies. None of Ali's recipients had dropped out of school, and they had all maintained high enough GPAs to continue in the program from year to year. Two were working on nursing and premed programs at the University of Arizona in Tucson.

"Any front-runners at the moment?" Leland asked.

Ali stood up, retrieved the two semifinalist folders, and sat back down with them in hand.

"Natalie Droman," she said, reading the name off the top file.

Leland nodded knowledgeably. "The girl from Cottonwood whose father has been diagnosed with ALS. Considering your own history with ALS, that's only to be expected. On the other hand, Natalie is an exceptional student regardless of what's going on in her family."

Years earlier, long before Ali had met Leland, her best friend from high school, Misty Irene Bernard, had died in a one-car motor vehicle accident when her aging Yukon had taken a deadly plunge off a snowbound cliff on Schnebly Hill Road. Because Reenie had been diagnosed with ALS a short time prior to the incident, her death had been categorized as a suicide until Ali had managed to prove otherwise.

She looked questioningly at Leland. "You have an encyclopedic knowledge of each of these kids, don't you?"

"I do my best," he agreed.

"And you're right," Ali added. "Natalie is an exceptional student."

"And the other one?"

Ali smiled and waved the remaining file in Leland's direction. "That would be your personal favorite, I presume," she answered. "Mr. Raphael Fuentes."

Athena, Ali's daughter-in-law who taught math at Sedona High School, had been the first of three teachers to nominate Raphael. His parents were divorced. His mother, left with three kids to raise, struggled to make ends meet with the help of sporadic child support and what she earned working as a receptionist in a small insurance agency. Raphael's father, whose engineering career and income had been seriously impacted by "outsourcing" was, as a result, unable to help his son financially, but he was nonetheless in the picture enough to pressure Raphael about going after an engineering degree.

There were several serious problems with that. Although Raphael was a good kid, his math skills were mediocre at best, and he had zero interest in engineering. His heart's desire was to attend Cordon Bleu and become a chef, a goal that his mother liked but couldn't help him achieve and one his father regarded with derision.

"Considering your own history," Ali added, mimicking what Leland had said earlier, "it's not too surprising that you'd be rooting for Raphael."

Leland Brooks knew as much as anyone about swimming against the tide of parental disapproval. His interest in cooking wasn't the only reason he had joined the Royal Marines as soon as he was old enough to sign up. He had spent most of the Korean War serving as a cook and had devoted his lifetime since then to honing his cooking skills and using them to good effect.

"I would like the lad to have an opportunity to better himself," Leland said. "But, of course, your policy has always been that the scholarships go to students attending a state-run college or university. Unfortunately, even though there's a Cordon Bleu branch in Scottsdale, it's nonetheless a private institution."

"It is private," Ali agreed. "But it's also a two-year program as opposed to a four-year one, making the total cash outlay not that different."

"I'm sorry," Leland apologized. "I shouldn't presume to lobby one way or the other."

"Why not?" Ali said with a laugh. "You've been part of this process since the very beginning, first for Anna Lee and Arabella and lately for me. Why shouldn't I have the benefit of your opinion?"

"It's not my place," he said.

"It is if I say so," Ali countered. "So how about if you set about issuing invitations to the tea?"

"Invitations as in plural?" Leland inquired.

"Yes," Ali said, making up her mind. "You've convinced me. This year we'll award two scholarships—one to Natalie and one to Raphael."

"Excellent," Leland said enthusiastically, standing up and gathering the coffee cups. "I'll consult your calendar and see to it right away. I assume you'd like me to use the Montblanc stationery Mr. Simpson gave you for Christmas?"

"Yes, please," she said. "And use my pen, too. You're far better at using fountain pens than I am."

Ali's cell phone rang just then, and her daughter-in-law's name appeared in the caller ID screen.

"Hey, Athena," Ali said when she answered. "What's up?"

"I need your help." Ali was surprised to hear Athena sounding close to tears. An Iraqi War vet and a double amputee, Ali's daughter-in-law was not the tearful type.

"Why?" Ali asked. "Is something wrong?"

"I just got off the phone with my grandmother," Athena said. "Gram has always been my rock. I've never heard her as upset as she was just now on the phone."

"What's going on?"

"Gram says someone tried to kill her last night. Someone came into her house while she was asleep. They turned on the gas burners on her kitchen stove without lighting them. The whole house filled up with gas. If it hadn't been for Princess, Gram's little dog, they both might be dead by now."

"Look," Ali said, "if we're talking attempted homicide here, your grandmother needs to report the incident to a local law enforcement agency and let them investigate it."

"That's part of the problem," Athena answered. "She already did that—at least she tried to. They pretty much told her she's nuts. They claim she's so old and frail that she probably turned the burners on herself and doesn't remember doing it. They didn't even bother sending someone out to check for prints. You've met Gram. Did she strike you as nuts?"

Ali did know Athena's grandmother. In fact, Betsy Peterson was the only member of Athena's family who had bothered to show up for Chris and Athena's wedding. Athena was estranged from her parents, Jim and Sandra, who, in the aftermath of Athena's divorce, had, for some strange reason, cast their lot with their former son-in-law along with his new wife and baby.

The summer following Chris and Athena's wedding, soon after discovering they were expecting, the newly-weds had taken a trip to Minnesota. Ali had hoped that the visit, including the prospect of the fast-approaching arrival of grandchildren, would help smooth over what-ever had caused the estrangement. The hoped-for rec-onciliation hadn't happened, and the arrival of the twins had made no difference in the status quo, either. Ali had never been made privy to the gory details of the trip to Bemidji. Once Chris and Athena returned to Sedona, they had been completely closemouthed about it. Ali gathered from their silence on the topic that things had been difficult, but she had resisted the temptation to pry.

"That's the other part of the problem," Athena con-tinued. "Donald Olson, the Beltrami County sheriff, and my folks are great pals. They went all through school together, and they belong to the same Rotary group. That might influence the way the incident is being treated. Do you think you could speak to Sheriff Olson and find out what the deal is?"

"It's not my place," Ali said.

"Please," Athena begged. "Can't you just say that you're my mother-in-law. I'm concerned about Gram, but since I'm stuck in school and can't call, I told Gram I'd ask you to do it for me. Besides, it's true. I can't call. I have to get back to class."

"What's the name of the county again?" Ali asked.

"Beltrami."

"Give me your grandmother's number, then," Ali conceded. "I should probably talk to her about this before I go poking my nose into a hornet's nest."

Athena reeled off the number. Ali jotted it down on the outside of Raphael Fuentes's file folder. After hanging up, she sat with the phone in her hand for some time before finally breaking down and punching in the number.

"Athena?" Betsy asked when she answered the phone. She sounded anxious.

"No," Ali explained. "It's Ali Reynolds, Athena's mother-in-law. We met at the wedding."

"Of course," Betsy said. "I remember you. When I saw the unfamiliar number on caller ID, I thought maybe Athena was calling me back from a phone at school."

"I just finished speaking with her," Ali replied. "She told me a little about what happened last night. Is there anything I can do to help?"

"If the local authorities won't lift a finger, I can't imagine what you can do from all the way down there in Arizona."

There were no awkward pauses in Betsy's replies. If she was operating with a few screws missing, Ali would have thought there'd be at least a momentary bit of confusion or hesitation about who Ali was or where she was. Ali had been impressed by the woman when she had met and interacted with her at the wedding. Betsy Peterson had seemed sharp enough back then, and Ali's first impression now was that she hadn't lost any ground.

"What do the local authorities say?" Ali asked.

"They insist I've lost my marbles. They claim I turned on the gas burners on my own stove my own darned self and never bothered to light them. The deputy they sent out overnight somehow got the idea in his head that I had tried to use the stove-top burners to warm up the house—something I would never do, by the way. Even if I had been that dim, I certainly would have been smart enough to light them. I've had that same stove top for almost thirty years, from back when my husband and I first moved in here. It's the stove Alton insisted we get for that very reason—that there were no pilot lights. The burners all have to be lit by hand. I hated them then, and I hate them now, but there's no sense tossing the stove out on the scrap heap since it still works perfectly."

"It's cold there, I take it?" Ali asked.

"Not that cold," Betsy answered. "It'll probably get all the way up to the twenties today, but we had a blizzard last night, so we've got at least six inches of new snow on the ground."

In the twenties with six inches of snow sounded cold to Ali. "But not so cold that you would have turned the burners on to warm the place up?"

"I have central heating and cooling," Betsy replied indignantly. "Doesn't anyone understand that? Why on earth would I try heating the house with the burners on the kitchen stove? It makes no sense at all. It's not something I would do."

"You said it snowed. If someone came and left, wouldn't he have left tracks?"

"The snow was just starting when I got home from bingo. If there were any other tracks, they're completely covered over. The only tracks Deputy Severson seemed to be interested in were mine. He was all hot and bothered that I went outside in the snow in my bare feet. I was afraid the house was going to be blown to smithereens, but he thought I should go back to the bedroom to put shoes on? My idea was to get the hell out."

According to Athena, her grandmother was a plain-spoken woman. That appeared to be true. "Did anyone come back this morning to investigate?"

"They did not, even though I begged them to please, please send someone out first thing this morning to dust for prints or collect DNA. Sheriff Olson told me that would be a waste of time. He made it sound as though I had made the whole thing up. After all, since I had enough presence of mind to turn the burners off before I went outside, the gas was long gone by the time Deputy Severson showed up. The way that man—the sheriff—spoke to me, I wanted to reach through the phone lines and wring his scrawny neck. Why on earth would I grab my dog and go running barefoot out of the house into a snowy yard if I hadn't been scared to death? And what did he expect me to do, leave the gas running until one of his slowpoke deputies managed to get himself over here?"

Betsy's umbrage at being told she was imagining things hummed through the phone.

"Do you know of anyone who would wish you harm?"

Betsy thought about that for several seconds before she answered. "About a year ago I had a disagreement with Sarah Baxter over the way she handled the glasses after Communion. After Sarah's turn at cleaning up, the next time I set out the Communion glasses some of them still had lipstick smears on them. It was unsanitary. I took her aside and told her that if she wasn't prepared to do the job properly, she shouldn't volunteer to do it at all. I tried to keep the matter private, but she took offense and turned the whole thing into World War Three. She ended up getting the entire congregation up in arms."

Nothing like a little "neighbor loving thy neighbor" to keep things interesting at church, Ali thought.

"But that's all water under the bridge now," Betsy continued. "I regret to say that Pastor Anders had to be called in to settle things. It turns out Sarah was having problems with cataracts and so was I. We both decided to resign from the Communion Committee and that took care of that."

"It doesn't sound like the kind of issue that would cause someone to break into your house and try to do you in."

"Sarah is out of town at the moment, so it couldn't have been her," Betsy said. "Besides, there was no break-in involved. I have no idea how the criminal or criminals got in or out of my house."

"Do you have an alarm?"

"Yes."

"Was it set?"

Betsy sighed. "No, it wasn't," she admitted. "My son would have a conniption fit if he knew I turned it off when I got home and left it off when I went to bed. When Princess needs to go out overnight, the last thing I need is to have that blasted alarm shrieking at us the whole time she's out in the yard trying to pee."

"So maybe whoever came into the house followed you inside when you first came home and then let themselves out again after you fell asleep. What kind of dog?"

"Princess is a dachshund," Betsy replied, "a sweet little wiener dog."

Ali remembered Athena's mentioning something about her grandmother having a dog that was a near look-alike to Bella. "Did Princess bark at all last night?"

"Not really. She whimpered rather than barked when she smelled the gas. At least, I think that's what woke her up, and that's when she woke me up. She's fourteen. Like me, she's probably more than a little deaf. Fortunately her sense of smell hasn't gone the way of her hearing. Now that you mention it, Princess did bark at Deputy Severson once he showed up." She paused and then added plaintively, "Do you believe me?"

Ali thought about it and then nodded to herself. "Yes," she agreed aloud. "I think I do."

"Thank you for that," Betsy said with a grateful sigh. "Thank you so much. You have no idea what a boost that is. I was beginning to think that maybe everybody else was right, and I was starting to go bonkers."

There was a buzz in Ali's ear—probably a call-waiting signal on Betsy's phone rather than Ali's.

"Sorry," Betsy said. "I have to take this, but thank you. Athena was so right to have you call me. You've been a huge help, even from that far away."

2

A matter of moments later, Ali located the number for the Beltrami County sheriff and dialed it. It took jumping through a number of gatekeeping hoops before her call was finally put through to Sheriff Donald Olson. "Who is it?" he asked.

Ali's husband, B. Simpson, was a huge fan of the Coen brothers, and of all their films, including *The Big Lebowski*, but *Fargo* was B.'s all-time favorite. He and Ali had watched the movie together numerous times, and B. could recite many of the lines verbatim. When B. used the expression "He's a funny-looking little guy," it was definitely not high praise.

Sheriff Olson's distinctive manner of speaking, with its emphasis on the word "isss," made him sound as though he had stepped straight off the set of *Fargo*.

"My name is Ali Reynolds," she answered. "I'm calling from Sedona on behalf of Betsy Peterson and her granddaughter, Athena."

"Oh, that," Sheriff Olson said dismissively. "The whole 'somebody's trying to kill me routine.' And now it sounds as though she's calling in reinforcements. Who are you again, and what's your interest in all this?"

"I'm Athena's mother-in-law," Ali replied. "She's at school right now and can't call herself, but she spoke to her grandmother earlier. Athena said Mrs. Peterson sounded very upset, and she asked if I would call to get an idea of what's really going on."

"What's really going on, Ms. Reynolds, is that Betsy Peterson is a frail, elderly woman who has no business staying on in that big old house way out in the country all by herself. Jim and Sandra, her son and daughter-in-law, are worried sick about her, but they can't do a thing about it. My mom pulled the same stunt—wouldn't leave the family farm no matter how much she needed to. I talked myself blue trying to get her to see reason, so it's not like the Petersons have a corner on the market when it comes to having issues with aging relatives."

"It sounds to me as though you're discounting what happened to her."

"What she *claims* happened to her," Sheriff Olson corrected. "Athena's always been a bright girl. If she'd care to read Deputy Severson's report, I'm sure she'd agree that nothing about Betsy's wild imaginings rings true. My deputy examined the scene and there was nothing to be found—including no evidence at all of a break-in. It snowed here last night. He found no unusual tracks leading to or from Betsy's house—no sign of any vehicles and no sign of anyone on foot, either, other than some footprints in the snow out in the backyard. Those belonged to Betsy herself, by the way. She evidently went running around out in the backyard, barefoot in twenty-degree temperatures. If that's not nuts, what is? If she had wandered off into the woods like that—in her bare feet and wearing nothing but a robe and a nightgown—she would have been dead as a doornail by morning, gas or no gas."

32 J.A. JANCE

Ali didn't like the man's tone. "In other words, on the basis of her fleeing a possible gas explosion without returning to the far end of the house to retrieve her shoes, you're prepared to disregard her claim that someone entered her home, turned on the gas, and tried to kill her?"

"As I said, 'claim' is the operant word here, Ms. Reynolds. By the way, when Deputy Severson arrived at the scene, there was no sign of any gas—none at all. He thinks she made the whole thing up, maybe just to gain a little attention. Or else it could be something else like the first stages of dementia. That's what those folks do, by the way. They wander around in the middle of the night doing things that make no sense and that they never remember doing. They claim things happened that never happened."

"Has Ms. Peterson been diagnosed with any form of dementia?"

"Not to my knowledge and not officially, I suppose," the sheriff conceded. "But I've heard from Jim that odd things have started to happen. Betsy lost her hearing aids a while back. Weeks later Sandra found them in the freezer in a bag full of chopped-up Jimmy Dean sausages. Then Sandra stopped by Betsy's house one day and found medications for her yappy little dog mixed in with Betsy's. No telling what would have happened if Sandra hadn't straightened that mess out. Betsy could have died or else the dog could have. Oh, and then there was the thing with her reading glasses. She left them in a gadget drawer in the kitchen."

"And you know about all this because . . . ?"

"This is a small town, Ms. Reynolds. People know their neighbors. We talk. Maybe you're not accustomed to that kind of thing where you live. Jim Peterson and I are lifelong friends. Our parents are aging, and a lot of the folks in our generation are dealing with the same kinds of issues. We're all in the same boat, don't ya know?"

Ali could see that Sheriff Olson's being in the same boat with Jimmy Peterson meant that he was far too close to Betsy Peterson's situation to be an impartial bystander.

"How long was it after the 911 call before your officer arrived at the scene?"

"Forty minutes or so. Why?"

"Was the door open or closed?"

"The front door was closed when Deputy Severson arrived, but the back door was still wide open."

"Wouldn't that open door, added to a forty-minute delay, allow for the gas to dissipate?"

"I suppose," Sheriff Olson allowed grudgingly, "but that presumes the gas was present in the first place. Now look, Ms. Reynolds, I have places to go and things to do. You might mention to Athena that if she really cares about her grandmother, she'll use her influence to talk Betsy into letting go of that big house and moving into one of those assisted-living places where she'll be properly looked after."

Ali felt her temper rising. By the time her parents, Bob and Edie Larson, sold their Sugarloaf Café, they had both spent a lifetime cooking for other people. Done with cooking, they had moved into Sedona Shadows, a retirement community that came complete with a dining room where someone else handled the daily meal service. As far as Ali could see they were having a blast living there.

Although the move had surprised Ali at the time, her parents had made the decision on their own, in their own good time, and far earlier than expected without any prompting from what her mother had laughingly referred to as "the peanut gallery."

Listening to Donald Olson, Ali suspected Betsy Peterson's situation differed greatly from that of her parents. In Bemidji, the peanut gallery seemed to be holding all the cards.

"Thank you, Sheriff Olson," Ali said, struggling to keep a civil tongue in her mouth. "I'll be in touch."

The sheriff didn't have to say "don't bother" aloud as she ended the call. His tone of voice made his opinion of Ali's unwelcome interference entirely clear.

She was still glaring at the phone in her hand, as if holding it responsible for her bad mood, when it rang again. This time her husband's phone number showed in the screen.

"Boy," she said, "am I glad to hear from you. Are you still in Switzerland?"

"I am at the moment, but I'm leaving for New York City tomorrow afternoon. I have a day and a half of meetings there. I should be home in time for dinner on Friday."

"Good," she said. "I've missed you, and so has Bella. She moped around here for days after you left. What do you want for your homecoming dinner?"

"My first choice would be some of Leland's meat loaf."

"Fair enough," Ali said. "I'll make sure meat loaf is on the menu."

"After that," he said, "I'd like to spend the rest of the weekend having a little quiet downtime with my wife and my dog."

"Sounds perfect," Ali said. "That's what Bella and I are hoping for, too."

"What's happening on your end?" B. asked.

She told him about her call from Athena and her subsequent conversation with Sheriff Olson.

"So Betsy says somebody tried to kill her and everyone else says she's losing her marbles?"

"That's about the size of it," Ali agreed glumly.

"What do you think?"

"Betsy didn't sound out of it to me—not in the least."

"What are you going to do?"

"I already did it," Ali replied. "Athena asked me to call and talk to the sheriff, and that's what I did."

"Fair enough," B. said. "Now let it go at that. This is Athena's problem, not yours—Athena's and Betsy's. We already know there's plenty of bad blood between Athena and her parents. If you get involved with all this, there could be even more spillover. You're better off not being sucked into the middle of it."

"Right," Ali said. Just because she said she agreed with him, however, didn't mean she meant it. After all, just like her mother, Ali Reynolds had never been much good when it came to minding her own business.

3

Enid Tower sat in the dusty waiting room, dreading the sound of the nurse calling her name. She hated the process of going into the examining room and having to strip off her clothing. She hated the idea of having Dr. Johnson examine her body—of him touching her breasts and her belly with his bony hands and asking probing questions about how she felt.

If he had been just another doctor, that might have been okay, but on Sundays, when Enid had to sit in front of him and his family in church, he was Brother Johnson rather than Dr. Johnson. Sitting in the pew with him right behind her, knowing that he was staring at the back of her neck, always made Enid burn with shame. It was almost impossible to pay attention to the sermon or whatever else was going on in church when someone who had seen her naked and had touched the part of her body that shouldn't be touched by anyone but her husband was seated in the very next pew.

This time, though, it wasn't just the examining room Enid dreaded—it was what would come after the examining room. Bishop Lowell always talked about having the courage of your convictions. When the bishop talked like that, he was usually referring to the way The Family lived—apart from everyone else, following their own beliefs and customs no matter what the outside world said or thought about them. Today was the day Enid would test the courage of her own convictions in a way she knew would not meet with Bishop Lowell's approval.

The baby in her belly seemed to catch her mother's disquiet and began turning what felt like somersaults. Enid rested her hand on her stomach, hoping that the pressure would quiet her baby girl's restless tumbling. That's what Dr. Johnson said she was going to have—a girl—and that was why Enid was leaving. She knew what her life was and what it would be if she stayed in The Family. She didn't want that for herself, and she certainly didn't want it for her little girl.

Enid stole a glance at Aunt Edith. The woman was not really Enid's aunt, at least not as far as Enid knew. Given the way The Family worked, however, she might as well have been, because everyone who lived in The Encampment seemed to be related to everyone else. In this case, the word "aunt" was a reflection of Edith Tower's marital situation. "Aunt" was how younger wives were expected to refer to and honor the ones who had come before.

The custom was true for Enid and Abigail Crowden, too. They were two years apart in age, had grown up as best friends—doing chores together, playing tag, jumping rope, wading in the water on those rare occasions when the washes ran. For a time they had been Abby and Enid, a pair of inseparable pals with a not undeserved reputation for being a pair of troublemakers.

Then Abigail had married Gordon on her fifteenth

birthday—The Family's age of consent—although they had been betrothed long before that. In the two years since, Abby had already had one baby and was expecting another. Like Abby's, Enid's wedding—complete with a white gown and veil—had occurred on her fifteenth birthday. Now, as Gordon's youngest wife—his newest wife—Enid was forced to address her once beloved friend Abby as Aunt Abigail. She'd had to grieve over losing Abby's friendship as well, because now that they were wives together, they were no longer friends.

Aunt Edith drowsed, with her head leaning back against the wall and her mouth hanging open. Enid wondered how old she was. Probably not much more than thirty or so, although she looked far older. Her face was swollen. The corners of her mouth turned down rather than up. Because she was missing several teeth, she hardly ever smiled. An angry, forbidding frown permanently adorned her forehead. Oh, and she was pregnant, too, although not as far along as Enid. Aunt Edith's body was swollen under her shapeless homemade dress, and so were her ankles. Enid had heard Dr. Johnson's nurse talking to Aunt Edith, warning her in a low voice that if they didn't get her blood pressure under control, she might end up having to spend the rest of her pregnancy doing bed rest.

Enid tried to feel sorry for her. That was what Bishop Lowell said you were supposed to do—feel compassion toward others. This would be Aunt Edith's eighth baby, although Enid had heard she had miscarried a couple of times, too. As First Wife, or at least as the eldest of those who remained, she ruled her part of The Family with an iron fist. Aunt Edith kept a willow switch in a corner of the kitchen and wasn't afraid to use it on the younger

wives and on any of the children, especially if there
was so much as a hint of back talk or if assigned chores
weren't done to her satisfaction. Enid knew that if Aunt
Edith ended up confined to her bed, she would use that
confinement as a weapon to dish out misery to others. As
the youngest wife, Enid would be a natural target.

Enid understood why Aunt Edith hated her. Aunt
Edith may have been pretty once, but years of constant
pregnancies had robbed her of whatever good looks she
might have possessed. Enid, on the other hand, was still
young and beautiful. Right now, hers was the bed Gordon
preferred to any of the others. At night he wanted Enid
to stand in front of him naked while she let down her
hair. Then, after taking his fill of her—according to him,
pregnancy was only a problem if you let it be—Gordon
liked to sleep on his belly next to her back and with his
outspread hand resting on her swollen stomach, as if
claiming both her body and her baby's as his own.

Enid knew the other wives were jealous of the added
attention he lavished on her. One morning, after Gordon
had gone out to do chores, Aunt Edith had barged into
the bedroom and caught Enid standing in front of the
mirror, admiring the undulating waves the undone braids
had left in her waist-length hair.

Aunt Edith had stopped in the doorway and stared at
her. "I suppose you think your hair is beautiful like that,
don't you," she sneered. "It's beautiful all right—just like
the waves on a slop pail."

With that, she had turned on her heel, slammed
the door behind her, and stormed off downstairs. That
evening, Enid had begged Gordon to give her a key for
their bedroom. She claimed it was because some of the
little kids had been sneaking inside and going through

his things, but it was really so Enid could have a few moments of privacy.

To her surprise, Gordon had seen fit to grant that wish. She knew a big part of his doing so had to do with her being young and supple. She always let him have his way with her, and she never complained. Once she had the key to their room, she treasured it, wearing it on a string tied around her neck. Each morning, she waited until Gordon went downstairs, then she crept out of bed and locked the door behind him before she got dressed for the day. When she went downstairs to breakfast, she locked the door again.

One day Aunt Edith had caught Enid locking the door. "What do you think you're doing?" she had demanded. "Who said you could lock that door?"

"Gordon," Enid replied. "Gordon said so."

It was hardly surprising that Enid spent that day scrubbing floors on her hands and knees, but with the key safely hidden away under her dress, she hardly minded at all.

The door to Dr. Johnson's examining room opened and a woman and a girl about Enid's age came out. She was someone Enid recognized. Her name was Mary. She was fourteen and betrothed to Bishop Lowell. The wedding was due to happen the following month. Marrying the bishop was supposed to be a huge honor. From the desolate expression on the girl's face, Enid knew that she had just been forced to undergo the dreaded virginity test. Only virgins were allowed to marry Elders, and written certification of that from The Family's approved physician, Dr. Johnson, came only after he had determined the hymen was fully intact.

From the set of Mary's mother's jaw, Enid could see the woman was angry. As Mary walked past with eyes downcast and shoulders slumped, Enid understood that, for some reason, Mary hadn't passed. Enid put her hand to her mouth in a gesture of unspoken sympathy because she knew what came next. Mary would be taken back to The Encampment and locked in the concrete block cell behind the church. The next time the Elders met, there would be a trial of sorts, with Bishop Lowell serving as judge and with only the Twelve Elders allowed on the jury. Everyone knew it was all for show. There wasn't the slightest chance that Mary would be found innocent.

Cast-Off girls weren't allowed to stay in The Encampment for fear of passing their wickedness on to someone else. Once convicted, Mary would be stripped naked and forced to stand in the back of Bishop Lowell's truck in broad daylight while she was driven away from the church and out of The Encampment. Everyone in The Family would be there, lining the road and looking on in absolute silence while the truck went past. No one knew what became of Cast-Off girls after the truck disappeared from view, and anyone stupid enough to ask would soon be on the receiving end of a willow-switch beating.

No one was allowed to ask about what happened to the Not Chosen girls, either. They too disappeared, but without the same kind of shame or spectacle as the Cast-Offs. Not Chosens were the girls who, by age seven or so, were somehow deemed unworthy and, as a consequence, were not yet betrothed. Like unwanted kittens in the barn, one day they were there; the next they were gone.

That's what had happened to a girl named Judith, whose cot had been next to Enid's on the girls' sleeping porch. The two girls had been the same age but, because

Judith was Edith's daughter, they had not been friends. One night they went to bed in the usual way, but the next morning, when Enid awakened, Judith was gone. Her cot had been stripped down to the bare mattress, and the chest with her clothing and belongings in it was gone as well.

Enid had discovered later that Judith wasn't the only Not Chosen who had disappeared that night. Another five or six had vanished from other households as well—at least that's what one of the older girls said in a whispered conversation after church the next Sunday. Disappearing Nights happened at odd intervals during the year. After-ward, any discussion about them was strictly forbidden. That didn't mean that the speculation didn't happen, but it was conducted in wary secrecy.

After one Disappearing Night, one of the older boys claimed he had seen the girls being carried onto a plane that had flown away into the night. Another said the Not Chosens were transported to an island somewhere to be fed to cannibals. As unlikely as both stories seemed, Enid from age eight on had been grateful each morning to wake up in familiar surroundings. Back then terror of the Outside had been greater than the unrelenting drudgery of living under Aunt Edith's thumb. Now, though, at age sixteen, that had changed. Being Outside was what Enid Tower longed for more than anything, for herself and for her baby.

"Susannah," the nurse announced.

Aunt Edith stirred while another pregnant woman—someone Enid knew but not well and who looked as though she might deliver any day—levered herself up from her chair and waddled into the exam room. As soon as the door closed, Aunt Edith closed her eyes again.

Enid looked longingly at the dog-eared magazines scattered on the table in front of her. The ones she really wanted to study were the torn back issues of *National Geographic*. Even though she couldn't read most of the words, she had caught a few stolen glimpses of the photos—colorful photographs of strange, faraway places Enid hoped to see someday. There was also a single copy of something called *TV Guide*. She wondered about that. Members of The Family weren't allowed to watch television or see movies, so why did Dr. Johnson have that magazine in his office? As for the woman pictured on the cover? The clothing she wore was far too revealing and her teeth were impossibly white. The Family believed in Dr. Johnson, but they didn't believe in dentists or in toothpaste, either. Baking soda was it.

Even with Aunt Edith fast asleep, Enid didn't dare pick up the magazine. Anyone caught with what Bishop Lowell called "godless literature" in her hand could count on a willow-switch beating the moment she got home. Besides, all Enid would be able to do was look at the pictures. The children in The Family were all supposedly being homeschooled, but Bishop Lowell didn't think there was any need for girls to learn to read. He claimed there were too many books and magazines that would do nothing but lead them astray.

Hidden away in a closet on the younger girls' sleeping porch and using a purloined flashlight, Enid had managed to teach herself some reading skills by working her way through some of the younger boys' reading books. Even so, she knew she would never be able to read a whole magazine on her own. That was something she was hoping she would be able to give her daughter on the Outside—the ability to read.

Barely ten minutes later, Susannah came out, still buttoning her blouse. The nurse stood in the doorway, glancing at a list. "Enid," she announced.

Taking a deep breath, Enid stood up. She had no purse to carry. Purses were considered vain. Instead, womenfolk from The Family were expected to carry nothing more ornate than small homemade pouches made of cloth that were large enough to hold only a small Bible and a single hanky. As Enid crossed the room, she gripped the pouch tightly in both hands, hoping that Aunt Edith wouldn't wake up and spy the telltale bulges in the pouch that concealed Enid's "ill-gotten goods"—the small scissors, the spool of white thread, and the needle she had smuggled out of the Sewing Room.

She crossed the room hurriedly, more than half expecting Aunt Edith to lumber to her feet and raise an objection. She did not. When Enid had come to see Dr. Johnson for her first prenatal checkup, Aunt Edith had insisted on accompanying her into the examining room. It had been humiliating for Enid to be up on the table, with her legs spread open in the stirrups and with Dr. Johnson peering at her while Aunt Edith watched from the sidelines. That evening, in bed, after Enid had given Gordon everything he wanted and more, she had pleaded her case.

"If I'm old enough to have your baby," she said, "I should be old enough to see the doctor without having Aunt Edith in the room with me."

Thankfully, Gordon had capitulated. Aunt Edith was furious about it, but even First Wives had to abide by their husbands' wishes. Enid was counting on that.

In the second of the two exam rooms, she slipped out of her dowdy, ankle-length gingham dress and the homemade cotton slip. Some of the girls in The Family insisted that women on the Outside wore a garment called a "bra" that helped to keep their breasts from sagging. Seeing her overripe body in the mirror as she slipped on the ugly green gown, Enid wished she owned something like that. Maybe someday she'd have one.

Once gowned, Enid hitched her unwieldy body up on the end of the examining table and waited quietly while Vera, one of Dr. Johnson's wives as well as his nurse, took Enid's temperature, blood pressure, and pulse. Very few members of The Family were allowed to live outside The Encampment. Dr. Johnson was one who did.

"Pulse is a little elevated," Vera muttered. "Are you upset about something at the moment?"

"No," Enid lied, willing her heart rate to slow. "I'm fine."

Dr. Johnson came into the room. He was tall and thin, with a long narrow neck that made Enid think of a giraffe—a giraffe wearing a stethoscope.

"How's our little mama doing today?" he asked as he stood with his back to her, washing his hands at the sink. He didn't pretend that he knew Enid's name. He probably said the same words to every woman who came into the room, whether or not she was little. As far as he was concerned, the women involved—the mothers—were a biological necessity. As individuals they were of little consequence. After all, the babies were what mattered. The Family valued and rejoiced at the live birth of each healthy child and most especially girl babies. As for the unhealthy ones—the ones that weren't quite right? No one saw them again.

"Fine," Enid managed. She didn't want to do anything that might attract unwarranted attention.

"Let's have a look, then."

Vera had left the room by then. Dr. Johnson may have said "let's," but he was the only one doing any looking. He touched Enid's bulging breasts, pinching the nipples hard enough that she winced and almost cried out. She wondered if he would have done it had Vera still been in the room.

"These were quite small when you first started coming here," he observed pleasantly, "but they're coming along nicely. You won't have a bit of trouble nursing."

Along with toothpaste and dentists, baby bottles and formula were something else The Family didn't believe in. Mothers were required to nurse their babies until they were ready for solid foods. If it turned out that a previous baby wasn't quite weaned before the next one came along? Too bad. Both kids took turns nursing while the mothers had little time to do anything else.

Dr. Johnson ducked out of sight under the sheet that covered Enid's raised knees. She held her breath while his searching fingers—cold despite the latex gloves he wore—probed inside her.

"Yes, indeed," he said. "Other than a little bruising here and there, everything's fine as frog's hair. By my calculations you've got another six weeks to go. From now on, though, you might tell Gordon to ease up on you some. I'm sure you can find some other way to satisfy his needs besides spreading your legs."

Enid nodded. She knew exactly what Dr. Johnson meant as a substitute because she had done it before. She also knew that Gordon liked it and she didn't. "I'll tell him," she said.

"Good girl," he said, patting her tummy in a possessive way that made her want to squirm off the table.

"That's the spirit. You get dressed now while we see what's going on with Aunt Edith."

As Dr. Johnson left the room, Enid scrambled off the table and pulled on her clothing. She was in such a hurry that she buttoned the front of her dress wrong and had to undo it and start over. She pulled on the light jacket she had worn when she left home and checked to make sure that the cheese sandwich she had smuggled out of the kitchen was still safely in her pocket. So was that precious piece of paper, the tiny one that promised Enid and her baby had a future that wasn't a part of The Family. Last of all, she picked up the cloth pouch.

Enid was grateful that Aunt Edith was missing from the waiting room when she emerged from the examining room. Behind the counter another of Dr. Johnson's wives, this one named Donna, was intent on what appeared to be a game of cards laid out on her computer screen. Gordon kept a computer on the desk in his office. If Enid had ever been allowed to touch it, she wouldn't have wasted a moment playing cards.

Enid walked to the door, moving calmly and hoping to arouse no suspicion. "I'm going outside for a while," she announced over her shoulder as she stepped out onto the sidewalk.

"Sure," Donna said, giving her an unconcerned wave. "Go right ahead."

Enid stayed outside in the early afternoon overcast for only a minute or so before she opened the door again and stuck her head back inside. "Bishop Lowell just came by," she said. "Tell Aunt Edith I'm riding home with him."

"Will do," Donna said, again without looking up.

Enid closed the door behind her, then turned and walked away from the office, traveling in the same gen-

48

J.A. JANCE

eral direction as where she would be expected to go. She walked past the post office and the little storefront library filled with long shelves of books that she had never been able to check out or read. As she walked past the grocery store where Aunt Edith would stock up before driving the twenty miles or so of dirt road back to The Encampment, Enid couldn't help smiling. Aunt Edith would be furious when she learned that she'd have to push the grocery carts herself and load the bags and boxes into the minivan without Enid along to do the heavy lifting. Aunt Edith would be even more furious when she got home and realized Enid had played her for a fool.

Walking through town, Enid knew exactly where she was going, but it was a desperate gamble. She had no idea if her carefully thought-out plan would really work, and she knew that severe punishments awaited her if she was caught and taken back home. Rather than think about that, she concentrated on moving forward and doing so at a steady pace. Running would attract too much attention—something Enid Tower could ill afford.

Neither could her baby.

4

Ali wasn't surprised when the doorbell rang in the middle of the afternoon. Bella, having lived most of her life in a condo where there had been a knocker rather than a doorbell, had taken several weeks to learn that a ringing doorbell meant company. With B. out of town, the dog had taken possession of B.'s customary chair. When the bell rang, Bella bounded down and scampered to the door. Leland soon ushered Athena into the library with Bella barking at her heels. As Athena sank into the chair opposite Ali's, the dog leaped into her lap. Athena hardly noticed. Absently patting the dog's head, she looked distressed and uncertain. Ali was surprised to see her usually self-possessed daughter-in-law in such apparent disarray.

"Are you all right?" Ali asked.

"I'm not," Athena answered, "but thank you for talking to Gram. I called between classes. She said you made her day because it sounded like you believed her."

"I did believe her," Ali agreed, "and I still do. As soon as I called, she knew exactly who I was, and she had no difficulty keeping her story straight. I've learned a thing

or two about Alzheimer's in the last year or two, and Alzheimer's patients have trouble doing that. In fact, she
didn't seem impaired in any way. When I asked her if
she had any enemies or if she knew of anyone who might
wish her ill, she mentioned something about a disagreement over Communion glasses at church. That didn't
strike me as the kind of quarrel that would rise to the
level of an attempted homicide."

"Did you speak to Sheriff Olson?"

Ali nodded. "I did. He seems to be of two minds on
the subject. His first choice is that Betsy turned on the
burners herself and doesn't remember doing it. His second option is that the whole incident is a figment of her
imagination. He felt compelled to imply that anyone who
would go outside barefoot in the snow is a couple tacos
short of a combination plate."

"In other words, one way or another, he thinks this is
all Gram's fault. What do you think?" Athena asked.

"If my house was filled with gas and I thought it might
explode, I'd boogie out through the nearest door, barefoot
and stark naked, too, if necessary—snow or no snow."

"So you think someone really did try to kill her?"
Athena asked.

"I do," Ali answered.

"But who?" Athena asked.

"That's the question, isn't it. Let's think about that. If
you look at the homicide statistics in this country, most
of the victims and perpetrators are involved in some kind
of criminal enterprise. Drug users and drug dealers knock
one another off with wild abandon. Your grandmother's
not likely to be involved in any kind of illegal activity, so
we can discount the idea that this is some kind of criminal infighting."

Ali paused. "She has arthritis, right?"

Athena nodded.

"Elderly folks are often easy targets for druggies looking for stashes of narcotics. The problem with that is that after I spoke to Sheriff Olson, I also spoke to the deputy who responded to her 911 call. Deputy Severson said there was no sign of rifling or attempted burglary, and that Betsy could find nothing missing from the house—including checking her supply of medications, which were right there on the kitchen counter. In other words, we can disregard the idea that whoever did this intended to rip off her meds."

"What does that leave?" Athena asked.

"Jealousy, maybe?" Ali asked. "What about her love life?"

"Gram's love life?" a disbelieving Athena asked. "Are you kidding?"

From her expression, it was clear that Athena had never considered the idea that her grandmother might *have* a love life.

"Older people can fall in love, too," Ali said gently. "Maybe Betsy is caught up in some kind of love triangle."

"No," Athena said, shaking her head. "Not possible. I can't imagine Gram doing such a thing."

"We have to find out," Ali said. "You'll need to ask her."

"Me?" Athena asked faintly. "Why me?"

"Who else is going to do it? Right now you and I are the only ones who have Betsy's back and are taking her concerns seriously. To find out what really happened up there, you'll probably have to go there. You'll need to find out what's going on in your grandmother's life and who her friends are, including any possible love interests. Maybe Sheriff Olson is right. Maybe she has reached a point where she needs more help than she's willing to accept. And if it turns out she is having mental difficulties, you may be the only one who can help her make whatever arrangements are deemed necessary."

"I'm not a detective," Athena objected. "I wouldn't have any idea how to go about doing something like that."

"You're Betsy's granddaughter," Ali said. "You don't have to be a detective to ask those kinds of questions. In fact, it's an obligation, and you'd be remiss if you didn't. Which brings us to yet another possible motive."

"What's that?"

"Greed," Ali answered. "As in, follow the money. How well off is your grandmother?"

Athena shrugged. "She's okay, I guess. I mean, we've never really talked about her finances. It's not my place."

"Again, if someone tried to murder her and the authorities are brushing it off, it's your place now. For instance, is her home paid for?"

"I'm sure," Athena said, "and what's left of the farm is paid for, too. Gramps owned a lot of land around Bemidji, land he sold off years ago. What we still call 'the farm' is really just a house on twenty acres. It's not a real farm, not the way it used to be."

"Has she ever seemed hard up to you?"

"Not at all," Athena said. "Never. When Gramps was alive, he bought a new car every other year, and he always paid cash. He bragged that he never bought a car on time. After he retired, he and Gram took long road trips every year, driving all over the country, sometimes for as long as a month or more at a time. That stopped after Gramps died. That's also when Gram stopped getting a new car every other year, but that was her choice. It wasn't because she couldn't afford it. She said that she did so little driving on her own that she didn't need a new car every time she turned around."

"Tell me about your parents," Ali pressed quietly. In the years she had known Athena, she had said little about her parents. Ali knew Athena was estranged from them, but both Athena and Chris had been guarded about supplying any details. Now, however, the ground rules had shifted in Ali's favor. To help guide Athena through this current crisis, Ali needed more information—the backstory that Athena had previously been reluctant to share.

Athena's eyes filled with tears. "You remember when Chris and I went to Minnesota?"

Ali nodded. She remembered it well. She remembered hoping Chris would be able to help mend whatever fences needed mending.

"What happened?"

"You don't know my mom," Athena said. "We've never gotten along, ever. When I was little, she wanted me to wear dresses and play with Barbie dolls. I wanted to wear overalls and hang out with Gramps. When I'd go stay with them, he'd let me sit in his lap and drive a tractor. Mom was appalled. When it was time for college, Mom wanted me to go to the University of Minnesota and join the same sorority she belonged to. She made it clear that if I didn't do things her way, she and Dad wouldn't pay a dime of my schooling costs." Athena paused. "Mom's not big on unconditional love."

"I guess not," Ali agreed.

"The problem is, I'm not big on being bossed around, either, so we're not exactly a good fit. When I told them I'd choose my own school and that I had no intention of joining a sorority ever, Mom said that was it. If I wasn't going to do things the way she and Dad said, then I was on my own as far as schooling was concerned. I'd have to pay for it myself. That's when I joined the National Guard. That was a place where my early tractor driving with Gramps came in handy. I trained in a transport unit and ended up getting deployed to Iraq where I got blown up by an IED. I came home like this," she added, glancing down at her prosthetic arm and leg.

Ali nodded. "I know about that. I also know that your grandmother came to visit you at Walter Reed while your parents didn't."

"Yes," Athena said bitterly. "Their position was that I'd made my own bed and now should lie in it."

There are conversations mothers-in-law are allowed to initiate and ones they are not. Taking a deep breath of her own, Ali stepped into uncharted territory. "Tell me about your first husband," she said.

When Chris had first mentioned that he and Athena were dating, Ali had been concerned that not only was Athena six years older than he was, she had already been married and divorced.

Athena sighed and squared her shoulders. "Okay," she said, taking a deep breath. "Jack and I met in basic training. He was from Minneapolis, where he had been an all-star quarterback in high school. He was used to being a big deal. He joined up for the same reason I did—to get some help going to school. My dad's a dentist, and it was ironic that I fell for a guy who wanted to go to dental school. By joining the National Guard he hoped to get through school without accumulating a crushing amount of debt.

"It was a first relationship for both of us. You remember that old song with the line 'we got married in a fever'? That was us. We were in lust, not in love. We eloped right after basic training. I'm sure Mom thought we were pregnant. We weren't. What surprised me, though, was that the moment my parents met Jack, they adored him, my dad even more than my mom. I think Dad saw Jack as the son he never had."

"Did you love him?" Ali asked.

"Jack?" Athena shrugged and paused for a moment before continuing. "I cared about him, but what I felt for him isn't anywhere near what I feel for Chris. I can see now that I married Jack more to get back at my folks than anything else, and the whole thing blew up in my face. It turns out, karma is like that. Jack just graduated from dental school. The plan is that he'll gradually take over my father's practice so Dad can retire. And that's what hurts more than anything—the idea that my parents would choose an ex-son-in-law over their own daughter."

Athena paused again and seemed to be thinking about what to say next. "I can see now how wrong it was for us to rush into marriage. We were both too young. He wasn't ready to settle down; he still wanted to sow some wild oats—which he did, by the way. We ended up in different National Guard units. Mine deployed; his didn't. I found out he was cheating on me with Janice before I even shipped out. Jack started talking divorce while I was still in Iraq. He had me served with the papers while I was deployed, and the divorce became final while I was in Walter Reed. I didn't fight it because by then a divorce was what I wanted, too. Still, it blew me away to think that he and Janice were already married and expecting a baby before I got out of rehab and made it back home to Bemidji."

Ali remained quiet. She knew more than most how much loving and losing at a very young age can hurt. If there was more to this story, she needed to wait patiently until it finally spilled out.

"There was no way I was going to go back home and live with my folks, so I stayed with Gram instead," Athena went on. "She had a wheelchair ramp built on the front of the house and let me sleep in her downstairs bedroom. I felt guilty that she had to go up and down the stairs, but she said climbing stairs was good for her. I lived with her while I went through rehab, got fitted with my prostheses, and got my teaching degree. I was able to sign up for school with one of the earliest distance-learning programs, one that allowed me to take courses online and go at my own pace. I finished my degree in three years and took the first job I was offered—here in Sedona."

Ali nodded. "What happened when you and Chris went back to visit?"

Athena sighed. "I didn't tell my folks we were coming. I told Gram, of course, because we were going to stay with her, but I asked her not to tell my parents. I wanted to surprise them. They were surprised, all right, and so was I. It turns out that Janice now works in my dad's office as a receptionist, and Mom takes care of Jack and Janice's son, Jason, while they're at work. While Jack was away at school, Janice and the boy stayed with my parents, living in my old room. I found that out when I went by the house. Mom wasn't exactly overjoyed to see me. I left and haven't been back."

Ali already knew that Athena's parents had never bothered to acknowledge the arrival of Chris and Athena's twins, which made their betrayal of volunteering to look after a non-grandchild all the more hurtful to their daughter.

"That must have been a shock," Ali said. "Why didn't Betsy warn you?"

Athena shrugged. "She probably didn't know about it. She and my mother aren't exactly pals. Never have been; never will be. Mom and Dad try to boss Gram around the same way they tried to with me." Athena paused. "So what am I supposed to do now?"

Ali thought for a moment before she answered. "We make sure your grandmother knows that we're behind her—that we believe that someone did indeed try to harm her last night. Now, tell me. Does Betsy have a security system?"

"Yes, but she turned it off when she came home from bingo. She doesn't leave it on when she's at home because it's inconvenient when she has to take the dog out. Thank goodness Princess smelled the gas and woke Gram up."

"But she didn't bark earlier when whoever turned the burners on was in the house?" Ali mused.

"I guess not."

A dog that didn't bark? Ali didn't like where that thought was taking her. The last time that had happened it had been because the intruder had been someone the dog in question knew quite well.

"Okay," Ali said, without passing along that last conclusion. "Tell your grandmother that from now on, inconvenient or not, the alarm stays on."

Athena nodded.

"Is there anyone left in town that you trust who could stay with your grandmother for the next little while?"

"Not really."

"Does Betsy's house have Internet access?"

"It does. She had Wi-Fi installed while I was there,

but she may have discontinued the service. She had a computer, but it's most likely dead by now. She doesn't use it."

"Tell her she needs to reinstate her Wi-Fi because she'll have a new computer shortly," Ali said.

"Why?"

"Because your grandmother is about to become a client of High Noon Enterprises," Ali said with a smile. "I'll talk to B. and to Stuart and see what kind of security equipment is needed in this particular situation. Come to think of it, I may even have to go to Bemidji myself to oversee the installation."

"You'd do that?" Athena asked.

"Of course," Ali said. "Why wouldn't I?"

Athena glanced briefly at her watch, then she sprang out of her chair, came over to Ali, and bent down to give her mother-in-law a hug. "Thank you," she whispered in Ali's ear. "Thank you so much."

5

Walking close to the buildings with her eyes modestly lowered, Enid didn't worry about being recognized. People would know from her manner of dress—the ankle-length gingham dress and the heavy oxford shoes—and from the way she wore her hair—in long braids wrapped around the crown of her head—that she most likely belonged to one of the religious sects that had taken up residence in this far-flung corner of Mohave County.

When voters in and around Colorado City had suggested creating a local law enforcement district and hiring their own marshal, Bishop Lowell had organized enough opposition to defeat the proposal. For one thing, the Mohave County deputy they had now, Amos Sellers, was a member in good standing of The Family. When the next vacancy occurred, he'd most likely be elevated to the status of Elder. Besides, Bishop Lowell was opposed to having any more law enforcement scrutiny than absolutely necessary.

Even though women in The Family weren't allowed to vote, Enid had heard all the pro and con discussions before the election. She knew that the Colorado City area fell under the jurisdiction of the Mohave County Sheriff's Office, which was headquartered in the town of Kingman, a place she had never seen. Because the Grand Canyon—another place Enid had never seen and often wondered about—lay between The Encampment and Kingman, travel between the two places wasn't easy. The most direct route took four hours and required crossing three separate state lines. The other, all inside Arizona, made for a seven-hour one-way trip. Lack of law enforcement oversight was one of the reasons The Family and groups like them had chosen to settle in this remote part of the state.

Kids and women from The Family weren't allowed to spend time in town without being supervised. Just being caught walking alone on the street would have been enough to call for a public caning from Bishop Lowell. Although Enid didn't worry about people in town recognizing her, she was anxious that someone from The Family might see her—someone who had come to town that day to pick up a tractor part or stop by the bank. If the person who found her turned out to be one of the Elders, there would be hell to pay. As far as the townsfolk were concerned, though, the only people who knew her, other than the nurses in Dr. Johnson's office, were the clerks and bag boys in the supermarket and maybe, just maybe, the clerk at the gas station where Enid was headed.

On those occasions when Aunt Edith had stopped to gas up before heading home, Enid was allowed to go inside and use the restroom. She may have paused briefly to admire some of the items under the glass counters, but because she never had any spending money, she never bought anything. That made it unlikely that the clerk would know her on sight. Still, once Enid got to the station, she waited until several people entered the market at once and inserted herself in the middle of the group.

It was three o'clock in the afternoon. From her visits to the grocery store and from watching people standing in line at the checkout counter, Enid knew this was the time of day when tourists who had spent the day wandering the Vermillion Cliffs or the North Rim of the Grand Canyon headed south to Flagstaff or Phoenix. These were folks who loved taking their hulking RVs and minivans off the beaten track. Enid understood from what they said and from the curious glances they sent in her direction that Colorado City was definitely off the beaten path. She was hoping she'd be able to convince one of those hardy-type travelers to take her along wherever they were going.

The first group waiting for stalls in the restroom consisted of two families with several school-age children. Standing in line behind them, Enid gathered from their conversation that they were all on spring break—whatever that was—and they were heading home to Phoenix. The kids went into the stalls first. Then, after washing their hands, they ducked out into the market to buy treats. When the first mother emerged from one of the three stalls and went to the washbasin, Enid found the courage to speak to her.

"Is there a chance of getting a ride from here to Flagstaff?" she asked.

The woman looked her up and down, with her gaze pausing a moment too long on Enid's bulging tummy.

"Certainly not," she said firmly. "I've warned my children to never have anything to do with strangers, and I have no intention of setting a bad example."

Flushing with embarrassment, Enid fled into the

nearest unoccupied stall and stayed there. Once the group left, she stripped out of her dress. Then, wearing only her shift, she sat on the toilet and used the stolen pair of scissors from her cloth bag to remove a foot or so from the bottoms of both the dress and the shift. She didn't worry about the jagged cuts on the shift as she whacked that off just above her knee. After all, the shift wouldn't show. The hem of the dress was the problem.

The full gathered skirt contained plenty of material, and the scissors were small. By the time Enid had cut her way around the whole thing—trying to keep to the same line of checks as she went—her hand ached and a blister was forming on her thumb. She wadded up the discarded material and tossed it into the trash, then she took out the needle and thread. She could have done a better job of hemming if she'd had straight pins and an iron to work with, but the best she could do was turn up a tiny hem as she went, tacking it with long, efficient stitches.

As she worked on the dress, Enid tried to reassure herself, *Not all the people on the Outside will be like that.*

Several women came and went while she was sewing. One of them rattled the door on Enid's stall and demanded, "What are you doing in there, having a baby?"

Enid had to stifle a giggle because, in a way, that was exactly what she was doing—having an Outside baby.

With the hemming job complete, Enid slipped the dress back on over her head. The new length seemed strange. She wasn't used to seeing bare skin above the tops of her heavy-duty shoes. Ducking out of the stall, she examined herself in the mirror, but the one above the sink was too short for her to see the bottom of her dress.

More women came and went. Most of them were older women with silver hair and with varicose-veined legs sticking out from under Bermuda shorts. The weather seemed cold to Enid. She couldn't imagine why anyone would be dressed in summer clothes. They talked about places like Wisconsin and Minnesota— more places that Enid could hardly imagine. The women generally took turns using the single handicapped stall, although, as far as Enid could see, none of them looked handicapped. They met her requests for a ride with somewhat more gentleness than the first one had employed, but the answer was still the same—N-O.

In The Family, women were not allowed to wear jewelry of any kind except a plain gold wedding band. Any other jewelry, including watches, was considered vain, ungodly, and wicked. From fifteen on, boys were allowed to wear watches, while the womenfolk were forced to tell time by following the positions of the sun. There was no window in Enid's restroom refuge, so the sun's timekeeping abilities were lost to her. Even so, she knew that more than an hour had passed, and she was starting to grow anxious. By now Aunt Edith, finished with her errands, was probably at home or very nearly so. Soon someone would sound the alarm that Enid had gone missing, and the search for her would be on in dead earnest.

The restroom door opened again. The two women who entered wore boots and jeans and hiking boots. Their hair was cut short. They weren't wearing lipstick or makeup. In fact, they looked more like men than women, although they went inside the stalls the same way the others had. Through the intervening walls, they talked easily of the hike they had taken and how soon they would arrive back at their RV park. They weren't particularly threatening, and they seemed kind enough, nodding to Enid as they left. Still, their mannish appearances was so far outside her realm of experience that she let them leave without asking them for help.

The woman who arrived immediately after they left was an older Indian lady with iron-gray hair pulled back into a complicated knot at the back of her neck. Enid knew a little about Indians. The ones who came through town occasionally were mostly Navajo. The men wore jeans, cowboy shirts, and boots along with shiny silver and turquoise bolo ties or handmade belt buckles. The women often wore brightly colored dresses and amazing turquoise necklaces, similar to the ones that were for sale in this very gas station, where handmade jewelry was arranged in a glass display case near the register.

Boys from The Family always made fun of the "squaws wearing their squaw dresses," but Enid often found herself envying those brightly colored, flowing dresses that bore little resemblance to the bland, home-sewn shapeless things she and the other women in The Family wore until their colors faded away to nothing.

Some of the older boys liked to tease the younger girls, telling them that the Indians came to town looking for women and girls they could kidnap for their scalps and claiming that Indians liked blond-haired scalps more than any others.

Based on what she'd been told, Enid should have been terrified of the new arrival, but she wasn't. The old Indian woman had a wise, kind face that was creased with a network of sun-deepened smile lines. When she came out of the stall and went to the basin, she nodded at Enid's reflection in the faded mirror.

"I need to get to Flagstaff," Enid blurted out urgently, saying the words fast enough that there was no time to change her mind. "I'm looking for a ride."

Drying her hands, the woman turned to Enid with her brow furrowed into a frown. "We're not going all the way to Flag," she said. "Twenty miles this side, but you're welcome to ride with us that far if you want."

When Enid left the restroom at last, she scurried along beside the heavyset woman, hoping that the Indian woman's ample body and voluminous skirt would shield her from the curious glances of both the clerk and the customers gathered around the cash register. Once outside, the woman led the way to a dusty pickup truck, an older-model Ford. A scrawny Indian man in a white Stetson, a black shirt, faded jeans, and equally faded boots was finishing filling the gas tank and returning the hose to the pump.

He looked up at Enid questioningly as she and the woman approached the vehicle. "She's going to Flagstaff and needs a ride," the woman explained. "I told her we'll take her as far as we're going."

Under the wide brim of the Stetson, the man's bronzed face was impassive, registering neither surprise nor objection. He simply nodded, as though picking up strangers and giving them rides was the most natural thing in the world. He waited until the pump burped out a receipt that he folded carefully before putting in his wallet.

"Okay then," he said. "Let's go."

The woman climbed in first, taking the seat in the middle with the floor-mounted gearshift between her legs. Once seated, her body seemed to spread out in both directions, leaving just enough room for the driver and Enid to crowd into the cab on either side. It was a tight fit. Enid had a hard time closing her door. She was relieved when the old truck's engine rumbled to life and then purred smoothly as they drove across the paved lot and onto the roadway. The truck may have been older than most of the vehicles at The Encampment, but this one seemed to run better.

Enid sat pressed up against the door with both arms resting on her swollen belly. As they headed south in the gathering dusk, the road was familiar at first. Enid realized then that she had been inside the restroom far longer than she had thought. The sun was already setting in the west as they drove past the dirt track called Sanctuary Road that, two miles later, would arrive at the first houses built inside The Encampment.

From that intersection on, Enid was in territory that was wholly new to her. The dark sky overhead was familiar, and so were the emerging stars, but she knew nothing of the surrounding landscape. *Was the Grand Canyon just over there?* she wondered, looking to the west. *Was she riding past it in the dark without being able to see it?*

They rode for miles in utter silence. The woman was the first to speak. "When's your baby due?" she asked.

"A month and a half," Enid answered.

"A boy or a girl?"

"A girl."

The woman nodded, her smile visible in the reflected light from the dashboard. "That's good," she said. "Then when you have a son, he will always have an elder sister to look up to."

Enid thought about that statement. It didn't seem to jibe with the way things worked in The Family. Yes, little boys valued their older sisters when they were little and needed food to eat or to have their diapers changed, but there came a time when that was no longer true. That's when the balance of power shifted. It didn't take long for boys to start looking down on the very girls who had once cared for them. About that same time, though—about the time the girls were betrothed and sent to live with their future husbands' families—the boys left their birth homes, too, going to live in the boys' dormitories near the church where they were overseen by Bishop Lowell's wives and trained to work in the fields. After that, the only time The Encampment's boys and girls saw each other was during supervised events at church.

"Does your family know you're out here by yourself?" the woman asked.

Enid nodded. "My mother's in the hospital in Flagstaff," she said, surprised at how easily the lie came to her lips. "I'm going to see her."

The old woman nodded, seeming to accept Enid's statement at face value.

As the silence deepened once more, the size of Enid's lie seemed to grow around her, filling the cab of the truck, robbing it of air. She wished what she had said was true—that her mother *was* in a hospital someplace, but, of course, that wasn't likely. In Enid's heart of hearts, she hoped her mother was Outside somewhere—that she had somehow escaped life in The Family and that someday Enid might even be able to find her.

Enid had only the vaguest memories of her mother, or, at least, of the woman she thought had been her mother. She'd had blond hair, too, worn in braids wrapped around the crown of her head, just the way Enid wore hers. She remembered that a woman with blond hair, kind eyes, a sweet voice, and a wonderful smile had been part of Enid's childhood for a while. She was there for a time, and then she was gone. After she disappeared, Enid went to live with another family. Then when she was five and betrothed to Gordon, she had come to live in his household under the strict thumb of Aunt Edith. Once, when Enid had asked Aunt Edith who her mother was and where she had gone, Aunt Edith had replied that Enid's mother was dead. End of story.

Except it wasn't. Last summer, Enid had broken one of The Family's cardinal rules and had paid an unauthorized visit to the pig sheds. The two women who tended the Tower family pigs lived in a small tin Quonset hut near a similar building that housed their charges. Never referred to by name, they were known only as the Brought Back girls—girls who had attempted to escape The Family and had lived Outside before being returned home. According to The Family's strictures, they were considered wicked and evil and were not to be spoken to under any circumstances.

The Brought Back girls slept on straw mattresses in a shed with no electricity. They had a kerosene lantern and a wood stove. Their Quonset hut came with no running water or indoor toilet. The two of them wore faded, cast-off, and much-mended clothing that was handed down to them only when it was no longer fit for anyone else to wear. After dinner each night, they came to the back door of the kitchen to collect that day's slop bucket for the pigs, bringing along two tin plates for the scraps that were their own dinner. Never allowed inside the house, they stood in silence on the back step, waiting until whatever leftovers happened to be available were doled out onto their individual plates.

Older girls were assigned various household tasks and child-tending chores. Enid actually preferred doing dinner dishes to some of the other jobs—like sweeping, dusting, and shaking rugs. As a result, she was often in the kitchen when the Brought Back girls came to the house after supper to collect their evening meal—their only meal of the day.

Enid had noticed that when Aunt Margaret was in the kitchen overseeing the cleanup, the amount of food heaped onto the Brought Back girls' plates was far more generous than when Aunt Edith was in charge. The same thing held true for the other wives when it came their turn. They made sure that the Brought Back girls' helpings were stingier than they needed to be.

Curious, Enid had managed to ask enough questions to learn that one of The Family's two in-house exiles was actually Aunt Margaret's younger sister, someone who had once been betrothed to marry Gordon and who had run away months before the scheduled ceremony. No one ever mentioned how she had been found or returned to The Encampment, but clearly someone had gone Outside and retrieved her.

For the first time, Enid began to wonder. She knew that on the rare occasions when girls ran away from The Family and didn't come back, their disappearances were worse than if they had died. Their names were inked out of family Bibles and were never mentioned again. It was almost as though they had never existed.

One afternoon, when Enid was charged with looking after some of the younger kids out in the play area, the electric fence around the pigpen went down and some of the piglets escaped their enclosure. Enid and the children helped return some of the escapees to the pen, an act of kindness for which the Brought Back girls were effusively grateful. In the middle of all the excitement, Enid managed a quiet word with the one she had been told was Aunt Margaret's younger sister.

The woman's clothing was filthy, and so was she. Her footwear consisted of a pair of taped-together men's boots several sizes too large for her. Her hands were rough and callused. Her matted hair was spiked with twigs of straw. She was missing several teeth. Enid tried to estimate how old she was, but the hard life she lived made guessing her age impossible.

Enid waited until no one else was within earshot. "My name is Enid," she said quietly. "Did you ever know my mother?" She asked the question with little hope of an answer. Much to her surprise, the woman nodded.

"Her name was Anne—Anne Lowell. She was a year younger than me. She was married to Bishop Lowell, although he wasn't the bishop back then. He was still Brother Lowell at the time."

Enid was astonished. If her mother had been married to Bishop Lowell, did that make Enid one of his daughters? If so, why had he never acknowledged her in any way? She realized now that the bishop had never in her memory spoken so much as a single word to her. All through her childhood, in fact long before Enid married Gordon, she had been known as Enid Tower. In other words, The Family had first driven her mother away and then they had stripped Enid of her sole connection to Anne Lowell—her name.

"Aunt Edith told me once that my mother died. Is that true?"

The Brought Back girl shook her head. "Your mother and I were friends," she said. "Anne had two miscarriages after you were born. When she got pregnant again, she ran away. Anne was one of the lucky ones. Unlike Agnes and me, she didn't get caught."

"Agnes?" Enid asked. "That's your friend's name?"

The other woman nodded, then she looked worriedly in the direction of the house, clearly concerned that someone might see them talking together. Enid knew what would happen to her if she was caught—she'd be punished, most likely with Aunt Edith's willow switch. She realized then that the Brought Back girls would be punished, too, probably with something worse than a switch.

"What's your name?" Enid asked.

"They used to call me Patricia," the grimy woman said wistfully. "That was a long time ago."

"You're still Patricia to me," Enid declared. "Thank you for telling me about my mother, and I'm glad to know your names."

She had left the pigpen then, but that conversation marked the beginning of Enid's rebellion. She was struck by the injustice of the way The Family's boys were treated and the way the girls were treated. She was especially bothered by the unrelenting internal exile of the Brought Back girls. Once boys grew up, most of them chose to leave. Few came back, but the ones who did were always welcomed with open arms and a sermon at church about the return of the Prodigal Son. Some of the returnees were even allowed to marry the girls who had been betrothed to them years earlier. None of the boys who came back were sent off to live in Quonset huts and look after pigs.

If boys could leave The Encampment and then come back whenever they wanted, Enid wondered, why couldn't girls?

Now that Enid knew her mother's name, she thought about Anne Lowell all the time, wondering what had happened to her and to her baby. It was common knowledge in The Family that Bishop Lowell was beyond strict with members of his own family and with the boys in the dormitories, too. Helena, his First Wife, was known to be an absolute terror—a woman who made Aunt Edith look like sweetness and light.

Lying in bed next to her snoring husband that night, Enid thought about her mother—and about what her life must have been like, living under the thumb of Bishop Lowell and Helena. Enid could understand that things might have happened that would have provoked her mother into running away, but how could she do such a thing and leave Enid behind? For weeks, Enid tossed and turned, turning that painful question over and over in her head. Then came the day when Dr. Johnson did Enid's first ultrasound.

Since most of the girls in The Family married on their fifteenth birthday, they usually had their first baby before they turned sixteen. For whatever reason, that hadn't happened to Enid. The marriage part, yes, but she didn't become pregnant for almost a year after that. It was so long, in fact, that Aunt Edith had called Enid aside one day and asked her if she was doing something wicked to keep from having a baby. Enid wasn't, of course. She had no idea what any of those wicked things might be. For whatever reason, she had been a month past her sixteenth birthday when she made that first prenatal doctor's visit.

As soon as Dr. Johnson told her she was expecting a girl, it was as though someone had flipped a switch somewhere deep in Enid's soul. Suddenly she understood not only what her mother had done but also why. Anne had learned that she was expecting a girl. She must have realized even then that Enid was lost to her, but she refused to consign another girl child to live among people for whom girls were valuable only so long as they could go forth and multiply. Leaving had been the only way for Anne Lowell to escape the kind of tyranny that routinely dished out the kinds of punishments Patricia and Agnes were forced to endure while boys were free to come and go as they liked with no apparent punishment at all.

That day in Dr. Johnson's office, before Enid had even finished dressing to leave the examining room, she had made up her mind and reached the same conclusion Anne Lowell had reached—Enid would run away.

For months afterward, she lay awake in bed next to Gordon, all the while plotting her escape. One night, when everyone was asleep, she managed to creep out of the house undetected and make her way back down the path to the dark Quonset hut that was home to Patricia and Agnes. When she tapped on the door, Patricia, carrying a lit candle, came to the door.

"I'm going to leave," Enid said. "I wanted you to know, and I didn't want to leave without saying good-bye."

Patricia nodded. "Just a minute." She disappeared into the hut. When she returned, she thrust a tiny piece of paper into Enid's hand. Holding it close to the light from the flickering candle, Enid saw a string of numbers and a single name—Irene.

"What's this?" she asked.

"It's a name and a phone number," Patricia answered. "Memorize both and then throw the paper away. Better yet, burn it so no one can find it. When you get Outside, go to a phone and call that number. Ask for Irene. She'll help you. She tried to help me, but they caught me before I could get to her."

Enid memorized the string of numbers. Not quite trusting her memory, however, she also kept the slip of paper, hiding it away in a crack between the baseboard and the Sheetrock in the bedroom she shared with Gordon. It had been there for months. Today, just before she and Aunt Edith left for town, Enid had taken the tiny piece of paper out of its hiding place and slipped it into the pocket of her jacket along with the sandwich.

Enid had never used a telephone. She realized that was the first thing she would have to do once she was Outside—find a phone and figure out how to use it.

After all, it wasn't as though she had never seen one. There was a phone in the house—a heavy black thing with buttons on it—that sat on the desk in the room that was Gordon's office. Aunt Edith was the only woman in the household who was allowed to touch it. Enid had noticed that the men in The Family, the Elders and also Bishop Lowell, had little things that they carried around in their pockets that were evidently telephones, too. Enid knew they talked to one another on them, even when they were outside, but she couldn't imagine how the phones worked since they didn't seem to require wires of any kind.

She also knew that there was a phone at the gas station. She had seen it hanging on the wall just outside the restroom door. The problem was, that one had slots for money—coins—so you evidently had to pay to use that phone. Money was something Enid didn't have.

During the months of planning, worrying, and waiting, there were times Enid had doubted this day would ever come. Now it was here—a cold, overcast day with occasional flurries of snow. For good or ill, she and her baby— a girl she would name Ann after her own mother—were riding into the darkening night in a pickup truck belonging to a pair of complete strangers. Children in The Family were constantly warned to avoid contact with everything from Outside and most especially Indians. Strangers were evil heathens and were to be avoided at all costs. The problem was, this old couple didn't seem the least bit evil.

It was well past dinnertime by now. Nervous beyond bearing, Enid had been unable to eat any breakfast or lunch before the doctor's appointment. When Aunt Edith questioned her about that, Enid had said she wasn't feeling well. If you were pregnant, that was always an acceptable excuse for not eating.

Now, though, with her stomach growling, she fingered the pilfered cheese sandwich. After being crushed against the door and the armrest, it was probably much the worse for wear. She was tempted to pull it out and eat it but decided that would be rude. There wasn't enough to share, and she couldn't very well eat in front of these people who were kind enough to give her a ride.

The man took his hand off the wheel, reached over, and put his hand on the woman's ample thigh. Enid cringed. When Gordon touched her leg like that, she knew that he wanted her to hurry up to the bedroom as soon as dinner was over and her kitchen chores were done. In this case, the woman patted the man's hand in return and left hers resting on top of his. There didn't seem to be any underlying message in the man's gesture. They continued to ride along in what struck Enid as a perfectly comfortable silence.

Then, to Enid's surprise, a telephone rang. It sounded just like the one on Gordon's desk. She was astonished when the woman bent down and pulled a tiny device out of her purse. It looked just like the phones Gordon and the other Elders used, and the bright light from the screen lit up the cab of the speeding truck.

The woman did something to the screen and then held the phone to her ear. "Hi, Ramona," she said. "We're on our way. We'll be there in an hour or so. No, we haven't had dinner. Okay. See you then."

Enid remained focused on the phone in the woman's hand, amazed that on the Outside even women were allowed to use them. Perhaps the woman was some kind of Elder—but was it even possible for a woman to be an Elder?

The woman stuffed the device back in her purse. "Ramona's cooking dinner," she said to the man. "It'll be ready about the time we get there."

The man nodded and smiled, while the woman turned back to Enid. "Our daughter," she explained. "She and her husband run an RV park north of Flagstaff."

"Could I use that, please?" Enid asked, pointing toward the spot where the phone had disappeared into the woman's purse. "I don't have any money, but there's someone I need to call."

Shrugging, the woman retrieved the phone and handed it over. "You're welcome to use it," she said. "We have plenty of minutes. You don't need to pay."

Enid managed to locate the slip of paper and pull it out of her pocket, but once she had the phone in her hand, she looked at it in complete befuddlement.

"Don't you know how to use it?" the woman asked.

Enid shook her head.

The woman took the phone back. She did something to it, and it lit up. "Who do you want to call?"

Wordlessly, Enid handed over the slip of paper. One at a time, the woman punched the numbers into the phone. When she finished, she handed the device back to Enid. "It's ringing," she said.

With her hand trembling, Enid held the phone to her ear. "May I help you?" a woman's voice inquired.

"Irene," Enid managed. "I need to speak to Irene."

"I'm sorry," the woman answered. "Did you say Irene? I'm afraid there's no one here by that name, but if you're looking . . .

Enid didn't wait to hear more. With those few words her only source of hope had been snatched away. Irene was the only person Patricia had said might help her. Without Irene, Enid and her baby were Outside and completely alone.

Not knowing what else to do, Enid handed the phone back, and the woman returned it to the purse. As they continued south, Enid held her hand to her mouth and stifled a sob, but she couldn't hold back the curtain of despair. With Irene gone, Enid had no idea where she was going to go or what she was going to do.

Without anyone to help her, no doubt Enid would be caught and returned to The Family. Most likely she'd be sent down to join Agnes and Patricia in tending the pigs. If that's what happened to her, fine, but what would become of poor Baby Ann?

6

Once Athena left, Ali made a quick call to B.

He listened to what she had to say. "So much for not getting sucked into the middle of it," he said resignedly, "but it does sound as though she could use our help. Go ahead and give Stuart a call."

Stuart Ramey was B. Simpson's right-hand man at High Noon Enterprises. In person, Stuart's social skills were somewhat lacking, but his personal foibles didn't necessarily make themselves apparent in telephone or computer transactions. He had, with some difficulty, overcome his fear of flying, enough to make a few flights in the course of the last few months, but elevators were still an absolute no-no. He lived to work and mostly lived at work, which allowed him to schedule his life around whatever time zone B. was currently occupying.

In the past Stuart had lived in his office on an unofficial basis, making do on an air mattress on the floor of an office that was usually cluttered with leftover pizza boxes and other fast-food takeout debris. A few weeks earlier, while Stuart had been out of town on an enforced holiday, B. had taken advantage of his absence and had remodeled that corner of High Noon's warehouse space into a combination office/studio apartment, complete with a bathroom, shower, and tiny kitchenette.

Stuart had returned to an office/studio combination that was now truly his private domain, and he loved it. What Ali appreciated about the new arrangement was that Stuart's office now looked more like an office and less like a slovenly college dorm room. How Stuart's private apartment looked, now safely shut away behind a closed door, was none of Ali's business or anybody else's.

Ali's call to Stuart was answered by his new assistant, Cami—short for Camille. Cami Lee was a recent graduate of UCLA. She was a bright young Asian woman who had arrived at High Noon with a ready smile, boundless energy, and a cum laude bachelor of science degree with dual majors in both computer science and electrical engineering. To everyone's relief, she seemed able to take Stuart's lack of interpersonal skills in stride. Ali was thrilled that B. had managed to snap Cami up before anyone else could.

"Good afternoon, Ms. Reynolds," Cami said when she answered the phone. "Mr. Ramey is on the other line. Would you like to hold or do you want him to call you back?"

Marveling at how young Cami sounded on the phone, Ali opted for holding and looked out the window while she waited. Over the course of the afternoon, the sky had darkened. The winter storm the weather forecasters had predicted seemed to be blowing in from the west. With the phone to her ear, Ali stepped over to the gas-log fireplace and turned the flame up another notch.

By the time she returned to her chair, Stuart was on the phone. "Hey," he said. "What's up?"

Ali spent the next ten minutes summarizing the situation with Betsy Peterson in Bemidji. "What's our interest in all this?" Stuart asked when she finished.

"Since local law enforcement agencies are discounting what Athena and I regard as a real threat, I want High Noon to build a security safety net around Betsy," Ali answered. "I want fully monitored electronic surveillance of her home. How do we go about making that happen?"

"Well," Stuart said, "you've got a choice here. It can be done cheap, quick, or good. Pick any two."

"I'm choosing quick and good," Ali replied.

"As in spare no expense?"

"Yes," Ali answered. "Athena will be the official client, but the billing is to be sent to me. I'm assuming you'll have to locate some outside assistance."

"Absolutely," Stuart said. "I've been to Minnesota in the winter. I've no intention of going myself, but I've got a contact in Minneapolis, a guy named Joe. He's good. He's also someone we've worked with before, and he might be willing to handle the job."

"Okay," Ali said, "if he agrees to take this on, let me know before you make it official so I can clear it with Betsy."

"Right," Stuart agreed. "The only way to make this work is to have her full cooperation. Do you know if she has a computer?"

"According to Athena, probably not one that's up to date. I understand Betsy has Wi-Fi in the house that may not be functioning at this point. She most likely discontinued the account once Athena moved here."

"We need to find out for sure," Stuart said.

"Talk to Athena," Ali advised. "She'll be able to tell you what you need to know."

"The thing is," Stuart cautioned, "most ordinary computers won't have the kinds of advanced electronic capabilities we'll need."

"You have carte blanche," Ali assured him. "Plan on getting whatever we need to do the job right."

"Okay," Stuart said. "Will do."

Ali's call waiting buzzed. "Get back to me, please, Stuart. I've got another call."

Ali switched over. "Any room in the inn?" Sister Anselm Becker asked.

Sister Anselm, a Sister of Providence, was also Ali's best friend and had served as Ali's matron of honor at B. and Ali's Christmas Eve wedding at the Four Seasons in Las Vegas. It had taken a special dispensation from the mother superior at St. Bernadette's, Sister Anselm's convent in Jerome, for Sister Anselm to be absent from the convent on Christmas Eve.

When she wasn't at home in Jerome, Sister Anselm often operated as a special emissary for Bishop Francis Gillespie, head of the Catholic diocese in Phoenix, who for the past dozen or so years had routinely dispatched Sister Anselm to hospitals all over Arizona where she served as patient advocate to mostly impoverished people who had no one else to intercede on their behalf.

"Of course," Ali said. "We always have a spare bed for you. What's going on?"

"I'm still here in Jerome dealing with construction issues," Sister Anselm explained. "I have to be in Flagstaff for a meeting early tomorrow morning. With a storm blowing in, I don't want to be driving back and forth to Payson in ice and snow."

St. Bernadette's had been built by the Sisters of Charity in conjunction with a parochial school in the early

1900s while Jerome was still a thriving mining community. When the mines shut down, so did the school. After lying dormant for a number of decades, the convent had been reopened by the Sisters of Providence as an R&R center and retreat house for nuns from any number of orders who needed a place of quiet contemplation and respite where they could recover their mental and spiritual equilibrium.

The programs offered at St. Bernadette's, many of them facilitated by Sister Anselm, may have been up to the minute, but the physical plant itself, now over a hundred years old, was falling down around the sisters' ears. Months earlier, a building inspector had threatened to red flag the convent and throw the resident nuns out into the street.

At the time, B. Simpson had been worried about a badly injured teenager who had come to his attention. The kid, Lance Tucker, was a talented hacker. He was hospitalized in Texas having already survived one failed homicide attempt. Fearing another, B. had negotiated a treaty with his friend Bishop Gillespie. In exchange for sending Sister Anselm to Texas to look after Lance, B. had agreed to tackle the daunting project of bringing St. Bernadette's into the twenty-first century. Since Sister Anselm had already established a close working relationship with B., the mother superior, Sister Justine, had appointed Sister Anselm to serve as construction supervisor for the convent's complex remodeling project.

Rehab work had been scheduled to begin in early January. The nuns from St. Bernadette's had decamped to a diocese-operated retreat in Payson in order to be out of the way. The facility in Payson, usually open only during the summer months, was a camp of sorts where priests from Phoenix could go to escape the valley's all-consuming heat.

The displaced sisters from St. Bernadette's had anticipated that their stay in Payson would last for no more than a matter of weeks. But that time period had already stretched into months. Delays with obtaining building permits had postponed work for nearly a month, and construction had only now finally begun. In the meantime, the nuns were shivering their nights away in flimsy cabins never designed for wintertime occupancy.

Ali had driven the almost eighty-mile route from Jerome to Payson many times. The fifty miles on the far side of Camp Verde were dicey under the best of circumstances. Snow and ice could make those miles downright treacherous. And then to have to turn around and reverse course the next morning to drive all the way to Flagstaff? No wonder Sister Anselm wanted to stay over.

"You're in luck," Ali told her. "Mr. Brooks looked at the weather forecast last night and told me that if a winter storm was coming through, today would be a 'cassoulet kind of day.'"

"Cassoulet, really?" Sister Anselm asked. "You know what a treat that is!"

Although Sister Anselm had been born in the United States, she had spent decades of her life living in a small convent in France. Ali already knew that Leland Brooks's cassoulet was one of the good sister's all-time favorite meals.

"I'll go out to the kitchen right now and ask him to set another place," Ali told her. "When will you be here?"

"In about an hour," Sister Anselm answered. "The snow is due to start any minute. I want to be off the mountain before that happens."

The mountain in question was Mingus Mountain, which marked the far western end of the Verde Valley.

Once off the phone, Ali headed straight to the kitchen. Leland Brooks greeted her news about their unexpected guest with a confident grin.

"In that case," he said, "I'd best set about mixing up a batch of corn bread to go along with the cassoulet. As I recall, the last time Sister Anselm had some of that, she referred to it as 'heavenly.'"

"That's because it is," Ali assured him.

"And I'll set the dining room table for two, then," he added.

When Ali and Leland were at home alone, she often joined Leland in the kitchen at mealtimes, but she knew his sense of decorum would preclude serving company there.

"I hope you'll join us," Ali said.

"No, thank you," Leland replied. "Will you be having wine?"

"Sister Anselm is partial to Côtes du Rhône," Ali answered.

"Very well," Leland nodded. "I've had my eye on a particular bottle of a Châteauneuf-du-Pape. I'll bring that one in from the wine cellar."

With that settled, Ali ushered Bella outside for a walk. They had installed a fully fenced dog run outside the back door and a doggie door as well. The latter Bella stubbornly refused to use. She no longer had to be on a leash to do her duty outside, but she needed someone outside with her holding a leash even if it wasn't attached to her. It was annoying to have to accompany her outside in the cold for no good reason.

Back in the house, Ali returned to the library and

cleared her desk, then she went to her room and changed out of her sweats into something a little dressier. When the doorbell rang, Bella and Leland went to answer it. By the time Leland escorted Sister Anselm into the library, Ali was there as well, seated in front of the fire, with a copy of *Pride and Prejudice* open on her lap.

Sister Anselm entered the room wearing ordinary business attire—a dark blue knit pantsuit with a high-necked white blouse under the blazer. The only hint that she might be a nun was a crucifix suspended on a gold chain that she wore at the base of her throat. The nun was a tall spare woman without a hint of the widow's hump one might have expected for someone in her early eighties. Her iron-gray hair, thinning a little now, was cut in a short bob. Behind a pair of wire-rimmed spectacles, her bright blue eyes sparkled with intelligence and good humor.

Sister Anselm settled into the chair opposite Ali. Bella immediately darted into her lap to give her an appropriate greeting, after which she decamped to Ali's. At that point, Sister Anselm caught sight of a vivid white mark marring the outside of one of her pant legs. She tried dusting it off but with little effect.

"It's only plaster dust," she said resignedly. "It's everywhere. I guess I'm lucky this is the only place it ended up. I can see now that B. was right. Reverend Mother thought we should be able to stay in the convent during construction. B. insisted otherwise, and it's a good thing he did."

"How's it going?" Ali asked.

Sister Anselm shook her head. "Naturally there's a problem with the foundation. I suspected as much since we'd had so much cracking at one end of the house.

They're bringing in a soil engineer to find a way to shore up the foundation. That has to happen before any other repairs can be undertaken."

Leland turned up just then with a rosewood tray that contained two wineglasses and an already opened bottle of the cru he had selected. A glance at the label told Ali it was one of the rarer bottles that had come from her philandering second husband's extensive wine collection. Because her divorce from Paul Grayson hadn't been finalized at the time of his death, she had inherited the wine collection along with everything else. She never sipped any of what she thought of as "Fang's wine" without remembering that it was, in a very real way, the spoils of war.

Leland poured two glasses and handed them out. Ali raised hers first. "Here's to remodeling!"

Sister Anselm laughed. "I had a long talk with the electrician today. He's a young guy who had never before seen what they call 'knob and tube' electrical wiring. Now that the place is stripped down to studs, it's all painfully visible. From the looks of it, the wiring situation constituted a very real fire hazard. The electrician told me it's a miracle we weren't all burned to death in our sleep."

"How old is St. Bernadette's again?" Ali asked.

"It was built in 1910," Sister Anselm explained. "They remodeled it once in the twenties. That's when they installed both electricity and running water. Very little has been done since, other than necessary repairs, painting, and the occasional plasterwork. For years Sister Evangeline, the cook, kept a list on the fridge saying what appliances could and couldn't run at the same time. For instance, starting the microwave at the same time the coffeepot was going was a definite no-no. Ditto the toaster. Making toast at the same time as anything else was turned on meant we'd blow a fuse for sure. And since there was seldom more than one or two plug-ins in every room, we had little multi-outlet extension cords everywhere."

"Fire hazard indeed," Ali observed. She had been deeply involved in the remodel of this house, so she had some idea of the complex issues involved. Even though hers was half the age of the convent, upgrading and redesigning the electrical service had been a costly but important process.

"By the way," Sister Anselm added, "I called Bishop Gillespie earlier this afternoon to tell him about the problem with the foundation. My understanding is that rectifying the situation will be expensive and raise the cost of the remodel considerably. I know B. agreed to do this for us, but I'm not sure his generosity will stretch that far. The bishop said the two of them would discuss it."

"Don't worry," Ali said. "After what you did for all of us in Texas? I can promise you that there's enough give in the remodeling budget to cover whatever is needed. If B. can't pony it up, I certainly can."

Leland appeared in the doorway. "Dinner is served," he announced.

Taking their wineglasses with them, the two women followed him into the dining room. Once they were seated, he served generous helpings of thick stew into their dishes. Then, setting the soup tureen down on the sideboard, he brought a platter heaped with slabs of corn bread still steaming from the oven.

After serving, Leland coaxed Bella into the kitchen with him. The two women ate a companionable meal while falling snowflakes drifted past the dining room window. They spent most of the time comparing the hazards of remodeling projects and some of it discussing Ali's scholarship responsibilities.

They finished eating a little past eight. When Ali invited her guest back into the library, Sister Anselm declined. "In the convent, we go to bed with the birds and rise with the chickens. If you don't mind, I'll take a rain check."

While Leland cleaned up, Ali took the last of her wine and returned to the library with her dog, her comfy chair, her fireplace, and her book.

Yes, remodeling took time, money, and effort, but from where she was sitting right now, it was definitely worth it. She hoped that when the nuns from St. Bernadette's returned home from Payson to their newly rehabbed digs, they'd be able to say the same.

7

As the pickup moved steadily southward, they began to drive through flurries of snow. It was starting to stick on the sides of the road but not on the pavement itself. Enid knew that her lightweight jacket would be no match for the weather once she left the crowded warmth of the pickup. And what would happen when she did?

Just thinking of it was enough to fill her heart with dread. What should Enid do? What if she spoke up and asked the man to stop and let her out right now? What if she went back to The Encampment on her own before The Family had a chance to send someone out searching for her? Maybe she'd be able to beg Gordon's forgiveness. If she was lucky, perhaps he'd let her off with nothing worse than a beating. Then again . . .

Eventually the strain of the day was too much for her. Not intending to, she nodded off, allowing her head to loll over onto the Navajo woman's broad shoulder. She awakened and straightened up, seemingly much later, when the pickup began to slow.

"We're almost there," the woman said as Enid sat up

and rubbed her eyes. "Our turnoff is coming up in a mile or two. Do you have someone who will come get you?"

"I'll be all right," Enid said.

Shaking her head, the woman twisted around and retrieved a blanket from the narrow space behind the seat. "It's cold out there," she said. "You'll need something besides that jacket to keep you warm."

Enid fingered the rough wool. In the pale light from the dashboard, she glimpsed the colorful hues and complex designs and recognized them for what they were. She had seen Navajo rugs and blankets before. There was a special counter inside the general store where tourists could buy them, cheerfully paying amounts of money that seemed, to Enid, to be princely sums.

"I can't take this," Enid protested.

"You have to," the woman insisted. Her voice was gentler than Aunt Edith's, but it brooked no nonsense.

"But I don't have any money," Enid objected.

"What you have is a need for a blanket," the woman said firmly. "I can always weave another. Please take it."

Reluctantly, Enid accepted. "Thank you," she said.

The pickup pulled off onto the dirt shoulder and came to a slow stop. The snow had let up, although a few flakes still skittered here and there. They had stopped at a junction of sorts, under a single streetlight and next to a flock of mailboxes. On either side of the paved highway dirt roads led off to the east and west and disappeared into the distance. Directly across the road was a lonely gas station.

The woman pointed toward the road that went off to the right. "Our daughter's RV park is that way," she said.

Nodding, Enid fumbled for the door handle.

"Are you sure we can't call someone to come for you?" the woman asked as Enid climbed out.

"No," she said, stepping onto a dirt shoulder that was partially covered by a thin coating of snow. "Someone will give me a ride."

She looked back the way they had come. Far in the distance she spotted a pinprick of light, which meant that another vehicle was coming this way. As the wind bit through her jacket, she wrapped the blanket around her shoulders and was amazed at how well the tightly woven wool shielded her from the cold.

She stood for a moment longer, holding the door open. "Thank you for the ride," she said, "and for the blanket, too."

Moving to reclaim her part of the bench seat, the woman nodded. "You're welcome," she said. "Take care."

When the pickup drove off, Enid stood in the cold and dark, staring longingly at the gas station across the road. It would be warm inside. She'd be able to use the bathroom. Maybe whoever ran the place would let her stay there long enough to find another ride. The problem was, people stopping there might well be going in the other direction, back the way she'd come.

Fishing the squashed sandwich out of her pocket, Enid unfolded the waxed paper, shoved that back into her pocket, and then wolfed down the sandwich while trying to make up her mind. This was the moment of decision, the time when she either had to move forward toward the unknown or turn back and face whatever punishment The Family meted out. Convinced now of her kinship to Bishop Lowell, she knew he would want to make an example of her. He'd want to be sure the other girls saw her suffer.

No, Enid decided at last, whatever future the Outside held couldn't be worse than what awaited her back home at The Encampment. Polishing off the rest of the sandwich, she turned to look at the approaching vehicle whose headlights she had glimpsed when she first stepped out of the pickup. It was much closer now, speeding toward her. Wrapping the blanket around her shoulders, she faced north and stuck out her thumb. The vehicle turned out to be another pickup. It sped past without slowing, traveling so fast that she caught not the smallest glimpse of the occupants.

Resolutely, Enid turned back to the road, squinting through the darkness in hopes of seeing yet another southbound traveler. As a consequence, she didn't notice that, after the pickup sped past her, it slowed a quarter mile or so away, stopped, and made a quick U-turn. With the wind whistling in her ears, she didn't hear the returning vehicle as it approached from the opposite direction, although she did catch a glimmer from the headlights out of the corner of her eyes. When she turned to look, that's all she could see—a pair of bright headlights that belonged to a vehicle that had pulled over and stopped on the shoulder on the far side of the highway. It sat at an odd angle so the high beams were pointed directly at her.

A moment later, the headlights went out. There was another brief flash of light as a car door opened and closed. Then she heard something else—first the crunch of boots on snow-glazed gravel and then a singsong voice saying, "Here, piggy, piggy, piggy. Don't you think it's time you came home?"

Terrified, Enid stood her ground. The approaching man's voice seemed oddly familiar. Obviously he knew all about what awaited her back home. In the dim light from the overhead streetlight, she saw him striding forward, walking along the shoulder on the far side of the road.

The glow of the streetlight was enough that she caught a flash of something on the man's jacket. Was it a badge she was seeing? Suddenly he tripped on something, or perhaps his shoe slipped on a bit of icy gravel. He staggered for a moment before catching his balance.

"Dressed up like an Indian, are you, Enid?" he said, righting himself. "Come along now. Time to go home."

She knew who he was now. He spoke with the authority of one of the Elders, issuing commands that he fully expected her to follow. Because that's how things worked in The Family—men issued orders; women obeyed.

When the dim figure started toward her again, he was little more than a looming shadow. Focused completely on him, she failed to realize that what had made the difference was another set of bright headlights from yet another vehicle. This one, approaching from the south, overwhelmed the insubstantial glow of the streetlight.

Paralyzed with a combination of dread and indecision, Enid stood for several moments longer, watching and waiting. Her pursuer had crossed one lane of pavement and was within a matter of feet of reaching her when Enid finally sprang to action. Instead of obeying, intent on nothing other than making her escape, she wheeled away from him and ran, sprinting toward what she hoped would be the relative safety of the gas station. She never made it. She never saw or heard the vehicle approaching her from behind; never saw the blinking turn signal that indicated the driver was starting to slow in order to turn into the gas station. Unfortunately, he hadn't slowed enough.

She heard the squeal of brakes. A sharp pain shot through her body as the front bumper caught her hip and tossed her skyward. For what seemed like forever, she flew through air. When she came back to earth, she landed hard enough to knock the wind out of her before momentum sent her tumbling over and over across the pavement. For a long time after she came to rest, there was nothing but darkness. Then, from very far away she heard a single voice calling out to her through her pain.

"Oh my God! Are you all right? I didn't see you at all. You ran out onto the road right in front of me. I tried to stop, but there wasn't time."

This was a man's voice—a young man's voice—filled with concern and anguish. He was leaning over her. Enid could feel his warm breath on her face and his hand touching her shoulder. Her first instinct was to caution him that he shouldn't use the Lord's name in vain. If he was back home with The Family, Aunt Edith would cane him if she heard that, and so would Bishop Lowell. She opened her eyes briefly. Searching his chest, she was relieved to see no sign of the badge she thought she had seen earlier. It wasn't there. The man leaning over her wasn't the one who had called to her from across the road—the one sent to bring her back home.

The pain was astonishing. Enid closed her eyes, trying to blot it out. When she opened them again, the man was gone—he had disappeared completely from her line of vision. She thought for a moment that he had abandoned her and left her alone to die or else that he had gone away, leaving her at the mercy of the man wearing the badge. But then the young man's face suddenly reappeared, and she felt the comforting weight of a heavy blanket settle over her.

She was out again briefly. When she returned to consciousness the next time, she heard more voices gathered around her—urgent voices, frightened voices, questioning ones. She struggled to make them out, trying to tell if there was a familiar one among them, but there wasn't. The people who surrounded her now and who were coming to her aid weren't from The Family. They were strangers, Outsiders.

"She's hurt." She recognized the young man's voice, yelling urgently to someone behind him. "Hurt bad. Call 911. We need an aid car. Now!" Then he turned back to Enid. "Are you there?" he asked. "Can you hear me?"

With superhuman effort, Enid forced her eyes to open and her head to nod. At least she thought she nodded.

"Thank God," he whispered. "You're alive. The guy from the station is calling an ambulance. Stay with me now. What's your name?"

He'd done it again—used the Lord's name in vain. Enid tried to move her lips, to tell him her name, but they didn't work properly. She said Enid, but he must have heard something else.

"Okay, Edith," he said. "Don't move. The guy from the station is putting out flares. We'll wait right here for the ambulance, okay?"

She wanted to tell him that Edith wasn't her name. Edith was someone else entirely, but all she could manage was a single word. "Okay," she whispered.

"What the hell were you doing out here in the dark?" he demanded. He sounded angry now—angry and accusatory. "You ran out right in front of me. By the time I saw you, there was no way to stop. I barely had time enough to step on the brake."

She wanted to tell him the whole story, but she couldn't. It was too complicated. It was too hard to talk; too hard to keep the pieces straight in her head. The world around her was turning fuzzy.

"My baby . . ." she whispered.

"What baby?" he asked. Turning his gaze away from her face, he appeared to look down at the rest of her body for the first time. His eyes stopped and widened when they focused on the bulge in her stomach.

"Oh my God, you're pregnant! I'm sorry! I'm so sorry, but it wasn't my fault."

Enid felt something wet fall on her face. At first she thought it was a drifting snowflake, but then she realized it was a tear—a single tear. The young man was weeping—crying for her. She wanted to reach out and comfort him—to tell him it was all right, but a sudden surge of pain, a shocking brand-new pain, rocketed through her body, robbing her of the ability to speak. As suddenly as it had come, the pain subsided. Feeling the wetness between her legs, Enid knew exactly what it was.

In The Family, that's what women and girls were supposed to do—have babies, lots of them. As a consequence, that was something they talked about—having babies and about the banes of pregnancy—the unrelenting nausea of morning sickness, the swollen ankles and aching backs of the final months and weeks before the baby came, and the realities and indignity of having your water break and then going into labor. That was what had just happened to Enid—her water had broken. The baby was coming.

With a strength she didn't know she had, she somehow reached out from under the blanket and grasped the young man's hand in hers, grinding his fingers together in something close to a death grip.

"Help me, please," she whispered. "My baby's coming."

"Your baby's coming now?" he groaned. "You've got to be kidding! Please, God, this can't be happening. Please."

"It is happening," Enid insisted. "She's coming. Don't let them take me back home. Don't let them take her there," she urged. "Please, whatever you do, don't let them take us back."

Just then another labor pain roared through her, silencing her ability to speak. Her whisper turned into a howl of agony. When the contraction passed, Enid lay breathless and spent on the cold, hard pavement. She was covered by a Navajo blanket and comforted only by the grip of that one strong hand—a hand that belonged to the weeping young man—the Outsider—who knelt beside her.

For a brief moment, Enid longed to be back home in The Encampment's birthing room. There, at least, she would have been warm and covered with a clean sheet. Dr. Johnson would have been there with her. Her bed would have been surrounded by the comfort of familiar faces.

The image passed as quickly as it came, taking everything else with it—the pain, the sounds of concerned voices in the distance, and close up, the man—the Outsider—who was now sobbing brokenly beside her. Before the next contraction hit, Enid had drifted into blessed unconsciousness.

8

Ali was sleeping soundly when she heard the distinctive chirp of Sister Anselm's ringtone. The clock said it was one o'clock in the morning. Her first instinct was to roll over and go back to sleep. When she heard the guest room shower come on, she realized Sister Anselm was up and on the move. Crawling out of bed, Ali donned her robe. With Bella at her heels, she headed for the kitchen to start coffee. Slipping on a pair of clogs, she took Bella outside. The four inches of snow on the ground was deep enough that the dog came back in with her belly covered with snow. Since Bella had spent most of her life in snow-free Las Vegas, snow wasn't something she enjoyed in the least. She shook it off before going back inside.

Sister Anselm emerged from her room with suitcase in hand and purse slung over her shoulder. By then, Ali was waiting at the end of the hall with a cup of coffee already loaded into a vacuum-sealed metal coffee mug that was more thermos than cup.

"Sorry," Sister Anselm apologized. "I meant to sneak out without disturbing anybody. I've just been called out to St. Jerome's Hospital in Flagstaff. Someone got run over on a highway north of there. Tell Mr. Brooks that I've already stripped the sheets. Is it still snowing?"

"It's stopped now," Ali said, handing over the cup. "I didn't know which way you were going, but I checked road conditions on the Department of Transportation website in both directions. This is a weird storm. The worst of it came straight in from the west. The roads from here down to Phoenix are in worse shape than they are going north to Flag. It may be tricky getting down the hill from here to the main drag, but from there on, everything should be plowed, sanded, or both."

"I'll be careful," Sister Anselm assured her. "I won't be much help to anyone else if I'm laid up in the hospital, too."

"Humor me, though," Ali said. "No lead foot, and call me when you get there. I seem to remember that you and that 'arrest-me-red' MINI Cooper of yours have been pulled over more than once."

Sister Anselm nodded grudgingly. "You're almost as bad as the reverend mother," she said.

"From what I know about your reverend mother," Ali replied, "I'll take that as high praise."

"By the way, all I ever got was warnings."

"That's because young cops look at you—a sweet old nun—and figure they'll go to hell if they write you up."

Sister Anselm grinned and shrugged. "True enough," she said, "and I'm always careful not to disabuse them of that notion."

The two friends were still laughing about that as Ali ushered Sister Anselm out to the car. She drove away as it was coming up on one-thirty. Ali considered going back to bed, but after a moment, she glanced at her watch. It had two faces on it—a big one for her, and a second smaller one that she used to keep track of B.'s current time zone. Using a second watch was far easier than adding and sub-tracting time zones in her head. In this case, it was just past eight-thirty A.M. in Zurich. Time enough for B. to be up and dressed, but a couple of hours short of his having to head for the airport.

Ali went back to the kitchen. The giant-sized traveler cup she had poured for Sister Anselm had taken almost half of the small pot Leland kept on the kitchen counter. She poured the remainder of the coffee into a large mug and then made her way back to her favorite spot in the house—one of the easy chairs in the library. After turning on the gas-log fire, she pulled out her phone.

"It's the middle of the night where you are," B. ob-served. "What are you doing up at this hour?"

"Sister Anselm was staying over, but she just got called to look after an accident victim in Flagstaff. I thought I'd give you a call before your flight. I poured myself some of the coffee I brewed for her, and now I'm all yours."

B. heaved a relieved sigh as the worry in his voice changed to genuine pleasure. "With a call coming from you in the middle of the night like that, I was afraid it was bad news. Hang on a sec. I'll pour a new cup of coffee for me, too. It's not the most conventional way for a newly married couple to have morning coffee together, but I'll take it." He was off the line for only a moment. When he returned, he added, "I was just talking on the phone to Stu about the situation in Bemidji."

Ali laughed. "What a surprise. One of these days, if Stuart ever gets a life of his own, he won't be able to time his waking and sleeping according to where you happen to be on the planet."

"That's true," B. agreed, "but right now he is, and his early morning briefings are invaluable."

"What about Bemidji?" Ali asked.

"I think his idea of sending Joe out to assess the situation is the right one."

"Joe would be the guy from Minneapolis?"

"Yes," B. said. "His name's Joe Friday. We've used him before. Stuart said he'd clear it with you later today. I don't think either one of us thought you'd be up and about this early."

"Joe Friday?" Ali repeated. "Are you kidding? Like the 'just-the-facts' guy from that old *Dragnet* series?"

B. laughed. "That's the one. We went over all that when I first met the guy. He said his granddad was a big fan of the show. Since he had to miss the broadcast the night his son was born, and because their last name was already Friday, he said that was the only way to get even with the kid. When the son's first child came along, the name got passed along again, so this Joe Friday is actually a second-generation Joe Friday."

"Right," Ali observed dryly. "Whatever generation, I'm sure he appreciates being asked about his name the same way I appreciate being asked if I know about that New York Yankees pitcher from Tulsa, Oklahoma. At least that's a married name. My parents didn't do that to me on purpose."

"Joe gets a big kick out of it, actually," B. replied. "Names aside, he's designed this slick motion-activated video network, one he can install in places where no one will ever notice. It's a smart system that will send out an alert whenever someone's in the house."

"Is this something Betsy will have to turn off and on whenever she's home?" Ali asked. "That's why she didn't have the alarm engaged the other night. Every time she lets her dog in or out, she has to turn it off. And what about the dog? If Betsy isn't home and the dog is, won't that set off an alarm, too?"

"For one thing, the alert doesn't sound where Betsy is. It operates on her Wi-Fi system and sends the alert to the desk of one of our round-the-clock monitoring centers. She does have Wi-Fi, right?" B. asked.

"That's what Athena told me. It's probably not hooked up right now, but Stuart says it will be."

"Good," B. replied. "What's so slick about Joe's system is that it uses facial and form recognition. When he goes there to set it up, he'll create three-dimensional recognition files for both Betsy and the dog. When the camera spots one of them, no alerts are issued. As for anybody else? They're all fair game."

"It sounds as though you and Stuart have this in hand. Why does he need to clear it with me?"

"Because you asked him to do it, for one thing," B. reminded her. "For another, we're going to need you to talk Betsy into letting Joe into her house. She'll need to create a convincing cover story for his visit, because the whole point is having the system installed without anyone else knowing it exists."

"Because the dog didn't bark?"

B. laughed. "That's my girl," he said, "and that's it precisely. Whoever came into the house that night and turned on the gas most likely was someone the dog—Princess, I believe—wasn't worried about even though she should have been. So we're going to observe the movements of everyone who enters the house and see if we can spot any of them doing something suspicious."

"This sounds expensive," Ali observed, remembering

she had given Stuart the go-ahead to spend whatever was needed.

"It is," B. agreed, "but you get what you pay for. Besides, you weren't planning on billing either Athena or her grandmother for this, were you?"

"No," Ali admitted.

"That's what I thought," he said. "In that case, we'll care enough to send the very best. By the time Stuart talks to you later this morning, he'll have some idea of Joe's availability. After that, it's up to you to convince Betsy Peterson that this invasion of her privacy is in her best interest."

"If there are going to be cameras everywhere in her house, how is she supposed to shower or take a bath without feeling like people are watching her every move? It sounds like there will be cameras in her bedroom and in her bathroom, too. Is that really necessary?"

"Yes, it is," B. answered. "If someone were going to try to slip something into a bottle of prescription medication, for example, it's important that the cameras record whoever might be messing with the medicine cabinet. But again, that's where the smart part comes in. The system only records the movements of people who aren't in the official 3-D recognition file.

"I'm suggesting that you recommend to Betsy that for now she and Princess be the only two entities with recognition files. Anyone else who enters the house will trigger an automatic alarm and record because the cameras will follow them everywhere. It'll be easy enough to tell from the images if they're on the up-and-up or if they're not."

"Betsy struck me as being a bit cantankerous," Ali cautioned, "but she's also provoked that the authorities back there aren't taking any interest in what happened. In other words, I should be able to pull this off."

"Of course, you will," B. agreed. "I have complete faith in your powers of persuasion."

With the pressing items of business out of the way, they talked for a while longer. By the time the call ended, Ali's coffee cup was empty. She turned off the fire and went back to bed, thinking that with a caffeine high she'd be able to make great progress on Jane Austen. After a mere page or two, she put the book down on the bed, turned off the bedside lamp, and fell asleep. She did notice, though, that just as she dozed off, a little warm dog wormed her way under the covers and curled up next to her back.

9

Once on I-17, Sister Anselm was surprised that Ali's weather report proved to be entirely correct. After leaving Sedona, the farther north she went, the less evidence she saw of the storm that was still wreaking havoc from Sedona through Prescott and Cordes Junction and all the way down to the northernmost outskirts of Phoenix. It was an odd kind of weather pattern, to be sure, although she doubted anyone would be able to ascribe the lack of new snow falling in Flagstaff to evidence of global warming or the newest catch-all label—climate change.

Driving north, Sister Anselm spent the time praying for her two, and as yet unknown, patients. An unidentified young woman, possibly a runaway, who was also pregnant, had been struck by a motor vehicle twenty miles north of Flagstaff on Highway 89. The woman, injured and unconscious, had gone into labor. Her infant, a girl thought to be six to eight weeks premature, had been delivered by EMTs in the ambulance on the way to the hospital. The baby was now being treated in a critical care nursery while the mother underwent multiple surgical procedures—one to remove her ruptured spleen and another to reduce pressure on her brain from injuries to the back of her skull.

When Sister Anselm turned into the hospital entrance, it may not have been snowy, but it was bitterly cold. Patches of black ice covered the paved parking lot, making her grateful that she had been directed to go into the underground garage, where a space had been coned off for her. After being buzzed into the building, Sister Anselm made her way to the front desk, where a bleary-eyed overnight receptionist directed her to the fourth-floor maternity ward.

Stepping out of the elevator, Sister Anselm was greeted warmly by an energetic young woman who hurried out of the nurses' station to welcome her. "I'm Nurse Mandy, the charge nurse. You must be Sister Anselm."

"Yes, I am. How are my patients?"

"The baby is premature—critical but stable. She also has a broken arm, which has been set and placed in a soft cast. She was having some breathing difficulties when they brought her in, but she's doing better now. As for the mother? She's critical, too, and still in surgery. When she comes out of the recovery room, by rights they should take her to the surgical recovery floor, but given the circumstances, her doctors have agreed to send her here instead. That way she'll be closer to her baby."

"Has there been any progress on identifying her?"

Nurse Mandy shook her head. "Not so far. Her clothing and belongings are all under lock and key, but I've been authorized to allow you access to them in case that will aid you in sorting out who she is."

"Isn't the sheriff's department working on that?" Sister Anselm asked.

"Yes, but they're not making much progress. They've checked statewide missing persons reports, but so far nothing has turned up that matches our victim. The investigation into the accident itself is still ongoing, but it's most likely going to be termed unavoidable. In other words, no wrongdoing on the driver's part. Apparently, she darted into the road in front of him. Had it been a hit-and-run, that would be a different story, but the driver stayed around long enough to help her and give a statement to police. A witness from a nearby gas station backed up his story."

Sister Anselm understood that had the incident been ruled a hit-and-run, there would have been far more urgency on the part of some law enforcement agency to identify the victim.

"By the way," Nurse Mandy added, "the young man who hit her is just down the hall in the waiting room. He claims not to know her. Nevertheless, he's beyond distraught. I tried to tell him he should go home—that there's nothing more he can do here. Even so, he's adamant about staying."

"Do you think he knows her and is pretending not to?"

"Maybe," Nurse Mandy said. "I've certainly seen that happen before, especially in instances of domestic violence. The assailant sits there and pretends ignorance while the helpless victim is unconscious and unable to say otherwise."

"Why don't I go speak to him," Sister Anselm said. "After that I'd like to take a look at the victim's personal effects; maybe I'll find a clue that will help us identify her."

She walked down the hall to a small waiting room. This was a part of the job she liked the least, approaching supposedly grieving loved ones and trying to suss out who was lying and who was telling the truth.

On one side of the room was a long window that allowed waiting room visitors to see inside the nursery.

Several separate seating areas with chairs and love seats would have accommodated a fair number of visitors. At this hour of the morning, there was only one—a young man in jeans, hiking boots, and a Northern Arizona University Lumberjacks sweatshirt. He jumped to his feet as Sister Anselm walked toward him.

"Are you the chaplain?" he asked anxiously.

"No," she said. "I'm not the chaplain."

"Is she dead?"

The anguish on his face seemed genuine enough. "No one has died," Sister Anselm assured him. "My name is Sister Anselm. I'm a Sister of Providence. I'm also what's called a patient advocate. I'm usually summoned when someone is hospitalized with no apparent next of kin and no way of communicating his or her wishes to medical practitioners. Part of my job is to help locate next of kin for, in this case, two patients rather than one."

"Two?" he asked. "That means they're both still alive?"

Sister Anselm nodded. "So far," she said, "but would that be you, then? Are you their next of kin?"

"No," the young man said. "Not at all." His face, which had brightened momentarily, turned somber again. His shoulders drooped. "I'm the guy who hit them."

Sister Anselm trusted her people skills. The young man's anxiety could easily have been faked, but the naked relief that had flashed across his face at learning that both patients were still alive was absolutely genuine.

He sat back down, hard, shaking his head in obvious relief. "I'm so glad to hear they're both still alive. When she told me her baby was coming, I thought, 'Oh, no, I've killed them both.'"

"Well, you didn't," Sister Anselm said, taking a seat next to him. "Now, you know my name. What's yours?"

"David," he said. "David Upton. I'm a junior here at NAU."

"I've heard only the barest outlines of what happened. I'd appreciate it if you could tell me your side of the story. I understand you were driving the car that hit . . . we'll call her Jane Doe for right now. I also was told that the victim isn't someone you know."

David nodded. "That's right. She's a complete stranger. I'd never seen her before when she ran out into the road right in front of me. There was no time for me to stop. She was just there. I'll never forget the sound of the thump when I hit her. She went flying through the air like a little rag doll. It was awful."

David shuddered at the memory, and Sister Anselm gave his knee a consoling pat. "How about starting at the beginning," she suggested. "Where did this happen, and where were you going?"

"I was on my way to Vermillion Cliffs," he said. "Some of my friends go to school at BYU. We were going to meet up there for some rock climbing. It's more fun to do that before the weather gets warm and all the warm-weather tourists show up. I'm studying chemical engineering. My big lab days are Tuesdays and Thursdays. I figured I could spend tomorrow climbing and then be back in time for classes on Thursday.

"That's why I left so late in the afternoon. I have an afternoon lab, and then I had to do some other stuff before I could leave town. There's a little gas station on Highway 89 about twenty miles from here. It closes around ten o'clock, so it's sort of the last place for a pit stop and coffee when you're headed north late at night. That's what I was going to do—stop and get some coffee.

"I was starting to slow down when she ran across

the road directly in front of me. All I saw was someone wrapped in an Indian blanket running into the beams of my headlights. There was nothing I could do. I tried to stop but there wasn't time. I hit her dead-on."

He paused and shook his head, as though the very memory of the incident was enough to leave him shaken all over again.

Finally he continued. "I got out of my vehicle and ran over to her. She was just a kid. She may have been wearing an Indian blanket, but she wasn't an Indian. I don't know any blond-haired Indians. She was lying there on the pavement so still that I thought for sure I'd killed her. There was blood coming from the back of her head. I didn't dare move her for fear of doing more damage.

"I kept calling to her, hoping to get her to wake up, and finally she did. It was so cold, and all she was wearing was this lightweight jacket kind of thing. I had seen the blanket go flying when I hit her. I found it, brought it back, and used that to cover her. The whole time I had been with her, I had been so focused on her face that I didn't notice anything else. It wasn't until I came back with the blanket that I realized she was pregnant. She said something like, 'don't let them send me back, and don't let them send my baby back, either.' Call me stupid, but that was the first I realized she was expecting."

He paused again and took a deep breath. "And that's about the time her water broke. I mean it was like a flood. The next thing I knew, she was soaked and so was I. By then other people had turned up. The clerk from the gas station came out and started putting up flares because we were both still in the middle of the road. Somebody else called for an aid car and notified the cops. I don't know how long it took for the ambulance to get to us. It felt like forever."

"She spoke to you, then?" Sister Anselm asked.

David nodded.

"Did she say anything about who she was—what her name is or where she's from?"

"I asked what her name was. She tried to tell me, but she was having a hard time talking. It sounded like something that started with an E—Edith maybe? She didn't mention a last name. There was a lot of confusion when the EMTs got there. For a while, they must have thought I was her husband. That's why, when they cut her hair off so they could deal with the wound on the back of her head, they gave me these."

An athletic bag was stationed at his feet. He reached down into it and pulled out a clear Ziploc plastic bag. When he handed it over to Sister Anselm, she saw it contained long coils of braided and blood-soaked blond hair. The braids had been clipped off close to the scalp, but whoever had cut them off had first secured the top of each braid with a rubber band just below the cut line.

As Sister Anselm studied the braids, she was thrown back in time, thinking of another girl, years earlier, one who had also worn her long blond hair in braids just like this. Drawing a deep breath and forcing the memory aside, she turned back to the distraught young man seated next to her.

"She was unconscious by the time they cut off her braids?" Sister Anselm asked.

David nodded.

"Presumably, then," Sister Anselm concluded, "the EMT was an Indian."

David gave her a puzzled look. "I'm pretty sure she was, but how did you know that?"

"This is probably waist-long hair when it isn't braided," Sister Anselm explained. "When Indians used to be shipped off to boarding schools, the matrons cut their hair off first thing, whether they wanted it cut or not. Keeping the victim's hair from being lost was an act of kindness on the EMT's part."

"It's covered with blood," David pointed out. "I probably should have given it to the cops when they showed up, but they started giving me the third degree, and I forgot all about it. The cops didn't get there until after the ambulance had pulled away. They took the position initially that I was at fault—that I was someone who knew the girl and had run her down deliberately. Either that, or else I was drunk as a skunk. They gave me a Breathalyzer and were blown away when they saw the results, because I don't drink, not at all, except for too much coffee.

"Anyway, after hassling me for the better part of two hours, they finally let me go, but they impounded my car. They said that since this might turn into a fatality, they had to confiscate my vehicle until their investigation was complete. There was no way I could go on up to Vermillion Cliffs to meet my friends without my car, so I caught a ride with some of the people who had stopped to help and came here."

"To the hospital?"

He nodded.

"There's more than one hospital here in town. How did you know which one?"

"The EMT who gave me the braids told me. At the time, I think she still thought I was the husband."

"And you came here because?"

David shrugged and rubbed his eyes, bleary with fatigue. "Because I needed to know if she and the baby were okay. It wasn't my fault, but still, I'm the one who hit them. The problem is, nobody here will tell me anything. They asked me if I was her next of kin. When I told them no, they said there was some law that made it impossible for them to give out any information."

"HIPAA," Sister Anselm murmured.

"What?"

"That's the name of the law," she explained. "It's called the Health Insurance Portability and Accountability Act. One of the requirements prevents health-care providers from giving out a patient's information to anyone other than an individual the patient has designated to receive it."

"So being here is pretty much useless," David said despairingly, "because they're not going to tell me anything anyway." He paused. "She's just a kid, Sister, probably still in high school. What was she doing out there on her own, alone in the middle of the night in the middle of nowhere? And what about the jerk who knocked her up? Where's he? The father must be some kind of a bad guy, because that's what she said to me out there on the road. She begged me to keep anyone from taking either her or her baby back—wherever the hell back is!"

Sister Anselm studied the distraught young man and heard the outrage in his voice. As a patient advocate, she had taken a vow of confidentiality—one that had come long before the mid-1990s when someone in Washington, DC, had made HIPAA the law of the land. But this young man, related or not, was the only one here—the only one taking responsibility for and caring about what had happened. Depending on the seriousness of Jane Doe's injuries, for now and perhaps for the rest of her young life, David Upton was the closest thing she had to a next of kin. Sister Anselm was still holding the braids.

"Now," she asked, "do you want these back or should I put them with the rest of her effects?"

"With her effects, of course," he agreed at once. "I'm sure they shouldn't have been given to me in the first place."

"I believe that, for whatever reason, they were given to exactly the right person. Now then, Mr. Upton," Sister Anselm said, standing up, "you should go home. Try to get some rest. How far do you live from here?"

"Not far, just a few blocks off campus. I can walk. But what if something bad happens?" David asked. "What if she doesn't make it? I won't even know."

"Give me your phone number," Sister Anselm said, pulling her own iPhone out of her pocket. "I promise, if her condition changes, I'll keep you apprised of what's going on."

"But I already told you," David countered. "I'm not . . . you know . . . any kind of relative."

"You are now," Sister Anselm said with a smile as she finished keying his number into her phone. "Because I said so."

"You can do that? Didn't you just say that giving me any information about her is against the law?"

"Yes, that is what I said," Sister Anselm conceded, "but I can also give you the information if I deem it necessary. As of this moment and as far as I'm concerned, you are my patients' only known next of kin. That goes for both of them."

David nodded. "Thank you," he said, "although I'm not sure how you can get away with it."

Sister Anselm patted the gold crucifix that dangled from the gold chain around her neck. "You might say, Mr. Upton," she told him with a conspiratorial wink, "that I've been granted a waiver in that regard by someone much higher up the chain of command."

10

At half past ten the next morning, Ali stumbled into the kitchen in search of her first cup of coffee. She had obviously slept too late to suit Bella, who was already curled up in a ball on the small round dog bed next to the kitchen counter near where Leland stood rolling out rounds of dough for pasties. He smiled a good morning and then nodded in the direction of Ali's cell phone.

"When I came into the house this morning and realized that Sister Anselm had decamped overnight," he said, "it occurred to me that you'd probably had a less than restful night. I took the liberty of coming into your room, liberating your cell phone from its charger, turning off the ringer on your bedside phone, and taking Bella along with me."

"Thank you," Ali said, pouring a cup of coffee that wasn't nearly as fresh as it would have been had she awakened at her usual time. "Sister Anselm was called out to look after someone up in Flagstaff. Once she left the house, I took advantage of being awake that early and had a leisurely conversation with B."

"I trust all is well with him."

Ali nodded. "He's hoping you'll make meat loaf for dinner when he's home for the weekend."

"Always a pleasure," Leland said. "By the way, there've been a couple of calls already this morning—one from Stuart Ramey and the other from Sister Anselm. I told them both that you'd call back."

"I will," Ali answered, "but not until I've had some coffee and gotten my head screwed on straight."

She took her coffee over to the kitchen window and stared out at a landscape made unfamiliar by snow. The sky was blue overhead, but the temperatures were still cold enough that the sun had yet to melt the five inches or so of snow that had fallen. Across the valley, the bright red cliffs were made all the brighter by being framed in white.

Slipping onto one of the kitchen chairs, she glanced at the small television set that was built into a cabinet slot just above the microwave. It was tuned to a news channel with the local weatherman standing in front of a map featuring lots of blue that designated frigid weather in places not generally accustomed to it.

"I'm afraid it's been all weather all the time this morning," Leland explained. "The storm that came through here last night dropped measurable snow in Phoenix for the first time since 2006. The time before that was 1937. Now that same storm is causing trouble in southern New Mexico and on into Texas."

Leland put down the rolling pin and wiped his hands on the front of his flour-dusted apron. "Now, what would you like for breakfast? A cheese-baked egg perhaps? On a cold day like this, that's what's called for—something hot from the oven. That's why I decided today was just the day to make pasties."

Ali turned away from the TV set as the coverage switched over to images of a multivehicle pileup that had occurred in Texas an hour or so earlier. In her days as a television reporter in Chicago, Ali had covered plenty of those kinds of incidents. Other than the exact death toll, she already knew too much about what would come next.

"Cheese-baked eggs sound wonderful," she said. "Will you join me?"

Leland shook his head. "No, thanks. I had my breakfast hours ago."

"How long before the eggs will be ready?" Ali asked.

"Twenty-five minutes from start to finish, and I'll have a new pot of coffee for you by then, too."

"All right," she said, abandoning her almost empty cup and grabbing her phone off the counter. "I'll go shower and get ready to meet the day."

By the time she returned to the kitchen—showered, dressed, blow-dried, and reasonably made up—a single place had been set for her at the kitchen table. A small plate held a still steaming ramekin full of Leland Brooks's crusty-topped egg concoction. There was toast and jam and freshly squeezed orange juice as well as an empty cup and saucer, which was filled with coffee the moment she sat down. As soon as she did so, Bella abandoned her bed and came over to sit on the floor beside her in hopes that a treat or two might come her way.

"You do spoil me," Ali said as Leland returned to the counter to finish making the pasties.

"Isn't that why you keep me on?" he asked. "To spoil you?"

Ali nodded. For years Leland Brooks's presence in Ali's life had been an ongoing blessing, but she also understood that the only reason—the real reason—he was still toiling away in her kitchen was that he needed some-thing to do. Leland was a man who required a purpose in his life. For right now, spoiling Ali Reynolds was it.

Other than a month-long vacation earlier in the year when his long-lost friend, Thomas Blackfield, had flown over from England to tour the U.S., Leland hardly ever took any time off. By the time the visit was over and Thomas flew back home, Leland had been eager to get back to work. Ali hadn't the slightest doubt that putting him out to pasture permanently would be the end of him. Leland Brooks was someone who wouldn't do well in retirement.

"I talked to Sister Anselm briefly while I was getting out of the shower," Ali said, cutting through the cheesy crust on top of the dish and sticking her spoon into the whole hard-cooked egg hiding underneath. "She asked if I could come by the hospital to see her later today. I told her that would depend on road conditions. The Cay-enne is four-wheel drive, but just because it's roadworthy doesn't mean everybody else's vehicles are ready for win-ter driving."

"Jesus has already cleared and sanded our driveway," Leland said, referring to Jesus Gonzales, someone Ali had hired to handle the heavier outdoor work that was, in Ali's opinion, beyond Leland's physical capabilities. "He says that once you get down off Manzanita, the roads are fine."

"All right, then," Ali said. "As soon as I've finished breakfast and made a few more calls, I'll head out."

Stuart Ramey called before she managed to finish the last bite of egg. "I understand you spoke to B.," he said. "He mentioned that I was cleared to dispatch Joe as far as he's concerned, but not until I get the go-ahead from you.

The thing is, Joe has a clear spot in his schedule today and tomorrow, so if you'd like him to handle this now, we need to get the ball rolling."

"Sorry," Ali said. "I'm afraid I overslept. I can't give you the all clear until I talk it over with Betsy Peterson. I'll get back to you as soon as I do."

That was what Ali had been thinking about the whole time she was showering and getting dressed—about how she should approach Betsy Peterson and what she should or shouldn't say. Ali would, in effect, be casting suspicion on Betsy's nearest and dearest, and Ali wasn't at all sure how that conversation was going to go.

Leaving the table, she poured another cup of coffee and took it with her into the library, clearing her mind as she went. The gas-log fire in the library was already burning. Her newspaper and yesterday's mail, both brought up the driveway by Jesus, were laid out on the nearest end table. Settling into her chair, she sorted through the mail, setting the bills aside for B. to handle when he was home and consigning the advertising circulars to the recycle bin. After all, how many 20-percent-off Bed Bath & Beyond coupons did one household need?

Finally, taking her phone in hand, Ali located Betsy Peterson's number and pushed the Send button. Betsy answered after the second ring and before the third.

"Good morning, Ali," Betsy said at once. "I hope you don't mind my addressing you by your first name. That's how you showed up in my caller ID."

"Of course not. Calling me Ali is fine."

Betsy might be in her eighties, but she clearly wasn't flummoxed by using a cell phone.

"And you can call me Betsy. Now tell me, what have you found out?"

"We're working on it," Ali answered. "First off, have you heard anything at all from the local authorities?"

"Yes," Betsy said. "From what I've been told, they've determined that whatever happened the other night was an accident of some kind. As far as they're concerned, I'm nothing but a dotty old woman who needs to have her head examined."

"When was the last time you spoke to Athena?"

"Just a little while ago, during her planning period."

"Did she mention my husband's firm to you?"

"As a matter of fact she did, a security firm of some kind—an old TV show, maybe—*Gunsmoke, Have Gun Will Travel,* something like that."

"A movie rather than a TV show," Ali corrected. "High Noon. It's a security firm with clients all over the world. We mostly specialize in computer security issues, but we can do other kinds of personal security work as well."

"You work for them, too?" Betsy asked. "Does that mean you're some kind of private investigator?"

"I'm more PR than PI," Ali admitted, "but occasionally I do some investigative work as well. With that in mind, are you interested in having High Noon launch an investigation on your behalf?"

"Absolutely," Betsy declared without a moment's hesitation. "Since Donald Olson, our illustrious sheriff, is being such a piker about all this, I need all the help I can get. In fact, I barely slept last night. I was too busy worrying about who might be coming in and out of my house without my knowledge."

"All right, then," Ali said. "Here's what we'd like to do. High Noon wants to send out one of our associates. His name is Joe Friday, and he's located in Minneapolis. He'll come to your place there in Bemidji and set up a surveillance system that will keep your whole house under observation."

"My whole house?" Betsy repeated. "Even the bathroom and bedroom?"

"Those rooms especially," Ali responded.

"But . . ."

"Just wait," Ali hurried on. "Before you object, let me explain. Joe will record images of both you and your dog. The cameras will all be set to recognize your images. Those will not trigger alarms, and they will not be recorded, but everyone else who sets foot inside your house will be."

Betsy sighed. "I suppose," she said. "If you think it's necessary, but does it have to be so intrusive?"

"Yes, it does," Ali answered. "At least that's our assessment of your current situation."

Ali could have added what she already knew—that the earlier intruder had known his way around Betsy's current alarm system and, more important, he had also known his way around Princess. Rather than overplaying her hand Ali waited, allowing Betsy to draw her own conclusions and hoping she'd make the right choice. Eventually she did.

"Very well, then," the other woman agreed. "Send him over. I'm sure you people know better than I."

We do, Ali thought. "All right. I'll give Joe a call," she said aloud. "Once I have an ETA on him, I'll let you know. In the meantime, you're going to need a cover story."

"A cover story?" Betsy repeated. "How come? Like in one of those cloak-and-dagger spy movies?"

"Exactly," Ali said. "Joe will probably show up in a work van with a sign saying he represents some kind of electrical company. If anyone asks about his presence at your place, tell them that you've been having trouble with your electrical service, and Joe's been dispatched to repair it for you. I understand your home has been equipped with Wi-Fi, right?"

"It used to be," Betsy said. "After Athena left, I discontinued the service. There was no sense in paying for it when I wasn't using it."

"What about a computer? Do you have one of those?"

"I have one, but it died months ago. The screen froze up on me one day, and I haven't bothered to do anything about replacing it."

"Joe's surveillance system will require a state-of-the-art computer because you'll need that to operate as a server. You can tell anyone who asks that Athena insisted on your taking these measures after that last scare. Tell them she wants you to be online so she can stay in touch with you by e-mail and FaceTime."

"Do I have to?" Betsy asked.

"Yes," Ali insisted. "It's absolutely necessary."

"Do you have any idea how old I am?" Betsy demanded. "Athena has been after me about all that for years, but I have zero interest in learning about all those computer contraptions or using them, either."

"If you want us to help you," Ali advised, "you'll need to change your mind about that and develop some interest in a hurry. In fact, if I'm not mistaken, your life may depend on it."

That was followed by a long pause. "Very well," Betsy said, capitulating at last, "now that you put it that way."

"Good," Ali replied. "I'll contact Joe immediately and let him know that he's not to leave your house without making sure you can log onto and off the computer and that you're capable of sending and receiving messages.

That's going to be important, by the way. Otherwise, if your bad guy shows up and sees that you're not using the computer yourself, he's going to smell a rat and figure out that the computer was installed for some other reason."

"Okay," Betsy agreed. "I'll do my best, but one other thing. How much is all this going to cost? Do I need to sign a contract or something?"

"No," Ali answered. "Athena is going to handle it."

"Well, for goodness' sake, I'm sure with two kids to feed, Chris and Athena are struggling just to make ends meet. No doubt I'm in a better situation to pay the bill than they are."

"As I said, Mrs. Peterson, the bill is handled, but you've just brought up another question. Tell me about your financial situation."

"I already told you. Call me Betsy, but what do you mean?"

"I mean how are you fixed for retirement funds?"

"I'm not sure why you're asking, but I'm fine," Betsy said briskly. "More than fine."

"How fine is 'more than fine'?" Ali asked.

"Let's just say I have plenty of money to last me for my lifetime, probably with some left over. Alton always said that he wasn't going to cork off without leaving me well provided for. Believe me, he was a man of his word."

"What happens to the part that's left over?" Ali asked.

"It goes to Athena, of course," Betsy replied. "That was written into Alton's and my wills long before he passed."

"Your son and daughter-in-law are specifically excluded from being beneficiaries?"

"Absolutely. When Alton and I were watching our money and trying to turn it into a tidy sum, Jimmy and

Sandra were acting like money grew on trees and spending like crazy. Mind you, that was after we had paid for Jimmy's schooling all the way through dental school. Alton always said he'd rot in hell before he gave them another thin dime of his hard-earned cash. That's what our wills said when he died, and it's what mine says to this day."

Yes, Ali thought as she ended the call a few minutes later, as far as she was concerned, there wasn't a single thing about Betsy Peterson that sounded the least bit dotty.

Ali's next call was to Stuart. "Okay," she said. "Tell Joe it's a go, but you'll need to warn him. He's going to need to hang around Bemidji long enough to make sure Betsy Peterson can operate that new computer of hers. From what she just told me on the phone, she's not exactly computer savvy. That'll have to change."

"Should I tell Joe he can expect to earn some combat pay?"

"Yes," Ali agreed with a laugh. "That sounds about right."

11

Ali's intention to leave for Flagstaff soon after breakfast was thwarted by a reminder that popped up on her computer screen the moment she turned it on. She and B. had agreed on an arrangement where she handled all of High Noon's various public relations inquiries, and this morning she was scheduled to do an interview with a freelancer from the Bay Area who was writing a profile on Lance Tucker, one of High Noon's most recent employee hires.

Lance was a talented teenaged hacker from Texas who had run afoul of both the law and one of High Noon's cybersecurity clients. Until a few months ago, he had also been a jailed juvenile offender. Working with a high school teacher who subsequently committed suicide, Lance had developed a groundbreaking program, GHOST, which allowed people to surf the Dark Net undetected. Rumors about GHOST's capabilities had leaked out into the cyberworld, turning Lance into a desirable target for a flock of good guys and bad guys alike. B. had been one of the good guys. After High Noon succeeded in saving both Lance and his family from a group of murderous thugs, B.'s company had walked away with two valuable prizes—Lance Tucker and his program.

Despite the fact that Lance had lost a leg in the process, his once bleak future was bright again. Although he was officially on High Noon's payroll, his only duties at the moment consisted of undergoing rehab related to adjusting to his new state-of-the-art prosthetic leg and working full bore on a distance-learning program that would give him a degree in computer science in under three years rather than the usual four. And, because so much of the world's cybercrime originated in the former Soviet Union, he was also taking a crash course in Russian. In the meantime, his GHOST program was now a proprietary part of High Noon's arsenal of cybercrime-fighting tools.

This story was clear enough to Ali because she had lived through those harrowing days that had ended in a number of homicides scattered across the wilds of Texas. It was a whole lot less clear to the dim young woman conducting the interview. Much as Ali tried to turn the reporter away from the more inflammatory aspects of the case, she could already tell that the woman would write a piece that wouldn't be good for Lance Tucker or High Noon Enterprises. Ali found herself wondering if she had been as irritating an interviewer back when she was fresh out of journalism school and starting her career as a television news reporter. One thing she knew for sure was that she had been a much faster typist.

When the interview finally ended, Ali headed out. Leland stopped her in the kitchen on her way to the garage. "Here's a little something for you and Sister Anselm," he said, handing her a cardboard box that looked suspiciously like one the cleaners used to return B.'s laundered and folded shirts. The unexpected weight of the box indicated it contained something other than shirts, and since the bottom of the container was warm to the touch, Ali suspected this to be one of Leland's signature care packages.

"What's this?" Ali asked.

"I have a clear understanding about the grim reality of the food choices available from hospital cafeterias," he answered. "These are a pair of pasties, fresh from the oven—one for you and one for Sister Anselm. If I put them in a tightly sealed container, they'd end up steamed and soggy. Inside the box, they should be crisp and still slightly warm by the time you get there. You can have them for lunch. I know Sister Anselm loves pasties, and you'll also find paper plates, napkins, and plastic silverware in the box—everything you'll need for a hospital waiting room picnic."

"What makes you think I can be trusted with two pasties?" Ali asked. "What if I keep both of them for myself?"

"You won't need to," Leland said, "because you know there are more where these came from." With that he reached over to the counter and picked up the small thermal carrying pouch he used for bringing frozen vegetables back from shopping excursions in Prescott.

"Some bottled water," he explained. "It's just out of the fridge, and it'll stay cold for a long time in this."

"Thanks," she said. "You always think of everything."

Bella had hung around with Ali while she was getting dressed, but when Ali's purse came out, Bella headed for her bed in the kitchen and settled in, making it plain that she had zero interest in going. She was not a dog who liked car rides. That wasn't too surprising considering how traumatic her last few adventures in vehicles had been, including the latest one—a trip down to Phoenix to see a canine dental specialist who had removed several of her terribly decayed teeth.

Ali headed north in a Cayenne that smelled more like a traveling bakery than an SUV. When she pulled into the hospital parking lot forty minutes later, both pasties were still untouched, but leaving them alone had required willpower.

At the reception desk in the main lobby, Ali asked for Sister Anselm and was surprised to be directed to the maternity unit on the fourth floor. There were several people in the unit's waiting room—two anxious husbands whose wives were currently in delivery rooms, and one proud father with a gaggle of relatives, pointing proudly toward a red-faced baby sleeping peacefully in a bassinet that was parked close to the nursery window. Eventually Ali caught sight of Sister Anselm, seated on a rocking chair in a far corner of the nursery.

Retreating to a waiting room chair, Ali set down her purse and the box of pasties, and then sent Sister Anselm a text announcing that luncheon was served.

A few minutes later, when Sister Anselm emerged from the nursery, Ali was shocked by her appearance. Everything about Sister Anselm looked bone weary. The sparkle was gone from her blue eyes. Her normally perfect posture was marred by the slump of her shoulders. In the few hours between the time Sister Anselm had left Ali's house in Sedona and now, the nun seemed to have turned into an old woman.

Trying not to stare and looking for a way to cover her dismay, Ali attempted a bit of normal conversation. "Your patient's a baby?" she asked.

"One of them is," Sister Anselm said, sinking gratefully into a chair and lowering her voice so no one else in the room could hear what she was saying. "A baby and her mother."

Ali knew better than to inquire about the condition of the two patients. She didn't have to. She could tell from the grave expression on Sister Anselm's face that the situation was dicey at best. Not wanting to voice her concerns about Sister Anselm herself, Ali sought refuge in a less difficult topic.

"Leland has all your best interests at heart," she said. "He baked a batch of pasties this morning and sent two of them along for lunch."

"Bless him," Sister Anselm murmured, leaning back and closing her eyes. "That man is a wonder and a marvel."

"He is that," Ali agreed.

When Sister Anselm continued to sit with her eyes closed and with her head propped against the wall, Ali wondered if the nun had simply dozed off. Ali had known her friend for years, always marveling at her energy and industry. Usually she was able to stay at a patient's bedside for days on end, sleeping in short power naps that would have left your basic finals-cramming college student in the dust. Now though, with Sister Anselm looking beyond exhausted, Ali forced herself to swallow her concern and busied herself setting out the food. Only when the pasties had been set on plates and the bottled water opened did she touch Sister Anselm's shoulder. The nun awakened with a start.

"Sorry," she said. "I didn't mean to drift off like that."

"It's fine," Ali said. "You must have needed the rest."

For a time, they tackled their pasties without speaking. That wasn't out of character—the two women often shared long periods of companionable silence in each other's company. This time Ali sensed a disturbing undercurrent in what wasn't being said. Sister Anselm had summoned her for some particular reason, but with the room filled with people coming and going, this wasn't the time to ask.

Ali downed her pasty with relish, while Sister Anselm simply toyed with hers. The idea of Sister Anselm turning up her nose at one of Leland Brooks's pasties was unheard of. At last, with a sigh, Sister Anselm put the plate and the remains of her pasty back in the box.

"I'll put this in the fridge in the break room and finish it later," she said.

While Sister Anselm left to put away her food, Ali cleaned up the remains of their indoor picnic. When the nun reappeared, she beckoned for Ali to follow. Somewhat revived and walking with at least some of her customary bustle, Sister Anselm led the way into a tiny conference room that held a small table, three chairs, and a box of tissues. Ali guessed that this tiny private room on the maternity floor was intended for delivering bad news rather than good.

"Wait here," Sister Anselm said. She left the room, returning a few minutes later with a banker's box and a pair of latex gloves. After placing both on the table, she turned back to the door and closed the blinds before sitting down opposite Ali and peering at her over the top of the box.

"This contains the personal effects of one of my patients," Sister Anselm explained. "I'd like you to go through the items one by one and then tell me your thoughts. You'll want to wear these," she added, picking up the gloves. "In the meantime, I'll go check on my patients. I have their vitals on my iPad, but I like to check on them in person all the same." With that, she vanished out the door, leaving Ali alone.

Puzzled, Ali donned the gloves, removed the lid, and reached inside. First to emerge was a clear Ziploc bag. Inside were a pair of bloodstained blond braids, coiled around and around to make them fit inside the bag. Ali had worn braids until sixth grade when she had insisted on cutting hers off. Noting the circumference of the many coils, Ali estimated that the braids themselves had to be three to four feet long. Without the braids the hair would most likely be waist length or longer. Whoever had worn the braids had probably gone for over a decade without having a haircut.

Next up came a pair of shoes. Ali set them side by side on the table to examine them. They were cheap, off-brand men's oxfords, not the kind of shoes a young woman of childbearing age would be eager to wear. They were ugly, dusty, badly worn, and desperately in need of a coat of polish. The laces were threadbare. There were several knots in each of them where they had been broken and tied back together rather than replaced. Picking up one of the shoes, Ali noticed that the sole had been worn through in more than one place and then inexpertly patched.

Holding the shoe in the air, Ali realized how smelly it was. This was footwear that had seen long, hard use without the benefit of socks. She guessed they were probably the same as a woman's size eight, although the part of the shoe where the size might have been inked into the leather had been worn away long ago. There was no visible sign of blood on the shoes. Ali remembered that, as Sister Anselm was leaving the house, she had mentioned something about a traffic incident, so perhaps the shoes had been knocked off the victim's feet by some kind of impact.

The next item in the layered collection of belongings was a carefully folded Navajo blanket, which Ali lifted out of the box. Hefting it in her hand, she found it to be surprisingly heavy. The weight alone hinted that it was of the genuine handmade variety. Here and there on the blanket ugly stains had turned the vivid reds and whites of the patterns to a rusty brown. Ali didn't need a spray of luminol to tell her that the brown stains indicated where blood had soaked into fibers of the closely woven fabric.

She studied the blanket as she set it on the table next to the braids and the shoes. The three items told surprisingly contradictory stories. The shoes said that whoever had worn them was poor—too poor for new shoes or even new shoelaces; too poor for socks. The blanket, on the other hand, if it was genuine, was probably quite valuable. It indicated that the victim might have had some kind of connection to the Navajo nation, but the blond braids suggested otherwise—an Anglo victim rather than an Indian one.

Next came a bag—a homemade drawstring pouch, made of faded gingham and worn enough for the threads to be frayed at the bottom. Long ago Ali had made one just like it in Girl Scouts. Since the bag evidently functioned as a purse, Ali pulled it open and peered inside, expecting to find some kind of ID. That expectation was met with disappointment. The purse contained none of the usual jumble one would expect in a woman's purse—no lipstick tubes, compact, wallet, or wad of tissues. It contained only three items—a Bible, a small pair of scissors, and a spool of white thread with a single threaded needle poked into the side. Returning the contents to the bag, Ali focused once again on the box.

The next item out was a jacket—a lightweight, single-layer denim jacket, not the kind of heavy-duty outerwear yesterday's weather would have warranted. There were bloodstains on the jacket as well, especially at the back of the neck. It looked as though whoever had been wearing the jacket had lain in a pool of blood until the jacket was saturated through. There were also some stains on the front of the jacket, especially on the lower right-hand side. So perhaps the woman had suffered two separate wounds, a head wound and some kind of damage to her body as well.

As Ali refolded the jacket, she heard a small rustle that seemed to come from one of the side pockets. Reaching into it, she pulled out a piece of crumpled waxed paper. Then her searching fingers encountered something else. A tiny scrap of paper had been stuck so deep in the bottom seam of the pocket that it might easily have been overlooked. There was writing on the paper. Something barely legible had been scribbled with a dull number two pencil. Holding it up to the light, Ali saw a telephone number and a single name—Irene.

Ali suspected that the injured woman had yet to be identified. Had her loved ones been notified, no doubt they would have arrived at the hospital by now. Realizing that the scrap of paper might be a vital clue in the identification process, Ali set it aside. It was not her place to make the call. That would have to be up to law enforcement or else to Sister Anselm.

The next item to surface was a set of underwear, or at least what was left of them. A jagged cut ran down from the elastic top and then came to a T from leg to leg. Ali knew that drill. An EMT wielding a pair of scissors had made the cut to remove the victim's clothing and get it out of the way.

Closer examination revealed that the garment resembled men's boxers more than it did any kind of women's underwear. The legs were loose rather than tightened with elastic, and the elastic waistband had been stretched to the limit, most likely to accommodate the growing baby.

The material itself was stained and stiff. It looked as though it had been soaked through with some kind of a yellowish liquid and then laid out flat to dry. There was no manufacturer's tag saying "Made in China" sewn into any of the seams. In fact, there was no tag at all, and the jagged stitching around the thick elastic top told Ali that the panties were most likely homemade and sewn on a machine that was close to giving up the ghost. *So*, Ali asked herself, *who in her right mind makes her own underwear?*

The item that came next passed for a full-length slip, but it was really more of a simple, shapeless shift made of some lightweight cotton material. The shift, like the underwear, had been cut straight up the middle, from bottom to top, again most likely by an EMT. This item of clothing might have started out as white sometime in the distant past, but it was now a grimy gray and smelled as though whoever wore it had little access to soap and water, bleach, or even deodorant.

Ali stood up and held the shift in front of her. Whoever wore it was fairly tall—about Ali's height, perhaps. Then her eyes were drawn to the bottom of the shift. It had been cut off in a careless, ragged fashion. The small, jagged cuts indicated that scissors used for this had been much smaller and not nearly as sharp as the pair used to cut through the underwear and shift. Not only that, the way the cuts came together, with the back much shorter than the front, made Ali wonder if the person doing the cutting hadn't been wearing the garment at the time it was shortened.

Finally she removed the last item from the box and shook it out. It was an old-fashioned shirtwaist dress with buttons and buttonholes up and down the front, and with a billowy, gathered skirt. The EMTs had hacked their way through all that, too. The buttons were all still buttoned. The material was a faded check that might have been blue and white at one time but was now more of a dim shade of lavender and white. The buttons were the serviceable white kind that might have been snipped off a man's shirt and reused on something else. Like the other clothing, the dress was bloodstained, especially on the back of the fold-down collar, and stiffened with yellow on the skirt.

As with the shift, it was the hemline that drew Ali's attention. Examining it, she could see that someone had gone to a lot of effort to cut through the material and then bind the jagged edge into a rough roll of whip-stitched hem. There had been no need to make the bottom of the shift straight. The person who had cut that off had known the shift wouldn't show. But the dress? Ali stood up and held it in front of her. The faded garment had probably been much longer at one time, but now, with some of the material cut away and with a rudimentary hem, it came to just below Ali's knees.

Sister Anselm reentered the conference room just then, closing the door behind her, nodding as she did so. "I believe the two of you are about the same size in terms of height," she said.

Ali turned back to the box, expecting to find some-thing more, but it was empty. "No bra?" she asked.

"No bra," Sister Anselm confirmed. "What you found in the box is all there is except for her wedding ring."

She took a seat across from Ali, then placed her folded hands on the table. The gesture reminded Ali of tapes she had seen of law enforcement interrogations done in locked interview rooms. The words Sister Anselm uttered next made the resemblance all the more striking.

"This is all my fault," she said.

"Why do you say that?" Ali asked in surprise. "How's that possible?"

Sister Anselm sighed deeply. "My patient was struck by a moving vehicle near a gas station twenty miles north of Flagstaff. It happened about eight-thirty last night."

"At eight-thirty?" Ali interjected. "You were miles away at the time. In fact, I believe we were still sitting in my dining room and had just finished eating dinner. How can any of this be your fault?"

"Because this isn't the first time something like this has happened," Sister Anselm said in a voice that was little more than a whisper. "I've seen it before."

She stopped and didn't continue. "Tell me," Ali urged.

With effort, Sister Anselm gathered herself. "There was a similar case a dozen years ago. The victim was a girl probably a few years older than this one, seventeen or so. She was found naked and savagely beaten on a road lead-ing to the Hualapai Mountains. That Jane Doe wasn't as lucky as this one. She was taken to the hospital in King-man. Her baby was delivered by cesarean. The mother died a day or so later, and the baby a week after that. I cared for the baby through her all too brief life, and I was holding her when she died."

Overcome by the telling, Ali watched as two tears slid down Sister Anselm's cheeks and dripped unnoticed onto the Formica-topped table. Ali said nothing, not because she was unmoved, but because she could see that Sister Anselm's wound, whatever it might be, was too deep for mere words. Anything spoken right then would have been meaningless.

Noticing the tears at last, Sister Anselm took a tissue from the box on the table. She wiped her eyes, blew her nose, and then mopped up the tears that had dropped onto the table. Finally she continued.

"When Baby Doe died, her mother's body was still in the morgue in Kingman in the hope that eventually someone would turn up to claim her. After the baby died, Bishop Gillespie arranged for both mother and daughter to be buried in a single casket and with a single marker, one that reads 'Jane and Baby Jane Doe.' They're in a shady corner of Holy Name Cemetery near downtown Kingman. Whenever I'm in that area, I always visit the grave and I always pray that somehow we'll learn who they were and where they came from."

Sister Anselm paused and let her hand sweep over the table and the collection of items resting there. "I'm afraid this is God's answer to that prayer—another victim—a mother and her infant child."

Another long silence ensued. At last Ali said what was in her heart—the only thing that made sense. "This is not your fault."

"But it is," Sister Anselm insisted. "Don't you see? When the sheriff's department let that first case go cold, I should have insisted that they keep it alive. The victim had no family to intervene and make sure she and her child weren't forgotten. I was their patient advocate, and

I failed them. Now, that means I've failed them all—that girl, this one, and both babies."

"How do you know the two girls are connected?" Ali asked.

Sister Anselm reached across the table and picked up the Ziploc bag containing the bloodied braids. "These," she said. "The first girl wore her hair the same way—in braids wrapped around the crown of her head. It's a very distinctive style that tells me they must have come from the same place," Sister Anselm asserted. "They fled the same place, and, according to David Upton, last night's victim begged that neither she nor her daughter be sent back there."

"Who is David Upton?"

"The young man who hit her with his car. He may well be the last person she spoke to."

"Is Mr. Upton a suspect?"

"Not as far as I can tell. So far the investigation seems to bear out Mr. Upton's claim that he was already slowing down to pull over when she ran across the pavement directly in front of him. Hitting her was unavoidable. I've been told that the right-hand turn signal on his vehicle was still blinking when deputies showed up to do their investigation."

Ali studied her friend's face for some time. "That's why you wanted me to come today and look at all this, isn't it," she said. "It's also why you had me wear gloves. The victim's personal effects are here because she came in an ambulance and was admitted to the hospital. If she dies, everything here will become part of a police investigation."

Sister Anselm nodded almost imperceptibly.

"And you're hoping that somehow I'll be able to help identify her?"

"Yes," Sister Anselm answered.

"But why? Why not let the cops do it? She's the unidentified victim of a motor vehicle accident. I'm sure they'll do their best to ascertain where she came from."

"That's what I'm afraid of," Sister Anselm admitted. "I'm afraid they'll figure it out. At that point, the father will most likely assert his parental rights, and the baby—assuming she survives—will be taken back to the very place her mother tried so desperately to escape. It's possible the mother might be sent back there as well."

Sister Anselm gestured again at the paltry collection of items that had come from the box. "Look at this. The poor girl ran away with almost nothing—a jacket, a spool of thread, a scissors, a light jacket, and a Navajo blanket. She did that for a reason. Perhaps, if we can solve the puzzle before the sheriff's department does, we can marshal the resources to protect both mother and child. In both cases, these two girls chose death rather than going back to face whatever life they had lived before."

"Was there any DNA evidence collected in the course of that other case?"

Sister Anselm shrugged. "I wasn't privy to much of the investigation, but I assume so. However, there was no sign of a sexual assault, if that's what you're asking."

"And nothing was found with the first victim? No possessions of any kind?"

"None whatsoever. No shoes. No clothing. She was wearing a wedding ring—a simple gold band. The same kind of band last night's victim was wearing."

"You said you thought the Kingman Jane Doe was about seventeen?"

Sister Anselm nodded.

"So both of them were young, married, very pregnant, and very unhappy."

Sister Anselm nodded again.

It didn't take long for Ali to make up her mind. She was her mother's daughter after all. Over the years Ali had seen what happened whenever one of Edie Larson's friends asked for help. A request like that quickly morphed into a sacred duty.

"All right, then," Ali said. "It appears to me that we have three important clues here. Do you have any way for me to reach out to that young man you mentioned, David Upton?"

In answer, Sister Anselm read off his phone number, and Ali keyed it into her iPhone.

"Next we have the blanket," she said. Ali had taken off her latex gloves. Now she put them back on. Lifting the blanket off the table, she unfolded it, and held it up. "I'm no expert, but this one feels genuine. That makes it both rare and valuable. So how does a girl who has to knot her broken shoelaces together end up with a blanket worth hundreds of dollars? I want you to use my phone and take a picture of it."

"What good will that do?" Sister Anselm asked.

"As I understand it, each Navajo weaver uses her own particular designs and dyes. I have a friend over at the museum who may be able to identify the weaver. If we can figure out where the blanket came from, maybe we can also learn how this Jane Doe came to have it in her possession."

The picture-taking process took time. When it was finished, Ali carefully refolded the blanket and returned it to the box.

"And then there's this," she said, picking up the tiny scrap of paper. "I found this hidden in the corner of her jacket pocket."

Sister Anselm looked at it but didn't touch. "Irene," she read aloud. "And that's a Flagstaff telephone exchange."

"So maybe someone here in Flagstaff was expecting Jane Doe to show up last night. For all we know, they may have already reported her missing. Would you like me to make the call?"

"Please," Sister Anselm said.

Putting the scrap of paper down on the table, Ali keyed the number into her phone. It rang several times before the call was answered.

"May I help you?"

"I'm looking for Irene."

The operator's reply came as a shock. In a moment of astonishing clarity, Ali knew exactly who Irene was and also that she was totally unreachable.

"Sorry," she mumbled into the phone. "There's no need." With trembling hands she ended the call, nearly dropping the phone in the process.

Sister Anselm frowned. "What's the matter? Is something wrong?"

"I should have recognized the number before I dialed it," Ali answered. "Irene's not there. She's dead. She's been dead for years."

12

Princess did not like Joe Friday. At all. She followed him everywhere, going from room to room, barking like crazy. Betsy didn't attempt to shush her, because, for one thing, Betsy was more than half convinced that the dog's assessment of the situation was correct.

When that nice young man from Arizona, Stuart, had called her earlier that morning to say that Joe Friday would be stopping by early in the afternoon, Betsy had more or less expected a Jack Webb look-alike to show up on her doorstep. In her mind's eye, Jack Webb had never aged a day since she had first seen that handsome black-haired man on the black-and-white TV console Alton had installed in the living room. Even with an antenna planted on the roof, the images on the screen were hazy with snow, but she'd been able to see enough of the actor's features to think he was just the cat's meow.

The Joe Friday who rang her doorbell and later carted an immense tool kit into her living room did not resemble Jack Webb at all. He had black hair all right, but rather than being trimmed in a conventional manly way, it came all the way to his shoulders in shiny waves that a lot of women would have killed for. Joe had tattoos everywhere Betsy could see—which is to say everything that wasn't covered by his red plaid flannel shirt and raggedy jeans. She theorized there were probably lots more tattoos in places she couldn't see.

In other words, as far as Betsy was concerned, Joe Friday already had two strikes against him—long hair and tattoos—to say nothing of the nose ring. Why young people insisted on putting studs in their faces and rings in their noses was more than Betsy could understand. No doubt Alton would have sent Joe packing based on appearance alone. Unfortunately, Alton wasn't here, and Betsy knew she needed help. As a consequence she did her best to overlook that first bad impression. It helped, of course, that Joe Friday was unfailingly polite.

"Mrs. Peterson?" he inquired, when she opened the door holding Princess in her arms to keep the dog from racing outside and tearing into the hem of his pant legs.

"Yes," she said. "I'm Mrs. Peterson, and this is Princess."

"Cute dog," he said, glancing at the dog, removing his worn baseball cap, and holding out his hand to the dog in greeting. "I'm Joe, the one who called earlier. Stuart Ramey sent me."

He had indeed called earlier, asking a question that Betsy had considered odd—what color switch plates did she have on her light switches and electrical outlets? Were they black or white?

White was the answer. Decades earlier, when they had been doing a remodeling project, Betsy had lobbied for avocado-colored appliances and beige switch plates and outlet covers. Alton had vetoed both those ideas at once, saying they were just fads. Much as Betsy hated to admit it, Alton had been right on both counts.

Joe had repeated Ali's suggestion that if anyone asked what he was doing there, she should tell people she had hired him to bring her electrical service into the twenty-first century, and that the work would most likely take a day or two.

When he bent down and started to unlace his boots before entering the house, she told him not to bother. "Having a little melted snow here and there never hurt anybody."

Leaving his boots on, he picked up the heavy metal toolbox he had carted up onto her porch, lugged it into the living room, and opened the lid. Sitting on the couch and still holding tight to Princess, Betsy was amazed. Joe Friday may have been lacking in the dress-for-success department, but his toolbox would have won Alton over in an instant. It was neat as a pin.

"I have several more boxes to bring in," he said. "Are you sure you don't want me to remove my boots?"

"Your boots are fine. Just wipe them off on the mat before you come inside."

He dragged in several loads of cardboard boxes, setting off a new set of noisy objections from Princess every time he reentered the house. "All right," he said, setting down the last ones. "Show me where your breaker box is."

Betsy led him into the laundry room and opened the door to the metal box that hung on the wall above her washer. Next to each breaker switch was a neat label, printed in ink, in Alton's own hand.

"Are the labels all accurate?" Joe asked.

"Of course," she said indignantly without bothering

to look. "My late husband labeled them, and Alton was a very careful worker."

"I'm sure he was," Joe said with a grin, "but I'll check each outlet as I go, just to be sure."

"What are you going to do exactly?" Betsy asked. She had expected that the surveillance system would require unsightly cameras placed in full view all over her house.

"I'll show you," he said. Back in the living room, he opened two of the boxes. From one he removed what looked for all the world like an ordinary switch plate—a white one—wrapped in clear cellophane. He passed it over to her. After examining it, she shrugged her shoulders.

"It's a switch plate," she said. "Just like the ones I already have."

"Not quite," Joe said. "The base of the hole for the switch has been slightly enlarged. Once I get the Wi-Fi up and running, I'll wire pinhole cameras inside each switch plate with the lens aimed through that bit of extra space. Because the cameras will be wired directly into your electrical system, they won't require any batteries, making the actual devices that much smaller. Whatever the camera records will go through your new computer by way of an invisible file, but it won't be stored there. Instead, the material will be uploaded to High Noon's servers. An alarm will sound on our end and the cameras will start recording whenever an unidentified image shows up."

"But what Princess and I do won't be visible?" Betsy asked.

"Not at all," Joe assured her. "Once I do your 3-D photo shoot and have your images uploaded into the system, the two of you will be exempt. More people can be added to the exempt status at a later date, but we don't recommend that immediately, especially not now while we're still trying to ascertain who may have been here the other night and turned on the gas."

Betsy had longed for someone who would believe her version of the other night's disturbing events. Clearly Joe Friday did. You had to watch out what you asked for.

"What if I have company?" Betsy asked. "What if someone stops by for coffee?"

"Whatever they do inside your house will be recorded."

"That seems like a terrible invasion of privacy," Betsy objected. "I mean, what if one of my guests needs to use the powder room?"

"I understand your concerns about invading your legitimate guests' privacy," Joe said. "And I'm willing to go so far as to make the powder room a camera-free zone, but everywhere else is fair game because murder is the ultimate invasion of privacy, wouldn't you say?"

He had her there. Betsy nodded. "I suppose so," she agreed.

"Now," he said. "First things first. Where do you want me to set up your new computer?"

"There's a desk in my bedroom," she said. "As long as I have to have the dratted thing, I don't want it here in the middle of the living room."

"All right, then," Joe agreed. "That's where I'll start— the bedroom."

Just then the doorbell rang. When Betsy opened the front door, she was dismayed to see her daughter-in-law standing on the front porch. "What's going on?" Sandra asked, glancing over her shoulder at Joe Friday's work van parked prominently in the driveway.

Betsy's first instinct was to say what she really felt—*It's none of your business.* But with Joe in the house installing his hidden cameras and with his toolbox and boxes spread out all over the living room, she couldn't afford to get into a tiff with Sandra.

Biting back a sharp response and sticking to the story they'd agreed on, Betsy said, "I'm having some electrical work done, and I'm also getting a new computer."

"A computer?" Sandra asked. "You hardly ever used the one you used to have. The sign on the van says your contractor is from Minneapolis. Couldn't you find someone local? I'm sure Jimmy could have found someone to do the work at half the price."

"Yes," Betsy agreed. "I'm sure he could, but he's so busy these days. I didn't want to bother him with my concerns."

"Well," Sandra asked in her usual pushy fashion, "are you going to ask me in or not?"

"Not," Betsy said. "This isn't a good time, not with the power going on and off all over the house. I was about to call Marcia to see if she could pick me up and take me into town to pick up a few items from the store. Since you're here now, maybe you wouldn't mind. I could even treat you to an early dinner at the diner."

Unaccustomed to being told no, Sandra was momentarily taken aback. Then she glanced at her watch. "I could take you into town, I suppose, and wait while you have something to eat," she agreed reluctantly. "But no dinner for me. We have plans."

"All right, then," Betsy said. "You go wait in the car. I'll put Princess in the laundry room and get my purse." With that, Betsy closed the door in Sandra's face, leaving her standing on the porch, thunderstruck and sputtering.

Harold, Betsy's neighbor, had come by late in the afternoon the day before, apologizing for his tardiness in getting her driveway plowed and her walkway and wheelchair ramp shoveled and deiced. With her coat on and her purse on her arm, Betsy was happy to use the cleaned-up ramp to walk out to Sandra's Volvo. Cataracts or not, once in the passenger seat, Betsy had no difficulty in seeing the tight-lipped expression on her daughter-in-law's face as she jammed on the gas and shot past Joe's van.

"I can't believe you'd go off like this and leave a complete stranger working in your house."

"He's not a complete stranger," Betsy said. "He's a friend of Athena's." That was close enough to the truth to sound plausible.

"Oh," Sandra fumed. "I suppose that explains it."

Betsy took her own sweet time in the grocery store and the pharmacy both, using her magnifying glass to examine labels and making a show of having trouble making up her mind. She couldn't resist. Having Sandra pacing in the background and checking her watch was just too much fun. With a little thought she was able to stretch her errands until well into the afternoon.

When Betsy finished shopping, she insisted they stop by the café. Betsy ordered a roast beef sandwich and Sandra her cup of black coffee. Only then did Sandra finally get down to business and broach the conversation Betsy had been expecting.

"Donald came by and talked to James last night," Sandra said. "They're both very concerned about you, you know. We all are."

Betsy knew exactly where all this was going, but she played dumb. "Concerned?" she asked innocently.

"Of course we're concerned," Sandra said. "It's one thing for you to lose your hearing aids or misplace your glasses, but it's quite another to have the kind of episode that ends up involving law enforcement."

"Ah," Betsy said, as if only now realizing what this was all about. "The situation the other night where Donald Olson thinks the burners on my stove came on either by magic or else all by themselves. Which is wrong, of course. I think someone tried to murder me."

Sandra didn't actually say that she doubted Betsy's version of the story, but the message came through nonetheless. "That's what has us so worried—that you'll have a moment of forgetfulness or confusion and come to some kind of harm. James wants you to go see Dr. Munson and have a complete evaluation."

Betsy considered that last comment in silence. Elmer Munson was another one of Jimmy's good pals. He had earned a certain reputation among some of her fellow bingo players down at the VFW as the go-to guy in town when recalcitrant parents needed to be brought to heel by their baby-boomer offspring. In fact, some of the more outspoken retirees suspected that Munson had been the driving force behind having his own mother declared incompetent.

Betsy's food came. She tried a taste of it before she replied. The sandwich was just the way she liked it, thinly sliced beef on a piece of plain white Wonder bread instead of on a slab of whole-wheat cardboard some restaurants tried to pass off as "healthy eating." And the rich brown gravy slathered over the top was thick and tasty.

"When exactly would you and Jimmy like me to schedule this checkup?" Betsy asked at last.

The whole time they had been together that day,

Betsy had noted a kind of nervousness in Sandra that she had never exhibited before. Jimmy didn't like rocking boats, and Betsy wasn't surprised that her son had sent Sandra to do the dirty work rather than facing the music himself. No doubt Sandra had expected Betsy would object to the very idea, but Betsy's apparent willingness to consider it sent a look of relief flashing across Sandra's face. Betsy found that look more disturbing than the whole Dr. Munson scheme.

Sandra reached into her pocket and pulled out a business card. "James already called Dr. Munson's office and booked an appointment for you," she said, sliding the card across the table. "Monday afternoon—two-thirty. I'll be glad to pick you up and bring you into town for the appointment if you like."

Which was no doubt Sandra's way of making sure Betsy didn't ditch the appointment.

"Oh, no," Betsy said casually, pretenting to examine the handwritten time on the back of the card and then slipping it into her own pocket. "That's not necessary. I don't like causing you any inconvenience, especially since you were kind enough to bring me into town today. I'll call Marcia. She's always happy to earn a little extra cash by driving me around. With this much notice, she'll have no difficulty working me in."

Sandra took the rejection in stride. "If you want to have Marcia pick you up, that'll be fine," she said with a smile. "All the same, I'll plan on being at the appointment, too. For moral support, you know."

"Of course," Betsy agreed with a nod. "For moral support."

13

Ali was still shaken when she left the hospital a few minutes later. She had no doubt that Sister Anselm's critically injured patient had been on her way to Flagstaff hoping for help from Ali's good friend Irene Bernard when she ran away from home. But Reenie had been dead for years. How was it possible that the injured girl hadn't known that Irene Bernard was no longer available to help her?

Hoping for answers, Ali got in the Cayenne and drove straight to the YWCA. She parked in a visitor's space near Irene's Place, the domestic violence shelter that Reenie had founded and championed and that was now named in her honor. Ali was always struck by the irony in that because Irene had died as a result of an act of senseless domestic violence, too, albeit from an unexpected source.

Ali rang the security bell and identified herself before being allowed inside. She went straight to the office of Andrea Rogers. At the time of Reenie's death, Andrea had been Irene Bernard's assistant. Now she was in charge. In the intervening years, Andrea had honed both her public-speaking and management skills. Like Reenie, Andrea spent a good deal of her time out in public raising both awareness and needed funds. Like her predecessor, Andrea took an active and personal interest in every traumatized family that showed up on the shelter's doorstep.

When Ali tapped on the doorframe of Andrea's office, she looked up as if annoyed with the interruption. Recognizing her visitor, annoyance changed to beaming welcome.

"Well, if it isn't Ali Reynolds," Andrea said, hurrying from her cluttered desk to envelop Ali in a welcoming hug. "To what do we owe the pleasure?"

Intent on her errand, Ali didn't let herself get sucked into a long exchange of pleasantries. "I need your help," she said. "I've just come from St. Jerome's. We've got a critically injured but so far unidentified young woman there along with her injured newborn baby. When I was going through the victim's effects, I found a scrap of paper with the name Irene on it along with a telephone number. When I tried calling, the phone was answered here."

"Here at the shelter?"

"I didn't realize it at first," Ali explained. "When the call was answered, all the operator said was 'May I help you?' It wasn't until after I asked for Irene specifically that she offered to put me through to the shelter. That's when I realized I had reached the YWCA."

"Sharing the switchboard with the YWCA during daytime hours saves us a bunch of money," Andrea answered. "And we teach the operators who pick up on our line to answer with a simple 'May I help you?' Sometimes after domestic violence victims call us, someone else—often an angry husband—will call, too, because he's busy going through his wife's phone records, trying to find out what she's been up to. A simple 'May I help you?' allows us to hide the fact that the wife—and most often it is a wife— is someone who's come to us looking for help."

Andrea paused and sighed. "As for using Irene's old number as our hotline number? We did that as a tribute to her—to honor what she stood for. When Irene was running the show, she often took those calls herself. This way she's still taking them."

It was clear from the sadness in Andrea's voice that Ali Reynolds wasn't the only one who still grieved Reenie Bernard's passing.

Andrea straightened her shoulders. "This young woman you told me about, the one in the hospital. Is she a victim of domestic violence?"

"From what we know of the investigation, she was in-jured in a traffic accident. She ran into traffic and was hit by a passing vehicle while in the process of running away from a difficult home situation. So the answer to that is a possible yes."

"What about the driver or the car who hit her?" An-drea asked. "Sometimes so-called accidents aren't ac-cidental."

"Indications are the driver is a complete stranger."

"What makes you think she might have called here?" Andrea asked.

"We don't know that for sure," Ali admitted. "What we do know is that she had a slip of paper with Irene's name and phone number on it hidden in her pocket."

"Come with me, then," Andrea said. "Let's go check."

Talking as she walked, Andrea led Ali into the cor-ridor. "We log in the numbers of all incoming calls placed to our hotline. That way, occasionally in crisis situations, we know where to send law enforcement assistance. Having that information is also helpful when we need to track down an offender who is trying to reach one of our residents in violation of a protection order."

Ali and Andrea left the shelter and entered the YWCA part of the building through a locking door that clicked shut behind them. In a side office just off the main entrance, a young woman sat at a desk laden with old-fashioned PBX telephone equipment.

"Hey, Debbie, this is Ali Reynolds, a friend of mine and a good friend of Irene Bernard's as well," Andrea announced. "Mind if I take a look at the logbook?"

Debbie handed over a simple spiral notebook, which was anything but high tech. The day of the month was written on the top of the page. The current page had only one listing—Ali's. It included the time, her cell-phone number, and the word "Irene" followed by a question mark. That was all the information the operator had gleaned before Ali had ended the call.

She turned back to the previous page. That one listed five calls. As soon as she saw the last one on the page, Ali felt her heart skip a beat. A call from a 928 area code had come in at 4:56. The 928 designation meant it had originated from a phone purchased and activated somewhere in northern Arizona. But the telling detail, the one that took Ali's breath away was the final notation on the line: "Irene?"

"It's here," Ali murmured to Andrea. "She did call yesterday; at least she tried to."

"Is there a problem?" Debbie asked with a frown of concern. "Which call are you talking about—the one for Irene?"

Ali nodded.

"That's so weird," Debbie said. "I've had two calls like that in the past two days—someone who asked for a person named Irene rather than the shelter."

"The second call was from me this morning," Ali said. "What happened the first time?"

"I started to explain that was the name of the shelter rather than a person, but the caller, a young woman from the sound of it, hung up before I had a chance. I passed the information on to Mrs. Young, the resident assistant in the shelter, in case she called back overnight. According to this, she never did."

"Beverly Young is our overnight housemother," Andrea explained. "Calls are transferred over to her office in the shelter once the switchboard closes for the night. That way we have someone on-site for people needing assistance during nonbusiness hours."

Ali thanked Debbie for her help and then keyed the phone number into the message section of the phone.

"I don't recommend your calling," Andrea cautioned as they walked back toward her office. "In a volatile situation, a call from an outsider could make things that much worse."

"I'll bear that in mind, but since Jane Doe is already in the hospital in critical condition, I'm not sure how it could get any worse."

"You'd be surprised," Andrea answered.

Good to her word, once Ali was back in the Cayenne, she didn't call. Instead she e-mailed the number to Stuart Ramey with a simple request:

> *Can you give me a name and address to go with this number?*

Her e-mail announcement chimed before Ali made it back to the parking lot at St. Jerome's. The message was from Cami, Stuart's assistant, rather than from the man himself:

> Mr. Ramey is busy right now. He asked me to handle this. The phone leads back to someone named Tsosie Begay. The address listed is a post office box in Chinle, AZ. If you need anything else, let me know.
>
> Cami

Ali sat in her idling car for a full minute after reading Cami's e-mail. Begay was a well-known Navajo name, and the phone number was more likely to lead back to the source of the blanket rather than to one of Jane Doe's family members. After giving it some thought, Ali went ahead and dialed. The phone was answered by a soft-spoken woman. "Begay residence."

"Hello," Ali responded. "My name is Ali Reynolds. I'm calling for a Mr. or Mrs. Begay."

"I'm Evangeline Begay," the woman said in a voice that gave nothing away.

Ali took a deep breath before launching off. "I'm looking into a phone call that was placed from your number to a phone located in Flagstaff late yesterday afternoon. It may be connected to a young woman who was injured in a traffic accident last night. We're trying to identify her."

"You said the girl was injured?" Evangeline asked. "How?"

"She was hit by a vehicle north of Flagstaff. I'm attempting to locate her family."

"She was running away," Evangeline said.

"We've surmised as much, but we're trying to locate her relatives. At the time she was injured, she was wrapped in a blanket—a Navajo blanket."

"One of mine," Evangeline answered. "All she had on was a jacket. It was snowing and cold, so I gave her my blanket to keep her warm, help keep her safe. Is she all right? What about her baby?"

"As far as I know at this moment, they're both still alive," Ali said. "But can you give me any idea of where she's from?"

"I know she came from a bad place," Evangeline replied after a pause. "I don't think she wants to be found."

"What bad place?" Ali pressed.

"It used to be called Short Creek," Evangeline answered. "That's what the People called it long ago. Now it's called Colorado City. Do you know it? Do you know about the people there?"

Ali did, because with those two words—Short Creek—everything about the Jane Doe puzzle seemed to click into place. Colorado City was the center of commerce for an isolated part of Arizona just to the north of the Grand Canyon. Although officially part of Mohave County, the area was hours away from even the most rudimentary law enforcement oversight. As a consequence, Colorado City and its environs had become a geographical magnet for any number of oddball communes and religious groups, many of which were suspected of practicing polygamy.

"Where exactly did you find her?" Ali asked.

"My husband and I were coming back from a selling trip, dropping off my blankets and his silver and turquoise jewelry at trading posts and gift shops before the summer tourist season starts. The man who owns the gas station in Colorado City is one of our customers. While Tsosie was talking to him, I went into the restroom. That's where I found the girl, hiding in one of the stalls. She said she was going to Flagstaff and asked if we'd give her a ride.

"It was while we were driving south that she asked to use my phone. When I gave it to her, though, she didn't know how to use it, so I dialed the number for her. It was to a friend of hers, someone named Irene. When Irene didn't answer the call, the girl seemed very upset, but I didn't ask what was wrong."

"Where did you let her out?"

"At a junction north of Flagstaff where we turned off to go visit our daughter. The girl said she was hoping to catch a ride into Flag to see her mother, who was in the hospital."

"Thank you," Ali said. "You've been a big help."

"Where is the girl?" Evangeline asked. "I mean, what hospital?"

"St. Jerome's."

"If you talk to her, please let her know that Tsosie and I will be praying for her."

"I will," Ali said. "Thank you."

14

When Betsy arrived home, Princess came to the door to greet her. After putting away her purchases and the container of carryout she'd brought home from the café, she went looking for Joe Friday. He was in her bedroom, tinkering with a computer on her small desk. He had stripped out of his flannel shirt. The short-sleeved T-shirt he wore underneath revealed more tattoos than Betsy could count. Or wanted to.

"Almost got 'er done," he said. "I already captured the images I need of Princess. Once I finish with the computer and have all your passwords set, I'll do your photo shoot. Then I'll be able to get out of your hair."

"You'll have the whole thing installed tonight? Really? I thought you said it would take a couple of days." Betsy was a little disappointed. She had rather liked the idea of having someone around the house to look out for her for a while. In fact, she had been fully prepared to offer putting him up in her guest room if for no other reason than to rattle Sandra's chain.

"Up and running," he answered. "The sight lines were

less complicated than I thought. With all the angles covered, I'll have a few cameras left over."

"Well," Betsy said. "Don't feel obliged to rush. I had supper in town on the way home. I brought you a hot roast beef sandwich, unless you're one of those vegan types who doesn't eat meat."

"Definitely a carnivore," Joe said with a grin. "And a hot roast beef sandwich or even a warm roast beef sandwich sounds like just what the doctor ordered."

"Come on, then," she said. "We'll deal with all that password business later. What would you like to drink?"

"Coffee if you've got it," he said. "I need to drive back to Minneapolis tonight."

Joe followed Betsy back toward the kitchen, stopping off to wash his hands in the powder room along the way. He settled down at the kitchen table and began eating while she stood by the counter waiting for the coffee to finish brewing. It bothered her to think that while she was just standing there in her own kitchen, someone a continent away could be watching her every move.

"My son and daughter-in-law made an appointment for me to see a doctor on Monday," she said. "To have my mental faculties evaluated." Betsy was astonished to hear the words coming out of her own mouth. How could she make such an admission to a complete stranger?

Joe was quiet as she set a coffee mug in front of him and then sat down with one of her own. When she looked up, he was studying her intently.

"Mrs. Peterson," he said, "if you don't mind my saying so, your son is a complete jackass!"

Fortunately for Betsy, she had yet to take a sip of her coffee. Had she done so, it probably would have splattered all over the table. She found herself nodding and laughing at the same time.

"I've met a few dotty folks now and again," Joe continued. "You don't happen to be one of them. Do you know this doctor, the one they want you to see? Did you agree to go to the appointment?"

Betsy nodded yes to both questions.

"Do you have someone who could go to the appointment with you—to have your back if need be?"

"Not really," she said. "There's my granddaughter, of course, but she lives in Arizona. And she's a teacher. I couldn't ask her to come up here for something like this."

"Find someone else to go with you, then," Joe urged. "And don't, whatever you do, mention a word of the security measures we've installed to anyone, including the doctor. Now then," he added, standing up and pushing away from the table. "Let's go deal with those passwords."

She followed him into the bedroom and waited while he went to fetch her a chair. He placed it next to his so she had a full view of the screen.

"Here we go," Joe said. He punched a button at the bottom of the screen, which came to life. A bouquet of begonias filled the screen, moving in and out of focus. In the middle of the colorful flowers was a small box asking for her user name and password. Before going any further, Joe adjusted the font so it was easier for her to read. That done, they established her user name as Betsy.

"If you give me a password," she objected, "how will I ever remember it?"

Joe picked up a piece of black plastic that was lying next to the computer. "This is a mouse," he said.

"What about it?"

"You use it to manipulate your cursor, but that's not

the whole reason why it's here." Placing the mouse on the table, he moved it until it was directly in front of Betsy. "I want you to put your thumb on it, right here in the bottom right-hand corner. Hold it like that for a moment."

Betsy did as he asked.

"Okay," he said. "That's enough." He waited for a moment, staring at the screen. "All right. Now we need to confirm it. Do that again."

She did. After a second or two, the image on the computer screen changed from melting begonias into a seascape.

"The begonias are a screen saver," he said. "The computer is running in the background, but the only way to access it will be with your thumbprint."

"That's my password, my thumbprint?"

"That's right. All you have to do is put your thumb in the same spot long enough for the image to register. As you can see, it looks like the computer is calling for an ordinary password, the kind people type in. An unauthorized user typing in passwords won't get anywhere, and I doubt it will occur to them that a woman your age, living out here in the sticks, would be using thumbprint recognition technology. Now, do you have either an e-mail or Facebook account?"

"Not Facebook," Betsy said. "I used to have an e-mail address, on Gmail, I think, but I haven't used it in years."

"You're going to start using it now." Joe's fingers flashed over the keyboard before pausing. "Yes, here it is. Now, what's your password for that?"

For an answer, Betsy stood up, went over to the dresser, opened the bottom drawer, retrieved a jewelry box, and removed a tiny spiral notebook that she handed to him.

Joe thumbed through the ragged book, then looked at her in dismay. "Wait a minute; these are the passwords to all your accounts—your bank accounts, your checking accounts, your cell phone, everything."

"Alton knew I'd never be able to remember all these. He's the one who had me start keeping this book. As you can see, I write them in pencil in case I need to change one of them."

Joe shook the book in her direction as though disciplining a child. "Don't you understand? Anyone who gains access to your house and to this book would also have access to everything about you? Here's your Gmail password. Go ahead and put it in. We'll change it later."

"Where are you going?"

"Out to the van to get my portable scanner," he said. "We're going to put all this information in a secure file inside the computer. Another copy will be stored elsewhere—at High Noon Enterprises most likely—and will be automatically updated if this one is updated. In the meantime, I recommend that you spend the next few days changing the passwords on all your accounts. As you're doing that, is there anyone else you would like to have access to the passwords?"

"My granddaughter," Betsy said. "Athena Reynolds. Her mother-in-law, Ali, and her husband own that company—the one you just mentioned, High Noon."

"Now I get the connection," Joe said. "All right, I'll tell Stuart we'll need Athena's thumbprint, too. That way she can be added to both the computer and the account as a secondary user."

While Joe headed for his van, Betsy found herself still fuming at his offhand and entirely too dismissive remark—"a woman your age." Even at what Joe seemed to regard as terribly advanced years, Betsy was determined to show him that she could still do a thing or two on her own.

Thumbing through the notebook, Betsy used the magnifying glass she kept in her pocket to locate the listing for Athena's e-mail address. Not knowing if it was still good, she tried it anyway. Before Joe returned, she had typed and sent a message to Athena, letting her know her computer was up and running.

Another hour and a half sped by before Joe had scanned all the pages of the notebook, shown her how to access them in the cloud, and then deemed Betsy work wise in terms of running the computer. That was when they finally did the photo shoot, even though at that hour of the night, Betsy was sure she didn't look her best.

The last thing before Joe left, he went out to the backyard, uncovered Alton's long-unused Weber grill, tossed Betsy's password notebook onto it and set the notebook on fire.

"Remember," he cautioned. "All your existing passwords need to be reset because we have to assume that any numbers in the notebook are most likely already compromised. From now on, all passwords go in your cyber safety-deposit file and nowhere else. You don't have to make the changes tonight, but make them soon."

"Right." Betsy nodded. "I'll be sure to do that right away."

For Betsy, though, it wasn't just about the passwords. There was more at stake here, and she wanted all of it settled and in place long before there was ever any question of Elmer Munson declaring her incompetent.

Just after ten, Joe loaded his tools and boxes into his van and drove away. As soon as he was gone, Betsy returned to the kitchen. It was late, but not that late. She had been thinking about this all during the password debacle, and she wanted to do it now, before she lost her nerve.

She had to use the phone book and the magnifying glass to locate the number, but once she had it, she dialed immediately. It took several rings before someone answered at Sundowner's Assisted Living Center. She almost hung up while she waited to be put through to Howard Hansen's unit, but she didn't.

"Hello." She heard the wariness in Howard's voice. *Calls in the middle of the night often mean bad news, especially at our age,* Betsy thought, then she chided herself for being as bad as Joe Friday.

"It's Betsy," she reassured Howard quickly. "No, there's nothing wrong. I mean, there's no emergency. But I do need your help. My son, Jimmy, thinks I'm losing my marbles. He and Sandra have made an evaluation appointment for me with Elmer Munson for Monday afternoon. I was wondering if you'd go with me."

It wasn't such an odd request. For the folks who socialized over bingo and at the VFW, it was often an "us or them" mentality, with members of the older generation duking it out with the younger ones. Howard Hansen may have been Betsy's boyfriend long ago, but he had also been a GP in Bemidji long before Elmer Munson graduated from high school much less medical school.

"I'd like to help out," Howard began, "but I don't drive anymore."

"I'll get us a ride," Betsy said. "I want you with me during the appointment."

"In the examining room? Are you sure?"

"Yes."

"That's rather irregular."

"Look," she said. "Sandra and Jimmy are trying to sell me down the river, and they're bringing in Elmer Munson as a hired gun to pull it off. I'm sure you remember what happened to Elmer's mother."

Howard sighed. "Well, yes," he agreed. "There is that. But if I go to the appointment with you, people are going to talk, especially if I accompany you into that exam room. We won't even be out of Munson's office before word will spread all over town."

"So?" Betsy returned. "In the past few days, any number of people have gone out of their way to remind me about how old I am. And they're right. I'm so old right now that I don't give a tinker's damn about what they say. Now, are you in or out?"

Howard didn't hesitate. "In," he said. "Definitely in."

"Okay. I'll let you know later when Marcia and I will pick you up. We might even have some supper after the appointment."

"Sounds good," Howard said.

Betsy was smiling when she returned the phone to its hook. "Come on, Princess," she said. "Let's go for one last walk before we go to bed. When Sandra and Jimmy find out what I've done today, they are going to be fit to be tied."

15

Returning to St. Jerome's after her visit with Andrea, Ali paused in the parking lot long enough to take a call from Stuart Ramey.

"Things are moving," he said. "Joe Friday is on the job, and his state-of-the-art monitoring system is being installed as we speak."

"Good," Ali said. "Athena will be relieved to hear that." Stuart went on to say something else, but Ali had stopped listening. Instead, she was watching a man and woman walk past her SUV, heading for the hospital's main entrance. The man, dressed in a sheepskin jacket, jeans, and boots, strode ahead of a pregnant woman who followed him at a distance of several paces. She wore an ankle-length checked print skirt over a pair of worn oxfords as well as a light cloth jacket. Her purse was a cloth drawstring pouch. But what Ali noticed most was her fading blond hair. Shot with gray, it was braided and then fastened into a crown that encircled the top of her head.

Ali's first thought was that these were Jane Doe's parents, come to check on their daughter.

"Sorry, Stu," Ali said quickly. "I've gotta run."

By the time she made it into the lobby, the couple stood in front of the reception desk.

"My name's Gordon Tower," the man announced in a booming voice that echoed off the polished granite floor. "I understand you've got my wife and my baby in here— Enid and baby Sarah. We've come to take them home."

His voice was loud and his manner brusque enough that there wasn't a person in the lobby who didn't turn to look in his direction. Ali looked, too. The man's gray hair and weathered face hinted that he was probably somewhere in his sixties. The woman's age was more difficult to pin down. Her graying hair and sunken cheeks, the product of many missing teeth, hinted that she was the same age as the man, although her pregnancy suggested that she couldn't be more than forty. In truth, Ali realized, she might even be far younger than that.

Seeming to sense the weight of Ali's gaze, the man spun around and glared at her. "What the hell are you staring at, woman?" he demanded. Before Ali could frame a suitable response, he had already turned his fury back on the hapless clerk.

"I'm sorry," she was saying, "we have no patients listed under those names."

He slammed the palm of his hand down onto the counter with such force that the clerk flinched from him.

"The hell you don't!" he growled. "They were brought here by ambulance late last night, and they shouldn't have been. The Family doesn't condone the kinds of black magic medicine that goes on in places like this. I'm here to take them both home. If you don't tell me where they are right now, I'll take this place apart brick by brick."

A uniformed but unarmed security guard materialized out of nowhere, most likely summoned by a panic button located somewhere on the receptionist's desk.

"What seems to be the problem here?" he asked.

"The problem is you people have my wife and baby," Tower growled. "I want them back."

"I was trying to explain to Mr. Tower here that we don't have any patients answering to the names he gave me," the clerk said. "Even if we did, we're not authorized to give out information . . ."

"Did you hear what I said?" Tower demanded. "You've got my wife and my daughter imprisoned somewhere in this hospital. Now, are you going to turn them over to me, or am I going to go away and come back with an attorney and sue the socks off this place?"

"Please calm down," the guard said, attempting to defuse the situation. "I'm sure this is all just some kind of misunderstanding. If you and the missus here would just have a seat . . ."

"I won't have a seat and I won't calm down. I want to talk to whoever's in charge, not some self-important pretend cop."

With Tower's attention focused entirely on the security guard, Ali took advantage of his momentary distraction to make for the elevator, dialing Sister Anselm's phone as she went. Naturally her call went to voice mail. When the elevator doors swished open, Ali bounded out into the waiting room. Several people were gathered there, but Sister Anselm wasn't one of them. A moment later, however, Ali caught sight of the nun emerging from a room down the hall. Sister Anselm looked at Ali in alarm.

"Is something wrong?" she asked.

"There's a guy downstairs hassling the front desk. He says his name is Gordon Tower, and he's come to take his wife and baby home, by force if necessary."

"Put the floor on lockdown, Nurse Mandy," Sister Anselm called to a woman seated at the nurses' station. Ali was surprised to see a metal shutter glide silently down over the inside of the nursery window. At the same time Ali heard the distinctive click of a door lock.

"Hey," one of the new fathers in the room said. "I'm here trying to look at my baby. What's going on?"

"Is the elevator disabled?" Sister Anselm asked.

Nurse Mandy nodded. "Done."

"All right, then," Sister Anselm said, taking Ali by the arm and guiding her toward the stairwell. "If there's going to be some kind of confrontation, it won't happen here on the maternity floor."

Sister Anselm sprinted down four flights of stairs in a way that left Ali far behind. When Ali opened the door at the bottom of the last flight, she heard raised voices coming from the lobby. Hurrying out of the stairwell on Sister Anselm's heels, Ali saw that the crowd in the lobby had grown. Several new innocent bystanders had shown up and were gawping. Five people stood outside the elevator door, pushing impatiently on the Up button and waiting for an elevator car Ali knew wasn't going to come.

Sister Anselm made it to the clamoring group in front of the reception desk at the same time two uniformed Flagstaff PD officers rushed in through the front entrance. The cops were there; the security guard was there; a man in a suit who, Ali discovered later, turned out to be the hospital's chief administrator was there; but it was Sister Anselm who waded into the melee and took charge.

"What seems to be the problem?" she demanded, her voice cutting through the uproar.

Gordon Tower rounded on her. "Who the hell are you?"

"My name is Sister Anselm," she replied calmly. "I may be able to be of some assistance, but first I expect you to stop shouting."

A look of consternation crossed the belligerent man's face. He was not someone who was used to being spoken to in that fashion, and certainly not, Ali surmised, by a woman. The other men in the room were more than happy to step back and let the nun take over.

"My name is Gordon Tower," he snapped at her.

Sister Anselm turned to the woman cowering behind the man. "And you are?"

The woman seemed perplexed at being expected to join in the conversation. She glanced at the man and waited for his nod of assent before she answered.

"Edith," she said. "Edith Tower."

"And your relationship to the woman you claim we're concealing here?"

"I already told these people," Gordon interjected. "I'm Enid's husband."

Again, Sister Anselm focused her sharp blue eyes on the woman. "I asked about your relationship to Enid?" the nun insisted.

Again Tower answered for her. "Edith's relationship to Enid is of no consequence in the matter at hand. Now, are you going to give me back my wife and baby or not?"

"Enid was brought in by ambulance and wasn't carrying any identification at the time she was admitted to the hospital," Sister Anselm said calmly, withdrawing her iPad from the pocket of her smock. "We need to have a few details, starting with her date of birth and her full name."

Tower sighed and ground his teeth. "Enid Ann Tower. No E on Ann."

"Her date of birth?"

Sister Anselm stood with her finger poised above the keyboard, while an exasperated Gordon turned to Edith. "Well?" he demanded impatiently. "When's her birthday?"

"July," Edith offered timidly. "It's sometime in July."

Ali was astonished. She remembered the month, day, year, and hour when Christopher was born. How could a mother not know that?

Sister Anselm exhibited no surprise whatsoever. "How old will Enid be this coming July?"

"Seventeen," Edith answered.

"Which means she's sixteen now. And where was she born? Perhaps we can ascertain her exact birth date through hospital records."

"Don't you understand anything?" Tower grumbled. "That's what I've been trying to tell you people all along. We believe in God. We do not believe in doctors and hospitals. Enid wasn't born in a hospital. She was born at home—in the birthing room."

"You're raising your voice again, Mr. Tower," Sister Anselm admonished. "Now tell me, where exactly is this"— she hesitated—" . . . birthing room?"

"Colorado City," Tower growled. "On The Family's private property outside Colorado City, a place we call The Encampment."

"Mother's maiden name?"

"Why on earth do you need to know that?"

"It's part of the identification process," Sister Anselm said, aiming a questioning look at Edith. "It's part of the information we need to have."

"Her mother's name was Anne," Edith said softly. "Anne Lowell. With an E."

One of the people from the growing crowd by the elevator came over to raise an objection. "Is someone going to call about the elevator? People are stuck in it. I can hear them pounding."

"One moment, sir," Sister Anselm said. "There's a problem here."

"You're damned right there's a problem," Tower agreed.

"Now then," Sister Anselm said, turning to him with a beaming smile. "I'll need your full name."

"Why?"

"Assuming our patient turns out to be Enid, then I expect you'll be the one responsible for all her charges. To that end, I need your name, your Social Security number, and the name and number of your insurance carrier."

"Who said I'd be responsible? Who said I had insurance?"

"Don't you?"

"Why would I need insurance? We don't use hospitals."

"You're using one now," Sister Anselm countered. "And if the patient upstairs turns out to be your wife, she's already had two rounds of lifesaving surgery with more in the offing. Surgery costs money, Mr. Tower. Surgeons cost money."

"And you expect me to pay for all of it? Why should I? I didn't ask to have her brought here. I don't want her to be here. You can't make me pay for treatment I don't believe in and never wanted."

"Just because someone is brought here by ambulance doesn't mean their family is allowed to skate on their obligation to pay the bill. Once we determine who the responsible party is, we expect him or her to do just that—to take responsibility and pay the expenses."

"I am not paying!" Tower declared. Anger distorted his face as he shook his finger in Sister Anselm's face. "What I am going to do is go upstairs, one damned stairwell at a time if I have to. I'm going to find my wife and my daughter, bring them back downstairs with me, and take them home. Is that clear?"

Instead of backing off, Sister Anselm stepped into his space. "What is clear, Mr. Tower," she said quietly, "is that you are a bully and an ass!"

Goaded into unreasoning fury, Gordon Tower's reaction was as instinctive as it was predictable. The powerful slap that landed on Sister Anselm's cheek crackled through the room. She swayed briefly and then stepped away from her attacker. Ali was about to weigh into the fray when she realized that Sister Anselm was smiling.

"Officers," she said, "I believe that constitutes an assault. Considering the circumstances, I'm under no obligation to turn the other cheek."

The two uniformed cops stepped up as if shot out of cannons. Within a matter of seconds, Tower's arms were handcuffed behind his back and he was being led away while someone read him his rights.

In the meantime, Sister Anselm turned to Edith, who had backed away from the confrontation, sinking down onto the nearest chair. "Are you all right?" the nun asked.

Edith nodded numbly. "When will he get out?"

Sister Anselm looked at her watch and shrugged. "The courthouse is closed now, so probably not until tomorrow morning. Will you be able to get home?"

"He took the car key."

Sister Anselm dispatched the still hovering security guard to retrieve the car key before Tower could be hustled into a waiting patrol car.

"When is your baby due?"

"Two months."

"It's a long trip from here back to Colorado City," Sister Anselm observed. "You might be better off staying in town. If you don't have enough money for a room . . ."

"We're not allowed to stay Outside," Edith said. "We might fall into evil ways."

The security guard returned with the car keys followed by a burly man in a sheepskin jacket very much like the one Gordon Tower had worn. He hustled straight over to Edith.

"Are you all right?" he demanded. "What's going on? Is Gordon really under arrest?"

Edith nodded wearily and handed the car keys to the new arrival. "I'm going to need you to drive me home," she told him.

Without another word being exchanged, the man took her arm and led her away.

Ali walked up to Sister Anselm and saw that the vivid imprint of Gordon Tower's hand still marred the skin on the nun's pale cheek.

"Are you all right?" Ali asked. "He hurt you."

"I'm fine. He certainly didn't hurt me nearly as badly as he's hurt Enid," Sister Anselm replied. "And he'll hurt her a lot worse if he gets his hands on her again. We may have won this battle, Ali. Now we need to win the war."

16

ack on the maternity floor, things were getting back to normal. The metal shutters on the nursery windows had been raised. The doors were no longer locked. Nurses buzzed around the ward, reassuring both anxious patients and visitors that the crisis had passed. While Sister Anselm, ice pack on hand, hurried off to check on her charges, Ali took a seat in the waiting room and turned to her iPad.

A few moments after putting the words "Colorado City" into her browser, Ali found herself reading about the "Short Creek Raid." Seeing those words in print, she remembered that was what Evangeline Begay, the Indian woman Ali had talked to earlier on the phone, had called the place—Short Creek.

In the summer of 1953, Howard Pyle, then governor of Arizona, had called out the National Guard and ordered a raid on the polygamous group of fundamentalist Mormons who lived there. In the course of the raid, the entire community had been taken into custody. Of the 400 arrested, 263 were minor children, some of whom were put into foster care and never returned to their biological parents.

The resulting political fallout was disastrous, especially for Governor Pyle. The Short Creek debacle was thought to be, in large measure, responsible for his failure to win his bid for reelection the following year.

With Pyle's unfortunate history as an example, succeeding governors had simply turned a blind eye on the people who lived in the area and had ignored whatever it was those folks were doing or not doing. Short Creek, now renamed Colorado City, had continued to benefit from this seemingly deliberate lack of governmental oversight.

Once that original group was reconstituted, its members went about formally establishing the Fundamentalist Church of Jesus Christ of Latter-day Saints. The FLDS church, as it was now called, remained the largest denomination in the area, although a number of groups with similar belief systems had settled nearby as well. Colorado City had again burst on the national scene a few years earlier when one of the FLDS leaders, Warren Jeffs, had been arrested and imprisoned on charges of sexually assaulting underage girls.

And now it's happening again, Ali thought, *because it's easier for officialdom to ignore the problem than it is for them to fix it.*

She remembered that Gordon Tower had said something about an entity he called "The Family" and Edith had mentioned "Outside," but Ali's browser located no applicable references. If The Family was a real group of some kind, it was operating under the radar of the people running Wikipedia.

Sister Anselm came down the hallway and beckoned to Ali. "Time for a strategy session," she said. "Better to do that in private."

Back in the tiny conference room, Ali noted the still visible handprint on Sister Anselm's cheek, but the nun's narrow shoulders were straight and the fire was back in her eye. The confrontation with Gordon Tower had galvanized her out of her earlier lethargy.

"How are they?" Ali asked. Then, remembering Sister Anselm's vow of silence, she added, "Never mind. Sorry."

"What's your take on Edith?" Sister Anselm asked.

"When I first saw her, I thought she was Enid's mother, but no mother forgets her child's birth date. And Gordon about had a cow when you asked about Edith's relationship to Enid."

"I noticed that, too," Sister Anselm said. "Colorado City is known for harboring polygamous groups, but admitting it here, in what Edith referred to as the 'Outside,' is probably not encouraged."

"We're both on the same page on that score," Ali confirmed. "Edith is an older wife of Gordon Tower, while Enid, formerly known as this Jane Doe, is a younger one?"

"Yes," Sister Anselm said. "That's my take, too. What caught my eye was the way Edith wore her hair. Did you notice that crown of braids?"

It was Ali's turn to nod. "You're right. That's the one obvious common denominator for all three of them— Edith, Enid, and the Jane Doe you told me about who was left near the Hualapai Mountains and later died at the Kingman hospital. It's a distinctive hairstyle, and it suggests that they could all be from the same group. Finding out what we can about Enid's background may help us untangle the Kingman Jane Doe's history as well. From there, we might even be able to find her killer."

"This many years later?" Sister Anselm asked dubiously. "Is that even possible?"

Ali nodded. "Tell me about that case again. When was it exactly?"

"It happened about twelve years ago. The Kingman Jane Doe was found close to death by some passersby who had been hiking in the mountains. She had been stripped naked, savagely beaten, and left to die."

"That doesn't sound like an act of random violence."

"No," Sister Anselm agreed. "It wasn't random at all. I went so far as to mention that to one of the detectives at the time—that I wondered if it might possibly be a case of domestic violence. The detective wasn't having any of it, at least not if the idea came from me. Besides, it made no difference. Since the cops had no idea of who she was or where she came from, the investigation went nowhere. I'm sure they worked the case for a time, but I don't know how hard or how long."

"It turns out we have something the cops back then never had—a clue, those three matching hairdos," Ali said. "We also know, first from my conversation with Evangeline Begay and now from Gordon Tower himself, that Enid came from somewhere in or around Colorado City. I think the Kingman Jane Doe came from there, too. Is there a chance Enid might have known the other victim?"

Sister Anselm shook her head. "I doubt it. If Enid is almost seventeen now, she would have been only four or five at the time Jane Doe disappeared. Most likely she would have been too young to remember anything about it."

"But maybe she's heard stories about it," Ali suggested. "Kids remember stories, and having a girl from the group running away or going missing would have been big news. It would help if we could ask her about it. Are we going to be able to?"

Rather than answering Ali's question directly, Sister Anselm folded her hands and gazed out the window toward the waiting room. "Patients with traumatic brain injuries and with swelling issues may be kept in medically induced comas for a while. Recovery takes time, and how much they'll be able to remember is questionable."

On the surface, Sister Anselm appeared to be speaking about TBI patients in general, although Ali understood the truth of the matter. She was really speaking about one patient in particular—Enid Tower.

"Let's say then," Ali suggested, "that your first instinct was correct and Kingman Jane Doe's death was due to an act of domestic violence—that she died at the hands of a husband or a boyfriend. As you said, since the cops had no idea who she was, they had no idea about where to go looking for suspects.

"I think it's likely that DNA evidence was collected at the time," Ali continued. "But just because it was collected doesn't mean that it was ever processed. Processing DNA was very costly back then. Without family members prodding the cops to keep working the case, there's a good chance that evidence is still lying, unprocessed, in a sheriff's department's evidence locker. And even if they did run it at the time, technology available back then might have yielded inconclusive results. With the advances made in DNA technology in the meantime, samples deemed useless back then can now be used to create full DNA profiles."

"So?" Sister Anselm asked.

"I'm thinking about this group Gordon Tower called 'The Family.' It's likely to be a small, isolated group—one that wouldn't be welcoming to people from the 'Outside.' So if what happened near Kingman was domestic violence, maybe the offender is someone from that same group—a group with a very small gene pool."

"Are you saying genetic profiles taken from Enid and her baby might lead us back to the Kingman Jane Doe and to her killer as well?"

"Yes, or even to a near relative of her killer. Knowing that might at least enable us to point the investigators in the right direction."

"And you propose to get these samples how?" Sister Anselm asked.

"From you, of course," Ali said.

Sister Anselm's pale face went a shade paler, making Gordon Tower's lingering handprint that much more obvious. Ali knew she had stepped over an invisible boundary.

"No," Sister Anselm said at once, shaking her head. "Absolutely not. I couldn't possibly condone such a thing. Besides, what would you do with the samples once you had them? Pass them along to the nearest crime lab? Run them through that national criminal DNA database that we're hearing so much about these days?"

"Not a crime lab," Ali answered. "I have a friend in the UK who was a huge help in sorting out the long-unsolved homicide of Leland Brooks's father. The friend's name is Kate Benchley. She runs an outfit called Banshee Group, a nongovernmental organization that specializes in identifying the remains of victims of various cases of genocide, or as politically correct people like to call it these days, 'ethnic cleansing.'

"Banshee Group's brief is to return murdered victims to their families for proper burial. If we were to send Kate sample swabs from Enid and her baby, I have no doubt that her people will provide us with their profiles in private. Once Jane Doe's case is reopened, assuming there is usable DNA, we'll have DNA profiles ready and waiting for comparison purposes. We'll have them available to hand over to any Mohave County investigator who might have need of making a genetic match."

"All that presupposes you'll be able to get the cold case reopened," Sister Anselm objected.

"Yes, it does," Ali agreed. "I have an idea about how to make that happen. It's an avenue I intend to pursue regardless of your answer on the DNA question."

"Taking the samples seems like a gross invasion of my patients' privacy," Sister Anselm said.

"Well," Ali said. "You could bring me that box of Enid's effects, and I could clip off a tiny piece of the part of her shirt that was soaked in amniotic fluid. That would probably fill the bill."

Sister Anselm thought about that and then shook her head. "I just can't see any way to justify doing such a thing, especially without having Enid's consent. It's out of the question."

"Do you remember what you told me this morning, about your being afraid that these two new victims were an answer to your prayers for a solution to the Kingman Jane Doe case? You also mentioned the responsibility you felt that by not pushing to solve that case, you had somehow left these two new victims at risk."

Sister Anselm nodded.

"What if you're right?" Ali asked. "What if this whole state of affairs is an answer to that prayer—an exact answer? Just because we've made the connection between the two cases doesn't mean we're absolved from having to do something about them. We need to carry this thing forward. With what we know so far, we can go to the Mohave County Sheriff's Office and give them a reason to reopen Jane Doe's case, but I want to do more than that. I don't want them to simply reopen it. I want them to solve it."

"And you believe those samples might be the key?"

"I do. Of course, if Enid dies, this whole discussion is moot," Ali added. "At that point, her DNA would be collected during the course of an autopsy with or without her consent, and the end result may well turn out to be the same. At that juncture the Kingman Jane Doe's case may be solved without our help, leaving your conscience entirely clear. But please remember, Kingman's Jane Doe didn't consent to having her DNA samples taken, either."

"No," Sister Anselm agreed regretfully. "She did not."

"And what about this?" Ali asked. "If we could go into Enid Tower's room right now and ask her if she'd be willing to allow you to take DNA samples, what do you think she'd say, especially if she knew samples taken from her and her baby might help solve another case, the murder of another runaway girl very much like her?"

"I suppose she'd say yes," Sister Anselm conceded.

"I suppose she would, too," Ali agreed.

Sister Anselm stood up. "I'll have to think this over," she said with her hand on the doorknob.

"Pray about it maybe?" Ali asked.

Sister Anselm allowed herself a small fleeting smile. "That, too," she said. "Now I'd best go check on them."

Refraining from any additional urging, Ali simply nodded. After all, a possible yes was far better than an absolute no.

"One more thing," Ali said. "Did you attend Kingman Jane Doe's funeral?"

"Of course, but as I mentioned, Bishop Gillespie handled final arrangements for both Jane Doe and the baby. I was there as part of the bishop's delegation, but I doubt my presence was noted one way or the other. Why are you asking?"

"Right now I'm mostly thinking out loud," Ali told her. "How many interactions did you have with the detectives on the Kingman case?"

"Just the one I already mentioned—when I brought up the possibility of domestic violence. By then, though, the mother was dead and I was caring for the baby. She couldn't tell them anything."

"With Kate Benchley's help, she might be able to now."

"Yes," Sister Anselm agreed. "You might be right."

For a few minutes after the nun left the room, Ali stayed where she was, thinking. If Sister Anselm couldn't square her conscience with taking the DNA samples, Ali realized she'd need to find some other way to accomplish that goal. In the meantime, she set about tackling the next problem.

By then it was ten o'clock on the East Coast. When she called B., he answered immediately. "Hey," he said. "I just got back from a dinner meeting and was about to call you. I heard from Stuart that the Betsy Peterson matter is under control. The surveillance system is up and running."

"Great," she said. "Now I have another problem for you. It's a cold case or, rather two of them—the deaths of a young mother and her infant daughter twelve years ago near Kingman. They were both Sister Anselm's patients."

Ali spent the next several minutes explaining the specifics to her husband.

"Okay," B. said when she finished. "What does any of this have to do with us?"

"I want to call Bishop Gillespie and ask for his help," Ali said. "I'm hoping that, based on his connection to the Kingman Jane Doe and her baby, he'll be able to convince the Mohave County Sheriff's Office to reopen those two cases."

"Because he paid their burial expenses?" B. asked. "Is that enough of a connection?"

"Maybe not," Ali said. "But there's something else at work there. We didn't meet the Mohave County sheriff when we were in that mess back in November, but I remember seeing his name—Sheriff Daniel Alvarado. I just googled him. He's still in his first term, so he wasn't sheriff back when all this happened. Based on his name, I'm willing to bet dollars to doughnuts that he's a good Catholic boy."

"That sounds like some sort of racial profiling. Or religious profiling at least," B. said. "Do you want me to call Bishop Gillespie and ask?"

Ali knew that if B. asked, the bishop would agree. Ali had something else in mind.

"No," she said. "I'll call him myself, but I do need his number."

17

When Ali left the conference room, Sister Anselm was standing near the nurses' station talking to someone. She waved for Ali to join them.

"This is the young man I was telling you about, Ali," Sister Anselm said. "David Upton. And this is my friend Ali Reynolds."

"Yes," David said ruefully, holding out his hand. "I'm the bad guy here, the one who hit the poor girl and sent her to the hospital."

"From everything I've heard, what happened was unavoidable," Ali said with a reassuring smile. "And obviously it was anything but a hit-and-run. I mean, you're here now, aren't you?"

David nodded. "I came by because I remembered something else from last night. I don't know if it's important, but when I first got to her, she kept mumbling something about her brother and something about pigs. Like don't take me to the pigs. When I remembered that today, I wondered if she'd had some kind of run-in with the cops."

"Did you see anyone else out there?" Ali asked. "Anyone at all?"

"I saw at least one car—a light-colored pickup, I think. It went past when we were there on the road and before the guy from the gas station put up the flares. I wondered why the driver didn't stop to help, but I was so concerned about her right then that I didn't really pay attention."

"If she was talking about the pig situation at the time, it probably is important," Ali suggested. "You should mention it to the officers who investigated the incident."

David nodded. "All right," he said. "I will." He turned to Sister Anselm. "Thank you for letting me know that they're both still hanging in. When she wakes up, be sure to tell her I stopped by."

When Upton turned and walked away, Ali sent a questioning look in Sister Anselm's direction.

"I know, I know," Sister Anselm said. "But sometimes, rules are made to be broken. Including this one." With that, she shoved something into the pocket of Ali's jacket then hurried off down the hall in the direction of Enid Tower's room. When Ali checked the pocket, she wasn't surprised to find two Ziploc bags, each of which contained a single cotton swab. On one bag was a taped label with the words "Jane Doe" written in ink in Sister Anselm's distinctive handwriting. The other one was tagged with the words "Baby Jane Doe."

With the samples in her pocket, Ali left for Sedona. The road was bare and clear, but she stayed well under the speed limit on I-17. Minutes later, when the Cayenne's headlights picked out a herd of elk taking a leisurely stroll across the blacktop, she was glad she'd been taking it slow. She had just passed the elk when her phone rang.

"Hi," Athena said, "I just got home from a basketball

game." Athena was now the high school's varsity girls' basketball coach.

"Who won?" Ali asked.

"We did."

"You don't sound very happy about it?"

Athena took a deep breath. "There's good news and bad news," she said. "For one thing, when I got home tonight, there was an e-mail waiting for me from Gram, which was a huge surprise. I've been trying for months to get her back online. How did you do that? So then, when I called to tell her congratulations, she said something weird—a couple of things, really. She told me I need to go see Stu and have him take a copy of my thumbprint. What's that all about? And while I'm there, she says Stu is supposed to take 3-D photographs of me, too. Why? What's going on?"

"It's probably something to do with the security system we installed for her," Ali said. "But if the e-mail from your grandmother is the good news, what's the bad?"

"I just got off the phone with my dad. He says he wanted me to know that he and Mom have scheduled what he called an 'evaluation appointment' for Gram on Monday."

"What kind of evaluation, physical?"

"Mental," Athena answered bleakly. "Dad told me that with everything that's going on, he and Mom think it's time to take that 'next step,' as he called it. That if Gram's turning on stove burners and forgetting about doing it or mixing up her meds, she's no longer capable of living on her own. What astonished me is that Dad says she agreed to go for the evaluation. Why would she do that? If I were in her shoes, I'd tell the people trying to lock me up to go piss up a rope."

"I get the feeling that your parents aren't particularly close to your grandmother," Ali said. "Is that the case?"

"More my mother's problem than Dad's. And Mom is most likely the mover and shaker behind all this. That's just how she operates. She can be a super-manipulator at times, and my father goes along with whatever she wants because that's what he does. He doesn't like to make waves as far as Mom is concerned, even when she treats him like crap. Which she always has, by the way, for as long as I can remember."

In the last two days, Ali had learned more about what made her daughter-in-law tick than ever before, and she suspected those insights had been offered more because Ali had turned off her asking mode in favor of simply listening.

"Growing up in that kind of family dynamic must have been tough," Ali offered.

Even over the phone she heard the catch in Athena's throat. "Yes," she agreed softly. "It was."

"Okay," Ali said. "You asked for High Noon's help, and you need to let us do just that. Your responsibility in all this is to do exactly what your grandmother asked—get the photographs and thumbprint taken as soon as you can, tomorrow if possible."

"You don't think it can wait until the weekend?"

"Sooner is better than later."

"All right," Athena agreed. "I'll see if my assistant can handle practice tomorrow. Maybe I can run up there after school."

"Do that," Ali said. "In the meantime, what's the doctor's name again—the evaluation doc?"

"Munson," Athena answered. "Dr. Elmer Munson."

"Okay," Ali said. "Let me follow up on this. Don't

worry. Your grandmother has some good people in her corner. She's not in this on her own, and neither are you."

By the time Ali turned off I-17, there was a small strip of snow on either side of the pavement, but that was only the remnant of what had been plowed off the night before. The rest of the snow had melted into the desert. After years spent living in Chicago, that was one of the things Ali really appreciated about living in Sedona. It was a place where snow was relatively rare and usually stayed on the ground no more than a day.

Out of freeway traffic, Ali dialed Stu's number and wasn't surprised to hear that he was still up and working.

"Tell me about needing Athena's thumbprint and the photo," she said. "I'm assuming it's got something to do with the surveillance system."

"The photo does," Stu answered. "If Athena shows up at her grandmother's house, her image will be one of the ones that doesn't trigger an alarm. The thumbprint is something else. Mrs. Peterson had all her personal passwords, including her banking passwords, in a notebook in her bedroom. Joe Friday pitched a fit about that. He's established a secure cloud account for her to use for storing passwords. Betsy wants Athena to be the only other person with access to all her passwords."

"She's probably not wrong about that," Ali said, "especially considering what Athena told me just now. I want you to find out everything there is to know about Athena's parents, Dr. and Mrs. James Peterson of Bemidji, Minnesota. I don't know this for sure, but I suspect that one or the other of them is up to no good."

"Why?"

"They seem to have launched a concerted effort to have Betsy declared incompetent. She told me yesterday that Athena is the only beneficiary named in her will. That means if she dies, Jim and Sandra Peterson get nothing, but if they can make a competency hearing work in their favor, they may be able to gain control of her funds right now."

"How deep do you want me to go?" Stu asked.

"Deep," Ali answered. "And while you're at it, take a look at someone else—a Dr. Elmer Munson, also of Bemidji."

"Who's he?"

"The doctor doing the evaluation," Ali answered. "Call me a conspiracy nut if you want, but I have a feeling there's something rotten in Bemidji."

Minutes after ending the call to Stu, Ali was home. Bella had evidently heard the garage door. She was stationed just inside the kitchen door and scampered around Ali in ecstatic short-legged circles. Straightening up from greeting the dog, Ali spotted a note from Leland on the kitchen counter. She had tried calling him earlier in the afternoon to let him know she'd be coming home late. When he didn't pick up, she had left a message. His note said: "Couldn't tell from your voice mail if you'd eaten or not. Just in case, there's a pasty waiting in the warming drawer."

That was welcome news. The pasty Ali had eaten at lunchtime was now far too many hours in the past. She took the warm one out of the oven, poured herself a glass of milk, and sat down at the table to eat, sharing only a few morsels of pie crust with the dog.

Half an hour later, after taking Bella out for one last walk, Ali and the dog headed for the bedroom. Ali didn't bother pretending to pick up *Pride and Prejudice*. She was beyond Jane Austen's reach tonight. And she didn't try to boot Bella off the bed, either.

She went to sleep as soon as she turned out the light, but she didn't stay asleep. In one dream after another, her friend Irene Bernard was there, surrounded by a group of pregnant girls, all of them wearing crowns of braids on the tops of their heads. In the dreams, Ali was the only one who knew the girls were dead. Reenie had no idea.

18

After a night of ragged sleep, Ali wasn't exactly at her best at eleven the next morning when she arrived at Bishop Gillespie's residence in Phoenix and was ushered by his assistant into a book-lined study. The old-fashioned library table that served as a desk was situated in front of a metal mullioned window that looked out on a spacious lawn of winter-hardy green grass. Except for a wrought-iron gate on the drive, the lawn was completely surrounded by a thick hedge of twenty-foot-tall oleanders and punctuated by towering, fully skirted palm trees. Off in the distance was the distinctive hump-shaped rock formation that gave Camelback Road its name.

Bishop Gillespie, seated in front of a gas-log fireplace in what Ali assumed to be an original Stickley Morris chair, watched with interest as Ali paused long enough to enjoy the view.

"The gardener keeps asking for me to let him trim the palm trees," Bishop Gillespie said, "and I keep saying no. All those dead palm fronds provide a lot of habitat for doves, especially, and they also provide a lot of shade."

He gestured toward an oak and leather Morris chair

that matched his. The lumpy leather cushions were burnished with long use and cracked with age. Ali guessed that the chairs were probably about the same age as the bishop.

"Come and sit," he suggested. "Coffee?" He raised the cup and saucer that had been perched on the broad flat arm of his chair in Ali's direction.

"No, thanks," she said. "I'm completely coffeed at the moment. Thank you for agreeing to see me on such short notice."

Ali had called earlier that morning, a little after eight, asking for an appointment. She expected it would take a day or two to gain access. When she was told eleven that morning was the only time available, she made tracks to be there.

"What have you and Sister Anselm got up to now?" Bishop Gillespie asked, beaming at her. "I assume that's why you're here."

He listened to Ali's story in silence until she reached the point where Gordon Tower had nearly decked Sister Anselm. At that point the bishop laughed out loud.

"It sounds like she deliberately provoked him."

Ali nodded. "She did, and since the cops were right there, they were only too happy to cuff him, arrest him, and haul him away."

"It's not the first time," Bishop Gillespie observed. "That's one of the tools Sister uses when she's dealing with bullies. That way someone else locks the guy up, and she doesn't have to mess with him. It only works, though, if she has cops on hand to witness the assault."

Ali had known Sister Anselm for years, but Bishop Gillespie's revelation was news to her.

The bishop fell silent again and stayed that way until

Ali finished telling him the rest of her story. In doing so, she told the bishop about sending DNA samples from Enid and her baby to Banshee Group while neglecting to say exactly how those samples had been obtained—a sin of omission. She ended with the hope that Bishop Gillespie would be able to convince Sheriff Alvarado to reopen the Jane Doe case.

"You're thinking that a reexamination of the DNA involved in the Kingman cases will lead back to a perpetrator who's a member of the group you just mentioned, The Family or whatever—the one Gordon Tower is part of?"

"Yes, I do," Ali answered.

Bishop Gillespie considered for a time before he spoke. "My connection to the Kingman case is tenuous at best, but I know that this case in particular is one that has haunted Sister Anselm through the years. However, your assumptions about the connections between the two cases may well be correct. My asking might provide the necessary impetus to get the case back in the spotlight. I suspect, however, that the added expense of the DNA lab work may turn out to be a sticking point as far as Sheriff Alvarado is concerned."

"High Noon will cover that," Ali declared.

"You're sure?" he asked.

Ali nodded. "I'm sure."

A long silence settled over the room. Bishop Gillespie was the one who broke it. "On the one hand, reopening this case—if it does lead back to The Family—might suggest the authorities are indulging in a certain level of religious persecution. On the other hand, the extreme youth of the two pregnant female victims—Jane Doe and Enid Tower—is indicative of a history of sexual abuse, something of which the Catholic church is hardly blameless.

"So, yes, I'll make that call to Sheriff Alvarado," he continued. "Since you are far more conversant with the details of the current investigation and how it leads back to the Kingman homicide investigation, I'll suggest that he contact you directly. In the meantime, I'd like to know more about The Family. I'd like to know if they're part of that splinter fundamentalist group that still refers to itself as LDS or whether this is something else entirely."

"You're asking me to look into it?" Ali asked.

"Yes, I am," Bishop Gillespie answered. "I'm familiar, of course, with what happened there years ago—the Short Creek incident you mentioned earlier. That was a complete travesty. I certainly don't want to be responsible for bringing that kind of overreaction down on the heads of folks who may be innocent of any wrongdoing. On the other hand, we have two young women, twelve years apart, risking life, limb, and their children's lives in desperate attempts to escape. That would suggest that something is seriously wrong as far as The Family is concerned. I want to know what's really going on up there."

"All right," Ali agreed. "I'll see what I can do."

That was an easy commitment to make since she was way ahead of Bishop Gillespie in terms of searching out information concerning The Family. On her way down from Sedona, she had called Stu. Since she had struck out in locating any online information on The Family, she asked him to see if he could find any information on Gordon Tower.

"I'm busy working the Bemidji angle," Stu had said. "If it's okay with you, I'll turn this over to Cami."

There was a discreet knock at the door to the library and the bishop's assistant stepped back inside. "Excuse me, Bishop Gillespie," he said. "Your next appointment is here."

Taking the hint, Ali rose to leave, but Bishop Gillespie wagged an admonishing finger in her direction. "Remember," he said with a smile, "I expect both you and that bully-baiting friend of yours to stay in touch and out of trouble. I'm sure Mr. Simpson has my cell number, but I'll ask my assistant to give it to you as well."

Ali left the bishop's residence with his direct number added to her phone's list of contacts. On the way back to I-17, she stopped off at a FedEx office to drop off the envelope bound for Banshee Group. She was back in the car and headed north when her phone rang with a call from Cami.

"Making any progress?" Ali asked.

"Some. I started by searching county and state databases for Gordon Tower. Both his driver's license and his voter's registration list him as living on Tower Road in unincorporated Mohave County. Then I got a satellite photo of Tower Road. There's only one house on it, a massive-looking place, and several outbuildings—a barn, some Quonset-hut-looking things, and a few others. I found a driver's license listing at that address for someone named Edith Tower, but there's no voter registration listing for her.

"I figured if Gordon Tower lived on Tower Road, I'd check out some of the other roads as well, and I struck paydirt. When I went looking through voter registrations for a Johnson living on Johnson Road, I found one—a guy named Wendell Johnson Jr. at 114 Johnson Road. A search of the driver's-license database for that address shows two licenses, one for Wendell Jr. and one for Anita, but no voter registration for Anita. There's another set of

Johnsons in the area, a Wendell Sr. and Vera, but their home address is actually in Colorado City."

"Let me guess," Ali interjected. "Vera drives but doesn't vote."

"Right you are. That's true for the entire enclave—two driver's licenses per household—one for a man and one for a woman, but there are no voter registration listings for any of the women. At all."

"What enclave are you talking about?" Ali asked.

"That information came from the property records. A little under fifty years ago, a guy named Angus Lowell showed up and purchased three thousand acres of unincorporated land in that part of unincorporated Mohave County. He bought that acreage from the FLDS church. He must have paid cash for the whole shebang because there's no record of anyone ever carrying a mortgage. The entire property is still deeded over to the Lowell Family Trust."

"That's it," Ali breathed. "That's probably why they call it 'The Family.' Are you saying that none of the individuals you just named actually own the properties where they live?"

"Not that I can tell," Cami said. "They may pay rent to the trust, but if they do, I can't find any paper trail. My guess is the roads were unnamed until a few years ago when the state required mandatory compliance and all rural roads were assigned names. At that point, the residents must have opted for the simplest solution and named each road for the family that lived there."

Ali didn't say the rest of what she was thinking. If this was a polygamous situation, the oldest wife was the one female in each family who was allowed to drive, but not a single one of the women—not even the most senior—was allowed to vote. And if women in The Family weren't allowed to drive or to vote, Ali wondered, what else were The Family's girls and women forbidden to do?

"Is there a Lowell Road?" Ali asked. "If so, who lives on that?"

"No sign of a Lowell Road, but the largest set of buildings is on what appears to be the main drag, which is actually Angus Road. That one has the same kind of house, barn, and outbuilding arrangement as all the others, only the house itself is far larger. In addition, there are two possible public buildings, maybe a church or a social hall of some kind with plenty of parking nearby. There are several somewhat smaller structures in that compound as well."

"Who lives there?"

"Someone named Richard Lowell. The single licensed female driver at that address is named Helena."

"How many roads on the property in all?" Ali asked.

"I counted twenty-eight separate houses on the map. That would make for close to thirty families, including Wendell Johnson Sr., whose family evidently lives in town."

Ali's call waiting buzzed with a blocked number showing up in the caller ID window.

"All right," Ali said. "Thanks, Cami. I've got to take another call. Keep putting the pieces together. I'll get back to you." She switched over to the other line. "Hello."

"Is this Alison Reynolds?"

"Yes."

"My name is Danny Alvarado, Sheriff Alvarado from Mohave County. Your name sounds familiar to me. Weren't you involved in some kind of dustup over near Bullhead City a while back?"

"You have a good head for names, Sheriff Alvarado," Ali said with a laugh. "And yes. I was the woman in the car trunk."

"I just had a call from the Catholic bishop down in Phoenix—Bishop Francis Gillespie. I take it you know him?"

"Yes," Ali replied. "He's a family friend." She realized as she said the words that it was no exaggeration. Bishop Gillespie was a friend.

"He was asking me about two unsolved cases from here in Kingman years ago—a young woman and her newborn infant. It turns out I was one of the investigators on that case and remember it well. Bishop Gillespie mentioned there might be a possible connection between those cases and a new situation over near Flagstaff. He said that both girls appeared to be runaways who were very young, very pregnant, and who wore their hair in a similar fashion."

"Yes to all," Ali said. "The hairdos were very distinctive— long braids wrapped around the tops of their heads."

"As I said, I was one of the investigators in the Jane Doe matter, and I remember those very distinctive braids. What I'm not sure is how you came to know about them."

"I heard about them from someone connected to both cases."

"That would be the nun Bishop Gillespie mentioned?"

"Yes," Ali answered. "Her name is Sister Anselm. She's a special emissary of Bishop Gillespie's, and functions as a patient advocate where necessary. Twelve years ago, Sister Anselm served in that capacity for both your victims—Jane Doe and her infant. Yesterday morning, by sheer coincidence, she was called out to care for this newly injured mother and child."

"Has your victim been IDed?"

"Tentatively," Ali answered. "We believe her name to be Enid Tower and that she ran away from one of the polygamous communities up near Colorado City. While on the run, she stepped into the path of an oncoming vehicle. That's what put her in the hospital."

"Not Colorado City again," the sheriff said with a sigh. "Dealing with those people is a nightmare. Do you happen to know which group?"

"I believe they call themselves The Family," Ali answered. "I don't have much more information on them than that. From what I've been able to gather, the whole group consists of twenty-five to thirty families, give or take. At the time of your Jane Doe's death, Sister Anselm attempted to suggest to the investigators that her death was the result of some kind of domestic violence. That idea got no traction at the time. This new case isn't specifically domestic violence, either, but still . . ."

"The good sister was entirely correct in her assumption. Considering the degree of violence visited on our Jane Doe, that's what we suspected at the time—that it was a DV case. However, with no additional information as to her origins, we got nowhere. I can see how, with a new lead like this and with a small population to draw from, a near DNA match from either our two victims or yours could lead back to our Jane Doe's killer. Based on that, we'd be willing to reopen the case."

Stunned, Ali realized that she had won the DNA argument without having said a word.

"But there's a problem with that," Sheriff Alvarado continued. "After I got off the phone with the bishop, I went downstairs to bring the evidence box up from the basement. To my chagrin, it's nowhere to be found. It's probably just misfiled. I've got my evidence clerk on a search mission, but so far there's no sign of it."

"Was any DNA evidence from your crime scene ever processed? Even if the box itself is missing, the state crime lab might still have the results taken from the evidence itself."

Sheriff Alvarado sent a bark of humorless laughter into the phone. "My predecessor wasn't a great believer in technology. That's one of the reasons I'm sheriff now and he isn't. He kept his eye on the bottom line. Since DNA profiling was expensive back then, he thought of it as an unnecessary frivolity. I'm sorry to say that the answer to your question is no—our Jane Doe's evidence was collected but never processed.

"In the last two years, my administration has been trying to rework our collection of cold cases, but only as time, personnel, and money allow. Having said that, it may explain why the Jane Doe box is missing. Perhaps one of my guys started focusing on that case without letting me know. Once the box is located and on its way to the crime lab, I'll let you know."

"Great," Ali said.

"How are your two victims doing, by the way? Did you say the mother's name is Enid?"

"Yes, Enid Tower. I can't tell you much about her condition, but as far as I know, both she and her baby are still alive. The baby was premature, but so far so good."

"Excellent," Sheriff Alvarado said. "Glad to hear it. If you learn anything more, keep me posted, and I'll do the same."

"One more thing," Ali said. "What kind of a presence does your department maintain in the Colorado City area?"

"Not much. As you no doubt know, it's part of my jurisdiction but difficult to reach by car. Back in the old days, all of us had to pull a few weeks of duty over there every year, living in a beat-up mobile home that doubled as the local substation and taking care of whatever came up. Then, about ten years or so ago, the department hired a guy named Amos Sellers who actually lives there. Deputy Sellers spends part of his time working out of the substation and part of it working out of his own home. He's done a good job keeping a lid on things. Since he's part of the community, people there tend to trust him. I haven't had any complaints about him—at least none that made it as far as my desk."

"Was there any kind of missing person report called in to him at the time Enid Tower took off?"

"Not that I know of. Had there been, it would have been forwarded to my attention."

"All right, then," Ali said. "Thank you so much for your help. Let's stay in touch."

As soon as Ali hung up, she immediately called Cami back. "Tell me something, have you happened to come across the name Sellers anywhere in that bunch of names?"

Cami didn't have to think twice before she answered. "Just a few minutes ago. Sellers Road. The people listed there are Amos Sellers and a woman named Elizabeth. Same old, same old. She drives but isn't good enough to vote."

"Thanks, Cami," Ali said. "Thanks a lot."

Amos Sellers—Deputy Amos Sellers. According to Sheriff Alvarado, he was the law of the land in Colorado City, but if he was part of The Family, as Cami's research clearly indicated, how come Sheriff Alvarado hadn't pro-

vided that telling detail? And if Amos was the representa-
tive of law and order in Colorado City, that meant that
anyone being mistreated or abused inside The Family
would have nowhere to turn for help—nowhere at all.

As for Sheriff Alvarado? Ali was more than a little
pissed at him. When she had mentioned The Family,
since he hadn't mentioned that his deputy was part of
the group, was it possible that Alvarado himself had some
connections to The Family?

Ali called Cami back. "I know you're busy, but I need
one more thing. Find out what you can on Danny Alvarado, the sheriff of Mohave County."

Ali pressed on the gas, urging the Cayenne forward
and northward at a good ten miles over the posted 75
mph limit.

19

Despite her concerns about Sheriff Alvarado, the last thing Ali had expected was for him to be a willing ally in reopening the Kingman Jane Doe case. She was sure Sister Anselm would be surprised and gratified about that, too, especially considering her misgivings about collecting the current DNA samples. Once the Kingman Jane Doe evidence box was located, any DNA materials inside it could be sent out for processing with an excellent possibility of there being a match.

Instead of taking Highway 179 and going back to Sedona, Ali stayed on the freeway and drove straight to St. Jerome's in Flagstaff. When she arrived in the maternity floor waiting room, Sister Anselm was in the nursery, sitting in a rocker with a tiny wrapped bundle of baby cradled in the crook of one arm and a bottle of formula held in her other hand. Using baby formula in this instance made complete sense. The mother of a newborn, especially a premature newborn, couldn't be expected to nurse the child when she herself had undergone major lifesaving surgeries. Whatever kinds of pain medications were being administered to the mother would go straight through her system and into the baby's.

Ali was still waiting for the baby's mealtime to finish when Stu called. "Did Athena mention anything to you about her parents having financial difficulties?"

"No, why?"

"James and Sandra Peterson aren't paying their property taxes. The taxes on both their home and on the building where the dental practice is located were due six months ago, and a new bill would have been issued right after the first of the year. So far neither one is listed as paid."

"What does that mean?"

"In my experience, when folks run short of moolah and don't have enough to cover expenses, property taxes are the first thing they let slide. Tax collectors are a lot slower on pulling the collection-agency trigger than banks and credit-card companies are."

"Athena's in class right now," Ali said. "I won't be able to talk to her about any of this until after school is over for the day."

"Don't," Stu advised. "Let me get a little better handle on what's going on before you discuss it with her. In fact, don't discuss it with her at all. Once we have her thumbprint she'll have access to all her grandmother's financial dealings and so will we without anyone crossing over into forbidden territory."

Hacking into unauthorized servers was something Stu Ramey did very well, but there were always risks involved, and hacking into financial accounts when it wasn't necessary was stupid.

"Fair enough," Ali said as Sister Anselm emerged from the nursery. "Keep me posted."

Just then the elevator door whispered open and four people swarmed out of it. Gordon Tower led the way. He was followed by Edith Tower and a man in a suit who looked to Ali suspiciously like a defense attorney. Last to emerge was a paunchy and somewhat younger man, a guy in his mid- to late thirties, who was dressed in a red flannel shirt. Ali recognized him as the one who had volunteered to drive Edith Tower back home to Colorado City the previous evening.

Sister Anselm showed no dismay about coming face-to-face with the man behind the black-and-blue hand-print that now graced her cheek. "Good afternoon, Mr. Tower," she said, folding her arms across her chest and stepping directly into his path. "Nice to see you out and about."

Tower made a sour face. "I'm here to see my wife."

"I'm sorry," Sister Anselm countered. "Do you have any proof that my patient is your wife?"

"Of course, she's my wife! I already told you."

"Do you have any actual documented evidence?" Sister Anselm asked. "Something like a marriage certificate, for example, one that's actually valid in the state of Arizona?"

"I don't think my marriage certificate is any of your business," Tower sneered. "I want to see my wife."

"I'm afraid HIPAA prohibits that from happening."

"Hip what?" Tower demanded.

"It's a federal law that mandates patient privacy rules," Sister Anselm replied. "Only people specifically authorized by the patient are allowed to have access to either the patient or to the patient's records. I can assure you, there is no such list with Gordon Tower's name on it."

Nurse Mandy, emerging from the nurses' station, had

taken up a position just to the right of Sister Anselm. "The good sister's assessment is quite correct in that regard," the charge nurse said. "To my knowledge the patient in question has yet to authorize any visitors."

Because she's still unconscious, Ali thought, standing up to take a defensive position alongside the other two.

"That's a load of bull and you know it," Tower growled. "Then let me see my baby. Don't try to tell me she needs to sign some stupid visitors' form, too."

"The problem is," Nurse Mandy said, "mother and child came in as a unit. Until we're notified otherwise, the mother's wishes or lack thereof hold sway. Now, sir, it would probably be best if you left. Otherwise we'll be forced to summon security. Again," she added pointedly.

Other relatives in the waiting room, including two newly minted fathers, watched the escalating drama with growing alarm. Not only that, the three women barring Tower's way were also blocking the window to the nursery. Ali knew that Sister Anselm had left Enid's baby in a bassinet in the farthest corner of the room. Even if Tower gained access to the window, the baby would be out of sight.

Nurse Mandy's threat of calling security caused some of Gordon Tower's bluster to fade. He spun around, turning on the man in a suit. "You're a lawyer. Can't you do something about these obnoxious women? Doesn't a father have some rights here?"

"I'm afraid the law backs them up on this one," the attorney said quietly. "For right now, I don't think there's much to be done."

"There is one more thing," Sister Anselm said.

Tower turned back to her. "What's that?"

Jabbing at the keypad, she unlocked the door to the

nursery and ducked back inside. She returned a moment later holding a cotton swab, which she handed to Gordon Tower.

He stared at it blankly. "What's this for?"

"It's to swab the inside of your cheek," Sister Anselm explained. "It'll give us a DNA sample. That way, even without a birth certificate, we'll be able to determine if you're actually the baby's father or if someone else is."

Tower's eyes bulged. Ali could tell from the stunned expression on his florid face that the idea the baby might not be his had never crossed his mind. He paled slightly. Doubling his fists, he turned to glare at Edith, as though the possibility of Enid's having been unfaithful was clearly Edith's fault. The way she shrank away from him, as if expecting a blow, told Ali there had been blows before. When Gordon turned his furious glower back on Sister Anselm, Ali fully expected him to fling the swab into her face.

"You can tell from this?" he demanded, holding the swab in the air and shaking it in Sister Anselm's face. "From this little thing?"

"Yes," Sister Anselm assured him. "We can."

Without another word, he shoved the swab into his mouth, ran the end of it up and down his cheek, and then handed it back to Sister Anselm.

"There!" he said. "If I find out that little bitch cheated on me, I'll—" He stopped in mid-sentence without finishing the threat. Then he turned and led the way back to the elevator.

Once the door closed behind them, Nurse Mandy turned on Sister Anselm. "What in the world was that all about? Why do you need his DNA? Do you think the baby really isn't his?"

"I have no doubt that Mr. Tower is the baby's father," Sister Anselm said with a triumphant smile. "But now he does. It'll give him something to think about."

"Look," Nurse Mandy said angrily, "we already know how volatile the man is. You had no business provoking him. What do you think will happen to that poor girl and her baby when they finally have to go back home?"

"We'll have to see to it that they don't," Sister Anselm responded.

Unconvinced and shaking her head, Nurse Mandy stomped off to the nurses' station.

"I believe yanking his chain like that is generally referred to as getting a little of your own back," Ali observed.

During the confrontation, Sister Anselm's system had been fired with adrenaline. As that drained away, Ali was concerned at how weary she looked.

"Maybe a little," Sister Anselm agreed somewhat sheepishly. "After all, nuns are people, too. I'll need to address that in confession this week, but that wasn't the main reason I ran him up and down the flagpole."

"What was it, then?" Ali asked as Sister Anselm pulled another Ziploc bag out of her pocket, placed the swab inside, zipped it shut, and handed it to Ali, who stared at it for a time. "What am I supposed to do with this?"

"Do you think you could send this to that friend of yours, the one with the DNA lab? I'd like to have this one tested along with the others."

"Why?"

"As I said, to prove categorically he is the baby's father."

"But . . ."

"Just because Gordon Tower claims he and Enid are

married doesn't make it true—at least not as far as the state of Arizona is concerned. Married or not, however, fathers are expected to pay child support. You see, Enid has no intention of going back home ever, and I can't say that I blame her."

"You know that for sure? How?"

"She told me."

"She's talking, then?"

"Not really talking, more like semiconscious babbling. It happened overnight. I'm sure the jabber is partially due to the medications she's on, but enough of her story leaked out to start making sense. Evidently someone was chasing her, someone who was sent to find her and take her back home. That's why she darted into traffic—to get away from him."

"A him?"

"Yes."

"Did she mention a name?"

"No, but that's what she said, over and over. Don't let him get me. Don't let him send me home. They'll take my baby away. They'll send me to the pigs."

"To the pigs?"

"Yes."

"What does that mean?"

"I'm not sure, but based on the idea that people are threatening her life and well-being, I've taken some precautionary measures. She's terrified that the guy who was after her still is. It wouldn't surprise me that she's not the only one who's worried. Taking someone away against his or her will constitutes kidnapping. The guy who was after her will be concerned that once she comes around, she'll be able to point fingers and name names."

Ali nodded. "What kind of precautions?" she asked.

"As of right now, the nursery is on lockdown and can only be accessed by way of the keypad. Enid is still listed as being in the room she was in yesterday. The door to that room is to remain locked, but she'll be moved to the room directly across from the nurses' station. We can maintain that subterfuge as long as the original room isn't needed for another patient."

"Is there anything I can do to help?"

"Yes," Sister Anselm said. "There is. I finished off the rest of Mr. Brooks's pasty for breakfast, but that was several hours ago. I'd appreciate it if you'd stay here in the waiting room for a time and keep watch while I go check into my hotel room, freshen up, and have a bite to eat."

"Of course," Ali said. "Glad to. Stay away as long as you like. You look like a nap wouldn't be out of order."

Sister Anselm nodded. "No can do. Baby Ann is on a two-hour feeding schedule."

"Baby Ann?" Ali asked. "I thought Gordon Tower referred to his daughter as Sarah."

"Baby Ann is what Enid calls her," Sister Anselm replied. "That's good enough for me."

20

The elevator door had barely closed behind Sister Anselm when Ali's phone rang.

"Hi, Cami," she said. "What have you got for me?"

"Angus Lowell," Cami answered. "I found information about him on the Internet under The Lowell Family rather than The Family. Somewhere along the way they dropped the Lowell part."

"Who's Angus?" Ali asked.

"He was the great-grandson of a Scottish industrialist named Angus McCutcheon who made his fortune as an arms dealer. He was one of those money-grubbing guys who had no scruples about selling his wares to both sides in any given conflict. When his underhanded dealings started coming to light, he took himself and his fortune out of the UK, settling first in Morocco and later in the Cayman Islands. That's where the Lowell Family Trust is located, by the way, the Caymans.

"About the time he ended up there," Cami continued, "Angus's great-grandson and namesake, Angus Lowell, was living in the United States. He had flunked out of Stanford and gotten hooked up with some druggie fellow dropouts. After doing his share of LSD, he ended up living in a hippie commune somewhere in the wilds of Northern California. At that point, Angus the elder staged an early version of an intervention and carted the kid off to the Caymans, where he underwent a course of treatment of some kind, had a religious conversion, and became an outspoken back-to-the-earth kind of guy. When the old man died a few years later, he left his fortune to his great-grandson, bypassing both his daughter and granddaughter in the process."

"The old man was a bit of a chauvinist, maybe?" Ali asked.

Cami laughed. "Do you think?"

"Where did you find all this stuff?"

"Newspaper archives mostly. Angus returned to the U.S. in 1966, purchased the land near Colorado City, and established a church he called The Lowell Family. Then he went to California, where he rounded up a collection of like-minded individuals, probably old pals from his commune days, and brought them to northern Arizona with him. At that point they all seem to have disappeared from public view."

"Is Angus still in charge?" Ali asked.

"Probably not. The guy who signs the checks and whose name is on the motor vehicle registrations for their fleet of cars, trucks, and SUVs is someone named Richard Lowell."

"One of Angus McCutcheon's progeny?"

"That's my guess."

"What happened to Angus the younger?"

"No idea. Since someone else has taken over the helm, I have to assume that Angus is no longer with us, but that's another interesting thing about the group.

If they keep any kind of birth and death records, they don't bother passing that information along to Mohave County."

"How many families are we talking about?"

"Twenty-nine all told—at least that's how many we've been able to find with addresses on the existing named streets. There may be others, like the Wendell Johnson family, where with two generations, one lives in town and the other doesn't."

"Where are we now?" Ali asked.

"Once I finished creating my driver's license/voter registration list, I handed it over to Stuart," Cami said. "So far he's only checked on a couple of the names, but the results are interesting. Apparently, each family receives a small allowance from the church that goes to the head of the household. Members dutifully file an income-tax report on that, but none of them makes enough money to trigger any tax liabilities or to attract the attention of the IRS."

"Income-tax fraud?" Ali asked.

"Maybe, but it's doubtful," Cami said. "Without birth certificates or Social Security numbers, they wouldn't be able to claim any dependents. As for the houses? They evidently belong to the group rather than to the people who live in them. The property taxes are paid for by the church. Ditto for the fleet of vehicles. They belong to the church, too."

"So we're not dealing with some kind of Amish mentality where electricity and combustion engines are off-limits?"

"Definitely not."

"What kind of stipends are we talking about?"

"Stu's only checked on a few of the names so far. Two

of those were for ten thousand and the other one for twenty."

Ali did some math in her head. "With thirty families on the rolls that still amounts to a considerable outlay. Where does the money come from?"

"That's not clear. They evidently raise cattle and hogs. They consume some and sell the rest. They also do a certain amount of subsistence farming."

"You can't raise enough livestock on three thousand acres to bring in that much money a year," Ali said.

A call came in for Cami. She signed off. Ali sat with the still warm phone in her hand, thinking about the money question. Both times she had seen Gordon Tower, he had been dressed in relatively ordinary store-bought clothing—jeans, boots, a western-style shirt, a Stetson. None of it had struck her as particularly expensive. Still, what he wore was a big step up from the threadbare homemade goods Edith was wearing and from the flimsy clothing and worn-out shoes Ali had seen in the box containing Enid's personal effects. So maybe a small family stipend stretched a lot further if you were buying clothing for only one person while everyone else made do with ragged homemade castoffs.

Closing her eyes, Ali tried to put together the chronology. If Angus Lowell had bought the property in the mid-1960s, that was nearly fifty years ago, but only a dozen or so years after the Short Creek debacle. At the time, the lesson of what had happened to Governor Pyle would have been relatively fresh in everyone's mind. Wanting to avoid suffering a similar fate, the politicians who had come after Pyle had maintained an unofficial but strictly observed hands-off policy—creating a live-and-let-live atmosphere in that corner of the state. Had their wink-

and-nod stance allowed members of The Family to do whatever the hell they liked, up to and including, perhaps, getting away with murder?

Ali thought about that fifty-year interval. If young women in The Family started bearing children at age fifteen or so, that time period allowed for at least three generations of young women to have come of age—women who had been and still were being denied their basic constitutional, civil, and human rights. They weren't allowed to vote, or drive, or wear store-bought clothes. The problem was they weren't in some village in the distant mountains of Afghanistan. They were right here, living on three thousand acres, smack in the middle of the good old U.S. of A.

So where did The Family's money come from? That was the crux of the matter. Three thousand acres wasn't a large enough spread to feed and support a group of twenty-five to thirty families. Not nearly. And no matter how much money old man Angus McCutcheon had set aside, the trust couldn't last forever without being replenished. The money for all those stipends was coming from somewhere, but where?

That's when it hit her, taking Ali's thoughts straight back to her training days at the Arizona Police Academy. The basic philosophy of community policing dictated that by paying attention to the small things—to graffiti on walls, property thefts, turned-over trash cans, littering, juvenile drinking—police could prevent those kinds of antisocial behaviors from morphing into something more serious—into the big-time crimes of armed robberies, assaults, and homicides.

Was that what was going on here? The authorities had neglected to enforce the little things—like birth and death certificates, for example. By doing so, had those same authorities allowed some other kind of major criminal enterprise to grow and flourish unnoticed in their midst? Two young women had run away from The Family twelve years apart—one now dead and one barely alive. Ali understood that Sister Anselm was right to be concerned for Enid's safety. What if Enid had a chance to tell what she knew? Maybe the end result would be enough to expose to all the world whatever no-good The Family was up to.

Taking a deep breath, Ali picked up her phone and dialed Cami back. "When you were matching all those road names to people, were there any places where you came up empty—where there was no match between the name of the road and the name of the family?"

"How did you know that?" Cami said. "I did, but only once. There's one road called Fields that shows no sign of any residence. There are some buildings that look like big sheds of some kind, but they're clearly not houses. The other residences are all built the same way, with a kind of cookie-cutter design plan and layout. It's like a company tract housing where all the houses are just alike, including all the various outbuildings and what appear to be large garden plots."

"Is the satellite map you're using right now the most detailed one available?" Ali asked.

"Probably not," Cami admitted. "It's the first one I found."

"If you can find one that's better, please send me the link."

"Will do, Ms. Reynolds," Cami said cheerfully. "I'm on it. Oh, and I just sent you what was available on Sheriff Alvarado. It's not much, but it's what I could find on short notice."

21

As soon as Ali's e-mail alert sounded, she brought out her iPad. The first item from Cami was a brief bio of Sheriff Alvarado, probably lifted from an election pamphlet. It said that he'd been born in California. As a toddler, he had moved back to Kingman with his stepfather and had lived there ever since. He was married and had two teenaged children, a boy and a girl, both attending Kingman area public schools. His list of memberships included a local golf club, Rotary, the National Sheriffs' Association, and the Cessna 150-152 Fly In Foundation.

After scanning that message, Ali turned to the second, one with a link to the satellite photo. Once it opened, Ali took some time to orient her view of the image. Cami had helpfully placed a flag on a spot southeast of Colorado City where Sanctuary Road intersected with the highway.

Zooming in on that part of the map, Ali saw the network of roads leading off that one. The legend next to the map indicated that these were mostly primitive roads—graded dirt tracks that would probably be washboarded and potholed this time of year. Angus Road, leading off Sanctuary, appeared to be the only one of the bunch that might be paved. Ali followed the stretch of road to the compound Cami had told her was occupied by Richard Lowell. Comparing it to the home next door made it clear that, by virtue of square footage alone, Richard Lowell was most likely the group's current leader. The satellite view didn't allow for sorting out the exact purpose of nearby buildings, but Ali found it easy to go along with Cami's assessment that the several larger ones were probably gathering places of one kind or another.

Based on the network of surrounding roads, Ali realized that the larger compound, the one on Angus Road, was central to all the others. That made it the logical spot to locate a church or school. But did the children from The Family actually go to school?

It took time to locate the track called Fields Road. It was near the top end of the property line. Beyond that was a wide swath of public land with the initials BLM (Bureau of Land Management) emblazoned on it.

This was the dead of winter. If there were actual fields at the end of Fields Road, they weren't readily visible. What was visible were eight long rectangular buildings, lined up one after another. Hauling out her reading glasses, Ali determined that they were most likely greenhouses—the kinds of plastic-covered structures someone might use for raising starter tomatoes or other vegetables that could be moved outside once the weather warmed up.

The greenhouses were closest to the property line. There were several other unidentifiable smaller structures as well as a much larger one that appeared to have a small loading dock on one side. That would indicate a warehouse of some kind. So maybe this was how The Family stretched their food budget—by growing vegetables even during the winter months. Next to that was a large rect-angular building with a long straight stretch of pavement leading away from it. It wasn't hard to determine that had to be a landing strip of some kind and a long one at that. So perhaps the largest of the unidentified buildings was an airplane hangar.

"You certainly look engrossed," Sister Anselm observed, arriving silently at Ali's side. "Anything interesting?"

The nun looked somewhat refreshed after her short break, but she hadn't stayed away long enough to take a nap.

"This is where Enid is from," Ali said, shrinking the image a little, passing the iPad to the nun, and then pointing to the property owned by The Family. "Gordon Tower's place is the one there in the lower left-hand corner of that network of roads. His is the only house on Tower Road."

Sister Anselm studied the map and then nodded. "Okay," she said. "What about it?"

"Cami estimates that there are between twenty-five and thirty houses just like Gordon's on a three-thousand-acre property belonging to a group that calls itself 'The Family.' The road name in question generally coincides with the name of at least one of the families living on it."

"Twenty-five to thirty or so families as well?"

"Yes," Ali answered, "but here's something interesting. Cami has learned that each of the households has two licensed drivers. In Gordon Tower's case, he's one driver and Edith is the other. But each household has only one registered voter."

"I assume that, in the Towers' case, the registered voter would be Gordon?" Sister Anselm asked.

Ali nodded. "That's right."

"What is this," Sister Anselm demanded, "a stateside version of the Taliban?"

It was gratifying to Ali that Sister Anselm had come to the same conclusion she had. "That's how it looks to me," Ali replied. "According to Cami, each of these families receives some kind of stipend from the church. So my question is, where does the money come from? Is it possible there's some kind of criminal activity going on that keeps them afloat financially?"

Sister Anselm thought for a moment before nodding. "That could be it, and they're desperately afraid Enid might spill the beans. Think about it; by simply walking away, she caused enough concern that they sent out at least one searcher and maybe more to bring her back. And that was before she had us for allies."

"In other words," Ali said, "now that Enid has us, she may be even more at risk than when she was out on that road alone in the middle of the night."

"And that makes her our responsibility," Sister Anselm declared. "The only way they're going to get her back is over my dead body. Now, according to my monitor, Baby Ann is crying. I need to go tend to her."

Once Sister Anselm was gone, Ali resumed studying her iPad. If The Family was engaged in something illegal and doing their best to keep it away from outside scrutiny, it stood to reason that they'd be conducting that business, whatever it was, at a spot as far away from prying eyes as possible. That meant the structures closest to the BLM wasteland might be a good place to start looking, especially since that's where the airstrip was located. Time passed while Ali stared at the screen, searching for answers to the puzzle, but the static satellite image told her nothing.

"Ms. Reynolds?"

Ali looked up and was surprised to find David Upton standing there.

"Any word on how she's doing?" he asked.

Unwilling to give out unauthorized information, Ali shook her head. "Not so far," she said.

She glanced into the nursery where Sister Anselm was just returning Baby Ann to her bassinet.

"Sister Anselm will be out in a minute. Why don't we ask her?"

The nun emerged from the nursery, caught sight of David, and greeted him with a handshake and a warm smile. "You'll be relieved to know that the little one is doing very well, Mr. Upton. And Enid—that's her name by the way, Enid Tower—is improving. She hasn't fully come around yet, and she's sleeping right now, but she's had a few periods of wakefulness. Would you care to sit with her for a while? You're welcome to do so if you'd like."

Ali was stunned. Whatever happened to HIPAA? she wondered. David Upton, too, seemed shocked.

"Really?" he asked.

"Of course," Sister Anselm said. "I'll let you into her room. Be sure to use the hand sanitizer before you step inside."

"What was that all about?" Ali demanded when Sister Anselm returned to the waiting room. "I thought visitors were supposed to be approved family members only. He's a complete stranger."

"I put him on the approved list," Sister Anselm said. "The Good Samaritan was the real deal, and David Upton is, too. Besides, just because something's the law of the land doesn't mean it's necessarily a good idea. Mr. Upton's is the last face Enid saw before her world went

black. He's also, for whatever reason, the only person
to whom she confided her wish to never go home. I'm
hoping the jolt of seeing him might help jump-start her
return to consciousness. We need to hear her story, but
I suspect there's someone else who could supply that
information, too."

"Who?"

"The person who was sent to bring her back."

"Yes, of course," Ali said. "But how do you propose to
find him, and once you do, how do you expect to get him
to talk?"

Sister Anselm glanced around the waiting room before she answered. The place was surprisingly empty. "He
was sent to retrieve her, possibly to keep her from spilling
the beans about a group totally dedicated to keeping their
secrets secret. Having failed to deliver, it's safe to assume
that he's fallen out of favor with whoever set him that
task. To get back in The Family's good graces, there's a
good chance he'll take a second crack at her."

"Here?" Ali asked. "In the hospital?"

"Where else?" Sister Anselm asked. "They need to act
promptly, before she regains consciousness and before
she can tell anyone what she knows."

"Which might turn this maternity ward into a war
zone."

"Believe me," Sister Anselm replied, "if either Baby
Ann or Enid were ready to be transferred to some other
facility, I would have done so already. I'm afraid we don't
have any choice but to wait for someone to show up.
When he does, I trust that, between the two of us, we'll
give him more than he bargained for."

"Then why not draw them out on our terms?" Ali
asked.

"How?"

For an answer, Ali picked up her phone and called Cami. "Is there a Colorado City listing for the Mohave County Sheriff's Office?"

"Just a sec," Cami said. "Let me look." Ali heard Cami's computer keys clicking in the background. "Okay, I've got it."

"Message me the number," Ali said.

"Will do."

"You're calling a cop?" Sister Anselm asked. "Why?"

"I'm going to bring a little disinformation into play. This particular cop happens to be a member in good standing of The Family," Ali explained. "That means he'll want to keep Enid quiet, too."

When the message came through, Ali located the number and pressed it. After four rings, there was a click as though the call was being forwarded, then someone picked up. "Deputy Sellers."

"My name's Lisa Goodson," Ali said, plucking a name out of thin air and shifting the phone to speaker. "I'm a reporter for the *Flagstaff Record*. I've just come from a briefing with the Coconino County Sheriff's Department. They're investigating a motor vehicle accident that involves someone from up around your way. A young woman was injured. Since she's a juvenile, they're not releasing her name. They did say that an unidentified light-colored pickup was seen leaving the scene. I'm wondering if they've requested any assistance from your department in this matter?"

"Not that I know of," Deputy Sellers said. "Someone might have called the office in Kingman, but this is the first I've heard about it."

Ali's truth meter registered a little ping. Of course

Amos Sellers would have known about it. One of The Family's inmates had gone AWOL. The resident cop would have been the first person Gordon Tower would have called, maybe not on an official basis, but certainly on an unofficial one. Deputy Sellers would have known everything about it.

"I tried going by the hospital," Ali continued breathlessly, not giving him a chance to respond. "I was able to learn that the accident victim is being cared for on the maternity ward, so there must be a baby involved in all this. The problem is there's this impossibly bossy nun running the show, Sister Anselm. She sent me packing. Fortunately for me, I have a friend who works at the hospital. Thanks to her, I managed pick up a tidbit or two. They're expecting to transfer both mother and baby to a new hospital early tomorrow morning, to 'an undisclosed location,' like this was some kind of Secret Service mission or something. But no one's told you anything about it?"

"Not one thing," Deputy Sellers replied.

"Oh, well then," Ali said. "Sorry to be a bother. Thanks for your time."

When she ended the call, Sister Anselm was grinning at her. "Since you just lit the fuse on what may turn into a keg of dynamite, perhaps I'd better speak to the hospital administrator and see if there's a way to transfer the maternity patients to some other floor."

"You'll be able to do that?" Ali asked.

"I believe so," Sister Anselm said. "This is a Catholic hospital after all. When I drop Bishop Gillespie's name, people tend to listen."

22

With all the unexpected messing about with Joe Friday on Wednesday, Betsy had completely forgotten that she had agreed to spend most of Thursday working with the planning committee on the Women's Retreat due to happen in early April. Had Grace Hunter, her ride for the day, not called to remind her, she would have been caught completely flat-footed. As it was, Betsy barely had time to get herself pulled together before Grace showed up in the driveway.

"I heard you had some trouble the other night and that a deputy dropped by," Grace commented, once Betsy was belted in. "Hope it wasn't anything too serious."

That was the problem with living in a small town. Everyone knew everyone else's business. Since the cops hadn't believed Betsy's version of events, and since Jimmy and Sandra didn't believe her, either, Betsy decided that the less said about the gas burner issue, the better.

"Just a little misunderstanding," she said. "It's straightened out now."

"And the workman? I heard someone was here most

of the day yesterday. I worried that you might be having plumbing issues. There's a lot of that going around."

"Electrical," Betsy muttered, resenting this whole third-degree interrogation. "And I had the guy install a new computer."

"Why, for heaven's sake?" Grace said. "You haven't been online since Athena left. You'll have to give me your new e-mail address."

"It's the old one," Betsy said. "It turns out that one still works."

The planning meeting took all morning. Betsy hated being on committees. All the wrangling back and forth drove her nuts, but if someone didn't volunteer to handle things here and there, nothing got done. The Women's Retreat had been going on for more than forty years, and Betsy had more experience than anyone else about putting the annual program together. She worried about who would take charge of it once she was gone, but right now, she was still the one running the show.

When the meeting was over, she and Grace stopped by the diner for lunch, so it was mid-afternoon before she got home. Exhausted by three days of seemingly nonstop activity, Betsy let Princess out and then decided a nap was in order. She and Princess went to the bedroom, curled up under her down-filled duvet, and slept for the next three hours. It wasn't until close to six when she got up, fed the dog, and fixed a sandwich to have for supper. She couldn't shake the idea that everything she did was visible to someone sitting at a computer monitor somewhere far away. Joe Friday had assured her that her own image wouldn't be tracked or recorded or set off any alarms, but she wasn't sure she believed all that.

She had assured Joe that she'd get right after the password thing, but so far she hadn't. The day had been too busy and time had gotten away from her. Tomorrow, she'd call Marcia to come pick her up early so she could go to the bank before her hair appointment and before the fish fry. That way it would all be handled before Monday when she had her so-called evaluation.

Before she went to bed for the night, Betsy sat down at the table and forced herself to face her computer. It looked like it was on, but it wasn't until she put her thumbprint on the mouse that she was able to access the hidden computer screen where her files and e-mail account were kept. Once there, she was surprised to find two new e-mails—one from Grace and the other from Athena.

Grace's said only,

Welcome back to the world of e-mail. I hope you'll sign up for Facebook, too.

Athena's said,

Stu has my thumbprint and image. We'll talk tomorrow.

It was only nine when Betsy shut down the hidden screen, leaving just the original begonia-covered screen saver—the fake one—still visible. *Yes,* she told herself as she crawled back into bed. *Tomorrow will be plenty of time to talk.*

23

Bringing the hospital administrator around to Sister Anselm's way of thinking wasn't exactly a slam dunk. While Sister Anselm worked on that, Ali ordered a pizza and then went down to the lobby to wait for it to be delivered.

She had called Leland earlier to say she wouldn't be home for dinner, but now she called again, told him that she was downstairs waiting for a pizza, and gave him a heads-up about her probably not being home for the remainder of the night.

"I wanted to make sure someone would look after Bella."

"Of course," he said. "No problem there at all, but it sounds as though there's something seriously amiss. Can I be of assistance?"

Ali laughed. She and Leland had been through too much together for her to try lying to him about it. "Yes," she said. "There *is* something amiss."

She explained the situation in an abbreviated *Reader's Digest* fashion.

"I see," Leland said when she finished. "It sounds to

me as though you and Sister Anselm have served notice to some potentially bad people that the young woman they're after—someone with possibly incriminating evidence—will be moved elsewhere, presumably out of the bad guys' reach, tomorrow morning. Is that correct?"

"Pretty much."

"Which means you've given them a deadline. If you'll pardon my saying so, this seems especially foolhardy, even for the two of you. What about the other patients and employees at the hospital? What are the chances your actions might endanger them? And if there's some kind of criminal activity occurring in that place where the young woman is from, then you need to let the proper authorities know about it and let them handle it."

She hadn't mentioned to Leland that Deputy Sellers, the man she had just spoken to and who had blatantly lied to her, was someone who should have been considered a "proper authority." Not in this case. And there was no way to begin explaining to Leland what happened at Short Creek, now known as Colorado City, all those years earlier.

"We'll be careful, especially when it comes to other patients," she said. "Sister Anselm is in the process of emptying the floor, even as we speak. Chances are no one will show up. If they do, they won't be expecting to find two women who can rightly be considered armed and dangerous."

"No," Leland agreed. "I suppose not."

After ending the call, Ali sat for a time in silent contemplation. What if she was right? What if there was some kind of criminal activity going on within The Family? If she and Sister Anselm did somehow bring it to light, would anyone be willing to do something about it? And what about all those women and children? She remembered how Edith Tower had ducked out of the way of Gordon Tower's fist. Edith might have some control over what went on inside the home, but Gordon would always be the final arbiter of what happened and what didn't.

In the world of The Family, women apparently didn't count for much. But if the guys in charge went to jail for something illegal, what happened to the families once they were gone? If the women had literally been kept down on the farm in something close to involuntary servitude, what would become of them and their children if they were turned loose in the world? As single mothers, would they have any marketable skills? Would they even be able to read and write?

Cami had said The Family was made up of twenty-five to thirty separate households. If every husband had more than one wife and only the first one of those was a licensed driver, that meant there might be around a hundred women with young kids who wouldn't have cars or be able to drive. They'd be turned out of the only homes they had ever known and driven out into a world about which they knew next to nothing. If most of the men or even some of them were held accountable for some wrongdoing and went to prison, the cult might be dismantled. What happened to the women and children then? For the first time, Ali understood the magnitude of the problem and the real reason officialdom had turned a blind eye. Taking The Family down would mean turning the women and children who lived there into refugees— or perhaps into something worse.

Short Creek had been bad enough—an instance of law enforcement overreach where everyone, children included, had been taken into custody and families torn apart forever. Ali remembered seeing more recent coverage of unaccompanied migrant children being warehoused in inadequate facilities where they, too, were treated like little more than prisoners.

Even worse, Ali had distant but still vivid memories of what might prove to be a hauntingly similar situation— Waco. She had been sitting on the news-anchor desk in L.A. when the siege at Waco came to its horrific end. She had watched the awful videos as flames had engulfed the place. The fire, allegedly started by some nut job who refused to surrender, had burned the compound to the ground, killing seventy-six people in the process.

Up to now, the fact that The Family held women and children in what amounted to bondage hadn't seemed to register with law enforcement agencies or merited any official response, but what if all that changed? What if Ali's involvement unearthed evidence of criminal wrongdoing? What if the menfolk who appeared to be running the show were held to account and put in jail? In that case, Ali might be responsible for divesting those same women of everything familiar and driving them homeless into the world. What would become of them then? Who would help them?

Suddenly Ali Reynolds found herself in the same spot Governor Pyle had been in all those years earlier, dealing with a situation no one else had been willing to tackle ever since. Did she keep poking her nose into the problem or did she let it go? Do something about it or turn away? And was she prepared to deal with the consequences of both taking action and not taking action?

She picked up her phone and scrolled through her contacts list until she found the numbers belonging to

Andrea Rogers, the executive director of Irene's Place. It was late enough in the day that Ali didn't bother with the work number. She called Andrea's cell instead.

"Sorry to bother you at home," Ali said.

"What makes you think I'm at home? You should know that running a shelter has never been a nine-to-five job. What's up?"

"Have you ever heard of The Family from up near Colorado City?"

There was a long pause. "It sounds vaguely familiar," Andrea said at last. "Wait, yes. Now I remember. Irene mentioned it, but obviously that was years ago."

"Were there clients who came from there?"

"There may have been. At least that's the context in which it was mentioned. I don't remember any names or details, though. It's too long ago."

"Do you have records going back that far?"

"I'm not sure. Now everything is computerized," Andrea said. "We haven't had the time or money to go back and digitize those earlier records—the ones from when Irene was in charge. They're downstairs in the archives."

"Can you see if you can find anything?" Ali asked.

"I'll try," Andrea said, "but those old files are a mess, so don't expect miracles. Anything else?"

"Well, yes," Ali said. "There is one other question. What would happen if The Family got broken up and the women and children who lived there were left homeless. Would you be able to help them?"

"How many people are we talking about?"

"That's not clear. We estimate there are twenty-five to thirty families involved, but each of those families most likely includes more than one wife and probably several minor children as well."

"So seventy-five to a hundred women and maybe twice again that for the children?"

"That would be my guess."

Andrea took a deep breath. "Well, obviously we couldn't handle them all here, but we do have contingency plans with other shelters and agencies. What do you know of these folks' situations?"

"The girls aren't allowed to leave home or vote or learn to drive. Fifteen- and sixteen-year-olds are forced into arranged marriages and turn up pregnant."

"That sounds like a form of domestic abuse to me," Andrea said. "Of course we'd find a way to help them. Is this going to happen anytime soon?"

"I'm not sure it's going to happen at all," Ali answered. "But just in case, if I were you, I'd make a few calls and have your ducks in a row."

"I will," Andrea said. "And as soon as I hang up with you, I'm heading for the basement."

Reassured by Andrea's quiet strength, Ali turned to the next piece of the puzzle—how to find out what was really keeping The Family afloat. The first and most obvious source of easy cash would be some kind of involvement in the drug trade. A steady cash crop of marijuana could be worth millions, especially if there was no need to smuggle it across the border. Using those isolated buildings as grow houses suddenly made all kinds of sense. So did the airstrip. The problem was, all this was nothing more than conjecture on Ali's part.

Sheriff Danny Alvarado might be her best buddy as far as reopening that long-cold Kingman Jane Doe case was concerned, but without that missing evidence box, it would take compelling evidence to provide enough probable cause for Alvarado to stick his small department's finger into The Family's mess. Neither would the feds, up to and including the DEA, want to get involved without real evidence of wrongdoing. But if law enforcement's hands were tied, what about private citizens? If Ali drove up there to scope out the place, the worst she could be charged with would be trespassing. Entering from the BLM side would reduce the risk of being seen . . .

She stopped short because, in that very moment, she came up with an answer. Picking up the phone, she dialed Stu.

"What do you know about drones?" she asked.

Ali's own experience with drones had come about several years earlier when she had stumbled across someone who, under contract to dismantle military drones, had instead been rehabbing and repurposing them as vehicles to smuggle drugs into the United States. Compared to current technology, those models would all be completely out of date by now.

"Not a whole lot," Stu answered. "Don't fly 'em myself, but I know people who do. Why?"

"Did you happen to take a look at the satellite images Cami found of The Family's compound outside Colorado City?"

"Not yet. I've been pretty busy with Bemidji all day," he said. "I'm researching Betsy's son's and daughter's financials. As for Betsy? Her system is completely operational now. In fact Athena came by earlier to give me her thumbprint and 3-D image, so that's all out of the way, too. What do you need?"

"I'd like you to examine the images Cami sent me. Pay close attention to the structures that look like greenhouses at the northernmost section of the property. I'd like to have a better idea of what those are. The group is supposed to be fairly self-sufficient, so the greenhouses may be nothing more than a way of growing vegetables during the winter, unless, of course, they aren't."

"Is that why you're asking about drones?" Stu wondered. "You're looking for a drone operator who can fly in and out and take a look-see without anyone being the wiser?"

"That's it."

"Let me work on it and get back to you," Stu said. "Where are you?"

"In Flagstaff, with Sister Anselm," she answered. Giving Stu more detailed information than that risked having him pass it along to B. She fully intended to tell her husband what was going on, of course, but in her own good time. B. wouldn't be any happier on the course of action she and Sister Anselm had decided on than Leland Brooks was.

The entrance doors swished open and the aroma of pizza wafted into the lobby. Two people rose and stepped forward to intercept the delivery boy. That meant Ali wasn't the only hospital visitor ordering pizza for dinner that night.

"Gotta go, Stu," she said. "Our pizza just arrived."

"Mine, too," he told her. "Bon appétit."

"So you picked up a bit of French lingo on your trip to Paris?" she asked.

"A little," he admitted. "But good pizza isn't easy to find there."

24

Ali was still giggling about that as she went up to the reception desk to collect the pizza. As the delivery guy accepted the tip, he apologized. "Sorry for the delay. We kept yours hot, but when we ended up with two other deliveries coming here to the hospital, my manager decided to make it just one trip."

Ali was turning away with the pizza in hand when the entrance door opened again and two men walked into the lobby—a uniformed cop and a man in civilian clothing. The man in civvies—a suit and tie—was a complete stranger, but after a moment Ali recognized the second one. He hadn't been in uniform at the time, but he had been part of Gordon Tower's entourage during both hospital confrontations. He had said nothing but had stood in the background watching the proceedings. He had also offered to drive Edith Tower home. Ali knew his name even before he walked up to the receptionist and pulled out his badge.

"I'm Deputy Sellers," he announced, "and this is Richard Lowell. We're here to see a patient named Enid Tower. What room is she in?"

Goose bumps prickled the back of Ali's neck. The tale Ali had spun about Enid being moved to another facility had worked. Deputy Sellers's presence made it clear that someone inside The Family didn't want Enid moved anywhere out of reach. Knowing which house was his, Ali had an idea about who Richard Lowell was and why he was here. Enid represented a dangerous leak. He was there to plug it.

Ali glanced at her watch. Almost an hour had passed since she had come down to the lobby. Had that been enough time for Sister Anselm to clear the maternity floor?

"Ms. Tower isn't being allowed visitors at the moment," the receptionist replied primly after typing in the name and checking her screen.

"I'm not a visitor," Sellers replied. "I'm a police officer investigating a traffic incident. This man is Enid's father. Now, are you going to give me the room number or not?"

Richard Lowell was Enid's father? That was news.

Hoping not to attract any attention, Ali took her pizza in hand and bailed. She slipped across the lobby and into the elevator, then held her breath in hopes that the two men wouldn't follow her fast enough to join her in the elevator car.

When the door opened onto the maternity floor, Ali darted off. Sister Anselm was seated on a love seat. The coffee table in front of her held two cups of vending machine coffee, paper plates, plastic silverware, and a supply of paper napkins.

"Are we clear?" Ali demanded.

Sister Anselm looked startled. "Yes," she said. "Everyone's gone. Why? What's wrong?"

"Turns out the wait isn't nearly what we expected. Deputy Sellers is downstairs with someone who claims to be Enid's father. He's asking to see her. The cop is someone we've seen before, by the way. He was here earlier with Gordon Tower—both times. He just wasn't in uniform at the time. The other guy, the one claiming to be Enid's father, is Richard Lowell. From what Cami told me, I'm guessing he's The Family's head honcho."

"How interesting," Sister Anselm said. "Okay, have a seat. You dish up the pizza while I send a message." Picking up her iPad, Sister Anselm dictated into the machine. "Lockdown on the surgical floor, please. Now. And extra security to the lobby."

"Not here?"

"No," Sister Anselm said. "Let's see what they have to say for themselves. But just for argument's sake, turn on your iPhone's recorder."

By the time the elevator door opened again, both women were comfortably seated with plates loaded with pizza in front of them. Ali hoped that they looked as though they didn't have a care in the world.

The two men stepped off the elevator together. Deputy Sellers stopped short when he saw them. "That's her," he said, pointing in Sister Anselm's direction.

"Good evening, gentlemen," Sister Anselm said, putting down her plate. "May I help you?"

Richard Lowell stepped forward. "I'm here to see my daughter," he said. "Her name is Enid."

As if anticipating that someone might ask for documentation, he handed her a white leather-covered Bible. "This is our family Bible. You'll find Enid listed on page four, the third line down."

Sister Anselm paged open the book, ran her index finger down the page, and then handed it back. "I don't see any mention of her mother's name."

"Her mother is deceased," Richard Lowell said firmly.

"What was her name?" Sister Anselm asked. "Someone seems to have used Wite-Out to remove it. Is that customary where you come from?"

"It doesn't matter what's customary and what's not," Lowell growled. "The only thing that matters is that I'm Enid's father, and I demand to see her. I've been told that you intend to move her somewhere else in the morning. She's still a juvenile. As her father, I absolutely forbid it."

"I have no idea where you came up with the notion that Enid is about to be transported to some other facility. She's in no condition to be moved, and neither is her baby."

Lowell glowered at Amos, holding him responsible for passing along the erroneous information Ali had fed him.

"As for the rest? Your daughter happens to be a juvenile who is married and also who just gave birth to a baby," Sister Anselm observed. "According to this, she won't be seventeen for several months. So presumably you would have given your consent and signed off on it in order for her to obtain an underage marriage license."

"None of that is any of your business," Lowell insisted, "but of course I gave my permission."

"Good," Sister Anselm said, "because, unless Gordon can produce a valid marriage certificate, he may well be brought up on charges of statutory rape."

Richard Lowell visibly blanched at that. Like Gordon Tower, he was unaccustomed to being challenged in public, and most especially by a woman.

"Be that as it may," he said, "I want to see my daughter. Now. And, as soon as she's well enough, I fully intend to take her home."

"No," Sister Anselm said.

"What do you mean no?" he asked.

"I mean no, to both. You can't see her, and you can't take her home."

"You can't do that."

"I'm afraid I can. I'm Enid's patient advocate. She has given plain instructions that she has no intention of going back home or of letting her baby go back there, either."

"You've spoken to her, then?" Lowell demanded.

Sister Anselm gave him a grim smile. "What do you think, Mr. Lowell?"

Lowell turned to Sellers. "She's here someplace," he muttered. "Find her. If she's well enough to talk, she's well enough to travel. We'll take her home by force if necessary."

Tensing, Ali prepared to spring into action, but before Deputy Sellers could do as he'd been told, the elevator door slid open and Leland Brooks came into view. Ali was astonished to see him. When she had spoken to him on the phone from the lobby earlier, she was sure he had been at home in Sedona. She hated to think how fast he must have driven to make it all the way to Flagstaff in that amount of time.

Dapperly dressed and apparently unconcerned about his breakneck driving, he emerged from the elevator leaning heavily on the gnarled hickory cane he had purchased a few weeks earlier when he had slipped and twisted his ankle during a visit to the Petrified Forest. Limping into the maternity-floor lobby, he looked for all the world like a helpless doddering old man, but Ali knew appearances could be deceiving. Armed with that cane, he was every bit as dangerous as Sister Anselm was with her Taser and Ali with her Glock. Ali estimated that, in the scheme of things, Leland's presence more than balanced out Deputy

Sellers's sidearm and whatever else he or Richard Lowell might be carrying.

Leland glanced from face to face as if assessing the situation, then he grinned at Sister Anselm. "Oh good," he said. "I see I'm not too late for pizza, and I'm not the last to arrive, either. How soon do you expect the others?"

Sister Anselm immediately followed Leland's lead. "They should be here any moment," she said, peering at her watch. "I expected them half an hour ago."

Deputy Sellers sent a questioning glance in Richard Lowell's direction. He was rewarded with the tiniest of head shakes. Whatever the pair had intended to do wasn't going to work with a crowd of witnesses present.

"Let's go," Lowell said.

He turned and headed for the elevator with Deputy Sellers trotting at his heels. As the elevator door closed, Sister Anselm picked up her iPad and dictated another message. "Two coming down," she said. "Make sure security escorts them from the premises, and they are not to be allowed back inside."

"Well," Leland said, beaming at Sister Anselm after she sent the message and set her iPad aside. "It appears to me that reinforcements arrived just in the nick of time."

"I'm quite sure we could have handled them on our own," she said. "Bullies are the same the world over— they always back down, but thank you all the same, Mr. Brooks. Now let me go find another plate, and you can join us for pizza."

25

From the way Richard Lowell and Deputy Sellers had slunk off with their tails between their legs, it seemed unlikely that they'd show up for a return engagement. As a consequence, what followed seemed like a celebratory party.

"So this floor is entirely deserted at the moment?" Leland asked, enjoying his pizza and sipping at his own cup of vending-machine cappuccino.

Sister Anselm nodded.

"How did you make that happen?"

"After two rounds with Gordon Tower, the hospital administrator already regarded Enid's presence here a problem. I may have slightly overstated the danger I thought her family members might pose to other patients and staff members. His initial solution was to transfer her to another facility tonight, but I nixed that idea based on her current condition. After that, I had him."

"You did indeed," Leland agreed.

A moment later, however, Sister Anselm's face grew somber. "That Bible was evil, you know," she said.

"Evil?" Ali asked. "What do you mean?"

Sister Anselm shrugged. "Maybe it was just the man who handed it to me, but the idea of whiting out the name of someone who died—the name of the mother of your child? That's odd. And that's not all. As I was opening to the proper page, I scanned through the first couple of pages as well. A number of names were crossed out with the letters N.C. written next to each name. I can't imagine what that means, but I'll bet it's not good."

She stood up then, collected a new plate, and scraped the two remaining pieces of pizza onto it. "As late as it is, I doubt there'll be any more trouble tonight, so I'll go downstairs and relieve Mr. Upton. I'm sure he's been here far longer than he intended."

"Who's Mr. Upton?" Leland asked once she was gone.

"He's the guy who was driving the car that hit Enid."

"So the driver who injured the girl is allowed into her hospital room while her own father isn't?" Leland asked with a frown. "Has Sister Anselm gone barking mad on us?"

"So it would seem," Ali agreed.

Her phone rang, and B.'s photo appeared on the screen. "I'm home," he said. "There's no sign of you and no sign of Bella. Where are you?"

"You're home," Ali repeated. "I thought you weren't coming home until tomorrow."

"I wasn't, but another blizzard is due to hit the East Coast early tomorrow morning. It's predicted to be bad enough that I had a choice of ducking out of town tonight or being stuck in Manhattan for the whole weekend. When I managed to snag a last-minute flight, I canceled tomorrow's meetings and came home. I didn't call because I was hoping to surprise you. Turns out the joke's on me."

"I'm having a pizza party with Sister Anselm and Leland on the maternity floor of St. Jerome's Hospital in Flagstaff."

"And Bella?"

"Leland dropped her off with my folks. They're not allowed to own a dog, but this was regarded as an emergency."

"So maybe you should bring me up to date. I talked to Stu as I was driving up from Phoenix, but I have a feeling that there's a lot more to the story."

It was not a particularly happy conversation, and it took the better part of an hour. By the time it was over, Ali's iPhone was burning her ear, the battery power was down to 5 percent, and B. was over being pissed at her for, as he called it, "going off half cocked." By the time they said good night, though, things were better.

"All's well that ends well, I suppose," B. said finally, "but there goes that Leland—saving the day again. Whatever are we going to do with the man?"

"Keep him around, I guess," Ali said. "Now let me go. My phone's going to die any minute if I don't find my charger."

By the time she found the charger, an outlet, and had her phone plugged in, Ali realized that Leland was curled up on a nearby sofa, sound asleep. She prowled around the floor long enough to find a linen cart stocked with clean blankets. She collected several and took them back to the waiting room. She used a couple of them to cover Leland and wrapped one around her own legs. She didn't know if the temperature in the waiting room had really gone down or if she was simply dealing with the dissipation of adrenaline.

She was glad Leland was sleeping, and she hoped Sister Anselm was, but Ali herself was wide awake and

chewing on the way Richard Lowell had been dressed—
his spiffy suit and tie, as opposed to the homespun crap
and thrift-shop rejects in the box containing Enid Tower's
personal effects.

It was close to midnight when she sent Stu an e-mail,
copying Cami as she did so.

> *Richard Lowell paid us a visit at the hospital
> earlier this evening. I believe Cami said he was
> probably the guy in charge right now, since he lives
> in the house closest to the church. I want to know
> everything there is to know about him.*
>
> *Ali*

She had no sooner sent it than a response came back
from Stu. Didn't the man ever sleep?

> *Hey, I thought you'd be downloading some zzzzs
> about now, but I wanted you to know that I got
> the drone thing handled. A buddy of mine is using
> drones to do aerial surveys of all BLM land abutting
> Grand Canyon National Park. I asked him to do the
> job for us and made it worth his while. Since he's
> already done some work in that area, it won't be any
> trouble for him to get himself and his equipment
> where we need them. He'll be there bright and early
> tomorrow. Make that today.*
>
> *And yes, I'll start digging on Mr. Lowell. Cami's
> right. Since he lives in the big house, he's probably
> the big cheese.*
>
> *Oh, and did you know B. is home? He called me
> on his drive up from Phoenix, but he asked me to*

keep it a secret because he wanted to surprise you. Felt like I was caught between a rock and a hard place. Hope you don't mind.

                                                        Stu

Relieved to know the supposed greenhouses might soon give up their secrets, Ali sent her response immediately:

A tale of two bosses. Not to worry. Thanks.

                                                        Ali

Having done as much as she could do for the night, Ali rested her head against the back of the love seat and pulled the blanket more tightly around her legs. She had just drifted off when her phone startled her awake. When she picked it up and Kate Benchley's photo peered back at her from the screen, Ali realized that the bag with Gordon Tower's cheek swab in it was still in her pocket rather than in a FedEx envelope on its way to Banshee Group.

"You said it was urgent, and we treated it as urgent," Kate said when Ali answered. "I know it's the middle of the night there, but we've got a match, and I wanted you to know right away."

Ali was still on the groggy side. *A match?* she wondered. Of course there was a match. Baby Ann was Enid's daughter, after all. Why wouldn't there be a match? Maybe the note Ali had sent along with the samples hadn't been clear. She thought she had said she just wanted the profiles. But the urgency in Kate's voice put Ali on edge.

"Don't worry about waking me. I was still up, sort of, but what kind of match do you mean?"

"Two of them actually," Kate answered. "Not exact matches, but near matches."

Now Ali was truly mystified. "Matches from where?"

"One came from a victim from the tsunami in Thailand and the other from a mass grave at the scene of a Colombian drug cartel massacre. I'm looking at the forensics reports right now. Both were female and both were estimated to be no more than six or seven years old. One is a second cousin of the sample labeled Baby Ann and the other is a half sister of the one named Enid."

Ali was thunderstruck. "How's that possible?" she asked. "Baby Ann is barely two days old. She and her mother live with a group of people, a cult actually, that carves out a meager existence in northern Arizona. I can't imagine any relatives of theirs being able to travel outside the U.S. How could they?"

Kate took a long steadying breath. "I hate to be the bearer of bad news," she said. "Those girls didn't go traveling of their own free will. In the world of sex trafficking, girls that young are the crown jewels. I'd guess they were smuggled out of the United States and sold on the black market for a ton of money. The one in Thailand was found virtually intact and tossed up on a hillside days after the tsunami. The one in Colombia was skeletal remains only."

Kate was still speaking when Ali took the phone from her ear. For a moment she stared at it in disbelief. Then, as she tried to suppress her gag reflex, the phone clattered to the floor. Throwing off the blanket and scrambling to her feet, she raced for the nearest restroom. At least she managed to heave the last few undigested bits of her pepperoni pizza into the toilet rather than onto the floor.

26

When Ali finished in the restroom and staggered back out to the waiting room, Leland was sitting up on his sofa with Ali's cell phone clutched in one hand. His white hair stood on end, reminding Ali of that iconic photo of Albert Einstein, but she was too heartsick to mention it.

Seeing what must have been a desolate expression on her face, he immediately pushed himself to his feet and hobbled across the room to hand over her phone. "Madame," he said, taking her arm to lead her back to the love seat. "Whatever is the matter? Are you ill?"

"I am," Ali said. "I'll tell you in a minute. First I need to call Kate back."

She redialed the number. "What happened?" Kate asked. "It sounded like you dropped the phone."

"I did drop the phone," Ali said. "I had to. I was about to barf my guts out. The whole idea makes me sick to my stomach. How do you do what you do?"

"It's not easy," Kate replied. "And you're not alone in being disgusted by this. I've already been in touch with my contact at Interpol. His name's Sean Fergus, and he's part of their international Human Trafficking Division. I told him what I found, and I'm sending copies of the DNA profiles directly to him. Of course, he wanted more details. Since I didn't have any, I referred him to you. I'm sure he'll be in touch, probably later today. You need to be prepared, Ali," she cautioned. "There may be more near matches waiting out there."

Ali thought about the names in Richard Lowell's family Bible, the ones Sister Anselm mentioned that had been crossed out and designated with the initials N.C. The name of Richard Lowell's deceased wife, Anne, had been whited out of the list, but Ali now suspected that the N.C. notation represented a fate that was infinitely worse.

"You're right about that," Ali said. "I suspect those two victims may be just the tip of the iceberg."

"That was Kate Benchley on the phone?" Leland asked when Ali ended the call. "The young woman who did the DNA testing in my father's homicide when we were in the UK?"

"That's the one," Ali answered. "Sister Anselm obtained DNA samples from both Enid and her baby. We sent them to Kate in hopes that there would be some way of matching their profiles with ones from an unidentified mother and child who were murdered near Kingman years ago. Instead, we've found matches to two near relatives, young girls, whose unidentified bodies have been found years apart and half a world away. Kate thinks we've stumbled into some kind of international human trafficking organization."

"Oh my," Leland said. "And that Lowell person who was here earlier—you think he has something to do with it?"

"There's a good chance he's the person in charge."

During Ali's phone call, Leland had resumed his seat. Now he stood back up and paced back and forth. "If I'd had any idea," he said, brandishing his cane, "I'd have given that man a good thrashing on the spot!"

Sister Anselm returned and looked anxiously back and forth between them. "What's wrong?" she asked. "Has something happened?"

Ali gave her a condensed version of Kate Benchley's call. With an ashen face, Sister Anselm sank into the nearest chair. "What do we do now?" she asked.

"Kate says someone from Interpol, an agent who deals with human trafficking, will be in touch later today," Ali answered. "I guess we'll see what kind of suggestions he has to offer."

Sister Anselm rose to her feet. "I tried to convince Mr. Upton to go home, but he was adamant. Since he's still in the room with Enid and the baby, I believe I'll go down to the chapel and pray for direction."

The nun was almost to the elevator when her phone rang. She listened for a moment. "I'm sure that's fine," she said. Hanging up, she turned back to Ali and Leland.

"That was the hospital administrator. An expectant mother and father just showed up downstairs. Their doctor is demanding access to the maternity floor. The administrator has been forced to declare the crisis over and is in the process of reopening the maternity floor. He's also lobbying for Enid's safety and for the well-being of other patients and staff that she and the baby be transferred to another facility without delay."

"Are they up to being moved?" Ali asked.

"Possibly," Sister Anselm said. "I've spoken to their doctors and suggested the possibility of taking them by air ambulance to Physicians Medical Center in Tucson. If need be, once Enid and the baby are well enough to leave the hospital, they can stay with my friends at the All Saints Convent until it's safe for them to return to this area."

Recalling the time Ali had seen the nuns from All Saints in action, she knew that Enid and the baby would be in good hands at the convent.

"Also," Sister Anselm continued, "additional security personnel have been authorized for the remainder of the night, so if you two want to go back to Sedona . . ."

"Absolutely not." Leland sat back down and folded his arms across his chest. "I'm not leaving. If's there's even the smallest chance that either one of those vile men or some of their associates might return, I intend to be here to greet them in an entirely suitable fashion."

Despite everything, Ali couldn't help smiling at that. When it came to being in a tight spot, Leland Brooks was always a good guy to have around.

"If he's not leaving, neither am I," Ali added.

Resigned, Sister Anselm nodded. "Somehow I already knew that's what both of you would say."

27

Still churning over what she had learned from Kate Benchley, Ali didn't doze off until sometime in the wee hours. When she awakened, the first face she saw was B.'s. Standing over her and shaking her shoulder, he held out her phone.

"Call for you," he said. "A guy who claims he's from Interpol is asking to speak to you."

In his years of running what had become a global cybersecurity company, B. Simpson himself was accustomed to dealing with Interpol, but he was clearly puzzled about why someone from that agency would ask for his wife.

Ali took the phone in hand. "Ali Reynolds," she said, trying to sound as though she hadn't just awakened out of a sound sleep. While she had slept, the room around her had changed. The security screen on the nursery was no longer closed. Two new fathers had been added to the mix. Nurses were back on the floor, and Leland Brooks was nowhere to be seen.

"Sean Fergus here," the caller said. "Sorry to call so early, but this is a matter of some urgency. When Kate Benchley sent over those two profiles last night, it set alarm bells ringing. We have DNA profiles that are similar but not an exact match from over a dozen victims, scattered around the globe. Some of those come from crime scene evidence and autopsies dating back as long ago as the late seventies. Those samples predate DNA profiling and have only recently been brought out of storage to be processed. In other words, there may be more that have yet to be processed. Some of the girls may well be alive, and there may be more dead victims whose bodies have never surfaced. What we do know is this: None of these profiles match up with those of any known missing persons."

"That's because they were never reported as missing," Ali told him. "Just a moment. I'll need to go into another room to discuss this further."

Untangling her legs from the blanket someone had put over her, she got up and motioned for B. to follow. The maternity-ward conference room was unoccupied, and they made for that. Once B. was inside, she closed the door behind them.

"What do you mean they weren't reported?" Fergus was asking. "How is that possible?"

Ali set about answering that question. It was a good thing her phone had spent the night on the charger. The conversation with Sean Fergus took well over an hour. The phone was turned on speaker, so in the process of briefing Fergus, B. learned the rest of the story as well.

"You're saying we have no idea how many girls might have come through that pipeline or how many more are at risk?" Sean asked.

"That's correct," Ali answered.

"I believe you mentioned that the area where this group is located is rather remote. If so, how are the girls being transported?"

"We've recently learned that there's an airstrip located on the property," Ali answered. "My guess is the first leg of the journey is done by air. As to what comes after that and how they're smuggled out of the country? I have no idea."

B. held up his finger, signaling a need to add something. "B. Simpson here. I'm Ali's husband and also CEO of High Noon Enterprises. One of our security operatives did an aerial survey of the area around the airstrip earlier this morning and located several questionable buildings. Some of them appear to be greenhouses and are evidently being used to grow fresh vegetables for wintertime use. The largest of the buildings, however, is clearly an airplane hangar that is currently unoccupied."

"How long is the airstrip?"

"We measured it," B. replied. "It's long enough to accommodate a small jet. An aircraft as large as a Citation X could probably take off and land there with no difficulty."

Fergus processed that unwelcome information. "With no idea of when or even if another load of girls is due to be shipped out, I'm urging that we act without delay. I believe the DNA evidence we have in hand is sufficient for us to obtain warrants, but getting things to work across international and jurisdictional boundaries will take time. Before we hand this off to any other agency, I'd like to have more intel than we have now."

"Pardon the interruption again," B. offered, "but my company has done work for Interpol on numerous occasions, usually with a guy named Arturo Bernini in the Cyber Fraud Division."

"You know Bernie?" Sean asked.

"I didn't know that's what you called him," B. answered, "but yes, he's always been my point of contact. The film footage we have now, taken without benefit of a warrant, is most likely totally useless to you or anyone else. Check us out with Agent Bernini. If you can issue us with appropriately drawn warrants, we can send the drones back in to take another set of films, ones that will be admissible."

"Your company has drone capability?" Sean asked.

B. winked at Ali before he answered. "Doesn't everybody?" he said.

"Okay," Sean said. "I'll see what I can do. The next step, of course, is to notify local law enforcement agencies about what's going on and make sure we can count on them for help."

Remembering Deputy Amos Sellers standing just behind Gordon Tower and nodding at the other man's every word, Ali shook her head in response, even though B. was the only one to see the gesture.

"I'm concerned about that," Ali said aloud. "The Family is located in Mohave County. Their deputy, the local one who actually works that area, happens to be a member of The Family."

"You're saying we can't expect any help from that quarter?" Sean asked.

"Not from the local deputy," Ali answered. "If he's part of all this and knows an operation is in the works, there goes the element of surprise. I'm sure even folks at Interpol know about what happened at Waco."

"Indeed we do," Fergus agreed. "What about the deputy's superior?"

Ali thought about her phone conversation with Sheriff Alvarado. He hadn't exactly volunteered information about Amos Sellers's connection to the cult. The sheriff had also mentioned having spent time policing the area where The Family was located although nothing in his bio hinted that Alvarado himself was in any way connected to the group. Still, Ali had some concerns about him that she wasn't willing to voice aloud at this point. Instead, she chose to hedge.

"Amos Sellers's boss, Sheriff Daniel Alvarado, is headquartered in Kingman. That's a good four hours and more than two hundred fifty miles from where The Family is located."

"Big county," Sean murmured.

"Yes," Ali agreed. "It is. I've spoken to Sheriff Alvarado on a slightly different but related matter. When the topic of The Family first came up, he wasn't exactly forthcoming."

"What do you mean?"

"He didn't see fit to volunteer the information that one of his officers is part of The Family. I had to find that out on my own, and that worries me."

"It would concern me, too," Fergus agreed. "Are you implying that Alvarado may be connected to all this?"

"I'm not saying that for sure, but I am worried that once his department is notified . . ."

"That the deputy will give away the game. In which case, as you said, we'll have lost the element of surprise."

"Yes, so how do these joint operations usually go?" Ali asked.

"The most common scenario dictates that we start by notifying the FBI. An official notification from them will then be passed along to local authorities, apprising them of the operation. This case may call for a somewhat less direct approach. Is there any way you could deal with the sheriff on an informal basis and attempt to feel him out?"

Ali thought about that. "I suppose I could drive over to Kingman and have a chat with him."

"In my opinion, eye-to-eye contact is always better than over the phone," Fergus agreed. "Our primary concern is this. Regardless of what action is undertaken, no innocent women and children are to be harmed."

"Exactly," Ali said. "That's my position, too."

There was a rap on the conference room door, and Sister Anselm poked her head inside. "Enid's been restless and wakeful most of the night, but now she's come around enough to be able to identify her pursuer."

"From the other night?"

Sister Anselm nodded. "She says Deputy Amos Sellers, or, as she calls him, Brother Amos, was about to lay hands on her. That's what sent her darting into traffic."

"Amos Sellers?"

"What's that?" Sean said. "I heard someone else speaking, but I couldn't quite make out what was said."

"This is Sister Anselm," Ali said, beckoning the nun closer to the phone. "Enid Tower's patient advocate. She says Enid just identified the man who was after her the other night. Deputy Sellers, the man I was just telling you about. Not only did he force Enid into oncoming traffic, he didn't stop to render assistance, either."

"Did the incident occur inside his jurisdiction or outside?"

"Outside."

"He most likely didn't come forward because he didn't want anyone to know he was there."

"That would be my assessment," Ali answered.

"Was the young woman able to provide any further details?" Sean asked.

Since the question seemed to be directed at Sister Anselm, Ali passed the phone to her.

"She's been talking off and on all night about someone named Agnes and Patricia. She calls them the 'Brought Back' girls. Presumably they're previous runaways who were caught and returned to the cult. One of them was evidently instrumental in helping Enid make her escape, and she's worried that they'll be brought to account for it."

"What about younger girls?" Sean asked. "Did she make any mention of those?"

"Yes," Sister Anselm said. "Unfortunately, yes. She calls them 'Not Chosens.'"

"What does that mean?" Sean asked.

"Girls who end up unbetrothed are designated as Not Chosen," Sister Anselm answered. "Several times a year, those girls simply disappear overnight and are never seen again. When I got a look in one of the family Bibles, I noticed that several names with the letters N.C. beside them were marked through in red ink. I was puzzled about them at the time. Now, with Ms. Benchley's help, I'm afraid we all have a better understanding of the grim reality of what those letters mean."

"How many of those marked-through names did you see?" Sean asked when Sister Anselm finished relating that part of the story.

"At least seven or eight, just in the first two pages of Richard Lowell's family Bible," Sister Anselm said. "Since there are probably twenty-five to thirty families, that most likely means there are that many more family Bibles."

"And that many more missing girls," Sean muttered under his breath. "It just gets worse and worse, doesn't it? Okay then. Where are we?"

"Ali and I will drive over to Kingman together to try to assess whether or not we should bring Sheriff Alvarado into the picture," B. offered. "Unless, of course, someone else has already spilled the beans."

"If so, the leak didn't come from our end," Sean insisted. "In the meantime, I'll be checking in with Bernie and contacting my U.S. counterparts. I don't have any idea how long all this is going to take, but since you seem to be the one with the most intimate knowledge about the current situation, Ms. Reynolds, is it okay if I have them contact you directly as necessary?"

"Yes, please," Ali agreed. "Feel free to give them my contact information."

When the phone call ended, Sister Anselm consulted her watch. "We've made arrangements for the patient transfer," she explained. "The air ambulance is due here any moment. I'd best go make sure all the details are handled."

When Ali and B. left the conference room, Ali noticed that, except for two new daddies, the waiting room on the maternity floor was empty. "Where's Leland?" she asked.

"He looked beat," B. said. "I told him to go home and get some rest. You're not in such great shape yourself," he added.

A mirror hung on the wall outside the nurses' station. A glance in that told Ali that B.'s assessment of her appearance was on the money. Her hair and makeup were a mess. Her pantsuit had been slept in, and it showed.

She shook her head. "You're right," she said. "I look like hell, and I'm starving besides. Any chance of getting some breakfast before we head for Kingman?"

"I've got a better idea," B. said. "Knowing you'd been stuck here overnight, I brought along a change of clothing and your traveling makeup kit. They're out in the car. How about we rent a motel room so you can get showered and changed? Then before we head for Kingman, we'll stop long enough to have breakfast."

"You're a good man," she said, giving him a peck on the cheek. "In fact, you're a gem. If we weren't already married, I'd marry you on the spot!"

28

Betsy woke up early and pulled on her robe as soon as she got out of bed. The idea that people she didn't know might be watching her every move was still very disturbing. After walking Princess, she made a careful circuit of the house, checking the windows and doors, making sure nothing was out of the ordinary.

Once Princess was fed and the coffee finished perking, Betsy went over to the kitchen cabinet and opened what she liked to call her "dynamite drawer." The whole time she and Alton were married, he had carefully balanced the checkbook every single month—without fail. Alton had been a pretty sensible guy. Betsy had generally gone along with his programs without raising much of a fuss, whether the question at the time was about installing a new roof, purchasing a car, or selling off part of the farm. It wasn't because Betsy didn't want to voice a countervailing opinion so much as the fact that she had usually agreed with Alton's assessment of the situation at hand.

Once he was gone, Betsy still did most things his way, with one small exception—balancing the checkbook and savings accounts, and it happened that now there were several of those. Each account had been established to fund and handle some particular purpose. She checked the credit card bills each month when they came in just to be sure there were no oddball charges in addition to the ones that were on automatic or the occasional small purchases she herself made. Once she had surveyed those, she tossed the statements, along with the collection of bank statements that came in month after month, in the bottom drawer—the deepest one—in the kitchen cabinets. Finally, once a year and usually at the beginning of March, she hauled out the ledger—she still used Alton's old-fashioned ledger—and his calculator and did a year's worth of bookkeeping all at once before handing the whole shebang over to the accountant to sort out the taxes.

She and Alton had lived carefully if not exactly frugally. Having seen too much of what happened during the Depression, Alton had stayed away from the stock market. He had derided it as "gambling with other people's money." And he hadn't gone looking for investment schemes with high returns, either. But he did believe in banks. The tiny returns that came back on savings accounts were fine with him. He had created several and assigned a label to each—Household, New Car, Travel, Emergency, Home Improvement. Once one of them was full to the extent that it didn't exceed FDIC limits, he went on to create the next one, and the next, and the next—five in all. When it came time to pay bills, he—and, later, Betsy—would transfer the necessary amounts from the proper account into the checking account where Social Security checks were automatically deposited.

With the farm long since paid for, most of Betsy's day-to-day bills could be handled by that without having to resort to taking funds from one of the named accounts.

When she did have added expenses, like the credit card bills for her trips to and from DC to look after Athena and also her trip to Arizona for the wedding, those were transferred over on an as-needed basis only. Since those occasional expenditures were few and far between, Betsy had zero concerns about running out of money in her lifetime, just the way she and Alton had intended.

It was only February, a month earlier than usual, but since Betsy had to visit the various banks later on in the day anyway, she decided she could just as well get the onerous bookkeeping chore over and done with. Steeling herself for the task with a first cup of coffee on the table next to her and with Princess curled up in a cozy ball at her feet, Betsy settled down to work.

She dumped the whole drawer upside down on the table, so that the earliest statements would be the ones on top. In the very first statement—in the account Alton had labeled "New Car," Betsy saw something worrisome. There were four different $250 ATM withdrawal transactions posted to that account in a one-month period— one a week—a thousand dollars gone. The only problem was, Betsy Peterson had never made an ATM withdrawal in her life. She supposed you'd need some kind of card to make that happen, but she didn't have one. The only plastic she carried of any kind consisted of her trusty Visa and Amex cards, where she always maintained a zero balance.

With trembling hands, she tore into the next envelope—her Home Improvement account—only to discover the same thing, one withdrawal a week, $250 a shot, four times in the course of the month. And so it went, in every account. Betsy worked in a state of rising fury until she had the whole year's worth of statements

opened and accounted for. And there were the cold
hard numbers. In one year, someone had relieved her of
$60,000 without her knowledge or consent.

Too late she realized that Alton had been right to do
the accounting every month. Had she done that, she
could possibly have limited her loss. But now? Her first
instinct was to pick up the phone, dial the first bank, and
go to war with the manager. She had the phone in her
hand when she thought better of it and put the receiver
back on the hook. The bank statements for January had
not yet arrived. If she called the bank and alerted them,
that might also serve to alert whoever was doing it. She
wanted the guilty parties caught and punished every bit
as much as she wanted them stopped.

Instead, she tracked down the phone number for Joe
Friday, the guy who had installed what he had explained
was something like a distant band of guardian angels
there to watch over her.

"Good morning, Betsy," he said when he answered.
Obviously his caller ID was in good working order.
"What's up?"

"I've been going over my bank statements," she said.
"Someone has been making unauthorized withdrawals all
year long in every one of my accounts. They've been using
ATMs, which I've never once used. I'm mad as a wet hen
about it, and I don't know what to do."

"I'll call Stuart," Joe said. "Believe me, this kind of
thing is right up his alley. He'll be back in touch as soon
as possible."

When the phone call ended, Betsy reached down,
lifted Princess into her lap, and held her close. "See
there?" she told the squirming dog. "I wasn't just being
paranoid. Someone really is after me."

29

As Ali drove out of the parking lot, she caught sight of a departing air ambulance. She was relieved to know that both Enid and her baby were flying off to Tucson, well beyond The Family's reach.

The Crown Inn Motel just up the street from the hospital was convenient if not particularly inviting. What she needed that morning was a shower and some breakfast. The Crown Inn offered both because it came complete with an attached restaurant, the Pancake Castle.

The room itself was marginal at best, with a shower that offered little more than a dribble of water and clean but aged towels that were see-through thin. Rinsing the shampoo out of her hair under a chin-high shower head presented a challenge, but she managed to make it work. The mirror over the sink was so short that she had to lean over the basin to see enough of her face to put makeup on. Even so, when Ali stepped out of the bathroom, she felt like a new woman.

She emerged just in time to hear the end of a phone call. "Okay," B. was saying. "We'll stop long enough for breakfast, then I'll head out. I should be in Cottonwood about the same time the warrants arrive."

"Cottonwood," Ali echoed. "I thought you were driving over to Kingman with me."

"Sorry, babe," he said. "You're on your own. Warrants issued in Phoenix should be in Cottonwood sometime within the next two hours. I need to be on hand to sign off on them."

"That was fast," Ali observed.

"It's Interpol," B. answered. "The last part of that word may be P-O-L, but in my experience it really should be P-U-L-L. The fact that any number of kids may be in jeopardy means that everybody concerned is jumping through hoops. The warrants give us authorization to dispatch Stu's drone guy. The FBI has its own drone capability, but our guy is on-site, and theirs isn't."

"I was looking forward to having you along to back me up when I go talk to Alvarado."

"Hey." B. grinned. "Don't forget our agreed-upon division of labor. Stu, Cami, and I handle High Noon's geek stuff; you're in charge of PR. You make nice with Sheriff Alvarado, and we'll handle the drone issues."

Once inside the tackily turreted Pancake Castle, B. opted for the King—a full stack—while Ali took the Queen—a short one. Both breakfasts came with crisp bacon and coffee included. The pancakes turned out to be a bit thick for Ali's taste and not nearly up to the delectably thin ones her father, Bob Larson, used to serve at the Sugarloaf. Still, Ali downed hers with relish.

"Oh," B. said after they ordered. "I almost forgot. Stu just received a message from Joe Friday. Betsy called Joe in a blind panic this morning because she discovered that someone has spent the last year lightening her bank accounts to the tune of some sixty thousand bucks."

Ali whistled. "How did they do that?"

"By making unauthorized withdrawals using debit cards that Betsy somehow didn't know she had. It started in January of last year. Stu's in the process of tracking down the dates, times, and ATM locations that were used for the transactions. He's hoping to locate security tapes."

"If the withdrawals started in January," Ali asked, "how come it went undiscovered for so long?"

"For one thing, the amounts were small enough that they didn't raise any red flags. Betsy is one of those people who does all her accounting work once a year, just in time to meet the April 15 IRS deadline. Today was the day she tackled that job, and today is also when she noticed the problem."

"Did she go to the cops?"

"Not yet," B. said. "Surprisingly enough, she reached out first to Joe, who immediately put Stu on the case. Betsy evidently has issues with some of the local law enforcement folks and came to us instead."

"I don't blame her," Ali said. "When she was worried that someone had tried to kill her, the local sheriff came right out and told her she was nuts. What about Athena? Has Betsy mentioned any of this to her?"

"That's not clear at the moment," B. answered. "If she had, I'd think Athena would have called to discuss it."

"Betsy probably doesn't want to worry Athena any more than she already has."

"In that case," B. said. "I won't mention it, either, at least not until I get a clear reading from Stu and/or Betsy."

"Good thinking," Ali agreed.

Twenty minutes later, Ali hit the road, heading west

on I-40. She had spent most of the previous day and all of the night inside the hospital. During that time, the weather had taken a turn for the better. For the first twenty miles or so, a tall berm of plowed snow lined the roadway although the pavement was clear and dry. As the road gradually descended in elevation, so did the snow lining the highway until eventually it disappeared altogether. Ali was thinking about her upcoming meeting with Sheriff Alvarado when her cell phone rang.

"Good morning," Andrea Rogers said when Ali answered. "I'm slow getting started this morning. I stayed up way too late looking through boxes, and I ended up oversleeping. I turned the alarm off instead of punching snooze and went right back to sleep."

"Did you find anything?" Ali asked.

"Yes and no. Seeing some of the names made me realize we need to computerize those old files. It turns out in some cases, we're dealing with second- or even third-generation abusers, as in violence begets violence. There's one family where both the grandmother and her grandson's spouse have come through the shelter. Unfortunately some files we dismissed as being ancient history are all too current."

"Did you find anything leading back to Colorado City?"

"No, but I did run into Reenie's ancient computer. It's a tiny little thing—a Toshiba laptop, one that used those little floppy disks—the hard plastic ones. Why they called them floppies, I have no idea."

Ali recalled the long-ago era of floppy floppy disks, but now was no time to go off into a discussion of the history of computer science.

"So?" she asked.

"When Irene was starting the shelter, it was a one-woman outfit that operated out of a cubbyhole office down in the basement. She had no clerical help until the YWCA was able to give her a part-time assistant for a few hours a week. Up to then, that computer was all she had. It's dead as a doornail now, of course, but I found a small file box—a gray plastic container—that's loaded with floppy disks. There might be something on one of those, but I have no idea how you'd go about accessing the information."

"Maybe Stu can figure something out," Ali suggested. "Where are the floppies now?"

"I brought them home with me. Are you still in town?"

"I'm on my way to Kingman right now. I'll probably come back through town on my way home to Sedona. I'll stop by to pick them up then if that's all right."

"Sure," Andrea said. "Call me when you know your ETA. What about that other thing we talked about last night? My plan was to spend today alerting the folks in my network that our shelter may need overflow help at some time in the near future. Do you have any better idea how many women and children we're talking about and do you know what the time frame is?"

"No to both," Ali answered. "If we do need help, it may be sooner than later, but please, don't give out any details. Something big is about to happen in Colorado City, but the fewer people who know about it in advance, the better."

"Understood," Andrea agreed.

When that call ended, Ali wasted no time in dialing Stu. "Hey," he said. "Good to hear from you. I've got some news that will interest you. I've got a line on one of the ATMs used in many of those debit-card transactions. It's located in the lobby of the Setting Sun Casino northwest of Bemidji. I'd say that one or both of Athena's parental units has a serious gambling problem. I suspect they may be using Betsy's money to stay afloat or at least to hide the losses."

"Will you be able to prove it?"

"I'm requesting security-camera feeds," Stu said. "Those have to go through official channels. Without any personal connections, that may take time."

Ali laughed. "I didn't know there was anywhere on earth that you didn't have personal connections. But now I have another problem for you."

"What's that?"

"I'm on the trail of a box of nineties vintage computer disks from a long-dead Toshiba laptop that may have some bearing on the Colorado City situation. Is there any way you can retrieve data from those and turn it into currently searchable files?"

"No problemo," Stu answered. "You've never seen my storage unit, have you? It's chock-full of ancient computers, starting with my dad's first Commodore 600. I've got an Eagle or two, a few Epsons, a whole flock of Toshibas, an HP or two, and any number of Dells among others. They all work, too. At least, they were working when I put them in storage. We could use a simple USB-compatible external drive for the floppies, but I'd love a chance to play with the old beauties. You give me the floppies, and I'll give you the info."

"Will do," Ali agreed. "I'll pick them up tonight and have them to you first thing in the morning."

The remainder of the two-hour trip Ali spent plotting strategy. She decided her best bet was to approach the problem obliquely. By starting with the Deputy Sellers issue and assessing Alvarado's reaction to that, she hoped to gain some insight into how much more, if anything, she should tell him.

The responsibility Sean Fergus had laid on her shoulders was a heavy one. Lives were at stake. She was gratified that the Interpol agent had placed so much trust in her but puzzled about it, too. Eventually she figured it out. It was only because of her involvement, along with Sister Anselm's, that any of this had come to light. Sean needed to trust someone to make the right call, and she was it.

Squaring her shoulders, Ali paid attention as the GPS directed her off the freeway in Kingman. Within minutes she pulled up outside a long one-story building that bristled with antennas. Once inside the lobby, she told the desk clerk who she was and why she was there.

"Sheriff Alvarado is in a meeting just now. Was he expecting you?"

"No," Ali said. "I'm glad to wait."

Just to the left of the desk was a wall that held a glass display case that included photos of each of the men who had served as county sheriff. Only the most recent ones were in color. When she reached Sheriff Alvarado's photo at the far end, she stopped short. From his name, she had expected him to be Hispanic. But this guy had bright blue eyes and a mop of reddish-blond hair.

"Ms. Reynolds, I presume?" said a pleasant voice close to her shoulder. "That's probably not what you expected. You most likely pictured some roly-poly little Hispanic guy."

When Ali turned to look, she found herself facing the man whose features and uniform matched those in the photo. "You've got me there," she admitted.

Alvarado laughed. "You're not alone," he said, taking her hand and shaking it in welcome. "My mother came from Sweden originally as a military wife who was widowed when I was tiny. The man she married after that, my stepfather, Umberto Alvarado, grew up right here in Kingman. When my mom died a few years later, Umberto came back home to be close to his family. My stepfather's mother, my nana, raised me.

"Kingman may have been home for my stepfather, but growing up here wasn't easy for me. I was too Anglo to hang out with the Mexican kids and too Mexican to hang out with the Anglo kids. Alone in a crowd as it were. That's why I spent my senior year as an exchange student in Sweden and even got to meet a few of my mother's relatives. In a pinch, I could probably still speak some Swedish, but there's not much call for it here."

"Not too many Swedish tourists in Kingman?" Ali asked.

"Not many." He grinned. "By the time I got back to the States, I'd had a taste of a different world that left me with zero interest in going to college. Instead, I graduated from high school and hired on with the sheriff's office. I've been here ever since."

Listening to the brief recitation of his biography, Ali realized that most of what Alvarado had told her—including his exchange-student stint in Sweden—was information Cami had already passed along to her. As she followed the sheriff across the lobby, through a security door, and through a labyrinth of hallways to his private office, she wondered about that. Was he telling her his life's story in an effort to put her at ease, or was he attempting to deflect her attention away from something else?

After directing Ali into a visitor's chair, Sheriff Alvarado took a seat behind a desk that was awash in paperwork topped by a pack of Marlboros. With a glance in Ali's direction, he swept the cigarettes out of sight and into the top drawer of his desk. Then he leaned back in his chair with his arms folded behind his head.

"So what can I do for you this morning?" he asked. "If you're here about the Jane Doe evidence situation, you should have just called rather than driving all the way here. That evidence box still hasn't surfaced. Believe me, we've been searching heaven and earth."

"This isn't about that," Ali told him. "At least it's not only about that. What can you tell me about Deputy Sellers?"

A flash of wariness crossed Alvarado's face before he answered. It was there and gone, but not without her seeing it.

"Amos? What about him?"

"Enid Tower is awake and talking." Ali's comment elicited no visible reaction. "She told us Amos was chasing her at the time she was hit by the vehicle—that he's the one who forced her into oncoming traffic."

"That's not possible," Alvarado declared at once. "The site of that MVA was inside Coconino County, not Mohave."

"But Deputy Sellers was there," Ali asserted. "Even if he was off duty and just passing by, shouldn't he at least have stopped to render assistance?"

Alvarado had no answer for that.

"How long has he been a member of your department?"

Alvarado frowned. "Quite awhile. He must be close to forty now. That means he would have been in his late twenties when he signed on."

"What if the whole time he's been acting as a sworn deputy for you, he's also functioned as The Family's enforcer?" Ali asked. "What if Enid Tower isn't the only runaway Amos Sellers was sent out to retrieve? Maybe twelve years ago he was dispatched to collect your Jane Doe as well, except, instead of taking her back home, he ended up killing her. In fact, maybe that's why he went to work for the sheriff's office to begin with—to lay hands on any evidence that might implicate him in the crime. After all, there's no way of knowing how long that evidence box has been missing. He might have smuggled it out of your evidence room years ago."

"This is nothing but idle speculation," Alvarado declared. "It's also utterly absurd. Amos would never do something like that. What makes you think this girl is telling the truth?"

"What makes you think she isn't?" Ali countered.

They had reached an impasse. "Amos Sellers is a sworn deputy," Sheriff Alvarado said finally. "I trust him."

It was as simple as that. Alvarado trusted Amos Sellers and Ali didn't. Any operational intel shared with Alvarado would go straight to The Family via Sellers. It was time to back away from her real purpose in coming here and take shelter in the backup story.

Ali stood up. "Do me a favor," she said. "The next time you see Deputy Sellers, you might ask him about Jane Doe as well as that missing evidence box. If I happen to see him first, I'll do the same."

"Fair enough," Alvarado said. He started to rise.

"Don't bother showing me out," Ali said. "I can find my own way."

She waited until she was out in the parking lot before she called Sean Fergus's number and left a message on his voice mail. "Ali Reynolds here. Sheriff Alvarado stands behind his deputy one hundred percent. That means that, as far as I'm concerned, the sheriff isn't a trustworthy ally in terms of any operation launched against The Family. You asked for my opinion, and here it is. If you want to maintain the element of surprise, you'd best leave Sheriff Alvarado and his department out of the equation."

30

Ali filled up with gas before leaving Kingman. On the two-hour drive back to Flagstaff, she struggled to stay awake. She was on the phone to Andrea Rogers, telling her she'd be at the shelter around one, when a call came through from an unknown number. Half expecting it to be from a law enforcement official of some kind, Ali switched over immediately.

"Ali Reynolds here."

"Where did they go?" a male voice demanded urgently. "I can't reach Sister Anselm, and no one at the hospital will tell me anything."

It took a moment for Ali to recognize David Upton's voice.

"Oh, David," she said. "Yes. The hospital was worried about security issues. They suggested that Enid and the baby be moved elsewhere. They're on their way to a hospital near Tucson. I thought you knew all about it."

"Before I left the hospital last night, there was some talk about transferring her," David said, "but I had no idea it would happen this fast. What I don't understand is what am I supposed to do with Patricia and Agnes?"

"Who?"

"Patricia and Agnes," David said, "Enid's friends. She was afraid someone might figure out that they'd helped her, so I went and got them."

"The Brought Back girls from Colorado City?"

"Where else?"

"How did you find them?"

"How do you think?" David replied. "Enid gave me the address. My car is impounded. I drove up there in a borrowed minivan. I used the GPS on my phone to locate the address and followed that to hike in and find them. There was a third girl Enid was worried about—someone named Mary. Patricia showed me where she's being held—a jail kind of thing, right next to the church—but that was locked up tight. We tried to find a way to let her out but couldn't. By then it was starting to get light. We finally had to leave Mary where she was and get the hell out. I wanted to be back in the van and out of there before anyone noticed they were gone."

"Where are you now?" Ali asked.

"Back in Flag."

"Are Patricia and Agnes there with you now?" Ali asked.

"Not exactly."

"What do you mean, not exactly?"

"I left them in the van out in the parking lot while I came into the hospital," David said. "The way they are now, I couldn't bring them inside and I couldn't take them to my dorm, either."

"Why not?"

David sighed. "Because they're dirty. They're dressed in filthy rags and they stink. On the way down, cold as it is, I had to drive with the windows open just to breathe.

You wouldn't believe the way they were forced to exist, looking after the pigs and having to live with them, too. No wonder Enid was so afraid of being taken back home. The same thing would have happened to her. No telling what they would have done to her baby."

Unfortunately, Ali had an idea of the kind of fate that would have awaited Enid's child. She took a deep breath. "Do you know where the YWCA is?"

"I think so. Why?"

"Take them there. If you go around to the back of the building, you'll find an entrance to the women's shelter, Irene's Place. The director, Andrea Rogers, is a friend of mine. I'll call ahead and let her know you're on your way. I'm coming there, too."

"What's going to happen to them?" David insisted. "Enid is on her way to Tucson, so she's probably safe. What if someone comes after these two?"

"Did anyone follow you?"

"No," he answered. "At least I don't think so. I tried to keep an eye out. Patricia told me they usually don't talk to anyone until early evening when they go up to the house to get food. They gave the pigs an extra feeding before we left, but still, if the animals start acting up, someone may notice the girls are gone sooner than tonight."

"Okay," Ali said. "Go to the shelter. I'll be there as soon as I can. Andrea can help them get cleaned up and find something for them to wear in the clothing bank. After you drop them off, wait around in case I need to talk to you."

Ending the call, she immediately redialed Andrea and let her know what was happening.

"Don't worry," Andrea said. "We'll look after them."

Andrea sounded reassuring, but as far as Ali was concerned, looking after Patricia and Agnes wasn't the most pressing issue. Off the phone with Andrea, Ali immediately located the last call to Sean Fergus and punched that number. She was relieved when he answered the phone.

"Did you receive my earlier message?" Ali asked.

"Yes," he answered. "I did. Going around Sheriff Alvarado makes it tough, but I'm working on an alternate strategy."

"Good," she said without asking for details. "Right now we've got another problem."

"What?"

Trying to explain David Upton's connection to Enid was more than Ali could do right then. "A friend of Enid Tower's took it upon himself to hike into The Family's compound last night and bring out two of the women who were being held there. They attempted to bring out a third as well, but she's being held in some kind of lockup. The two he rescued, Agnes and Patricia, live apart from the rest of the population. It's possible no one knows that they've gone missing so far, but they will soon enough."

"There goes any chance of taking them by surprise," Sean muttered.

"Exactly."

"You say this person hiked in?"

"Yes. His name's David Upton."

"How did he gain access? Did he encounter any resistance going or coming—any guards or anti-intrusion devices?"

"Not that he mentioned. According to him, he parked somewhere along the highway and walked in and out."

"In that case," Sean said after a pause, "maybe losing the element of surprise isn't as big an issue as we thought. If this chap was able to gain access to the compound without being detected, he may be able to tell us what route he followed."

"All right," she said. "I'm almost to my exit. I should be meeting up with David in the next few minutes. I'll have him give you a call."

Ali pulled into the parking lot behind the YWCA and parked next to a dusty Dodge Caravan minivan. David, waiting in the doorway, came out to meet her.

"Is this what you drove up and back in?" Ali asked.

He nodded.

"Where are Patricia and Agnes?"

"They're showering and changing clothes," David answered.

"Okay," Ali said. "Why don't you take the van back to wherever it belongs. If someone did see you, there's no sense in advertising that you dropped someone off here."

"Right," David said. "The guy who owns it keeps it in a garage. In other words, once it's back inside, it won't be visible from the street. Do you want me to come back here after I drop it off?"

"Please," Ali told him. "These two women trusted you enough to come with you. They'll be more likely to talk to me if you're there than if you're not."

"Convincing them to come along wasn't easy," he said, "especially when I came snooping around in the middle of the night. I told them Enid was afraid they'd be in trouble for helping her get away."

"Why would anyone think that?"

"Because it's true," David answered. "Patricia had a phone number for someone on the Outside, a woman named Irene. Enid didn't know Irene's was a place instead of a person." He nodded toward the door where a discreet brass plaque attached to the wall read simply, IRENE'S.

It's actually both, Ali thought, remembering her lost friend Reenie Bernard—a person and a place. That explained the phone call Enid had made. She had called asking for Irene with no idea that Irene Bernard had been dead for years while the shelter that was her legacy lived on.

"Anyway," David continued, "Patricia and Agnes must have believed it, too, because they finally agreed to come along." He stood up. "I'll go drop off the car."

"Do you need me to follow you and bring you back?"

"No," he said. "It's not far. It'll only take me a few minutes to walk it."

"Do you have your phone with you?" Ali asked.

"Sure," he said, removing it from his pocket. "Why?"

"I need you to call someone," she said. "His name's Sean Fergus. Here's his number."

Ali read Sean's number from her phone and David dutifully keyed it in. "Who's Sean Fergus?" David asked. "And why do I need to talk to him?"

"He's an Interpol agent," Ali explained. "He's operating on the assumption that The Family is engaged in some kind of human trafficking operation. He's looking for any information you can provide on how you made it in and out of the compound this morning."

"Human trafficking?" David repeated. "Are you serious?"

"Very," Ali told him.

"Okay then," David said. "I'll give him a call."

As David set off to return the minivan, Ali rang the shelter's doorbell. After identifying herself over the intercom, the door buzzed open. She found a receptionist seated at a desk just inside. "May I help you?"

"My name is Ali Reynolds. I'm looking for Andrea Rogers."

"She's expecting you, Ms. Reynolds, but she's busy right now. You're welcome to take a seat."

"Thanks."

Ali had just settled down on a nearby sofa when Andrea hurried out into the waiting room through a door controlled by a keypad. Ali was relieved to see that Irene's Place was serious about security. Considering the dire circumstances surrounding some of the shelter's clientele, security was essential.

Andrea sank onto the seat next to Ali, shaking her head. "I'm sure it's been years since either one of those poor girls has had a hot shower. Scrubbing off years of grime takes time. I gave them each a bag filled with toiletries, led them to the shower room, and told them not to rush. I also found a couple of pairs of sweats and scuffs they can put on until we locate something more suitable for them to wear. They're both terrified, of course, afraid someone's going to come charging in here to drag them back. They mentioned somebody by name. Amos, I believe."

"That would be Amos Sellers," Ali told her.

Andrea looked surprised. "You've met him?"

"I'm afraid so. He's The Family's chief enforcer."

"Well," Andrea continued, "it seems Agnes and Patricia tried running away once before—a long time ago. Amos was sent out to find them and bring them back, which he did, and none too gently, either."

"Did they come here?" Ali asked. "To the shelter?"

"This happened years ago, long before the shelter

existed in its current form. All they had was Irene's name and phone number. Unfortunately, they were caught before they made contact. When they came here today, they fully expected to find Irene herself. I had to explain that Reenie was gone and that I had taken her place."

"How did they even know about Irene?" Ali asked.

Andrea shook her head. "I have no idea."

The doorbell rang. When the receptionist opened the entryway door, a delivery guy came in carrying a bag of Subway sandwiches.

"I sent out for some lunch," Andrea explained. "I asked what they wanted to eat. They said something soft. They both have severe dental problems. Once we get them decent clothing and have them settled into one of our apartment units, that's the next thing we'll tackle—getting them in to see a dentist. Fortunately, we have several who volunteer their services, but if these two are any indication of the kinds of difficulties people from that place are going to be dealing with . . ." She shook her head.

"I suspect there will be a lot more of same," Ali said. "Have you had any luck finding potential places to stow them if they do show up?"

Andrea sighed. "There's been such an influx lately. Many of the shelters are full of dumped-off women. They're not victims of domestic violence per se, but when they're stranded and penniless in a foreign country with no English, no money, no work skills, and no way to feed their children, what are you going to do, let them starve? Nobody I know in the shelter business is going to turn up their noses and tell them to come back when someone does them the favor of giving them a black eye."

Ali knew that Arizona and Texas were favorite dumping grounds for impoverished migrant women who were caught in limbo, with no way to return home and no way to survive in the United States without someone stepping up to help them. Andrea Rogers and women like her were the ones who did.

A door leading into the interior of the building cracked open. A woman poked her head out and peered cautiously around the room. "Is it okay if we come out? We're not really dressed."

"You're fine, Patricia," Andrea assured her, "but if you'd be more comfortable, we can go into my office. It's a little more private."

Self-conscious and tentative, the woman edged into the room. There was no way to determine her age. She might have been thirtysomething; she might have been fifty. Streaks of gray shot through dark blond hair that, still dripping wet, had been skillfully braided into a single plait that hung down beyond her waist. The fact that she was missing several teeth made her look older than she was. Years of living outside in all kinds of weather had tanned her skin to the shade of saddle leather and given her a permanent squint.

Ali held out her hand. "I'm Ali Reynolds," she said. "Irene was a good friend of mine. And your name is?"

Patricia looked down at the proffered hand as if unsure what to do about it. When she finally took it, Ali noticed that the skin was chapped, callused, and tough. This was the hand of someone accustomed to doing hard physical labor.

"Patricia Glenn," she muttered.

A second woman, one with equally worn and roughened features, stepped into the room. "And I'm Agnes— Agnes Gray," she said shyly, keeping her eyes downcast and without offering her hand.

Agnes and Patricia were similar enough in looks that they might have been sisters, although Ali thought it more likely that they were cousins of some kind. Like Patricia's, Agnes's hair was braided into a single long plait, and she, too, was missing enough teeth that her cheeks sank in on themselves, making her look far older than she was.

Andrea hurried into her small office. Unloading sandwiches from the paper bag, she offered them to Patricia and Agnes as they followed her into the room. Ali, bringing up the rear, was about to close the door behind them when the receptionist buzzed David Upton into the waiting room. Ali beckoned him into the office as well.

"Did you reach Fergus?" she asked as he went past.

David's reply was a curt nod. Once Patricia caught sight of David, she scrambled around Agnes and grabbed one of his hands in both of hers.

"Thank you," she murmured. "Thank you for bringing us here. It's like heaven. We even got to take a hot shower." Then, seemingly embarrassed by having said too much, she moved away and sat down abruptly on one of the visitor's chairs.

"I wouldn't go so far as to say it's heaven," Andrea said briskly, "but it's the best we can do. Just be assured that we all stand prepared to offer our help to you and to anyone else who may be interested in leaving The Family behind."

Patricia's eyes widened. "You'd help other people leave if they wanted to?"

"Yes," Andrea said. "Are there some of those—people who would like to leave?"

"Maybe." Patricia spoke warily, as if afraid of saying too much.

"What we need is information," Ali said, stepping

into the conversation. "How many people are involved in all this—how many families and how many women and children?"

"I'm not sure," Patricia answered. "Once we were brought back, we weren't allowed to go to church or to any of the gatherings, so it's hard for us to know exactly how many. I'd guess there are about twenty-five families, maybe more."

"How are you related to Gordon Tower?" Ali asked.

"My older sister, Margaret, is one of his wives," Patricia answered. "After Agnes and I ran away, her family wouldn't take her back and my family wouldn't have me. Margaret convinced Gordon to let us stay as long as we took care of his pigs and didn't make any trouble."

"Which we have, now," Agnes said quietly. "Made trouble, I mean. If they figure out we helped Enid, we can't ever go back."

"You don't have to," Andrea assured them.

"What can you tell us about the girls who are called the Not Chosen?" Ali asked.

Agnes and Patricia exchanged a wordless glance. "They go away," Patricia said finally with a shrug. "Usually in the middle of the night. You wake up in the morning and they're gone. No one ever sees them again."

"It happened to my little sisters," Agnes added in a whisper. "Christina and Donna Marie. Christina was sweet and never caused any trouble, but her eyes were crossed. Boys teased her and told her that her strange eyes made her ugly. She was six when they took her."

"They?" Ali asked.

Agnes nodded. "Three men came out onto the sleeping porch. One held the door while the other two collected Christina and Donna Marie. They took them out of their beds while they were sleeping. Someone came back later, stripped off their bedding, and gathered up their stuff. I knew about Disappearing Nights—I'd heard about them from the other kids, but that was the first time I'd seen it happen on my sleeping porch. I was already betrothed, so I thought I was safe, but I didn't dare move or say a word. I stayed like that for a long time after they left, afraid they'd come back for me, too."

Agnes broke off while two tears dribbled out of her eyes.

"Was there something wrong with Donna Marie, too?" Ali asked gently.

Agnes nodded. "She wouldn't talk or else she couldn't. I never knew for sure which it was. I hoped that wherever they went that they were together. Donna Marie could see better than Christina could and Christina did the talking for both of them."

"How was Donna Marie related to Christina?"

"We're all half sisters," Agnes said. "We all had the same father but different mothers. I was older, so I was in charge of looking after them. I cried for days after they went away. My father caught me crying and slapped me silly. He told me that it was God's will and that the Not Chosens went to a better place. I thought that meant they were dead and had gone to heaven." She added quietly, "I hope that's true—that they are in heaven."

Not prepared to address that issue, Ali turned to Patricia. "Why did you and Agnes run away the first time?"

"We were friends," Patricia said simply. "She was betrothed to Jack Adams. One day his first wife, Martha, claimed Agnes had sassed her. Most of the time first wives handle those things on their own, but Jack said he'd take care of it himself. He beat Agnes until she could barely move. The next week, Aunt Martha made Agnes go along to the grocery store, even though she was still black and blue all over. There was a woman in the store— someone from Outside—who told her about a woman who would help her if she needed it. She jotted a name and a telephone number on a scrap of paper."

"Irene's name?" Ali asked.

Patricia nodded. "We decided to run away together and ask Irene for help. Amos caught us while we were still on the highway."

"So that's Amos's job?" Ali asked. "To bring back runaway kids?"

"To bring back runaway girls," Patricia corrected. "Boys can leave whenever they want, and most of the time they don't come back. Unless they've been promised a place on the council or as one of the Elders, there's no reason to."

"How long has Amos been doing that?"

Patricia shrugged. "A long time. He gets paid for being a deputy, but he also gets paid for catching girls and bringing them home."

"He's a bounty hunter, then," Ali concluded. Patricia frowned as though the terminology was beyond her. Ali rephrased her comment. "What I'm asking is does he get a reward for bringing girls back—a cash award maybe?"

This time Patricia nodded.

"And how many are there?" Ali continued.

"How many Brought Back girls?" Patricia shrugged. "I suppose every household has one or two. After all, everyone has pigs that need looking after."

"Are there some that Amos misses?" Ali asked. "Some runaway girls who actually get away and don't come back?"

"A few, I suppose," Agnes said wistfully.

With every question and answer, a few more pieces of the puzzle shifted into place. Ali was about to ask another question when her phone buzzed in her pocket. With another unfamiliar number on the screen, Ali excused herself and left the office to answer.

"Alison Reynolds?" a voice asked.

"Yes."

"This is the governor's office. Would you please hold the line for a call from Governor Dunham?"

31

Out in the lobby, a police officer was in the process of delivering a woman with two toddlers and a baby into the care of the receptionist. The woman was crying and so were all three kids. Barely able to hear over the din, and despite having left her coat on the chair inside Andrea's office, Ali stepped outside. A frigid breeze had kicked up, blowing down off the mountains to the west. Ali huddled against the building while she waited for the governor to come on the line.

Ali knew Virginia Dunham's name, of course. Although Ali hadn't voted for the woman either time, Governor Dunham was in the last year of her second term in office. She was, by all reports, a woman with the reputation of being painfully direct.

"Ms. Reynolds?"

"Ali, please," Ali said into the phone. "Just call me Ali."

"And you're welcome to call me Virginia. Now that we have all the name business out of the way, I understand that you and your friend Sister Anselm have set off something of a firestorm up around Colorado City."

"That wasn't our intention," Ali answered, "but it's what happened."

"So far this morning I've had conversations with people from Interpol and from the FBI. I'm hearing stories about human trafficking, about people being run down on the highway, and about someone else threatening to bodily remove a seriously injured patient from a hospital room against doctors' orders. All told, it sounds like a hot mess, and you seem to be smack in the middle of it. So tell me, if you will, what the hell's going on up there?"

It wasn't a simple story to lay out, but Ali did the best she could.

"Sean Fergus mentioned that you didn't want the local sheriff's department informed about any of this," Governor Dunham said once Ali finished. "I have a stack of warrants here on my desk—thirty in all—that call for the collection of any and all of The Family's family Bibles, which may or may not include the names of some of the alleged human trafficking victims. The warrants also specify that we can take cheek swabs from all the adult residents in the community in order to conduct DNA comparisons of the people in The Family with the profiles of human trafficking victims.

"Incidentally, I've been informed that we've now located a total of twenty of those, most of whom are deceased. However, that number includes two young women who have been found alive. They ended up in an orphanage and stayed on in Nigeria when they were old enough to leave because they had nowhere else to go. Without passports or documents of any kind, they were stuck where they were."

"Twenty victims?" Ali echoed. "That many? The last I heard the count was just over a dozen."

"As I said, it's been a very busy morning," Governor Dunham replied. "Back to the warrants issue, however. When it comes time to execute them, I have a problem. Who's going to do it? That job should belong to the local sheriff's department, so what's your beef with Sheriff Alvarado? I can't ignore the man. The Encampment is located inside his jurisdiction."

"Are you aware that one of his deputies, Amos Sellers, is part of that community—a member of The Family?"

"I'm well aware of the situation with Deputy Sellers," Governor Dunham said. "As a matter of fact, I have a warrant with his name on it right here in front of me. What about him?"

"For an unknown number of years he's moonlighted as The Family's bounty hunter, tracking down runaway girls and bringing them back home. He's had that job longer than he's been a deputy. If Sheriff Alvarado's department is involved in whatever you're planning, I'm afraid word will get back to Amos and from him to everyone else. I can't see the whole group hitting the road for parts unknown, but I can see them herding everyone—women and children included—into the church or some other central location and turning it into a siege situation."

"You mean turn it into another Waco," Governor Dunham said. "That's what you're thinking, isn't it?"

"Yes," Ali admitted. "The thought had crossed my mind."

"Mine, too," Governor Dunham said. "I've been remembering images of that hellacious fire all day long. That's why the current plan is to execute the warrants in the dead of night when everyone should be at home fast asleep. We'll be using emergency response teams from several jurisdictions so the warrants can all be executed at once. That way, any resistance should be kept to a minimum and on an individual rather than group basis. I believe that will be safer for all concerned—law enforcement officers and civilians alike.

"But just because one of Sheriff Alvarado's people belongs to the targeted group doesn't mean I'm going to tar everyone with the same brush," Governor Dunham continued. "I'm also not going to overstep my authority and allow a duly elected law enforcement officer to be left out of the loop on a major operation being conducted inside his jurisdiction. I assure you, Ali, I have every confidence that Sheriff Alvarado and his people will conduct themselves in full accordance with the law. Understood?"

"Yes, ma'am," Ali said, feeling as though she'd just been chewed out by her high school principal.

"That said, however," Governor Dunham continued, "I'm not discounting your concern or the historical precedent, either. As I'm sure you're aware, long ago there was a very similar situation in which people living in a place called Short Creek, now Colorado City, were taken into custody while peacefully assembled inside their church and singing hymns. That was part of what gave Governor Pyle such a black eye and turned what he did into a PR nightmare—the fact that they were all in church and singing when they were arrested. Later on, the man had his ass handed to him by the voters when he ran for reelection.

"What happened to Governor Pyle turned Short Creek, now Colorado City, into a no-man's-land and left it virtually untouchable as far as state government and law enforcement are concerned. Out of sight was out of mind. Everybody—my administration included, I'm ashamed to say—went along with that program. We were all content to let the people up there do their own thing. After all, what's a little polygamy among consenting adults?"

"But they're not just consenting adults," Ali objected. "I already told you. Little girls are expected to be betrothed by the time they're six or seven. When they're in their mid-teens, they're forced into marriages with much older men and end up giving birth to children while they themselves are still juveniles."

"You know that to be the case?" the governor demanded.

"Yes, I do," Ali answered. "As for the ones who try to escape? If they're caught and brought back by Deputy Sellers, they're consigned to live lives of terrible privation."

Ali thought about mentioning the other girl then—the Kingman Jane Doe who hadn't survived long enough to be brought back. But there was no point. Ali knew that without the missing evidence box, Amos Sellers would never be held accountable for her death or for the death of her child.

"I take it you heard that from the two women you mentioned earlier," Virginia Dunham said, cutting into Ali's thought process. "I believe you referred to them as Brought Back girls? What are their names again?"

"Agnes and Patricia," Ali answered. "They've spent the last fifteen years living in a Quonset hut with no electricity, no heating or cooling, and no running water. They've been forced to sleep on straw mattresses and walk around wearing other people's cast-off rags and shoes. If the state of Arizona treated convicted killers the way they've been treated, the American Civil Liberties folks would be up in arms."

"I suspect the American Civil Liberties folks will be weighing in on this matter all too soon," Governor Dunham observed, "and not in a good way, either. They'll be far more concerned with how we treat the guys we place under arrest than they will be about how the women and children were treated.

"The problem is," she continued, "my blind eye went away early this morning when Sean Fergus's phone call landed on my desk. As long as I'm the chief executive of the state of Arizona, known instances of human trafficking will not be tolerated. Holding people in what amounts to involuntary servitude will not be tolerated. Denying women and children their basic civil and human rights will not be tolerated—not on my watch. Because I'm not Governor Pyle.

"When this term of office is over, I'm done. I'm not standing for reelection for this office or any other. Politics and I are finished, so I'm going full speed ahead on this, Ali. The raid I've authorized is on. It's going to happen— tonight, most likely. Sheriff Alvarado's department will be charged with executing some of the warrants but with the proviso that Amos Sellers is to receive no advance warning whatsoever. Is that understood?"

Nothing Governor Dunham said dispelled Ali's misgivings about Sheriff Alvarado's involvement, but it wasn't her call to make. "Yes, ma'am," Ali said.

"I'm expecting that, one way or another, arrests will be made," Governor Dunham went on. "At least one person—the head honcho, a guy named Richard Lowell, will be going to the slammer. Interpol made it clear to the various banking institutions involved that cooperation would be in their best interest. All the financial transactions lead directly back to Lowell's name and no one else's. He's the one listed on all the accounts. He's the one who disperses the money and writes the checks. That means that once he's taken down, The Family's financial underpinnings will go away as well. Whether or not some or all the men go to jail, it's likely that their families will be dispossessed."

Just then the cop left the shelter and returned to the patrol car he'd left parked in front of the building. A glance inside told Ali that the distressed woman and her equally upset children had been ushered through the waiting room and into the area beyond the security door. Shivering from the cold and trying to keep her teeth from chattering, Ali buzzed to be let back inside. Once inside she found the receptionist was on the phone discussing what sounded like a complicated personal issue. Ali hoped that the conversation was engrossing enough that she'd be able to continue her own without every word being overheard.

Governor Dunham was on a roll. "Human trafficking issues aside, let's address the displaced persons part of the problem. My understanding is that this group has chosen to remain almost completely isolated from the modern world. That's going to change in a heartbeat. How do we help these people make that difficult transition? For instance, the two women you mentioned before—Agnes and Patricia. What's happening with them right now?"

"I'm friends with Andrea Rogers, the executive director of Irene's Place, a domestic violence shelter here in Flagstaff. Agnes and Patricia have been fed. They've also taken showers and been given a change of clothing. Most likely, they'll end up in one of the no- or low-cost housing units Irene's has at its disposal. They're fish out of water.

They're nervous and scared, but what scares them more than anything is that someone will force them to go back to The Family."

"That's not going to happen," the governor insisted. "Do either of them have any marketable skills?"

"I doubt it," Ali answered. "They've spent the last fifteen years of their lives looking after a herd of pigs. My expectation is that most of the others won't be any better prepared for life on the outside."

"According to the number of warrants on my desk," Governor Dunham said, "we're dealing with thirty-one residences in all—twenty-nine on the property and two in town. If each household consists of a husband and three or four wives, that comes to one hundred and fifty, give or take."

"From what Patricia said, each family probably has its own contingent of Brought Back girls, too."

"That would add sixty more," the governor said. "How many kids?"

"Lots," Ali said. "That's my impression, anyway. Women are there to do the housework and bear children, the more of those the better."

"So let's estimate eight to ten children per household. That's another two hundred fifty to three hundred. The drone footage reveals something that functions as a dormitory of some sort. It apparently houses young males in their teens. We got an unofficial playground count on them of forty-five to fifty. That brings us up to more than five hundred destitute individuals with no place to stay, nothing to eat, and no marketable skills, right?"

"That's how I see it," Ali agreed. "Some of the family units may want to stay together. Others may not. The Brought Back girls who've been treated as untouchables will most likely need to be handled as a whole separate category."

"All right," the governor agreed. "What's the name of your friend again, the one who runs the shelter?"

Ali gave Governor Dunham Andrea's contact information. "Do you have any idea about the number of units Andrea has available?"

"Not really," Ali answered.

"I'll speak to her, then," Governor Dunham said, "but trust me. Her organization won't be left to shoulder this load alone. My office will be assisting them and, if you agree, so will you."

"Me? How?"

"I'd like to appoint you to serve as a special deputy in this matter," Governor Dunham said. "By the time tonight's raid is over, people in The Family will feel like they've been subjected to a military attack. They won't be far from wrong. They'll be traumatized and terrified.

"This is a joint task-force operation put together in a hurry to prevent another possible load of girls from being shipped out of the country. To make sure of that, an FBI SWAT team will move in from the north after dark. They'll be bivouacked on the BLM land that lies north of The Encampment and tasked with guarding the landing strip. If an aircraft flies in, the team has been directed to allow it to land but under no circumstances are SWAT members to let it take off. That team will be coming down from Salt Lake rather than up from Phoenix. Once I'm off the phone, my deputy will be contacting the emergency response teams in nearby jurisdictions and assigning them specific targets."

"What do you need from me?" Ali asked.

"You and I and whoever else we can round up will be

there to win hearts and minds," Virginia Dunham said. "We'll be the rear guard, going in after the raid itself and after the cops have finished doing their jobs. Our task will be to convince the folks left behind that we mean them no harm. If you can persuade Patricia and Agnes to come along, they might be able to demonstrate to some of the women and most especially to the other Brought Back girls that we're there to help. They're going to need what we have to offer, but I expect we'll have to convince them to accept it."

Ali didn't have to think long or hard. "If you want me as your deputy, I'm in," she said. "Tell me where and when."

"We'll assemble at the Department of Public Safety headquarters in Flag at six P.M.," Governor Dunham said. "I'm told it's a four-hour drive from there to The Encampment. People will leave in convoys of two or three vehicles, starting at seven. If too many head up the road all at once, it'll be far too obvious. We should all be in position before midnight; that's when the fireworks start."

"I'll be there," Ali said. "With any kind of luck, Patricia and Agnes will be there, too."

32

Ali went back into the office. Andrea looked up at her with a tentative smile, which quickly faded. "Is something wrong?"

Ali nodded. "Yes. I just got off the phone with the governor of Arizona." She looked at David Upton. He nodded slightly, a gesture that indicated to Ali that he already had some idea of what was coming. Ali's problem was figuring out a way to start the conversation.

"Patricia and Agnes," Ali said. "Have you ever heard of DNA?"

Their blank stares were answer enough. Somehow she doubted that their educations had included much in terms of biology.

"You know that your bodies are made up of cells—skin cells, blood cells, bone cells, right?"

They nodded in unison, but Ali was afraid the nods came out of their being agreeable rather than any kind of real understanding of what was being said. She continued anyway.

"Inside each of those cells are tiny bits of material that lead back through the generations to your furthest ancestors. DNA tracks back to your mothers and fathers. You share DNA traits with your brothers and sisters, cousins, aunts, and uncles. In other words, people who do what's called DNA profiling are able to examine the family tree that is planted inside each of your cells."

That was a great oversimplification, but it was the best Ali could do. "When Enid and her baby were first admitted to the hospital, we had no idea who they were or where they were from. In an effort to find out, we took a sample of Enid's DNA and of her baby's, too. We sent the samples to a friend of mine who runs a company that specializes in DNA identification. They ran a check and found that their DNA is closely related to that of several young women and girls whose unidentified bodies have been found in places far from here—on the other side of the world.

"The person who called me on the phone a few minutes ago was the governor of Arizona, a woman named Virginia Dunham. Investigators from Interpol, which is an international police organization, and elsewhere have now connected twenty victims, some dead and a few still alive, who originally came from The Family."

Patricia frowned. "How's that even possible? Girls from The Family aren't allowed to travel."

"Have you ever heard of human trafficking?"

Again Patricia and Agnes replied in unison, this time shaking their heads.

"Human traffickers specialize in taking young girls, some as young as six or seven, and selling them to the highest bidder."

Agnes looked puzzled. "They sell them?" she asked. "Why?"

"For sex," Ali answered. There was no way to sugar-coat the explanation, so she plowed on. "There are evil people in this world who prefer having sex with children rather than with adults. I think it's likely that the young girls in question were sold to people like that."

Patricia made the connection first. "The Not Chosens?" she gasped. "The girls who disappeared? Is that what happened to them?"

Ali nodded. "That's what we believe," she said. "Governor Dunham is planning on taking immediate action to prevent another group of Not Chosens from being sent away."

"What kind of action?" Andrea asked.

Instead of answering, Ali looked closely at Agnes. "You mentioned that several men were involved the night your half sisters were taken, right?"

"Yes."

"The assumption is that most of the older men in the group are either involved in what's happening or know about it. The raid tonight will be to collect family Bibles, which we hope will contain records of the girls who disappeared—names, birth dates, et cetera. There will also be warrants to obtain cheek swabs for all the adult males in hopes of connecting the DNA dots between them and some of the unidentified victims."

"A raid," Patricia asked, looking horrified. "You mean like with guns and everything? I remember hearing about something like this. It happened a long time ago. The old bishop—Bishop Lowell's father—used to preach about it in church. He said there was this group of people who believed in polygamy just like we do. He said they all got sent to jail, even the little kids."

"This is a lot more serious that just practicing polygamy," Ali said. "The human trafficking element makes all the difference. Governor Dunham is determined that what happened at Short Creek, the incident you're talking about, won't happen again—at least we hope it won't. To make that work, though, we'll need your help and Agnes's, too."

"Our help?" Agnes said faintly. "What kind?"

"It's likely that many of the men will be taken into custody or at least in for questioning, on the basis of the ages of some of their wives if nothing else. The people left behind—the women and children—will be frightened. We'll need you to convince them that we may be from the Outside, but we're not their enemies. You'll need to help explain that if they want to stay where they are, they'll be allowed to do so, but if they want to leave—as you two did—they'll be allowed to do that as well—that there will be people on the Outside, like Andrea here, who will help them find places to live, food to eat, and suitable clothing to wear. From what you've told me about the way you and Agnes were treated, I suspect there are other Brought Back girls who will want to leave."

Patricia nodded thoughtfully. "The others might stay, especially mothers with children, but I think most of the Brought Back girls will want to leave."

"I'm trying to grasp the scope of the problem here," Andrea said. "How many Brought Back girls are there?"

"I'm not sure. We know there are others, but we're not allowed to communicate."

"Do any of the Brought Back girls have children?" Andrea asked.

"If some of the others do have children, those children would be living with other families, not their mothers, but most of the girls who run away do so before they have kids—before they get pregnant. That's what Agnes and I did, anyway."

"But not Enid," Ali said. "Her baby was due in a month or so."

"And not her mother, either," Patricia said.

Ali was surprised. "Wait, you mean Enid's mother ran away, too?"

Patricia nodded. "Anne Lowell was a year or two younger than we were. She told us she was leaving. We wanted to help her, and we tried to give her Irene's information, but she said she didn't need it—that she had someone on the Outside who would help her." Patricia shrugged. "I guess that's what happened. Anne must have gotten away. No one ever saw her again."

Ali had serious doubts that Anne Lowell had made good her escape, but she needed to know more.

"So Enid was already born and her mother was pregnant with a second child when she ran away? She just took off and left Enid behind?"

"She was scared. She didn't think her husband, Brother Lowell—he wasn't Bishop Lowell then—was the father, and she was terrified about what he'd do to her if he ever found out she'd been with someone else. I don't blame her for that. Bishop Lowell pretends to be a minister, but under the white robes he wears, the man's a monster. There's no telling what he would have done to her."

"Did Anne give you any hints about who that other man might be?" Ali asked.

Patricia shook her head. "No. After she left, there were rumors that she'd been seen with someone from Outside, but that was all just gossip."

"Do you remember exactly when Anne Lowell took off?"

Patricia considered before she answered. "I'm not sure. Without a calendar to keep track, it's hard to tell how much time has passed, but Enid was little when her mother left, not more than three or four."

Ali did the math. Enid was sixteen now. The Kingman Jane Doe, most likely another refugee from The Family, had been found dead twelve years ago. What if Jane Doe turned out to be Enid's mother? The time lines might just match.

"You said Amos Sellers was the one who brought you back?"

Patricia fidgeted before she answered. Ali could see that Patricia wasn't at ease discussing any of this. "Brother Amos wasn't a deputy sheriff back then. He got hired to do that a few years later."

"Would he have been the one sent out to retrieve Anne Lowell?"

Patricia shrugged. "I'm sure he looked for her, but he never found her." She frowned. "Why are you so interested in Anne?"

Ali wasn't prepared to answer that question, not right then, so she deflected it. "Looking for connections is all. Did Enid know any of this?"

"I told her who her father is," Patricia admitted. "I thought she had a right to know that. I didn't tell her all of it. It was bad enough that her mother ran away. Knowing the rest wouldn't have done her any good. If anything, it might have made things worse. Besides, it was more gossip than anything else."

"Look," Ali said, changing the subject. "It was brave of you to leave with David here last night. It was also smart of you to trust him. I think you could tell immediately that he meant you no harm, but those other women at The Encampment have most likely spent their entire lives being taught that everything outside The Family is evil.

Will you go with us this evening and help convince them otherwise?"

"Yes," Patricia said at once. "I'll go."

Agnes had to think for a moment; then, rather than speaking aloud, she simply nodded.

Ali turned to Andrea. "It's going to be cold up there tonight, and we'll probably be outside a lot of the time. Can you have someone take them shopping for clothing suitable for that—for coats, boots, and whatever else is needed? Whatever it costs, I'll handle."

"I could take them shopping," David Upton offered, "but I don't have a car right now."

Without a word, Andrea handed him a set of car keys.

"Okay," David said. "Tell me where we're supposed to go when we finish."

"Their apartment should be ready in about an hour or so," Andrea said. "It's being stocked with linens, pots and pans, and a minimal supply of food. Come back here, and I'll give them the key."

Ali reached into her purse, found her wallet, and handed David a fistful of cash. "Thank you for handling this," she said. "It's a big help."

David exited the office, taking Patricia and Agnes with him, and leaving Ali and Andrea alone.

"What's the real score?" Andrea asked.

"According to Governor Dunham's estimate, there's a good chance that, before the evening is over, you'll have between four and five hundred displaced homemakers and children dropped in your lap. Some are bound to want to stay where they are, but we have to be prepared for the worst. I expect you'll be hearing from the governor in person. I gave her your name and number."

"Okay," Andrea said. "I've made a few calls and already have some contingency plans in place. This isn't an exceptionally busy time for tourists, and I know if there are vacancies, a lot of the hospitality folks will step up until we can make permanent arrangements."

There was a tap on the door. The receptionist stood in the doorway looking uneasy. "Excuse me, Andrea," she said. "Sorry to interrupt, but the governor's office is on the phone."

As Andrea reached for her phone, Ali headed for the door. "Wait," Andrea said. "What about that box of floppies? Do you still want them?"

Ali stopped in the doorway. "Thanks, but no thanks," Ali said. "We don't need them. I thought if we searched through them, we'd find out how Irene's phone number ended up in Enid's pocket. Now, thanks to Patricia and Agnes, we already know. Good luck with Governor Dunham. See you later."

33

Ali had turned her phone ringer on silent when she finished speaking to Governor Dunham. During her talk with Patricia and Agnes, Ali had felt the buzz of at least three incoming calls and had ignored them all. Now checking the recent call list, she found two calls from B. and one from Sister Anselm. She called B. first.

"It's a fine mess you've gotten us into this time," he said. "We have two drones in the air with secure feeds going to both the Department of Public Safety and the FBI. One is keeping an eye on the landing strip until a SWAT team shows up, and the other is working its way around the perimeter of The Family's property, looking for signs of disturbances that would indicate places where anti-intrusion devices might have been installed."

"Finding any?"

"Not so far. I've also had two phone calls from someone who's apparently a close personal friend of yours—Governor Virginia Dunham. She tells me you've been appointed to be some kind of special deputy."

"The DNA trail has led to twenty human trafficking victims at last count," Ali told him. "This joint operation is being launched to forestall any attempt to smuggle one last load of girls out of the country. Governor Dunham wants to roll up the operation before that happens rather than after."

"Does The Family have any idea about what's coming?"

"I hope not."

"I'd prefer a straight-out no," B. said.

"Believe me," Ali said. "So would I."

"Even after your meeting this morning, you're still worried about Alvarado?"

"Very much so, but my opinion on that score doesn't carry much weight. The governor insists that since Colorado City is inside his jurisdiction, the sheriff and his department must be part of the program."

"If someone leaks intel to The Family, then anyone going there tonight may be walking into a trap," B. said. "Please don't tell me that you're going, too."

Obviously B. Simpson knew Ali far too well. "Don't worry," she said. "I won't be on the front lines. I'll be with the governor as part of a rearguard action. Our job will be to convince members of The Family who are interested in leaving the cult that they are free to do so. Patricia and Agnes, the two Brought Back girls David Upton walked off with last night, have agreed to come along and reason with the others. And guess what? Now, thanks to them, we have a solid lead about the identity of Sister Anselm's Kingman Jane Doe. I believe DNA comparisons will reveal her to be Anne Lowell, Enid Tower's birth mother."

"I don't understand. Why do you have to be so personally involved?" B. insisted.

"Because Sister Anselm and I are the ones who started this whole saga. We both feel responsible. That's why she took Enid to Tucson. That's why I'm going to Colorado City. Don't worry, B. I'll be safe."

"I'd rather you stayed out of it."

"I still have my bulletproof vest," Ali said. "It's in the back of the Cayenne."

The vest was a relic from her brief stint with the Yavapai County Sheriff's Department.

"Being safe would mean avoiding places where you might need a bulletproof vest," B. countered. "Still, the more I say, 'Do not go in the basement,' the more likely you are to go there anyway, so why don't I shut up and save my breath? But here's the deal. If you're going to be part of a 'rearguard action,' so am I."

Ali started to argue the point but stopped. If B. wasn't going to try to talk her out of going, she wouldn't badger him about it, either.

"Okay," she agreed. "We're to meet up at the DPS headquarters here in Flagstaff at six P.M."

"What are you planning to do between now and then?"

"Do we still have that hotel room we paid for earlier this morning?"

"We paid for it by the day not the hour. Why?"

"Because I think I'm going to go there and grab a nap. I didn't get much sleep last night. Tonight won't be much better."

"Do you still have a key?"

"I never had one to begin with."

"All right. I'll call and tell them that you're coming and that you've lost your key."

"Thanks for throwing me under the bus," Ali said with a laugh. "See you at six."

"Wait," B. said. "Don't you want to hear Stu's and my news?"

"What news?"

"He managed to collect some images from the security tapes on those ATMs at the casino in Minnesota. He ran them through a facial recognition program, and we now have a good idea of who's been lifting the money out of Betsy's accounts."

"Who?"

"Her daughter-in-law, Sandra."

Ali sighed. "I wish I could say I was surprised. Have you told Athena?"

"Nope," B. said. "This is your investigation. As far as I'm concerned, that means delivering the bad news is your job. After all, as you pointed out to me just a moment ago, you're the one with the bulletproof vest."

Ali hung up then and dialed Sister Anselm. "I think we have a possible identity on the Kingman Jane Doe."

Her announcement was greeted by a sharp intake of breath. "No! Are you serious?"

"I am. I have reason to believe Jane Doe is a girl named Anne Lowell who ran away from The Family compound when her daughter, Enid, was three or four."

"Jane Doe is Enid's mother?" Sister Anselm's shock was audible. "However did you learn all this?"

"Last night, after David Upton left the hospital, he drove up to Colorado City and rescued two of Enid's friends."

"Agnes and Patricia, the two Brought Back girls?" Sister Anselm asked. "Enid spent the whole night muttering about them, saying that they might be in danger, but I thought it was just the meds talking. I didn't pay that much attention."

"David did," Ali answered. "They're the ones who gave Enid Irene's number. They must have been worried, too, because when David showed up and offered to bring them here, they didn't hesitate."

"But how did they get Irene's number in the first place?"

"Someone from here in Flag—someone who knew Irene—offered Irene's information to Agnes when she showed up at a grocery store in Colorado City with a crop of fresh bruises showing. When Patricia and Agnes took off a few weeks later, they had Irene's number with them. They never got this far, but they kept the number. When Anne Lowell was getting ready to run away, they offered the number to her, too, but Anne said she didn't need it. She claimed someone on the Outside was helping her. Now, all these years later, Patricia and Agnes are the ones who gave Irene's decade-old information to Enid."

"You said someone on the Outside was helping Anne," Sister Anselm interjected. "Do we know who?"

"A boyfriend most likely. At the time she was married to Richard Lowell, the guy who's now in charge of the compound. She evidently had a relationship on the side with someone who wasn't her husband—maybe even with someone outside the cult—and was afraid of what her husband would do to her if he found out about the affair."

"That's why she ran away—because she was carrying another man's child?"

"So it would seem."

"Should I tell Enid? She's sleeping right now, but she's improving."

"No," Ali answered. "Don't tell her anything yet, not until we know for sure that the Kingman Jane Doe is Anne Lowell."

"How do we ascertain that," Sister Anselm asked,

"especially since the evidence box in that case has gone missing?"

"The box may be missing, but Jane Doe and her baby aren't. They're right where you left them in a common grave in Holy Name Cemetery in Kingman, Arizona."

"What are you suggesting?"

"We have a possible ID," Ali answered. "Bishop Gillespie is the one who paid Jane Doe's burial expenses. If we can't get a court order to have the body exhumed, maybe his previous involvement will give him leeway to request an exhumation."

"It's a Catholic cemetery," Sister Anselm mused. "He might be able to make that work, but won't he need a court order? How would he get one of those?"

"I'll check with my new BFF, Governor Dunham. She's busy with planning tonight's raid, but I'll ask her to look into the exhumation problem as soon as possible."

"Wait," Sister Anselm interjected. "Did you say raid? What raid?"

"How long have you been gone?" Ali asked. "It turns out a lot has happened."

She spent the next ten minutes telling Sister Anselm everything that had transpired, ending with her long conversation with Governor Dunham.

"So you'll be going to Colorado City tonight?" the nun asked when Ali finished.

"Yes."

"I wish I could be there, too," Sister Anselm said.

"But you can't. We need you to look after Enid. Let other people handle the rest of it."

Once off the line with Sister Anselm, Ali spent the next fifteen minutes on hold with the governor's office, waiting to be put through to Virginia Dunham. By then more than an hour of Ali's four-hour naptime window had evaporated, and she had yet to make it back to the Crown Inn.

"Yes, Ali," Virginia Dunham said finally. "Sorry to leave you on hold so long. I was trying to clear up the tour bus situation. For arrestees, I'm bringing along a Department of Corrections bus that's used to transport prisoners back and forth for court dates. I've also hired two motor coaches. They'll be available to handle the transportation needs of any residents who wish to leave the compound immediately. The coach company was giving my chief of staff fits about possible liability issues. I'm afraid I had to get involved and kick a few asses to make it happen."

Ali couldn't help smiling at that. Governor Dunham was definitely living up to her advance notices.

The governor listened patiently while Ali laid out the most recent wrinkle in The Family's complex history.

"It sounds to me," Governor Dunham said when Ali finished, "like you're using the Kingman Jane Doe thing to go after Sheriff Alvarado again. You really don't like the man, do you?"

"Liking has nothing to do with it," Ali asserted. "And it's not just the sheriff. There are things inside his department that don't pass the smell test, Amos Sellers being a prime example. His being a deputy and The Family's bounty hunter at the same time isn't right. In fact, it's a conflict of interest. I'm worried that Sellers may have been personally involved with what happened to Anne Lowell. He may also be the person behind the disappearance of that critical evidence box."

"Let's cross one bridge at a time," Governor Dunham cautioned. "I can see that having DNA evidence constitutes a new lead in the Kingman Jane Doe case. No matter what the fallout is from tonight's raid, I owe you an enormous debt for bringing this ungodly mess to my attention. So please let Sister Anselm know there's no need for her to involve Bishop Gillespie in this matter. My attorney general has a cold case unit that operates statewide. I'll turn this exhumation issue over to him, but not today, mind you. My whole team, including the AG, are up to their asses in alligators at the moment. You'll have to trust me on this."

"I will," Ali said. "Thank you."

"See you at six?"

"Yes, ma'am," Ali said. "Wouldn't miss it."

On the way back to the Crown Inn, Ali called Sister Anselm back and told her she could stand down from tackling Bishop Gillespie—that the exhumation problem had been handled. Once off the phone, she realized it had been a very long time since breakfast. She would have stopped by the Pancake Castle to grab a bite of lunch, but they closed at two-thirty. It was more than an hour and a half beyond that.

B. may have called ahead, but getting let back into the hotel room wasn't easy. The discrepancy between B.'s last name and Ali's was noted and required a detailed explanation. Ali could tell by the disapproving frown on the clerk's face that she was better off claiming their having married recently for the name difference. She had a feeling that the gray-haired woman behind the counter would not approve of someone who had no intention of ever changing her name.

Once Ali managed to talk her way into the room, she was sorry. The bed hadn't looked all that inviting early in the morning, and nothing had changed in the intervening hours. The faded flowered bedspread was well beyond its expiration date, and even from a distance the lumps in the worn mattress were clearly visible. Ali turned off her ringer, placed the phone on a charger, and set the alarm on her iPad for five-fifteen. Then, slipping off her shoes, she lay down on top of the covers and pulled her coat over her to keep warm.

With so many pieces about to be set in motion, she more than half expected to toss and turn. Instead, she fell asleep instantly. When the alarm went off, she awakened from a dreamless sleep, rested and ready for action.

She and Sister Anselm had started this, and now was the time to finish it.

34

While Ali slept, a text had come in from David. He said he'd been called away, but he had taken Patricia and Agnes back to their new temporary housing unit and gave Ali their address.

When Ali rang the bell at an upstairs apartment, the Patricia who answered the door was barely recognizable from the woman Ali had first seen; Agnes looked totally different, too. David Upton had done exactly as he'd been asked, and the Brought Back girls were transformed. The clothing he'd helped the two women purchase was inexpensive, off-the-rack-type fare, most likely from Target, but it worked. Dressed in jeans, sweaters, and lace-up boots, the two Brought Back girls looked like normal thirtysomething Americans rather than bewildered immigrants from a bygone era.

Somewhere along the way, both women had visited a salon, coming away with short bobs to replace the long cumbersome braids. The thing David hadn't been able to fix were the neglected and missing teeth, which were still front and center.

"I've never worn pants before or boots, either," Patricia said, looking down at her legs a little self-consciously. "Women in The Family aren't allowed."

Wearing pants and boots aren't the only things you weren't allowed to do, Ali thought. She said, "Are you ready to do this?"

Patricia nodded. "Do you think people will even recognize us?"

"They will," Ali assured her. "They may also be more than a little envious. Come on."

Patricia and Agnes donned a pair of down-filled ski jackets and followed Ali out to the car, where they had to be reminded and helped to put on their seat belts. When Ali pulled into the parking lot at the DPS headquarters on the dot of six, the place was full to the brim with unmarked patrol cars from any number of jurisdictions. That made sense. The thinking was that having an army of readily recognizable marked cars heading north would be far too noticeable. Parked on the street were two immense chartered tour buses along with the converted school bus, complete with barred windows and a Department of Corrections logo, that would be used to transport prisoners.

What Ali found most surprising was the total lack of any media presence. She wondered how an operation of this size and complexity had been organized and thus far operated completely under the media's radar. She guessed that Governor Dunham had held more than a few feet to the fire to make that happen.

Inside, the spacious lobby was packed. Cops in and out of uniform chatted amiably, making the room look like the site of a mini-law-enforcement convention. No doubt the officers' emergency response team gear was stowed in the vehicles parked outside. Faced with the crowd, Agnes and Patricia hesitated in the doorway. Ali scanned the room, recognizing a few familiar faces before finally spotting B. He stood head and shoulders above most everyone else, talking with her friend Dave Holman, a homicide detective from Yavapai County.

"This way," Ali said, urging the Brought Back girls forward and into the crowd. "I want to introduce you to my husband."

Before she had a chance, however, Virginia Dunham's voice came over a loudspeaker. "May I have your attention, please."

Looking up, Ali saw that a lectern had been set up on the landing of the marble stairway that led to the building's second story. Virginia Dunham, clad in boots, jeans, and a fringed leather jacket, took her place behind the microphone.

"For those of you who don't know me, I'm Governor Dunham," she continued, donning glasses and reading from a prepared text. "Thank you all for being here on such short notice. You're about to participate in an important operation that will take most of the night and maybe part of the morning as well. That means it'll be a long haul. As you leave here, you'll find a supply of boxed lunches next to the door. We're going to Colorado City, where I'm not expecting a welcome mat or any open restaurants. Feel free to take two boxes with you, one for now and one for breakfast. I've got a taco truck that will be on-site later, but it isn't scheduled to arrive until after the main event, which is planned for midnight.

"We have credible evidence that offenders from a group called The Family have been running a human trafficking organization. Earlier today, there were some doubters and naysayers when I began putting this op-

eration together and telling people that we needed to
act quickly to prevent another group of girls from being
shipped off into the sex trade. I want you to know that we
now have intel that corroborates my concern. The FAA
has informed my office that a charter company has filed a
flight plan for a Citation X that's due to land on The Family's private airstrip at one A.M. for a scheduled two A.M.
departure.

"By the way, the final destination on the flight plan
is listed as Caracas, Venezuela. Venezuela happens to be
a country with which the United States has no extradi-
tion treaty. If either the victims or perpetrators make it
that far, they'll be completely beyond our reach. That's
why I've put this together in such a hurry—to make sure
that doesn't happen. An FBI team is being assembled to
handle the airstrip aspect of the operation. The suspect
aircraft will be allowed to land, but it won't be taking off
again.

"Throwing the plane's scheduled arrival and departure times into the mix means that we must hold to our
midnight timetable. No delays. It's a four-hour drive
from here to there. The FBI is overseeing the entire
operation. Their command and control vehicle is on the
way already and should be in position well before the
rest of you arrive. Teams one, two, and three will depart
ten minutes after the conclusion of this briefing. Other
higher-numbered teams will launch off in groups of three
at ten-minute intervals. We can't afford to have a north-
bound traffic jam. Stick to the speed limits. Don't attract
undue attention. Maintain radio silence in case someone
is monitoring police channels. The tour buses and my
Sprinter will be the last ones to depart and head north."

Ali was struck by the new information that a plane

was scheduled to arrive at The Family's landing strip—a charter capable of long-distance flying. Her gut told her that was more than a coincidence. If The Family had scheduled a flight out for sometime tonight, wasn't it likely that they knew something was up and suspected that a raid was coming?

While Governor Dunham continued to lay out team assignments, Ali broke away from B. and Dave and wandered through the crush of cops, searching in vain for Sheriff Alvarado.

"The FBI has called down satellite surveillance of the area," Governor Dunham continued. "So far it appears that no one is behaving as though they've had any advance notice of our intended arrival. Each three-man team has been assigned a number that corresponds with the operations number assigned to each of the targeted residences. At the back of the room, just before the box-lunch table, you'll find an additional table where team captains will collect their assignments, complete with addresses, GPS coordinates, and communications routings to the C and C vehicle. Most of you will be parking outside The Family's property and hiking in to your target, so plan on using GPS technology. Teams with the greatest distances to cover on foot have been scheduled to depart first. Fortunately, preliminary surveys of the area show no sign of anti-intrusion devices. Is everyone clear on that?"

There were nods all around. When no one raised a hand to ask a question, she went on.

"As I said, every team should be in position and prepared to take action at the stroke of midnight. Launching all the raids simultaneously allows our targets the least opportunity for organized resistance, and that is something we want to avoid if at all possible. Authorization for carrying out this operation has been more flexible than it would have been otherwise due to the fact that we strongly suspect that another group of girls is in immediate danger of being transported out of the country.

"The search warrants you'll be carrying specify two things—the first authorizes the collection of family Bibles from each of the residences. The Bibles are thought to contain the names and birth dates of suspected trafficking victims. The second specifies that the men named on the warrants are required to undergo cheek swabbing for DNA testing. If they refuse or put up any resistance, they're to be taken into custody and individually transported to this location for questioning. By the time they arrive back here, we should have people from the FBI on hand to conduct the interrogations.

"You'll find that the adult women in the community aren't named on the warrants primarily because we don't have legal names on the vast majority of them. The women are welcome to provide DNA samples but cannot be compelled to do so. However, any who interfere with the execution of the warrants are to be taken into custody.

"Each family unit may have its own collection of what are commonly referred to as Brought Back girls. These are women who have attempted to run away and who have been returned to their families. These girls—women really—are kept as virtual prisoners. If any of them or any of the other women express a desire to leave the community, let them know that they will be allowed and helped to do so. We'll have transportation available to bring them back here to Flagstaff, where we're making arrangements with a local shelter to locate temporary housing.

"I'm not sure how many of you are aware of the incident at Short Creek in the early fifties. There, in an early-morning raid on a polygamous community very similar to this one, every person involved was arrested, minor children included. Many of those children were put into foster care and never reunited with their families. We're attempting to avoid that outcome here. That's why Irene's Place, a local domestic violence shelter, is assisting us in this operation. Where possible, please treat the affected women and children with kindness and consideration, although again, interference on their part in execution of the warrants will not be tolerated.

"You may have noticed that there's a notable lack of media presence here. That's a deliberate call on my part. I've asked all affected agencies and personnel to maintain strict secrecy in advance of this operation. That includes maintaining radio silence and limiting the use of cell phones. I have it on good authority that there are people out in the world who make it their business to track and listen in on cell-phone signals. Your continued cooperation in keeping this operation under wraps is essential. Now, be safe out there. Go with God."

By the time the governor removed her reading glasses and stepped away from the lectern, Ali was waiting for her at the bottom of the stairway.

"Where's Alvarado?" Ali asked without greeting. "Other department heads are here. He's not."

"You must be Ali," Governor Dunham said. "I understand there was some kind of delay in his being able to leave town—a family emergency, I believe. Sheriff Alvarado has his own Cessna. He'll be flying over to Colorado City and meeting up with us and his officers there. Since the Mohave County teams are part of the last group to leave here, he most likely won't depart Kingman for a while yet. I offered to pick him up in the Sprinter at the airport, but he told me he keeps a vehicle there that he can use as needed."

Ali shook her head. "This is a major operation due to occur in his jurisdiction. Aren't you the least bit worried about his not being here for the briefing?"

"He may have missed the briefing," Governor Dunham said, "but he'll still be there for the operation. What's your problem with all this?"

"What if he's involved?" Ali replied. "If he let Amos Sellers in on the operation, then it's a good bet The Family is in on it, too."

"Do not worry about Deputy Sellers," Governor Dunham assured her. "That situation is being handled, even as we speak. As for The Family's having been alerted? Our satellite recon shows no unusual activity anywhere inside the compound. As far as we can see, they're still entirely unaware of our intentions. Now, where are Patricia and Agnes? They'll be riding along with me in the Sprinter so they'll be on hand to intercede with other residents, but I'd like to at least meet them before then. You'll be riding with us, too?"

"I expect so," Ali said. "Agnes and Patricia are over there with my husband." As she turned in that direction, a cell phone rang behind her. She looked back at Governor Dunham, who had stopped long enough to answer.

She listened for a moment and then nodded. "Excellent. Deputy Sellers is already here in town? Great. Yes, have him wait there. Put him in an interview room and tell him you'll bring Patricia and Agnes up from the jail shortly. Once the first of the FBI interview teams arrives, we'll send one of them right over with the Amos Sellers warrants in hand."

Ali was astonished. "Deputy Sellers is here in Flagstaff? And what's this about Patricia and Agnes being in jail? I already told you. They're right over there."

"I heeded your earlier warning about Deputy Sellers possibly compromising the operation," Governor Dunham said, "so I took steps to remove him from the board by simply appealing to his greed. Knowing his bounty-hunter function, I took the liberty of having my chief of staff, Bill Witherspoon, pass along a phony tip about Agnes and Patricia's supposed whereabouts. Bill told Deputy Sellers that the two runaways had been arrested here in town and charged with shoplifting. He was led to believe that they were being held by the Flagstaff PD and needed someone to post their bail.

"That call didn't exactly rise to the level of filing a false police report, but it was close, uncomfortably close. Bill was still worried about it, right up until Sellers took the bait. He was on his way here in two shakes of a lamb's tail, hotfooting it out of Colorado City in his personal vehicle rather than in a patrol car. That's a pretty good indicator that he wasn't traveling in any official capacity. As of right now he's cooling his heels in an interview room at the Flagstaff PD. I trust that puts at least some of your concerns about him to rest. Now, if there's nothing else . . ."

"There is," Ali said. "I'd like to talk to him."

"To Deputy Sellers? Why?"

"Kingman Jane Doe," Ali answered. "Amos Sellers was already The Family's enforcer back when Anne Lowell ran away. At the time there were rumors that the baby Anne was carrying didn't belong to her husband. Supposedly she had a boyfriend on the Outside who was going to help her. Instead, we believe both she and her baby ended up dead. Of all the people in The Family, Amos was more Outside than in. What if he did both—fathered the baby and then killed Anne to cover it up?"

The governor thought about it. "Anything he tells you won't be admissible in a court of law, you know," Governor Dunham warned, "but it might answer a lot of questions. You're saying what you're interested in has nothing to do with tonight's operation?"

"Nothing."

Governor Dunham shrugged. "Go ahead, then. Since you're not a cop, I don't see any harm in asking. Just be back here in plenty of time for us to head north."

Ali hurried back to where Patricia, Agnes, and B. had been joined by Andrea Rogers. "The governor says we'll be departing in a little over an hour. If you don't mind, Patricia and Agnes, B. and I will leave you here with Andrea long enough for us to run an errand."

"What kind of errand?" B. asked, dutifully following behind as Ali threaded her way through the still packed room.

"We're going to go talk to Amos Sellers. He's currently in an interview room at the local cop shop."

"He's one of the bad guys, isn't he? Won't talking to him be dangerous?"

"No," Ali assured him. "His weapons will be locked away in a gun locker, and so will mine."

"All right, then," B. said. "Let's do it."

The trip from the DPS headquarters to the Flagstaff PD took seven of the sixty minutes Ali had allowed herself. Once inside the building, she was surprised to learn she and B. were both expected. Governor Dunham had called ahead and cleared the way. Leaving B. and a uniformed officer to watch through the two-way mirror, Ali entered the interview room alone.

Amos Sellers rose to his feet. "What are you doing here?" he demanded. "I was expecting a cop. He's supposed to be bringing two prisoners over from the jail so I can post their bail and take them back home."

"They're not coming," Ali said. "They've already been released."

"Then I'm leaving, too." He started for the door.

"No, you're not," Ali said. "That door is locked. Sit down."

"Wait a minute," Sellers said. "You're not a cop. You can't order me around."

"Sit," she said. "An FBI team is on its way to interview you."

"Interview me?" Sellers asked, sinking back down on his chair. "About what?"

"Human trafficking. About how The Family's Not Chosens are routinely shipped out of the country and end up being sold as sex slaves all over the world."

"That's not possible," Amos insisted. "The Not Chosens go to other families, other homes."

"Who says?"

"Bishop Lowell."

"And you believe him?"

"Why wouldn't I?"

"Then you're a lot dumber than I thought," Ali said. She glanced at her watch. The minutes were ticking by.

"A team from the FBI is due here any minute to discuss that with you. Right now, though, I'd like you to tell me about Anne Lowell."

Hearing the name caused a subtle change in Amos Sellers's features. His jaw tightened. His eyes narrowed. "What about her?"

"You tell me."

He shrugged. "She was married to Bishop Lowell at one time, but she ran off. It happened a long time ago. Nobody ever heard from her again."

"That long time happens to be twelve years," Ali corrected. "My understanding is that you were sent out to get her. That's your job, isn't it—to bring The Family's runaways back home?"

"I never found Anne Lowell," he answered. "Like I said, she ran off and never came back."

"She never came back because she's dead."

Amos reacted to that bit of news with a visible tremor, as though a jolt of electricity had passed through his body.

"How? When?"

"About the time she left home presumably," Ali said. "She was found badly beaten but still alive in the desert outside of Kingman. She was hospitalized but didn't survive. Neither did her baby. They were buried together in a common, unmarked grave and have only just now been identified."

"I never knew she was dead," Amos said, shaking his head.

"Didn't you?" Ali countered. "I'm wondering if it's possible that you were the father of that baby. Anne ran away. You went after her, found her, and decided to kill her rather than bring her back home."

"I didn't," Amos insisted. "I wasn't the father of her baby, and I didn't kill her, either."

Ali shrugged. "Maybe you know who did, then. I've heard rumors that Anne had a boyfriend on the Outside. That wouldn't have gone over well with a cuckolded husband who was about to move up into a leadership role in The Family's hierarchy. Maybe you caught Anne, handed her over to her irate spouse, and let him do the job himself."

"I'm telling you, Richard Lowell didn't kill Annie, and neither did I. I had no idea she was dead until just now when you told me."

"You called her Annie a moment ago," Ali observed. "Annie, not Anne. Were the two of you friends?"

There was a long pause before Amos answered. "Yes," he said finally, "we were. When I was a little kid, I came down with pneumonia and was really sick. Annie was the one who took care of me instead of my mother. After that the two of us became friends. We stayed friends when we were older, even though we weren't supposed to be. That's why I helped her."

"Helped her how?"

"To get away. As far as The Family is concerned, adultery is a serious offense. If Bishop Lowell had found out that the baby wasn't his, he would have been the one to cast the first stone."

Ali felt a chill down her spine. "Literally?"

Amos nodded. "I didn't want Annie to die. I knew that, as soon as she went missing, I'd be the one sent to retrieve her. When I drove away to go look for her, nobody had any idea that she was hidden in the trunk of my car."

"Where did you take her?"

"To Kingman," Amos said. "To meet up with her boyfriend. The last thing she said to me when she got out of my car and into his was that he loved her and was going to take good care of her. She believed it, and I didn't have any reason not to believe it, either."

"You saw the boyfriend?"

Amos nodded.

"He was someone you knew?"

Amos nodded again.

"So maybe the boyfriend's the one who killed her."

"I asked him about her once, years later. He said she'd had the baby—a little girl—and that they had moved to someplace in California—San Diego, maybe. He said they were both fine."

"But they weren't," Ali added.

Another nod, this one with a resigned inevitability about it.

"Tell me about the boyfriend," Ali said.

"He was just a deputy back then, stuck in Colorado City for a couple weeks at a time. I don't know exactly how they met, but they did."

"Was the boyfriend married?" Ali asked.

"Yes."

During the lengthening silence, Amos Sellers visibly struggled to come to grips with the idea that Annie had been both betrayed and murdered. Meanwhile, Ali began to connect the dots. She knew by Sheriff Alvarado's own admission that he had once done patrol duty in Colorado City. He was already married back then. For a man with ambitions of rising in the department, having a pregnant girlfriend show up in town would have blown his world apart. No wonder that critical evidence box about the Kingman Jane Doe homicide had disappeared. With it gone, Sheriff Daniel Alvarado must have figured he was in the clear.

Noticing that Amos Sellers had so far avoided mentioning the boyfriend by name, Ali did so herself. "Is that how you ended up being a deputy—because you had something on Sheriff Alvarado?"

It was pure bluff, but it worked.

"I didn't blackmail him, if that's what you mean," Amos declared, clenching his fists and laying them on the tabletop. "A year or two later, he put in a good word for me is all, but I never knew he killed her. I never knew she was dead. Like I told you, she was kind to me. That's the thing about Annie—she was kind to everybody, not just me."

Ali watched in amazement as two tears leaked out of Amos's eyes and coursed down his cheeks. She was even more surprised to find herself placing a comforting hand on one of his knotted fists. "You thought you were saving her," she said quietly. "You had no way of knowing that you were handing her over to a killer."

Amos bit his lip. "No," he agreed. "I didn't."

"We're just talking here," Ali said. "There's nothing official about this conversation, one way or the other, but let me ask you this. If you were called upon to do so, would you agree to testify to what you just told me?"

Amos Sellers nodded. "Yes, I would," he said softly. "Anne Lowell was my friend. He told me she was fine."

As Ali stood up to leave, Amos Sellers buried his head in both his hands and wept. She touched his shoulder with her hand as she went past.

"Sorry," she murmured, before buzzing to be let out. "Sorry for all concerned."

35

That was a bombshell," B. said as Ali exited the interview room. He followed her back out to the evidence locker, where she retrieved her Glock. "What are you going to do about it?"

"Nothing for right now," she told him. "Let's deal with one crisis at a time."

Nodding, B. glanced at his watch. "Catching up with Governor Dunham's Sprinter is going to be tight. I was planning on driving up on my own, but when I spoke to Andrea, she told me that I've now been officially invited to join the governor's 'rearguard' action. Governor Dunham is of the opinion that having a couple of males from the Outside along for the ride might be a good idea. Bill Witherspoon, her chief of staff, will be there, and so will I."

As they exited the building, two men in suits were entering. Everything about the new arrivals said FBI, but there was no time to stop and chat. By the time Ali and B. drove back to the DPS parking lot, Virginia Dunham's Sprinter along with the two chartered buses were the only vehicles left behind. Ali paused long enough to grab her

Kevlar vest from the back of the Cayenne before climbing aboard the Sprinter. Although Ali took the vest with her, with a four-hour drive between then and the scheduled engagement, she didn't bother putting it on immediately.

"It's about time," Governor Dunham grumbled, motioning them into the last two seats. "We were about to leave without you."

The interior of the Sprinter had been converted into something that reminded Ali of the cabin of a small jet. It had four captain's chairs around a polished-wood fold-away table. There was a long sofa of bench seating along one wall. The tiny galley at the front of the vehicle, just behind the cab, came complete with a granite countertop and backsplash. A door to the right of that opened and closed, shutting off the cab and allowing people in the cabin complete privacy. At the opposite end of the vehicle were two doors. One apparently led to a traveling restroom and the other to a baggage compartment and rear exit. With plenty of electrical outlets and a built-in printer, the vehicle was nothing short of a traveling office well suited for long official road trips.

The Sprinter's interior may have been luxury itself, but the mood of the occupants was less than cheerful. Andrea Rogers, along with Patricia and Agnes, had claimed three of the four spots on the sofa. Concerned about what awaited them back home, the Brought Back girls huddled together in subdued silence. The governor was seated in one of the four captain's chairs with her chief of staff at her side. It wasn't until after Ali and B. had settled into the two opposing seats that they were properly introduced to Bill Witherspoon.

"Was the interview successful?" Governor Dunham asked.

"Yes," Ali said.

"Anything I need to know?"

Ali took a deep breath. "Amos Sellers is under the impression that Danny Alvarado was the father of Anne Lowell's baby. They must have gotten together back when Alvarado was a deputy and pulling occasional patrol duty in Colorado City. Amos and Anne were friends. When she got knocked up by someone who wasn't her husband, she was desperate to get away. In The Family adultery is a capital offense, punishable by stoning."

"Stoning?" Governor Dunham asked. "Seriously?"

Ali nodded. "Unfortunately, yes. Amos says that when Anne came to him for help, he's the one who helped her get away. He claims he took her as far as Kingman and dropped her off with her boyfriend."

"He mentioned Sheriff Alvarado by name?"

"Yes. The sheriff told Amos later that Anne had her baby—a girl—and had moved on to San Diego, where, presumably, she and her baby were hunky-dory and living happily ever after."

"Except they weren't," Governor Dunham said grimly. "They weren't at all."

A long silence settled over the vehicle while the governor processed this latest revelation.

"All right, then," Virginia Dunham said at last, "there's nothing to be done about any of this right now. We'll handle it later. First things first. At the moment, there's been another development. Satellite imaging shows lots of back-and-forth movement between the various residences, the landing strip, and the church up at The Encampment. Because we don't have any idea of what's normal around there, the movements may be just that— normal. Bill here, on the other hand, shares your concern,

Ali, that our targets may have somehow become aware of our intentions. My decision is that we move forward with the operation regardless. If something bad happens, I'm prepared to accept full responsibility."

Not full, Ali thought. *Some of that responsibility will be Sister Anselm's and mine.*

The Sprinter was moving steadily northward through the night. "All right," Governor Dunham said, resuming control. "As of now, we're going dark. Please turn off all electronic devices, iPads and cell phones included. We won't light them up again until after we're in position and the operation is under way. At that point, maintaining secrecy will no longer be an issue."

Knowing how much information could be gleaned from tracking electronic devices, Ali and B. both complied without protest, although Ali wished she'd had time to call Leland and let him know a little about the situation before the no-communication edict went into effect.

"Now," Governor Dunham said, switching seamlessly from command mode to hostess mode, "how about some dinner? The box lunches aren't exactly gourmet fare, but they're better than going hungry. They're in the fridge drawers under the coffee dispenser."

B., seated on the aisle, hopped up and retrieved two of the lunches and a pair of chilled sodas as well. By now, it had been a very, very long time since breakfast. Ali didn't pause before tearing into hers. Bologna had never been high on her list of preferred sandwich fillings, but since she was famished, that dry sandwich was nothing short of divine. Ditto for the small bag of chips and tiny container of mandarin orange slices tucked into one corner of the box.

When her lunch was gone, Ali wrapped herself in a blanket that had been thoughtfully folded over the back of her chair. As the Sprinter rumbled north through the night, Ali should have been wide awake and worrying about what awaited them at the end of the road. Instead, once the carbs from the box lunch were absorbed into her system, she was out like a light. Only when the van began to slow more than three hours later did she return to her senses. B. continued dozing and didn't wake up completely until the van came to a complete stop.

Peering out through the window, Ali discovered that a full moon had lit up the high desert landscape. The van was parked on a wide spot next to the paved roadway in a graveled area lined by an array of mailboxes. Across the highway, a narrow dirt road led off into the distance. Here and there silvery patches of unmelted snow glimmered in the moonlight.

The lights in the cabin had been dimmed, but a glance at the luminous dial on her watch told Ali that it was twenty past eleven. The three-hour fifty-seven-minute drive had taken just that. As Ali settled in for an interminable forty-minute wait, B. reached out to take her hand and squeezed it reassuringly. She squeezed back. She was glad to have him here with her; glad that however this turned out—for good or ill—they were in it together.

The door between the cabin and the cab popped open, and the driver appeared in the doorway. "Going outside to stretch my legs, ma'am," he said to Governor Dunham.

"Don't be too long," she warned him.

Ali had carried her vest onto the Sprinter when she boarded and had dropped it on the floor next to her seat.

Picking it up, she turned to the governor. "I could use a pit stop, too."

"Good idea," Governor Dunham said, gesturing toward the left-hand door at the rear. "Help yourself."

Slipping her vest on as she went, Ali made for the restroom. She had finished what she needed to do and was washing her hands in the tiny sink when a door somewhere behind her slammed open with such force that the whole vehicle shuddered.

"Hands where I can see them!" an unseen but clearly angry male voice shouted. "Now."

Ali froze where she was. With the restroom door shut, she could hear what was going on out in the cabin but she couldn't see it. Those chilling words told her that an armed assailant had somehow disabled the driver, stormed aboard the vehicle, and now was holding the others hostage. Drawing her Glock out of her holster, Ali stood in front of the flimsy pocket door, holding her breath and waiting for it to slam open, too. It didn't.

"Who are you?" Governor Dunham was speaking. "What do you want?"

"I think you know who I am. The name's Lowell. I'm the guy you're after," the man replied. "The guy outside was armed, so I'm guessing some of you are, too. Hand them over—weapons and cell phones. All of them. You"—he addressed one of them—"take that box and gather 'em up."

Ali felt the Sprinter wobble slightly. She had no idea which member of the group had stood up in response to that spoken command, but someone had. Holding her breath, Ali waited, realizing eventually that Lowell had no idea that someone else was on board the vehicle. As long as Ali did nothing to give away her presence, she was relatively safe. She also understood that she was the court of last resort for all six of the people being held prisoner on the other side of that all-too-insubstantial door.

"Hey," Lowell was saying. "Someone with two cell phones and a revolver in her purse. Give me that gun. It could come in handy. A man can't have too many guns."

Ali knew that the Brought Back girls wouldn't have been armed, and she doubted that Andrea Rogers would have been, either. That meant that in addition to Ali, only Governor Dunham had been carrying a weapon.

"I was planning on hiking the whole way, and then I saw this rig," Lowell continued. "At first I thought you were just a bunch of stupid campers, spending the night, but when I found out the driver was armed and carrying a security-detail badge, I realized this has to be some kind of command vehicle. So I would guess the lady with the gun is the one running the show?"

"More or less," the governor said. "My name's Governor Virginia Dunham. I'm one of the people running the show, Mr. Lowell, but only one of them. There are plenty of others. It's over, Mr. Lowell. This is not going to end well for anyone. Give it up."

"I'm supposed to surrender on your say-so? Are you nuts? Who's the one holding the weapons here?"

Ali glanced at her watch. It was just now twenty-five minutes past the hour. Thirty-five minutes to go. Moving slowly, she put her own weapon down long enough to ease her cell phone out of her pocket. An emergency 911 call this close to zero hour might put the entire joint operation in jeopardy, but she needed to alert someone about their dire situation. Instead, praying that Stuart Ramey was still up and working, she forced her trembling fingers to type a text:

> EMERGENCY. DO NOT REPLY OR CALL. HELD
> HOSTAGE IN SPRINTER BY LOWELL. RECORD
> WHAT'S SAID. NOTIFY DPS. SEND HELP. DO NOT USE
> REGULAR 911 CHANNELS.

Then she dialed Stuart's number. He answered after half a ring.

"Ali, I got your text. What's up? How can I help?"

At the sound of his voice, Ali's knees almost buckled out of sheer gratitude. Instead of replying verbally, Ali turned the call volume to max. Then she sent another text:

> FOLLOW SIGNAL. LOWELL ARMED AND
> DANGEROUS. ACTING ALONE, I THINK. GOV'S
> DRIVER MUST BE DOWN. SIX HOSTAGES, INCLUDING
> GOV AND B.

Ali allowed herself a deep breath. If Lowell ended up gunning them all down, Stuart would at least be able to provide an audible recording of what had happened.

"If you have a quarrel with anyone, Mr. Lowell," Governor Dunham said, "it's with me. Let the others go."

"Nobody's leaving," Lowell replied. "Everybody stays."

Ali's opinion of Governor Dunham moved up several notches. Despite having a gun pointed in her direction, she sounded poised and utterly calm.

Ali hurriedly sent Stuart another text:

> ARE YOU HEARING ALL THIS?

Stuart's response was almost instantaneous.

> LOUD AND CLEAR

So was Ali's.

STAY WITH US.

Ali stuffed the cell phone into her bra and picked up her weapon in time to hear more of what was happening beyond the door. She heard Lowell's sudden change of focus when he finally either noticed or recognized the Brought Back girls.

"You two are behind all this, aren't you? I should have known you'd be involved. As soon as Amos told me that you'd run off, I knew there'd be trouble. Whatever happens, it's all your fault."

"You're evil," Ali heard Patricia mutter.

"You'll never get away with this," Agnes added.

"Right," Lowell said. "Another station heard from. Who says I won't get away with it? Out of the pigpen less than a day and already you've cut off your hair and started wearing godless clothing. Just because you're wearing pants now, young lady, what makes you think I'll listen to you? You may have forgotten your position in the world, but I haven't. Besides, you and Patricia there won't be around to cause trouble for much longer. Now shut the hell up."

"Leave them be," Governor Dunham said.

"You shut the hell up, too," Lowell ordered again. "In my world, women speak only when spoken to."

"Wait a minute," Bill Witherspoon interjected. "You can't talk to her that way. She's the governor of Arizona!"

"Watch me," Lowell replied. "Just watch me."

With the phone put away, Ali had the Glock back in her hand. The earlier trembling that had afflicted her texting ability had diminished, but she had no idea what to do. She was painfully aware that, with the door shut, she was blind to what was going on just beyond the door. She had no idea where Lowell was standing or what kind of weapon he had in hand. Most likely some kind of automatic. How else could he assume he'd be able to hold six people at bay and impel them to do his bidding?

As for Ali, if she emerged from the bathroom to face him, she'd most likely be walking directly into his line of fire. She had confidence in her shooting ability, but with him looking straight at her, he'd have the drop on her. In addition, in the close confines of the cabin, any stray shots risked the possibility of hitting the marble backsplash and ricocheting into the very people Ali was hoping to save.

"Who are you?" Lowell demanded.

Ali was riveted when she heard her husband's answer. "I'm B.—B. Simpson."

"Well, Mr. Simpson, the driver of this vehicle seems to be otherwise occupied. Can you drive this thing?"

"I suppose."

"Do it, then," Lowell ordered. "Go up front and get us the hell out of here."

B. rose and headed toward the cab. "Where are we going?" he asked.

"Leave the connecting door open. I'll give you directions as we go, but if you try anything funny, like running us into a tree or a fence post or a utility pole, I'll put a hole the size of a dinner plate in the middle of the governor's chest. Got it?"

"Got it," B. replied.

The body of the Sprinter shifted as B. moved forward. Ali imagined Richard Lowell sitting with his weapon still trained on Virginia Dunham's chest. With B. in the cab, he was somewhat protected from bullets shot from Richard Lowell's weapon but not from Ali's.

"You don't need the rest of these people," Governor Dunham asserted once again. "Let the others go."

"Like I said, you don't get to tell me what to do."

A few seconds later, B. shifted the idling Sprinter out of neutral. Ali shifted her stance, leaning against the wall for support lest some sudden jerk or bump betray her presence. They lurched onto the pavement and, after a moment, were speeding in what seemed to Ali to be a northerly direction. For a time no voices came from the cabin. The only sound was the rumble of moving tires on pavement.

"Where are we going?" Governor Dunham asked several minutes later. "What are your intentions?"

"Where I'm going is none of your business, but my intention is to use you and the others as an insurance policy to get me there." After a pause Lowell continued, "Hey, driver. Take the next right and stop at the security gate. After we drive through, the gate will close automatically."

"What's your name?" Ali heard Lowell ask.

"Bill," the chief of staff answered. "Bill Witherspoon."

"Okay, here's the deal. When we stop, you hop out and key in the code 1556. Come right back once the gate opens or somebody dies."

The vehicle slowed. When it came to a stop, Ali felt a slight wobbling as someone moved through the vehicle. A door opened. As Witherspoon's two-hundred-plus pounds exited the vehicle, it shifted slightly when the load lightened. Now there were only four hostages left in the cabin. That meant fewer people in immediate danger, but still plenty of people at risk. The van moved forward and stopped again. For a moment, Ali hoped Bill Witherspoon would take advantage of being outside and make a run for it, but he did not. The vehicle shifted again as the chief of staff returned, pulling the door shut behind him.

"Go to the third hangar on the right," Lowell ordered.

Standing in the dark, it was only then that Ali realized they had come to an airport of some kind. Since they had only just pulled off the paved highway, she doubted that it was the landing strip at the top of The Encampment. It had to be an airport somewhere else, but where? Colorado City, maybe?

The Sprinter was moving forward when she heard Lowell's voice again. He sounded disturbed. Upset.

"Who the hell would be coming in at this time of night?" Lowell demanded. "Hey, driver. Get us out of sight, quick. Pull into the slot between the second and third hangars and douse the lights. Do it now! As soon as that plane lands and the pilot goes away, let me know."

Ali was gratified to hear Lowell sounding uneasy, both surprised and rattled. Wherever they were, he hadn't anticipated having unexpected company. Ali knew that the runway at The Encampment was large enough to accommodate a small jet, but she had a hard time imagining that Colorado City boasted another nearby airport with runways long enough to handle a Citation X.

And what about the plane that was landing? This close to zero hour Ali felt there was a good chance the new arrival might be Sheriff Danny Alvarado, but was he there as a friend or an enemy? Was he coming to support his officers or to help Richard Lowell make good his escape?

Ali glanced at her watch for at least the hundredth time. Eleven forty-five. Twenty minutes had elapsed since the Sprinter had first pulled off the paved highway onto the shoulder. Less than that since Ali had sent her text to Stuart. Was that enough time for him to have summoned help?

The Sprinter stopped again and sat idling when Ali heard Governor Dunham speak again. "What about that other plane, Mr. Lowell?" she asked. "What about the jet that's due to land on your private airstrip and then head off for Caracas?"

"I diverted it," he answered. "I don't know where you found that group of Keystone Kops pretending to be a SWAT team, but I can tell you for sure—they're a bunch of useless city-slicker losers. City people always forget that kicking up dust out here in the desert is a dead give-away.

"When they started bringing in their vehicles and equipment earlier this afternoon, those plumes of dust were as plain as the nose on my face. They told me something wasn't right, so I went up and had a look-see. They're parked just out of sight and waiting for that flight to come in. Sorry to disappoint. There won't be a plane showing up tonight, but there'll be plenty of excitement to keep them occupied. When that tankful of Jet-A goes up, those guys will get their money's worth."

His last words set Ali's heart pounding. Lowell had convinced some poor sap to set fire to a tank of aviation fuel?

"What tankful of Jet-A?" Governor Dunham demanded. "Are you saying you have aviation fuel stored on your property and you're going to set it on fire?"

"Not me, personally," Richard Lowell said. "Robbie Miller's in charge of that operation and happy as a clam about it, too. I gave him a stick of dynamite and some matches and told him exactly what to do—wait for my phone call. When I give the word, he's to light the fuse and toss the dynamite in a big puddle of fuel that has somehow leaked out onto the ground."

"You can't make Robbie do something like that!" Patricia shrieked at him. "You can't!"

The Sprinter rocked back and forth momentarily as if some kind of struggle was occurring out in the cabin.

"Sit back down, bitch!" Lowell ordered. "One more outburst from you and you're a goner."

Another rocking motion shivered through the rig. It was easy for Ali to imagine someone, Andrea Rogers most likely, bodily restraining Patricia and returning her to her seat, but the woman's outrage was still audible.

"You gave Robbie dynamite?" she demanded. "He has no idea how things like that work. What if he dies?"

Even though Ali was still focused on the conversation, the blindness of being in that locked, darkened room had fine-tuned her other senses. Because she was still leaning against the interior door, she felt another slight tremor in the vehicle and another slight shift—as though someone had once more exited the van. Holding her breath, she listened to see if anyone else had noticed.

"If he dies, he dies," Lowell replied disdainfully. "As for making him do it? Don't be silly. I don't have to *make* that dimwit kid do anything. He volunteered. Everybody knows how much Robbie loves fire. He's followed me around like a puppy for years. It's about time he made himself useful. He may be dumb as a stump, but he'll follow orders, and once he sets that Jet-A on fire, your troop of SWAT guys will be so busy trying to rescue those girls that . . ."

Ali's heart constricted in her chest. Governor Dunham must have been on the same wavelength.

"What girls?"

"The girls your guys think are heading out on that plane with me tonight," Lowell crowed proudly, reveling in the idea that he had somehow managed to outwit everyone. "I figured the Brought Back girls wouldn't have gotten away all on their own, and that told me it was time to get out. A load of girls was due to leave tonight, anyway. I decided to turn that full load into a partial. Couldn't do a full one with me on board the same plane, but there was no sense leaving all that money on the table."

Governor Dunham had called that shot completely. A load of Not Chosens had indeed been set to go out tonight. Now instead of being shipped off into the sex trade, it sounded as though they were doomed to be burned alive.

"Where are they?" the governor demanded urgently. "Where?"

"In a locked room at the back of the hangar. I handled the deliveries myself over the last several hours, just to give the SWAT team something to watch while they were waiting. When I boogied out the side door of the hangar, I left my car parked inside. As far as they're concerned, I'm there, too. By the time the fire cools down enough to sort through the bodies, they'll be astonished to learn I'm not part of either group. By then, it'll be too late and I'll be long gone."

"Wait," Governor Dunham said. "Are you saying other people are dead, too? Who?"

"Does it matter? Now tell me, isn't your little party due to start real soon?" He paused and chuckled. "That's another thing. For this kind of operation, you need people who know a thing or two about being out in the boonies.

You need people smart enough to walk through the wilderness without waking the dead. I heard your guys bumbling around in the dark and talking on my way down. I heard enough to know that midnight's the witching hour—five minutes from now. Then all hell breaks loose." There was another pause before he added, "Hey, driver. Is the pilot of that other plane out of here yet?"

They all waited for B.'s response. None was forthcoming.

"Driver?" Lowell called again. "Hey, what's going on up there?"

Half sick with relief, Ali realized B. must have somehow managed to exit the vehicle without attracting any attention.

"You're coming with me," Lowell growled ominously. "Now."

"Leave her be," Witherspoon objected. That was followed by the distinct sound of something hard striking flesh, a loud groan, and a sickening thump as someone crumpled to the floor.

"Come on now, Gov. Move it. You try anything and this AK-47 is going to cut you into tiny little pieces."

That's what Lowell was wielding—an AK-47? And the only weapon Ali had available was a measly Glock? Once again, Ali felt a shifting of the vehicle, as though several people were moving around at once. A front passenger door clicked open. That could only mean that Lowell and Governor Dunham were both up front, on the far side of the partition between the cab and the cabin. If Ali was going to do anything about this—and she wasn't sure what—now was the time to do it.

Holding her breath and with the Glock in hand, Ali cracked the bathroom door open and emerged into the

cabin. Andrea was on her knees, trying to help Bill Witherspoon as he struggled to his feet. Agnes and Patricia
seemed rooted to their seats.

"Everybody out," Ali hissed in an urgent whisper,
opening the door to the luggage compartment and beckoning them toward it. "Go out the back door and make a
run for it."

They did it at once. Bill Witherspoon was the last
of the four to disappear through the opening. Ali moved
forward through the cabin. She had just ducked into the
galley alcove next to the doorway into the cab as an ear-
splitting blast of automatic gunfire filled the air.

For a moment, Ali was rendered completely deaf. Her
hearing was starting to return when she heard another
shot—a single one this time—followed a moment later
by another. Then the air filled with the sound of a woman
screaming. "Help me, please," Governor Dunham cried.
"Please help me. I've been shot."

Ali started to step forward to do just that—to go
help—but then the Sprinter shifted again. She knew
what that meant. Someone had just climbed back inside,
and she thought she knew who. Freezing in her hiding
place, she pulled herself back into the kitchen alcove.
She knew Richard Lowell. She had seen him at the hospital when he had come there trying to lay claim to Enid.
But what if B. was the first one to come through the
door? Or what if someone else did?

When a man wearing a sheepskin jacket suddenly
barreled through the doorway, Ali knew it was Richard
Lowell. He appeared to be injured. He held an AK-47 in
his left hand while his right hand and arm hung uselessly
at his side. Intent on something else, he darted past Ali
without a glance in her direction. When he reached the

captain's chairs, he slammed his weapon down on the tabletop.

His back was turned to Ali. She could see a bright red spot leaking through his jacket and blossoming into a fist-sized stain just below his shoulder. Richard Lowell had been shot and was bleeding profusely. Grunting in pain, he struggled to pull something out of his jacket pocket. Only when Ali saw the phone did she realize what he planned to do. Richard Lowell may have been shot, bleeding, and maybe even dying, but he was intent on going out with a bang—by making the phone call and setting Robbie and the airplane hangar on fire.

It took a second or two, but finally Lowell had the phone clenched in his left hand and was clumsily attempting to operate it with his thumb. Only then did Ali step up behind him.

"Drop it!" she ordered. "Drop it now."

"You wouldn't shoot me, would you?" he panted.

"Try me," Ali said.

Richard Lowell was not a tall man. Looking over his bloodied shoulder, Ali could see the face of the phone. His thumb was already poised over the top number on his list of recent calls when Ali did what she had to do. She simply pulled the trigger.

Richard Lowell slumped to the floor. The phone flew out of his hand and disappeared under one of the seats. Without the phone, Ali had no way of knowing if he'd managed to complete the call or not. Looking at the man's suddenly still body and realizing that she'd shot him full in the middle of the back, Ali didn't need to check to see if he was dead. She already knew.

"Drop your weapon and get on the ground!" someone ordered.

Ali turned to see a man in full SWAT regalia appear in the rear door opening, the one through which Witherspoon and the others had exited. As he moved toward her, weapon held at the ready, Ali complied. She laid the Glock on the galley's counter and dropped to the floor.

"You need to check on Governor Dunham," she urged as the officer fastened her wrists behind her with a pair of cuffs. "She's outside the cab somewhere. She's been shot."

36

What followed was a forty-five-minute period of total chaos. For most of that time, Ali sat in one of the captain's chairs with her hands cuffed behind her back and with Richard Lowell's lifeless body on the floor at her feet. Through the window next to her Ali watched as a group of EMTs swarmed toward the Sprinter and then left again on the run, pushing a gurney that they loaded into a medevac helicopter. It had arrived on the scene so promptly that Ali theorized that it had most likely been summoned by Governor Dunham herself and then held in reserve somewhere nearby, awaiting any possible casualties from the upcoming joint operation.

The helicopter had barely taken off when a grim-faced FBI agent who introduced himself as Agent Malovich stepped into the van. The first thing he did was remove Ali's cuffs. After that, he popped her Glock into an evidence bag. That was a mixed message. Ali couldn't tell if she was in the clear or not.

"Is the governor going to be all right?" she asked.

He shook his head. "Too soon to tell. There was a struggle over a revolver the guy had tucked in his pants.

Governor Dunham went for it, and so did he. Looks like she got him in the shoulder but ended up shooting herself in the leg. We put on a tourniquet before the EMTs even got here, but I don't know if they'll be able to save the leg. Now, how about if you tell me what went on here."

"Do I need a lawyer? Are you going to read me my rights?"

"No Miranda warning, and you don't need a lawyer. We already talked to the people outside—three women and a man. According to them, this guy was armed, dangerous, and badly in need of being put down. They all say you're a hero."

"First tell me about my husband," Ali insisted. "He got out of the van earlier. He's out there somewhere. With all the gunfire, I'm worried about him. Is he all right?"

"B. Simpson? Let's just say he's not hurt, but he's not all right, either. The other guy's dead. Your husband says it's his fault."

"What other guy?"

"The county sheriff—a guy named Alvarado. He tried to bluff Lowell, pretended the place was surrounded even though his backup was minutes away. Lowell unloaded on him with his AK-47. Cut the poor guy to pieces."

"B. doesn't even own a weapon. How can it be his fault?"

"You'll need to ask him about that, but later. He's being interviewed now, too. So please, tell me what went on. I'm the first person you're talking to about all this, and I certainly won't be the last. Do you mind telling me what happened here?"

"What about the hangar? Did it burn down or not?"

"No, ma'am," Malovich said. "We located the kid with

the dynamite and the cell phone. He was still waiting for orders to set it off."

Ali closed her eyes in gratitude. She had pulled the trigger in time. Richard Lowell hadn't managed to complete the call.

It didn't take long for her to tell the story of how, with Ali in the restroom, Lowell had broken into the Sprinter and taken its passengers hostage. Malovich listened but without taking notes. Knowing she'd be interviewed in far greater detail later when what she said was being recorded, Ali hit the high spots of what had happened, ending with her ordering Lowell to drop the phone and pulling the trigger when he didn't.

"Okay," Agent Malovich said at last. "All that jibes with what everyone else is saying. You can go now. You should probably go check on your husband. He's in the hangar right next door, and he's pretty shaken up. Oh, and you'll have to go out the back way and walk around to hangar number one. The space between two and three is an active crime scene."

It was three o'clock in the morning as Ali made her way to hangar number one. On the far side of number two she could see the generator-powered floodlights that had been set up around the crime scene. She didn't need to go there. Remembering visiting Sheriff Alvarado and with him totally at ease in his office hours earlier on the previous day, there was nothing she wanted to see.

She found B. sitting just inside the door to the hangar, hunched into a plastic lawn chair, with his face buried in his hands.

"Sorry," she murmured, walking up to him and laying a comforting hand on his shoulder. "So much for being part of the out-of-harm's-way 'rear guard.'"

B. nodded without looking up. "I signaled with the headlights as he was taxiing to his tie-down. Three shorts, three longs, three shorts—SOS. Sheriff Alvarado saw the signal and came right over to me, as soon as he got out of his plane.

"I told him what was going on and that the guy was inside, holding hostages and threatening to kill them. By then Alvarado knew the SWAT team was coming, but they were still two minutes out. He told me he wanted to get closer so he'd be able to give his guys a better idea of what was going on inside the Sprinter. That's when the door opened. Lowell came out, holding Governor Dunham in front of him. Alvarado was caught out in the open. Lowell opened fire and cut him down just like that."

Ali heard the futility in B.'s voice and her heart ached for him. "It's not your fault," she said.

"If I hadn't signaled him to come over, he wouldn't be dead."

"You don't know that. Neither does anyone else."

Looking around the hangar, Ali located another chair—an ancient wooden desk model on creaky casters. She pushed that over to B.'s chair and sat down beside him. Then she reached out and took his hand.

"I heard the governor got shot and was airlifted out," B. muttered after a minute or so. "Is she going to be okay?"

Ali shook her head. "Don't know," she answered. "We'll have to wait and see."

"I tried to come see you, but they wouldn't let me back inside the van. Dave Holman told me you shot Richard Lowell."

"I did," Ali admitted. "I didn't have a choice. He was about to make a phone call that would have killed a kid and set fire to a tank full of jet fuel. I shot him in the

back, and I'm not sorry about it, either. Did Dave say anything about how the search warrants went?"

B. looked up at her questioningly. "You haven't heard?"

"Heard what? I've spent the better part of two hours
locked in the van with Lowell's body and then being interviewed by an FBI agent. Nobody's told me anything."

"I've been interviewed, too," B. said, "but my guy let
something slip, and Dave told me the rest. It turns out
the men named in the search warrants are all dead."

Ali was taken aback. "Dead? All of them? What was
it, some kind of suicide pact?"

"Not exactly," B. answered bleakly. "As far as I know,
Amos Sellers is the only one still alive. Everywhere the
teams went, they were able to lay hands on the Bibles
with no problem because none of the men was home.
Lowell had evidently summoned all the heads of households to what was supposedly an important meeting at
the church.

"There's a bunker in the basement. He lured all but
two of them into the bunker, then sprayed them with the
automatic weapons fire, probably from the same AK-47
he used here. It was a bloodbath. The other two, the
guys who weren't in the basement, were found up at the
airstrip, parked in the airplane hangar, inside in a pool of
aviation fuel. Both of them had been shot execution style.
The men in the basement died earlier in the evening. The
men in the car probably died a while later."

"How many dead?" Ali asked as the weight of the
death toll sank into her soul.

"Twenty-nine from the family," B. answered. "Dave
says Lowell must have been trying to get rid of everyone
who might know any of the details about the human trafficking operation."

"What about the girls?" Ali asked. "The ones at the hangar?"

"There were only six of them, and they're fine—frightened but fine. At least that's what I was told. When Alvarado ran up the flag here, they split the SWAT team into two groups. Some came here and the others stayed behind to look out for the girls. They've called in a hazmat unit to clean up the spilled Jet-A before it leaks down into the water table."

Dave Holman walked into the hangar and came over to where they were sitting. "DPS is sending a helicopter over to Kingman to notify Sheriff Alvarado's next of kin. They asked me if I wanted to go along. I told them I wanted to check with you first. It's been a hell of a night; if you need any help getting back home . . ."

"Come to think of it, we do," Ali said at once. "We rode up in the governor's Sprinter, and that's not going anywhere anytime soon. Andrea Rogers and the two Brought Back girls are in the same fix."

"The governor's chief of staff assigned a DPS officer to do The Family's next-of-kin notifications. My understanding is that Andrea, Patricia, and Agnes will be assisting with that."

"We should probably help with that, too."

Dave shook his head. "No," he said. "You two have done enough."

Ali glanced at B.'s ashen face. "You're sure it's no trouble to drive us?" she asked.

"None at all," he answered. "Between doing a next-of-kin notification and getting my friends back home to Sedona, which one sounds like a better idea to you?"

37

The Phoenix-area taco truck that Governor Dunham had summoned to provide refreshments for her teams of officers had now arrived on the scene. It was parked on the shoulder of the road, just outside the entrance to the airport. With cops of all descriptions coming and going, the place was doing land-office business. Once convoys of hastily dispatched media vans started to arrive, it would be even busier.

Dave pulled over and stopped next to the food truck. "It's a long way back to Flag from here," he said. "After what you've both been through, you're going to need food, and it's on me. What do you want?"

"Whatever's good," B. said. Because of his need for legroom, he was in the front passenger seat. That put Ali in the back of the patrol car—behind the screen and in a part of the car with no interior door handles—something she found unsettling.

Looking at the mob lined up at the window, Ali's assessment was more realistic. "Whatever they have left," she said. "Since a few of the people waiting in line are early-bird reporters, it's probably best if B. and I stay in the car."

Dave left to place their orders, returning a few minutes later with three brown bags of food and another filled with cans of soda. "They're about to run out of everything. All they had left are bean-and-cheese burritos, so that's what I got. We all have a single burrito and cans of Diet Coke. Hope that'll work for you."

As soon as Ali smelled the food, she realized she was once again starving. In terms of hours, the box lunch she had eaten as the Sprinter came north from Flagstaff wasn't that long ago. In terms of life experience, it was epochs away.

"This is fuel for us," Ali said, unwrapping her burrito and taking a bite while the beans were still hot. "What about gas for the car?"

"Someone in authority convinced the guy who runs the trading post on the south side of Colorado City that it would be a good idea for him to do an unscheduled opening," Dave answered. "He's got all his gas pumps up and running. I filled up immediately. If demand ends up outstripping supply, I don't want to be one of the people left stranded until the next gasoline tanker truck shows up with a delivery."

They headed south a little before four. A few minutes into the drive, when Ali unconsciously reached for her phone to let Leland Brooks know what was happening, she remembered it was gone. So was B.'s phone and both their iPads. B.'s had been in his briefcase. Ali's iPad had been in her purse, and both purse and briefcase were still in the impounded Sprinter. As for her iPhone? Agent Malovich had commandeered that as evidence documenting the call she had made to Stu. With all their electronic devices under lock and key as part of a crime scene investigation, Ali started to ask to borrow Dave's phone. But then, noticing the time, she didn't.

"So how did you get mixed up in all this?" Dave asked Ali as they drove under a moonlit high desert sky. "B. gave me the shorthand version earlier before we left Flag to come here, but I have a feeling there's a lot I don't know."

Between them, Ali and B. told the story, a little at a time. By the time they finished, the sky was beginning to brighten in the east. For a while, the only sound in the vehicle was the whine of all-weather tires on the pavement.

Dave was the one who broke the silence. "There you have it," he said. "In one fell swoop, Sheriff Daniel Alvarado goes from being an unindicted homicide suspect to being a full-fledged hero. So do you still think he murdered the Kingman Jane Doe?"

"I do," Ali said quietly. "I most certainly do."

"What are you going to do about it?"

"I'm not sure," Ali said.

The problem of dealing with that had been banging around in her head the whole time she and Dave had been telling the story. "Alvarado may look like a hero right now, but Anne Lowell and her baby are still dead."

"Are you going to go through with the Doe exhumation, then?" Dave asked.

"I'm not sure," Ali said again.

"What's the point?" B. asked quietly.

"We'll determine once and for all if the Kingman Jane Doe is Anne Lowell," Ali answered. "We'll also know if Daniel Alvarado was the father of her baby."

"But knowing that won't tell us who killed her," B. objected. "With the evidence box missing, we'll probably never know. The only people who'll be hurt by all this are Daniel Alvarado's widow and kids. Right now he's a hero. Can't we let him stay a hero?"

"It may come up later," Dave cautioned. "Other people know that the Kingman Jane Doe most likely came from The Family. The human trafficking investigation will require putting DNA samples of all the victims into the system. There's no telling what'll happen when they get a match."

"That'll be somebody else's decision, then," B. said. "It won't be ours."

Given the circumstances, it didn't surprise Ali that B. was turning out to be one of Sheriff Alvarado's staunchest defenders.

"All right," Ali agreed. "I can live with that."

At six o'clock in the morning, a time when Leland usually showed up to start breakfast, Ali borrowed Dave's telephone to call home.

"Oh, madame," he said, "so good to hear your voice. We've all been worried sick."

"All?"

"Well, yes. Athena tried to reach you. Your mother tried to reach you. When neither you nor Mr. Simpson answered your phones, they both called me. I take it something serious has occurred. How can I be of service?"

Ali closed her eyes. She was bone weary. She had a choice to make. If she told the story to Leland on the phone right now, she'd end up having to repeat it at least two more times, once each with Athena and her mother and maybe with Chris and her father, too.

"What day is this?"

"Saturday."

"Just a sec." She covered the phone with her hand. "What do you think?" she asked B. "Should we invite everyone to breakfast, tell them the story all at once, and get it over with?"

B. thought for a moment and then nodded. "Have Leland set up a separate table out in the kitchen for Colin and Colleen. This isn't a story that's good for little ears."

Ali took her hand off the speaker. "How about if you invite everyone over to an early brunch," she suggested to Leland. "B. and I should be home around nine or so. That way we can say it once and be done with it."

"Of course," Leland agreed. "I shall do so immediately."

"Oh, and set a table for the little ones in the kitchen, please."

"Of course."

Once off the phone with Leland, Ali dozed off. Two hours later Dave drove them through Flagstaff to DPS headquarters. When he dropped them off, the parking lot wasn't nearly as full as it had been the night before, but given what all was going on up in Colorado City, the place wasn't exactly a deserted village. The collection of media vans—many of them with national news outlet logos—told Ali that what had gone on in Colorado City was big news. Doing his best to be unobtrusive, Dave dropped B. and Ali as close as possible to their respective cars. With her purse still in Governor Dunham's Sprinter, Ali was missing both her driver's license and her car keys. B. had a spare key for her to use, but no spare license.

Alone in the Cayenne, Ali wrestled with the enormity of what had happened. Twenty-nine members of The Family were dead, twenty-eight of them gunned down by one of their own. Governor Dunham's driver had perished as had Sheriff Alvarado, and Virginia Dunham was gravely injured.

Richard Lowell, the man most directly responsible for all that death and destruction, was dead, too. Ali had pulled the trigger that took him down. She felt absolutely no guilt about that—not a whit. As for the others? That was another story.

The operation at The Encampment, an action designed to bring human traffickers to justice, had ended in disaster—not the one Ali or anyone else had anticipated, but a disaster nonetheless. As far as Ali knew, the tour buses Governor Dunham had ordered to transport refugees from The Family were still there waiting, parked just up the road from the bustling taco truck. Who knew how many of The Encampment's residents, including other Brought Back girls, would choose to leave The Family in the face of this sudden and tragic turn in all their circumstances. The jury was definitely out on that score.

By now, the Department of Corrections bus, no longer needed, had most likely been recalled to its place of origin. The men it had been sent to transport were all dead. Twenty-nine of the thirty men named in the human trafficking warrants would be leaving Colorado City in a convoy of medical examiners' vans. They would never see the inside of a jail or a courthouse; they would never have their guilt or innocence determined by a judge and jury.

Unlike the raid at Short Creek, none of The Family's children had been taken into custody, but, with the exception of Amos Sellers's kids, they had all been left fatherless. Ali had heard Governor Dunham say she would take full responsibility if anything went wrong. In the upcoming news cycle, there would be plenty of comparisons between Governor Dunham's actions at The Encampment and Governor Howard Pyle's long-ago actions at Short Creek. The Short Creek raid had been publicized as being all about religious beliefs. With The Family, religion had been nothing but a thin veneer over an ongoing criminal enterprise. Governor Pyle had lost his election after Short Creek. Ali suspected that even with the death toll, Governor Dunham would come out smelling like a rose. The fact that she had been carried away from the incident with life-threatening injuries almost guaranteed that her glowing political legacy would continue to shine.

But what about Sister Anselm and me? Ali wondered as she turned off Manzanita Hills Road and onto her driveway. *What happened may be Governor Dunham's responsibility, but it's ours, too.*

38

The space at the top of the driveway was full of cars—Chris and Athena's new Ford Flex, Ali's mother's blue Buick, and a bright red Ford Fusion Ali thought belonged to Cami Lee from High Noon. Colin and Colleen came racing out of the house, followed hard upon by Bella. The kids were in the lead as they left the porch, but Bella beat them to and through the gate. By the time Ali opened the car door, Bella made an impossible leap, scrambling into the vehicle and up onto Ali's lap. Laughing through a barrage of doggy kisses, Ali exited the Cayenne and bent down to greet the kids.

"Where were you?" Colleen demanded, greeting Ali with a serious frown. "Mommy was worried about you and so was Daddy."

B. arrived on the scene and swung Colin up onto his shoulders. "And well they should have been," he told them. "It's been a tough night."

"Daddy said you were chasing bad guys. Did you get them?" Colin wanted to know.

"I think so," Ali told him. "I hope so."

By then the adults had made their way out of the

house. First came Ali's parents. Edie Larson pulled her daughter into a tight hug. "You've got to quit scaring us this way," she ordered.

"Sorry, Mom," Ali said. "Didn't mean to."

Bob Larson hugged his daughter, too. He said nothing, but his silent reprimand made Ali feel far more guilty than her mother's straightforward chiding.

To Ali's surprise next up were Stuart Ramey and Cami Lee. Somehow Ali managed to keep from mentioning how surprised she was to see Stu out of his natural habitat in front of a computer terminal.

"How come you guys went dark on us?" Stuart grumbled. "Aren't we supposed to be on the same team? I know everything went to hell in a handbasket up there, but as yet no details are being made public. Once your call to me ended, we've been shut out of the information loop along with everyone else."

Stuart liked to sit at his computer terminal and feel like he was in tune with everything that was going on. Being out of the know didn't work for him.

"I'm afraid that's all Governor Dunham's doing," Ali said. "When we headed north to Colorado City, she made us all shut down our devices so they couldn't be traced, and I'm sure the information embargo is part of her game plan, too."

"Right," Stuart said. "Everything was fine when they needed information from our drone. Now, though, it's all hush-hush. That's not fair."

Ali turned next to her daughter-in-law and was surprised to see Athena's eyes suddenly fill with tears.

"What's wrong, Athena?"

"I started trying to call you about eight o'clock, right after I got off the phone with Gram. When it kept going to voice mail and I couldn't reach B., either, I called Stuart. Gram told me some of it. Stuart told me the rest—that my mother's been stealing money out of Gram's accounts. Mom also has a boyfriend who happens to be the doctor who's supposed to do the competency evaluation on Monday. When I learned all that, I was ready to get on a plane last night and go home to punch Mom's lights out. Chris made me promise that I wouldn't go until after I talked to you and B."

"Yeah, Mom," Chris said, stepping up for his turn. "I told her she needed cooler heads to weigh in on all this. Yours and B.'s are the coolest heads I know."

Considering what had just happened in Colorado City, Ali almost objected to Chris's kind words. Instead she turned back to Athena.

"We'll talk this over," Ali said. "Don't worry. We'll figure it out. All of it."

Leland Brooks appeared on the porch. "Come on in," he said. "Breakfast is served."

Colin and Colleen stayed in the kitchen eating their chocolate chip Mickey Mouse–shaped pancakes under Leland's occasional supervision while everyone else tucked into coddled eggs and croissants at the dining room table.

"There's a breaking news alert on TV about what happened last night," Leland announced when he went around the dining room replenishing coffee cups. "I turned it off in the kitchen, but if you want to see it somewhere else . . ."

"Any word on the governor?" Ali asked.

"Hospitalized," Leland said. "Guarded condition."

No one leaped up to go see what the talking heads had to say. It would most likely play out as "another act of random gun violence, with thirty-one dead, including the shooter." That's how the media usually portrayed such things. News commentators would make a big deal of the governor's involvement, debating whether or not this was a case of governmental overreach. By the time the DNA details were sorted out and the human trafficking issues at the background of the case came to light, the media would have lost interest and moved on to something else. After all, who cared what went on in some remote corner of northern Arizona?

"What's going to happen to all those people, the women and children who have been left behind?" Athena wanted to know. "Where will they go? How will they live?"

"I have no idea," Ali said. "Whether they stay where they are or move into town somewhere, they're going to need huge amounts of assistance. The governor said she'd do everything in her power to help them."

"If she lives," Bob Larson cautioned. "But what makes you think she's a straight shooter?"

"The gun that was tucked inside Richard Lowell's pants was evidently one Governor Dunham took out of her purse when he demanded his hostages turn over their cell phones and weapons. While he was busy killing Sheriff Alvarado, she tried to take him down with that."

"Okay then," Bob said heartily. "Any woman brave enough to try to take down a guy armed with an AK-47 is a woman who gets my vote."

"Mine, too," Ali said. "But she'll have to run for something in order for that to happen."

39

After that, the conversation veered back to the situation with Betsy Peterson. In the end, the breakfast table discussion convinced Athena that it would be a good idea to have at least one cooling-off day before she went rushing off to Bemidji to kick butts and knock heads. They arranged for a further council of war on the following day, one where they would have access to any additional information Cami and Stuart might have dredged up in the meantime.

Once the company left, B. and Ali were done. They went into the bedroom, fell into bed, and slept. Neither of them noticed when Bella burrowed under the covers with them, but she was still there, late that afternoon, when they finally woke up. There had been no phone calls to awaken them. B. had had brains enough to turn off the landline extension before they crawled into bed, and if anyone was attempting to reach them by cell phone, those calls were being put through to devices locked in an evidence locker somewhere far out of hearing distance.

Prowling out to the kitchen, they found a note from Leland saying that he had thawed out the last two of the pasties he'd made earlier in the week. They were on a plate in a warming drawer and ready to eat. Ali remembered the day the pasties had been hot and fresh out of the oven and she had taken a pair of them along to Flagstaff to share with Sister Anselm. That seemed like an impossibly long time ago.

At the bottom of the note was a PS: "Please call Sister Anselm. She's waiting to hear from you."

On the kitchen counter they found two new cell phones, two new iPads, and a note from Stuart. "Picked these up for you this afternoon. I transferred all the info and numbers over from your old phones and iPads, including the High Noon security protocols. The old devices are bricked. Anyone trying to access them for any reason will get nowhere."

Ali sorted out which phone was hers and called Sister Anselm's number while B. logged onto the new iPad to see what fires needed to be put out in the larger world of High Noon Enterprises.

"I'm so relieved to hear from you," the nun said. "When I couldn't reach you, I talked to Mr. Brooks, so I know some of what went on, but tell me everything."

"That could take some time."

"No problem. The nuns from All Saints are looking after Enid and Baby Ann, and they'll go stay at the convent in Tucson for a few days once they're released from the hospital. I'm driving back to Payson right now, Bluetooth in my ear. I've got time."

Ali told her all of it. There was a pause when the story finally came to an end.

"We lit the fuse on this," Sister Anselm said quietly. "We didn't mean to, but we did. Our getting involved caused all those deaths."

"I'm afraid that's true," Ali agreed. "Richard Lowell was a woman-hating rabid dog. I'd shoot him again in a minute if I had the chance. But the others? Amos Sellers claimed to be completely in the dark on the human trafficking business, and maybe the others were, too. Maybe they were all true believers living their lives the way Lowell told them to."

"Like Jim Jones and the Kool-Aid," Sister Anselm observed. "And then there's the problem with Sheriff Alvarado. He's most likely the father of Anne Lowell's baby and her murderer as well, but without the evidence box, that case will never be closed, especially since, in the eyes of the world, the man died a hero."

And B. would prefer to keep him that way, Ali thought, but with B. sitting right there within earshot, she didn't say that aloud.

"I still want to know for sure Anne and Jane Doe are one and the same," Sister Anselm said. "I want to know that for Enid's sake and for mine as well."

The landline phone rang. Caller ID said Caller Unknown, but with everything that was going on, Ali felt a need to answer it. Besides, she had talked on the new cell phone for so long that it was burning her ear. "I need to take this."

"Bye," Sister Anselm said, and she was gone.

Ali picked up the other phone and was surprised to hear Andrea Rogers's voice. "Thank you," she said.

"Thank you?"

"For what you did. If you hadn't gotten us out of the van when you did, Bill Witherspoon, Patricia, Agnes, and I would have been sitting ducks."

"You're welcome," Ali said. "I didn't recognize your phone number."

"That's because I don't have my cell—none of us do—and I'm also out of the office. I had a free moment, though, and wanted to know how you're doing."

"B. and I just woke up," Ali said. "What's going on?"

"Patricia, Agnes, and I did our interviews and then spent the rest of the night and part of the morning helping with next-of-kin notifications. Understandably, the women from The Family are beyond distressed over what happened. I'm not sure how we would have managed if Patricia and Agnes hadn't been there to run interference.

"I rode down from Colorado City to Flag with the first busload of displaced women and kids. A dozen of those were Brought Back girls. One of the passengers was a girl named Mary who was being held in solitary confinement in a cell at the church. Patricia tells me she was a Cast-Off girl, someone who was betrothed to Richard Lowell and failed the required virginity test. The rest were women with three or four kids apiece. They're all temporarily settled in donated hotel rooms with volunteers from Irene's Place helping them get cleaned up and into suitable clothing. Bill Witherspoon has been a huge help, by the way. Governor Dunham gave him a blank check to handle whatever is needed."

"With state money?" Ali asked.

"No, he's authorized to use her personal funds."

"Speaking of Governor Dunham," Ali said. "How's she doing?"

"Out of surgery. She's in serious condition—serious but stable. Her husband told Bill that her doctors are hoping to save her leg. If the SWAT team guys hadn't used a tourniquet on it when they did, the leg would have been lost for sure.

"Anyway, the bus went back to pick up another load,

and I stayed here to streamline arrangements. It's complicated. Some of the so-called wives who also happen to be mothers are considered juveniles out here in the regular world. I'm walking a fine line making housing arrangements for them. Patricia may end up being turned into a de facto housemother."

"What about Agnes?"

"I believe she's staying on up at The Encampment for now. She said someone needed to look after the pigs and other livestock. I went toe-to-toe with a woman named Edith Tower. She was evidently Gordon Tower's first wife, which makes her his first widow, too. When she started throwing her weight around, I told her that Agnes is staying on voluntarily and she is to be allowed a room in the house—Enid's vacant room as a matter of fact. I also let her know that, if she made any attempt to force Agnes back into a state of involuntary servitude, there would be severe consequences."

"How many of the widows are going to stay and how many will go?" Ali asked.

"There's no way to tell that right now. We'll cross that bridge when we get to it. I know we're going to need more help."

"Take down this number," Ali said before reciting a number from memory. "That's my good friend Sister Anselm. She may be able to conjure up some additional help for you. We both have a vested interest in making sure these women are dealt with in the most humane way possible."

"Oops," Andrea said. "The bus is just pulling in. Gotta go."

Ali put the phone down.

"How about one of those pasties now?" B. asked.

"Good idea," she said. "I'm ready."

40

By ten o'clock Monday morning Ali and Athena were belted into a Citation X. According to the computerized map on the bulkhead, they were somewhere far above Colorado on a three-hour flight from Flagstaff's KFLG airport direct to Bemidji. Athena had been prepared to go and beard her mother in her den all on her own. Together, Chris, Ali, and B. had nixed that idea. They wanted her to have backup when she walked into a difficult situation with information that would likely turn a bad situation into a war zone.

Had Athena flown commercial from Phoenix, the trip would have taken the better part of three days. Flying direct, using B.'s jet card, meant they could come and go in a single day.

They were traveling with an iPad loaded with a collection of incriminating photos of Athena's mother, Sandra, and of Elmer Munson, who, judging from the many surveillance photos of the two of them together, was more to Sandra than just the family doctor. There were photos of the two of them at various cash machines where Sandra was lifting money out of her mother-in-law's bank accounts.

There were front desk photos of them checking into hotel rooms at various casinos in the area. There were photos of them laughing it up at blackjack tables—blackjack being Sandra's preferred game of chance, although given the sizes of her losses, it probably shouldn't have been.

The capper, though, and by far the most damning, was the video clip that showed Sandra paying a surreptitious visit to Betsy's house on Friday evening. Joe Friday's surveillance camera had worked its magic. The video feed, complete with a time and date stamp, showed Sandra, alone this time, entering Betsy's house while Betsy would have been in Bemidji at the fish fry. Sandra had spent most of the time in the bedroom, browsing through her mother-in-law's jewelry box. Alerted by Stuart the next morning, Betsy had done her own jewelry box inventory and discovered that her mother's antique cameo was missing, as was the pair of uncharacteristically extravagant diamond earrings Alton had given Betsy for their fiftieth wedding anniversary.

Athena hadn't told her grandmother she was coming, so this was to be a surprise visit. The plan was to arrive at Dr. Munson's office at the same time Betsy did. Ali was concerned about Athena's intention of confronting the two miscreants together, but she was only along as backup. This wasn't her fight. What happened during the encounter at Dr. Munson's office would determine if Betsy's next step would be filing a police report or simply demanding restitution.

On the way, Athena spilled out her heart. Athena had been at odds with her parents from a very early age. The battles were waged mostly between mother and daughter. Athena's father, Jim, had always taken Sandra's part, while his parents, Betsy and Alton, had functioned as their granddaughter's safety net and refuge. Athena knew that Betsy and Sandra had been on the outs for decades, but it was only this current crisis that had brought into sharp focus the seriousness of the rift between them.

"Until just the other day, I had no idea of Gram's intention to write them out of her will."

"I'm pretty sure your mother knew," Ali offered. "If she and your father were to be appointed Betsy's guardians, Sandra would have used her influence with your father to gain control of that money long before it ever got to you. She was probably also hoping to cover up what she's been doing for the last year."

"Which is stealing," Athena said. "My mother is a thief."

"And a liar and a cheat," Ali added. "I guess that's why you turned out to be the way you did. One way kids rebel is to be the opposite of their parents. That explains why you're who you are, but now I'm worried about Colin and Colleen. Will they be throwbacks to your mom?"

"I hope not," Athena said, and she wasn't laughing about it, either. The idea that her sweet little twins might grow up and turn into chips off her mother's block was clearly a disturbing possibility and one Athena had never before considered.

They landed in Bemidji and picked up their rented car with a good hour to spare before Betsy's two-thirty doctor's appointment. With Ali behind the wheel, they did a quick drive-by tour of the place, with Athena offering directions, pointing out the sights, and providing narration.

The sky was overcast, and the weather had veered into the high thirties, a temperature Athena said locals would regard as a regular heat wave. They drove through town and saw the schools Athena had attended, the house where her parents still lived, and her father's dental office on Paul Bunyan Drive.

"That red Miata parked outside belongs to Jack," Athena said, biting her lip.

Ali knew the fact that Athena's parents continued to maintain a close connection with her ex, Jack Carlson, was an ongoing emotional issue for Athena. Having Jack now installed as a full partner in her father's dental practice made things that much worse.

"I guess we won't be stopping in to visit, then?" Ali asked.

"I guess not," Athena answered in a pained but wry way that made Ali grateful Athena hadn't attempted this difficult journey on her own.

They parked outside Dr. Elmer Munson's office on Bemidji Avenue at two-fifteen. They were early enough to see Betsy, accompanied by an elderly man with a cane, clamber out of a battered Kia. The man had stepped out of the front passenger seat and then held the back passenger door open while Betsy wrestled herself out of the vehicle.

"That's Marcia Lawson's Kia," Athena explained as the vehicle moved away from the curb. "She drives Betsy around when she needs to go somewhere."

"Who's the man?" Ali asked

"I have no idea."

The old couple had already made their dignified way into the building when Sandra Peterson arrived. After a hasty job of bad parallel parking, she bustled in after them.

"Showtime," Athena muttered.

By the time Ali and Athena located the office and entered the waiting area, there was already a palpable feeling of tension in the room. Betsy and her unknown friend sat next to each other against one wall by the receptionist while Sandra, looking put out, sat on a love seat on the far side of the room.

"Hey, Mom," Athena said, waving a casual greeting. "How's it going?" Then she turned to Betsy. "Hi, Gram."

Sandra half rose from her chair. "What on earth are you doing here?" she demanded. Then, as if she knew, she sank back down into her chair.

Betsy struggled to her feet and limped over to give Athena a fierce hug.

"I heard Gram might be having some mental health issues," Athena said, turning to answer her mother's question. "Ali and I decided to fly up and see what's going on." Athena next stepped forward to hold out her nonprosthetic hand to the man with the cane who was rising from his chair and tottering over to greet her. The old guy had to be eighty if he was a day.

"I'm Athena," she explained. "Betsy's granddaughter."

"Just call me Howard," the old guy said. "You might say I'm BA and AA," he added with a chuckle and a quick glance in Betsy's direction. "That stands for Before Alton and After Alton. If I'd played my cards right way back then, maybe there wouldn't have been any Alton at all."

"Hush," Betsy said, giving him a playful shove with her arm.

A nurse stepped into the room from a corridor that led to the examining rooms. "Betsy Peterson," she announced. "This way, please." She stopped short when everyone in the waiting room, with the exception of Ali, rose as if to follow.

"Wait," the nurse said. "You can't all come in here."

"I'm Howard Hansen," Howard said. "Doctor Howard Hansen. It's probably a little before your time, but I was a GP here in town for many years. I came along today as Betsy's friend and to offer my services as a disinterested bystander in terms of this competency situation."

"You can't go into the examination room with her," the nurse objected.

"Exactly," Sandra agreed, trying to push her way past Howard.

"If Betsy here wants me in the examination room, I most certainly can be," Howard replied with a smile. "In fact, it might be best if you consulted Elmer himself on that particular issue."

The nurse's eyes narrowed. "I'll see what the doctor has to say."

The nurse had obviously taken offense at the idea that anyone would have the temerity to call her boss by his given name. She stalked off, returning a moment later with a man Ali easily recognized as a face in the rogues' gallery of photos Stuart Ramey had collected from various surveillance photos. Dr. Munson was wearing a lab coat and a stethoscope.

"What seems to be the difficulty here?" he asked, frowning.

"Hello, Dr. Munson," Athena said.

"Do I know you?"

"Probably not," Athena said. "I'm Betsy's granddaughter, Athena Reynolds. I know who you are, though. I recognize you from your photos. Several of them, in fact."

Swiping her iPad to on, she then held it out for him to see while she scrolled through several of the damning photographs. When Elmer Munson realized what he was seeing, his eyes widened, and he glared at Sandra.

"What's going on?" he asked.

"I don't know . . ." Sandra began, but then she caught sight of one of the photos, too. Her eyes bulged, too. "What's the meaning of this?"

The nurse, arms folded across her chest, stood behind

the doctor and watched the unfolding drama with rising interest.

"I have no idea what you think you're doing, young woman," Munson said to Athena. "It would be a good idea if you left now."

"We'll do just that," Athena said agreeably. "I can't imagine that any of your findings about Gram's ability to manage her own affairs will pass muster once the judge sees a sampling of these photos."

With that, Athena turned on her mother. "As for you? My independent investigators have established that a minimum of sixty thousand dollars has gone missing from Gram's savings accounts in the past year. It was withdrawn by way of fraudulent ATM transactions. That money is to be returned, with interest, as are Betsy's cameo pin and the diamond earrings that were removed from her jewelry box *by you* on Friday night while she was at the fish fry."

Sandra's mouth fell open. "How can you say such a thing?"

"Easy," Athena said. "Because I happen to have the video. Care to see it? This isn't a court of law, Mother, and I'm not a journalist, either. I'm not using the word 'alleged.' I don't have to. I'm your daughter. Right now this is still a family matter, but if you don't return every dime of what you've taken, it will become all too public. As for telling Daddy about your friend here? You probably don't need to." She glanced meaningfully in the direction of the mesmerized nurse and the openmouthed receptionist. "I'm sure people will be lining up all over town to give him the news."

Grim faced, Munson pushed past his nurse and disappeared down the hall, slamming an invisible office door behind him. The receptionist was still slack-jawed while Sandra stared at Athena in tight-lipped fury.

Unconcerned by her mother's reaction, Athena took Betsy's arm and led her grandmother out of the room. Howard followed, with Ali tailing along behind. Before the door had time enough to close entirely, it opened again and Sandra marched out, leaving a storm of conversation behind her in the waiting room.

"By God!" Howard said out on the sidewalk with a chuckle that was more a cackle than it was a burst of laughter. "That's more fun than I've had in years! You certainly put that mother of yours in her place!" he declared. "Good on you, Athena, girl. Good on you."

Betsy was smiling, too, but a moment later the smile disappeared and her expression turned serious. "We'll need to find a bench somewhere. I told Marcia to come back in an hour," she said. "We'll need a place to wait."

"No waiting," Athena said. "We'll give you a ride. We'll call Marcia and let her know that she won't need to come back to pick you up. How about an early dinner before we catch our plane home?"

"By all means," Howard said. "We're just in time for the blue-plate special at the diner. My treat."

It turned out that the blue-plate special—served on honest-to-God blue plates—consisted of passable meat loaf accompanied by lumpy mashed potatoes with parsnips lurking inside them. The rest of the plate was covered with a pile of pale green beans. By color alone, Ali determined the beans had come straight from a can. Canned or fresh didn't seem to make any difference to Howard. He cleaned his plate with obvious relish while Betsy barely nibbled on hers.

"Jimmy must have known what was going on the whole time," she said at last. "How could my own son betray me like this?"

"Trust me," Athena said. "My guess is he didn't know. In fact, I doubt he had any idea. This is all Mom's doing, Gram—all of it. We don't have tapes of her coming into your house and turning on the gas, but I'm sure she did that, too. She may not have been trying to kill you, but her intent was to do you harm. She drove you out of your house and into the snow in the middle of the night with no care at all about what might happen. It's a wonder you didn't catch pneumonia."

Betsy still looked pensive and lost. "What's going to happen when Jimmy finds out your mother has been stepping out on him?"

"He won't unless somebody tells him," Athena said. "In fact, I doubt he'll ever figure it out on his own. Mom has betrayal down cold. As far as Dad is concerned, what she says goes. She'll convince him that no matter what anyone says, you included, nothing happened between her and Elmer Munson. She'll claim people are telling lies about her, and Dad will believe every word that comes out of her mouth. And you know what? It doesn't matter because I don't care anymore. As long as she pays back every cent of the money she stole from you, what she does is none of my concern. And if she doesn't pay you back? Then we go to the cops, plain and simple, and she goes to jail."

"What about turning the other cheek?"

"No," Athena said decisively. "Not with her." She paused, then asked, "But what about from here on out, Gram? It makes me sick to think that anyone, especially my own mother, would take advantage of you this way, but what if someone else tries to do the same thing? You need someone looking out for you, someone closer. I'd like to see you out of that house—a place where you live all alone in the middle of nowhere. I'd like to see you in a spot where you'll have people around who can help you in case you're in trouble or having issues of some kind."

"I've invited her to come live with me at my assisted-living place," Howard interjected, "but she always turns me down."

To Ali's amazement, Betsy blushed at that remark. "They don't take dogs," she said, primly. "I won't leave my Princess behind."

"I'm glad you mentioned that," Athena said. "I did some checking before we came here. Sedona Shadows, the place where Ali's folks live, doesn't take dogs either, but I've found another facility that does, and they happen to have a two-bedroom unit that just became available."

"Why would I need a two-bedroom?" Betsy asked. "Besides, Sedona is too far away from home."

"Having a guest room is always a good idea, because you just might have company," Howard said, with a smile that was one short step from conniving. "I wouldn't mind checking out of this joint and coming south in the middle of the winter for a visit. Just for a day or two, of course, nothing more."

"Of course," Betsy said, but the way she said it sounded as though she was warming to the idea.

"When school's out, the kids and I can come north, help you sort things, and get your place listed," Athena continued. "Then we'd hire movers to pack your stuff into a van to move it to Arizona. Meanwhile, you and Princess would drive back to Sedona with us. Easy-peasy."

Betsy looked across the table at Athena. "I'll think about it," she said finally. "I really will."

41

For the next six weeks Sister Anselm and Ali spent most of their waking hours working hand in hand with Andrea Rogers and the other Irene's Place volunteers, shuttling The Family's displaced women and children to new homes. The Encampment was now mostly deserted. Inspections of The Family's housing facilities had revealed that they'd been built without permits and with little or no effort to meet building codes. Now all of them had been condemned. Rather than being sold, the structures were due to be demolished.

As The Family's collection of livestock was sold off, the proceeds from those sales were placed in escrow to pay for some of the former residents' care and keeping. Everyone knew that considerable funds were still squirreled away in Richard Lowell's banking accounts in the Grand Caymans. The problem was, authorities were still trying to decide how much of that money was a result of a criminal enterprise and how much was legitimate. Once all that was sorted out, some legal determination would have to be made about who inherited the money.

As one of Richard Lowell's direct descendants, Enid Tower might one day be in a position to inherit some of it, but decisions about that were most likely years of legal wrangling away.

Six weeks after what the media continued to refer to as the Encampment Massacre, Andrea Rogers from Irene's Place took the shelter's passenger van and drove Patricia and Agnes to Phoenix's Sky Harbor International Airport in Phoenix. Enid Tower, fully recovered and with Baby Ann properly strapped into a car seat, came along for the ride.

Ali and Sister Anselm made the same trip, driving down from Sedona in Ali's Cayenne. Their reason for going was a joyous one, but memories of the lives lost on that cold February night made for a heavy burden and robbed them both of the easy camaraderie they usually shared on car trips. It was the Monday after the scholarship tea, and chatting about that gave them some much-needed neutral conversational ground.

Arriving at Sky Harbor twenty minutes or so after everyone else, Ali and Sister Anselm joined the others in the arrivals lounge just outside customs as the transatlantic flight from Amsterdam landed and deplaned.

The family Bibles, confiscated in Governor Dunham's raid, had worked their magic. Two of the Not Chosens, both listed in the late Donald Gray's family Bible, were Agnes's half sisters, Christina and Donna Marie.

Sean Fergus, fast-tracking The Family's DNA testing, had learned early on that the two half sisters—one who spoke and one who now wore thick glasses—were two of the very few human trafficking survivors. Shipped off to Nigeria, they had somehow managed to stay together.

They had been bought by someone in Lagos. What happened next was unclear, but they had been rescued and taken to a local orphanage. With no way to explain who they were or where they were from, the two girls had lived in the orphanage as children, cared for by the attendants. When they were too old to be orphans anymore and without papers that would allow them to go elsewhere, they had stayed on, becoming caretakers for the younger children.

Now, through the intervention of Sean Fergus and Interpol, Donna Marie and Christina had been issued U.S. passports. They were coming home to the place from which they'd been spirited away at the age of six—a place they barely remembered.

As passengers from the flight made their slow way into the customs area and sorted themselves into lines, Agnes stood with her face pressed against the plate glass, looking down at the process.

"Will they recognize me?" Agnes asked anxiously. "Will they know who I am?"

"I'm sure they'll remember you," Ali said reassuringly.

Sister Anselm nodded. "The face of kindness is something a child never forgets."

A minute later, Agnes spotted them. "There they are! It's them. They just got into the far line on the left."

The two women in question wore loose-fitting, brightly colored dresses that flowed when they walked. Their feet were clad in flip-flops, but their dark blond hair was braided and pinned in a crown around their heads.

Ali's first thought was that Christina and Donna Marie were far better dressed than Enid had been when she had shown up at the hospital.

Ten minutes later, the new arrivals stepped warily onto an escalator that carried them upstairs. As they rode up, Agnes hurried to station herself just outside the sliding glass doors at the top of the escalator.

They stepped through and then stopped abruptly, staring at the soaring but unfamiliar room around them. Only when Agnes stepped forward to greet them did the one wearing glasses notice her. A moment later, the three of them were gathered into one another's arms, weeping and laughing in a warm embrace.

Ali was struck by how much younger the two newcomers looked. Difficult as their lives might have been at the orphanage, they'd received better care there than The Family's Brought Back girls had received at home.

Finally, Agnes said something. As they broke free, Agnes led them to meet the other people in the welcome party. "These are my friends," she said. "Patricia, Enid and her baby, Ann, Ali, and Sister Anselm. And these"— she smiled at the young women—"are my sisters, Christina and Donna Marie."

The new arrivals shook hands with Ali and Patricia and bowed formally to Sister Anselm. Ali realized that somewhere along the way, a Catholic sister of some kind must have impacted their lives.

"Agnes says she's my sister," the one called Christina said, nodding in Agnes's direction. "I remembered her all this time. I always thought she was my guardian angel."

There was a stir behind them. Ali turned in time to see Bill Witherspoon wheeling Governor Dunham toward them in a wheelchair. Her leg was wrapped in a toe-to-hip cast, but at least it was still attached. There was some hope that she would one day be able to walk again without the aid of crutches or a cane.

"Actually," Ali said, "Agnes is only one of your guardian angels. Here's another. Her name is Virginia Dunham, and she's the governor of Arizona." To the governor, she said, "These are Agnes's sisters, Donna Marie and Christina."

"I'm so happy to meet you both," Governor Dunham said, smiling and holding out her hand in greeting. "Welcome home."

Turn the page to read
the first Ali Reynolds/Joanna Brady novella

NO HONOR AMONG THIEVES

Also available as a Pocket Star ebook

When Sheriff Joanna Brady's distinctive rooster ring tone jarred her awake at oh-dark-thirty in the morning, she grabbed the phone off the bedside table and shot a guilty glance at her sleeping husband before she answered. After years of being married to a county sheriff, Butch Dixon had become accustomed to Joanna's being summoned to some incident or another in the middle of the night. At first he had made it a point to get up with her and make sure that, wherever she was going, she'd at least have a cup of freshly made coffee along for the ride.

Right now, though, the poor guy was fighting a deadline on his next book and had come to bed barely two hours earlier. "Just a minute," Joanna whispered into the phone.

In the old days, Joanna would have had to scramble across a pitch-dark bedroom while dodging the prone body of her rescued Australian shepherd, Lady, who had formerly slept as close to Joanna's side of the bed as possible. Now, though, Lady had put herself in charge of Butch and Joanna's four-year-old son, Dennis. All her instinctive herding proclivities had been turned full bore on keeping track of the boy. Lady spent all her waking and sleeping hours guarding him devotedly—enough so that both Joanna and Butch worried about what the dog would do with herself in the fall when Dennis went off to pre-kindergarten.

Once inside the bathroom with the door closed, Joanna

switched on the light and sat down on the closed toilet lid. "Okay," she said to Tica Romero, the Cochise County Sheriff's Office's overnight dispatcher. "What's up?"

"A Border Patrol officer called in a fatality MVA that may turn out to be a homicide," Tica replied. "A guy driving a delivery truck tore through the guardrail where Highway 92 crosses the San Pedro and ended up upside down in the riverbed. But the officer who called it in, Agent Bill Cannon, said the truck looked like something straight out of a war zone. He says the cab was riddled with bullet holes that appear to be from automatic weapons fire."

"Automatic weapons?" Joanna echoed. "Are you kidding me? Sounds like a serious smuggling operation of some kind, probably a couple of the drug cartels duking it out inside my jurisdiction. About the victim: Do we know what killed him? Did he die of a gunshot wound or from the wreck itself?"

"No way to tell at this time," Tica replied. "I've dispatched Detectives Carbajal and Howell as well as Dave Hollicker to the scene."

Jaime Carbajal and Deb Howell were two of Joanna's three homicide detectives. Dave Hollicker was part of her two-man—well, one man and one woman—CSI unit.

"Detective Carbajal is already on the scene and he wanted to know if you're coming, too."

Years earlier, Joanna's first husband, Cochise County sheriff's deputy Andrew Roy Brady, had been running for the office of sheriff when he'd been gunned down by a drug cartel's hit man. In the aftermath of Andy's death, Joanna was encouraged to run for sheriff in his place. Most people—including the voters who had elected her—expected Joanna to be sheriff in name only. After all, being the daughter of a sheriff—D. H. Lathrop—and being married to a deputy sheriff didn't exactly qualify Joanna to be a police officer or sheriff in her own right. But once she was elected, she did her best to get qualified, including sending herself to the Phoenix for a course of police academy training. One of the main things that won her the respect of those under her command was that whenever there was a homicide in Cochise County, Sheriff Joanna Brady was on the scene.

"Affirmative on that," she said. "I'll get dressed and head out. Let everyone know I'll be there as soon as I can."

"One other thing before you go," Tica said hurriedly before Joanna could end the call.

"What?"

"I don't know if any rental agencies are open about now. Maybe there's one in Sierra Vista, but you're going to need a truck."

"A truck? Why?"

"Because the truck landed so hard that it broke apart on impact, spilling a whole load of LEGO boxes and scattering them everywhere. If the San Pedro had water running in it today, there'd be a flotilla of *Star Wars* LEGO sets floating upstream."

"LEGO boxes?" Joanna repeated. "As in toys? As in those little plastic thingamajigs that kids stick together to build things?"

"Yes, ma'am," Tica replied. "Those are the ones. Evidently that truck was chock-full of them."

"Okay," Joanna said. "While I'm getting dressed, why don't you try you locating a rental truck. That's not going to be easy in the middle of the night."

She ended the call and jumped in the shower. She wore her red hair short on purpose. There was enough natural body to it that, if she combed it out wet, it would dry in some reasonable order without needing a blow-dry. Her mother, Eleanor Lathrop Winfield, thought the whole idea of wash-and-wear hair was too scandalous for words, but Joanna had too many demands on her time and energy to keep up with a complicated hairdo. Ditto for her makeup applications, which her mother regarded as hit-or-miss.

Joanna had her face on and was dressed in her uni-form, out of the house, and in the car less than twelve minutes after the phone call. She had taken the time to leave a note for Butch, but she hadn't waited long enough to make coffee.

The clock on the dashboard of her county-owned Yukon said it was 3:03 as she turned off High Lonesome Road and onto the highway. The night before, she'd been caught up in the first meeting of her reelection commit-tee, and it had kept her up far past her usual bedtime. As she accelerated, Joanna realized how rummy she felt. She needed coffee in the worst way. Luckily for her, the Cochise County Justice Center was on her way to the crime scene.

She dialed up the radio. "Hey, Tica," she said. "Any luck on that truck?"

"I contacted Frank out in Sierra Vista," Tica said. "Turns out one of his officers has a brother-in-law who operates the local U-Haul franchise. Frank is seeing if they can roust the guy out of bed and have him come handle the rental. If so, he'll give us a call."

Frank was Frank Montoya. Frank had been one of

Joanna's two opponents in her run for the office of sheriff. When he lost out, she was smart enough to appoint him to be one of her two chief deputies. In recent years, however, Frank had been lured away from that job when Sierra Vista offered him the position of chief of police.

"Bless his heart," Joanna said. "If anyone can make it happen, Frank is the guy. One other thing: What are the chances of getting someone to go down to the break room and make a fresh pot of coffee? If I swing through the front parking lot, maybe they could bring a cup out to me. I'm maybe three minutes away."

"You bet," Tica said. "Believe me, you wouldn't want to drink the crap in the bottom of the pot right now. That stuff is thick enough to kill you."

Minutes later, as Joanna turned into the Justice Center entrance drive, Sergeant Kevin Crane, her nighttime desk sergeant, was already hobbling down the wheelchair ramp with a covered paper cup of coffee in hand. While still a deputy, Crane's legs had been severely injured in a line-of-duty accident in which his patrol car had been T-boned by a drunk driver. At the time of the wreck, Kevin was divorced and remarried and had two sets of kids to support. He was supremely grateful when Joanna offered to move him over to a desk job rather than forcing him into early retirement.

"It's hot," he said, gingerly handing the thermal cup in through the window.

It *was* hot. It was all Joanna could do to get it transferred to the cupholder without burning her fingers.

"Thanks, Kev," she said. "If someone from Sierra Vista comes up with a truck we can rent, give them my departmental Amex card. I know Deputy Stock is off duty tonight, but wake him up and ask him to pick up the truck. He does still live in Sierra Vista, doesn't he?"

"As far as I know," Crane said. "Are you going to need additional help?"

"Probably. I'm told the crime scene is littered with a truckload of spilled LEGO boxes. If you can spare a patrol officer or two to come help gather them up, I'd be most appreciative."

"I'll see what I can do, but we're stretched pretty thin tonight."

With her coffee too hot to drink, Joanna drove through town and west on Highway 92 on the far side of Huachuca Terraces, still puzzling over what she had so far learned about the incident. How could a load of LEGO sets be worth a fatality firefight, especially one with assailants armed with fully loaded automatic weapons? Was that even remotely possible? Had the cartels started using phony toy boxes as a way of transporting drugs?

When she estimated the coffee was cool enough to drink, she tried a sip. It may have been fresh, but it tasted vile. If this was what the new coffee in the break room tasted like, the old stuff would have been far worse. Disgusted, she put the cup back in the cupholder and left it there.

The glow of flashing emergency lights, visible from miles away, guided Joanna to the crime scene. Parking on the shoulder of the highway just behind the ME's van, she stepped out of her SUV and gazed down at the artificially lit scene. She saw moving beams of flashlights here and there, as well as the occasional brilliant flash from someone shooting crime scene photos.

The high-desert chill of early April bit through the

shirt of Joanna's uniform and ruffled icily through her still-damp hair. Suppressing a shiver, Joanna reached into the Yukon's backseat and pulled out a brown leather aviator's jacket bearing an arm patch imprinted with the Cochise County Sheriff's Office logo. She was shrugging into its welcome warmth as Deputy Armando Ruiz walked up to her with his own blazing Maglite in hand.

"It's still pretty dark, Sheriff Brady. Are you going to go straight down the embankment from here or would you rather walk around?"

"Are you going down?" she asked.

"My assignment is to stay here," Deputy Ruiz replied. "I'm in charge of directing traffic, not that there's much of that at the moment. That'll change once the sun comes up. In the meantime, I've been walking up and down the road, looking for skid marks."

"And?"

"There aren't any. Looks to me like he made no effort to stop. He just veered across the centerline and crashed into the guardrail at full speed."

Joanna reached into the front seat and retrieved her own Maglite. Grateful she had worn a pair of sturdy hiking boots, she nodded toward the spot where the mangled iron guardrail had been ripped apart as the truck crashed through it. "I guess I'll take the straight down option," she said.

Maglites, heavy enough to be used as batons in a pinch, were designed to be used by cops much larger than Joanna's diminutive five-foot-four-inch frame. She appreciated the way the flashlight illuminated the tricky rock-strewn downward path, but the weight of the device made it difficult for her to maintain her balance. The last few feet down the incline were done on her butt in a very unladylike fashion. She was glad Deputy Ruiz hadn't announced her arrival beforehand. Once she reached the bottom, she needed a moment to brush herself off before anyone else spotted her.

The generator-operated work lights created pockets of bright illumination that alternated with places that were pitch-dark, making it impossible for Joanna's eyes to adjust. The first figure who emerged out of that unsettling mixture of light and dark turned out to be Detective Deb Howell.

"How are things?" Joanna asked.

"This is one night that makes me happy Maury and I finally got around to tying the knot," Deb replied with a grin. "Used to be when I'd get a call-out like this, I'd have to jump through hoops to find a middle-of-the-night babysitter for Ben. Having a husband right there and on call makes life a lot simpler."

Years earlier, Deb had met Maury Robbins, a 911 dispatcher from Tucson who was also an ATV enthusiast, during a homicide investigation at an ATV park near Bowie. They dated for a long time and finally got around to marrying a scant two months earlier. Since the wedding, the newlyweds had simplified their living arrangements by having Maury move into Deb's house in Old Bisbee. From there he made the hundred-mile-each-way commute back and forth to Tucson three days a week.

"That isn't exactly what I was asking," Joanna said with a smile.

Deb gestured toward the scene behind them. "We're stuck in a holding pattern right now, waiting for the ME to finish her preliminary exam."

For years a man named George Winfield had served as Cochise County's medical examiner. He and Joanna had maintained an excellent working relationship right up until George hauled off and married Joanna's widowed mother, Eleanor. That complicated things immensely, especially since Eleanor wanted a retired husband rather than one who was fully employed. When George resigned the post of ME, his replacement, Dr. Guy Machett, became a royal pain. Then, several months ago, Machett himself was murdered in an horrific attack. The new ME, Machett's replacement, was a tall, serious-minded black woman named Dr. Kendra Baldwin, who arrived in town the same weekend Deb Howell and Maury Robbins married.

This was only the second homicide Dr. Baldwin had investigated for Joanna's department, but Joanna had been part of the vetting process for the new ME, and she had every confidence that Kendra Baldwin's abilities would live up to her five-star credentials. Not only that, Joanna had been delighted when, in the course of their first interactions, Kendra suggested that they drop the formal "'Doctor' and 'Sheriff' BS," as she put it. "I'm Kendra, and if you don't mind, I'd like to call you Joanna."

After years of dealing with Guy Machett's unyielding objections to being called anything other than a strictly formal "Dr. Machett," Joanna welcomed Kendra Baldwin's brand of straightforward informality.

Just then, Kendra herself emerged from the circle of generator-powered artificial illumination. "There you are, Joanna," she said. "I've told my guys to take him back to the morgue. Once he's gone, the truck is all yours."

Joanna nodded her thanks, smiling as she did so. Guy

Machett had never referred to his morgue assistants by anything other than the formal term, "dieners." The fact that Dr. Baldwin called them "her guys" was also a mark in her favor.

"What can you tell us?" Joanna asked.

"Driver's license in his pocket identifies him as Fredrico Arturo Gomez from Bakersfield, California. He signed up to be an organ donor, but that's not going to happen. I found multiple gunshot wounds in his body, all of which penetrated the victim's left side. Any one of them could have done the trick. I'd say he was dead long before the truck smashed through the guardrail and hit the ground. From what I could see, a barrage of bullets entered the cab of the truck through the passenger side with enough force to penetrate both the truck and the victim."

"We're talking real firepower, then," Joanna observed.

"Right," Kendra agreed. "If the victim was traveling at sixty miles per hour or even sixty-five, we'd have to be talking either a whole troop of shooters or else an automatic weapon of some kind for there to be that many hits."

"Since the entry wounds are all on the victim's left side, that means the shooter was either on the left-hand shoulder of the highway, waiting for him," Deb suggested, "or else in a vehicle that was passing in the left lane."

"That could be, too," Joanna said. "Shooting from a passing vehicle makes more sense than coming from opposite directions. If each of the two meeting vehicles was doing sixty, that adds up to 120 miles per hour. The split second the two would have been side by side wouldn't allow enough time for multiple hits, even with an automatic weapon. There's a posted no-passing zone right there where he went through the guardrail, but if someone was out to kill the guy, a solid yellow line on the pavement wouldn't count for much. What we know for sure is that, one way or another, this guy was ambushed. Either the shooter was following him, or else he knew the exact time he would be traveling this particular section of roadway. So where's the brass—still on the pavement or on the shoulder somewhere?"

Joanna pulled out her phone and dialed Sergeant Crane's number. "We need some manpower out here," she said when he answered. "The targeted vehicle went off the bridge on Highway 92 at the San Pedro River. From the damage to the guardrail, it looks as though he was headed east, but we don't know exactly where the shooting took place. That part of the highway is fairly straight. The shooting might have happened as far away as a mile or so, and it took the truck that long to finally veer off the road. We need people out here combing the highway on both sides of the crime scene looking for brass and, if we're really lucky, maybe some usable tire prints."

"Is this a situation where we should bring the old duffers into play?" Sergeant Crane asked.

Recently a group of local seniors, several of them still in possession of Eagle Scout badges from long ago, had erased the natural dividing lines between the Kiwanis, Rotary, and Lions Clubs and shown up at Joanna's office offering to form a group of senior citizen reserve officers. Officially dubbed the SCRs (Senior Citizen Reservists), they had all gone through citizens' academy training and had done a number of patrol ride-alongs. Some of them helped out with routine filing and clerical procedures at the Justice Center. They had also proved to be invaluable in helping locate several vulnerable adults when the sheriff's office posted Silver Alerts. This, however, was the first time any of them would be deployed on a search for evidence.

Not surprisingly, George Winfield—the retired ME and Joanna's stepfather—was their leader. Joanna glanced at her watch: four twelve A.M. A phone call to George at this hour wouldn't faze him in the least, but it would put her mother in a complete snit. Joanna knew from personal experience that having Eleanor Lathrop Winfield get up on the wrong side of the bed wouldn't be good for anyone. That was the truth of the matter, but she also didn't want to spill those kinds of family beans in front of Sergeant Crane.

"Now that you mention it," she said, "calling out the SCRs is an excellent suggestion, but there's no sense having them out here milling around in the dark. If they're going to be conducting a search of both sides of the roadway, I'd rather wait until daylight before putting them to work. George is an early riser. Give him a call at five. Tell him what's up and that I'd like his people here right around sunrise. Before he comes out this way, though, ask him to stop by the Justice Center and pick up our supply of metal detectors. At last count, I think we had ten or so. And remind him that anyone turning up for this operation needs to be wearing orange reflective vests. Understood?"

"Roger."

About then, several flashlight beams came bouncing toward the spot where Joanna, Kendra Baldwin, and

Deb Howell stood conferring. At the center of the group were four men—Kendra's two dieners and two of Joanna's deputies—lugging a loaded and unwieldy gurney across sandy terrain that rendered the wheels useless.

"Do you want to see him?" Kendra asked.

Joanna shook her head. "Not right now," she said. "I'll see him later at the autopsy."

"Go ahead and load him up, then" Kendra told her attendants. While they struggled to do so, the ME turned back to Joanna.

"So you're coming to that?" she asked. "I thought only detectives viewed autopsies."

"It's my job, too," Joanna told her. "When do you plan to do it?"

"Probably first thing this morning," the ME replied. "Will eight work for you?"

"That's fine. Both Detective Carbajal and I will be there," Joanna said. "In the meantime, I'll put Deb here in charge of tracking down the victim's next of kin. Was the guy carrying a cell phone?"

"I didn't see one," Kendra answered. "Probably got thrown out of the truck in the crash."

"Don't worry," Joanna said. "We're going to be combing through this scene with a fine-toothed comb. If he had a cell phone in that vehicle, we'll find it. What about the Border Patrol officer who called it in? Where is he?"

"Agent Cannon," Kendra answered, pointing. "His vehicle is there on the right, just beyond where the truck came to rest. The last I saw of him, he was talking to Detective Carbajal."

"Cannon drove through our crime scene?"

"Don't be too hard on him," Kendra said. "He got here

within five minutes of the incident. At the time, he was far more focused on possible survivors than he was on preserving evidence."

"Point taken," Joanna agreed.

As Kendra started back up the embankment, someone else was coming down. In the glow of Kendra's flashlight, Joanna caught a glimpse of a bristling electrical-socket hairdo and had to stifle the urge to groan aloud. The last thing she needed at the crime scene was reporters of any kind. Among those unwanted reporters, Marliss Shackleford of the *Bisbee Bee* sat at the top of the list.

"You've got no business being here, Marliss," Joanna said coldly. "This is a crime scene. Go back up top where you belong."

"Come on, Sheriff Brady," Marliss said. "Do we have to do this? Can't you just tell me what's going on? I heard that a truckload of LEGO boxes had been hijacked or something."

"'Or something' is the operant phrase for the day," Joanna told her. "This is an open investigation. Until we're ready to give a full press briefing, there will be no comment at all from anyone in my department."

"You can go ahead and deny it all you want," Marliss prodded. "The point is I already know that a truckload of LEGO sets is involved. If you're going to go the 'No comment' route, you'll have to live with the story the way I tell it."

Joanna knew then that Marliss had probably been listening in on a police scanner and had learned enough to send her out in the middle of the night ready to do her stint of on-the-scene reporting.

"I'm not confirming or denying," Joanna insisted, "and I'm sticking with 'No comment.' Now, go back to your vehicle and get out of here. You're interfering with a homicide investigation."

As soon as the words were out of her mouth, Joanna knew she had screwed up, but it was too late to take them back.

Marliss perked up instantly "Did you say 'homicide'?" Marliss asked. "I was under the impression it was nothing more than a motor vehicle accident."

"Go," Joanna insisted. "Go now, before I have one of my deputies to escort you away."

"That's all right," Marliss said. "A homicide with LEGO sets on the side sounds intriguing enough. I should be able to do something with that."

She left then, scrabbling, unassisted back up to the highway. Joanna turned to Detective Howell. "Would you follow her and make sure that if anyone up there talks to her, especially people in my department, they understand that they will have to answer to me."

While Deb hurried away to do as she'd been told, Joanna turned and walked across the sandy riverbed to where Jaime Carbajal in plain clothes and Bill Cannon in his Border Patrol uniform stood leaning against the front bumper of Bill's marked SUV.

Border Patrol was a booming business in southern Arizona these days. Back when Joanna's father, D. H. Lathrop, had been the sheriff of Cochise County, he would have known all the local Border Patrol guys, the names of their wives, and probably the names of their kids, too. Now, however, with agents cycling in and out of the Tucson sector with astonishing regularity, Joanna knew no more than a handful on sight or by name, and Agent Bill Cannon was one she had never met.

Approaching the two men, she held out her hand. "Sheriff Joanna Brady," she said, introducing herself. "I understand you've been a big help here tonight."

Agent Cannon, with dark stains on the shirt of his uniform, turned out to be a young guy, not more than twenty-five or so. He was short and stocky and wore his blond hair in a crew cut. "Glad to meet you, ma'am," he said. "I wish I could have done more. I was just up the river a ways, walking the bank, trying to spot footprints, when I heard gunfire. I made tracks back to my vehicle and was almost there when I heard the crash. Tearing through that guardrail made a hell of a racket."

"How long between the gunfire and the crash?"

Agent Cannon thought about that for a moment before he answered. "Twenty seconds or maybe thirty at the most. When I came up the riverbed, I spotted the truck right away because the headlights were still on. The truck must have gone end over end a couple of times, because it came to rest a long way from the base of the embankment. And for the cargo box to split apart the way it did when it hit the tree trunk, the driver had to be going way over the speed limit when he hit the guardrail."

Detective Carbajal nodded. "Deputy Ruiz tells me there aren't any skid marks up above. I'm wondering if maybe the guy was already dead. His foot could have been deadweight on the gas pedal at the time it went off the road."

Nodding, Joanna stood for a minute examining the wreckage. The truck had evidently been airborne as it plunged off the embankment. It landed nose down in the dirt and then flipped over at least twice before the bed of the truck slammed into the trunk of one of San Pedro's venerable old cottonwood trees. The blow was forceful enough to split the cargo box in half and send an eruption of cellophane-covered LEGO boxes exploding in every direction. The delivery truck turned out to be larger than Joanna had envisioned, making her wonder if the single U-Haul truck she had ordered would be big enough to contain this unconventional cargo spill.

Joanna turned her attention back to the conversation in time to hear Jaime Carbajal say, "We'll need you to leave your vehicle here until we're finished processing the crime scene."

"Okay," Cannon agreed. "Let me know when you're done. In the meantime, I'll let my supervisor know that I need someone to come give me a ride so I can go home and clean up."

For the first time, Joanna realized that the stains on Agent Cannon's uniform were most likely bloodstains. Since he had been the first one the scene, that made sense, Joanna supposed, but still . . . The person who called in a homicide often had something to do with it.

"And you'll stop by the department later today to give an official statement?" Jaime continued.

"Sure thing," Agent Cannon said. "My shift ends at eight A.M. Give me a call after that and let me know what time is convenient."

"Will do."

Joanna watched Cannon walk away. "He's the one who called it in," she said quietly. "You don't think he's involved, do you?"

"I doubt it," Jaime responded, "although, just in case, I asked Deb to request a copy of his radio transmissions from Border Patrol."

"We won't have those anytime soon," Joanna observed.

She got along fine with the local Border Patrol folks, but relations between her and the headquarters folks for the Tucson sector weren't always the best. TSA routinely ignored or else delayed responses to requests for information from local jurisdictions. The message being that they were the feds, and everyone else could take a number and get in line.

"Maybe sooner than you think," Jaime Carbajal said with a grin. "Deb can be quite the bulldog once she sinks her teeth into something."

Donning a pair of Latex gloves, Joanna reached down, picked up one of the boxes, and shook it, listening and hearing the sound of rattling. The corners of the box were crumpled but not torn. The cellophane wrapping on the outside was still intact. She suspected that all this careful packaging meant that everything inside was still fine, including any drugs that might be hidden there. Turning on her flashlight, she discovered she was holding something that purported to be the TIE fighter with 1,685 pieces.

Joanna had no idea what a TIE fighter was. In their family, Butch Dixon was the resident expert on all things *Star Wars*, but she guessed that this model was probably worth a fair amount of money. Even the small LEGO sets Dennis lusted for on the shelves in Target were pricier than Joanna thought reasonable. This one was probably somewhere in the $200 range.

But examining the colorful box itself offered no hints about why the driver of a vehicle hauling LEGO sets would have been traveling on an out-of-the way route that wasn't a direct connection to anywhere else. Nor did it explain why the truck had been ambushed and taken down with automatic weapons fire. Shaking her head, Joanna returned the box to what seemed to be the same place she'd found it.

"We'll have to wait for sunrise to finish the crime scene photos," Jaime observed. "That's a little over an hour away."

Joanna nodded. "And I've asked for the SCRs to show up and search the roadway for brass. I want to know exactly where those shots came from and what kind of weapon was used."

"Take a look at the cab," Jaime suggested.

Together, Joanna and her detective approached the passenger side of the truck. The door lock had given way, leaving the door dangling on its hinges. A cursory survey of both sides of the door reminded Joanna of a cheese grater: smooth indentation on the outside and jagged ones on the inside.

"That's a bunch of holes," Joanna said. "Have you found any spent bullets?"

"Not yet," Jaime replied. "The CSIs have been working the scene but they haven't started on the truck. They'll probably have to wait until the truck is towed to the impound lot before they can finish up."

Joanna stepped away from the truck, shaking her head. "I don't need a team of CSIs to tell me what's really going on here," she said. "I already know."

"What's that?"

"Whoever the shooter is, he has way more firepower than we do and he's not afraid to use it. Not only do we need to find him fast, we'll have to be careful as all hell when it comes to taking him down."

• • •

Ali Reynolds was peacefully asleep when her husband's cell phone buzzed them both awake at seven A.M.

"Hey, Stu," B. Simpson said. "What's up?"

B. Simpson's company, High Noon Enterprises, had started off years earlier as a locally owned and operated cyber security company located in Sedona, Arizona. Since then it had grown exponentially, morphing into a well-respected international firm that numbered some of the world's leading companies among its clientele. Stuart Ramey, a high-functioning Asperger's syndrome guy with a brilliant head for computers and abysmal people skills, was B.'s second-in-command.

"We just got a hit on our LEGO media scanning program."

As part of their security process, they maintained a constant search for any media hits involving one of their clients. Media hits often meant that some kind of security issue was brewing, and keeping a multilingual worldwide watch for trouble was one of the services High Noon offered.

"What kind of hit?" B asked, switching the phone to speaker as Ali got out of bed and ushered Bella, their recently rescued miniature dachshund, over to the patio door to let the dog out. Because of the presence of too many nighttime critters in Sedona's semi-wild environs, Ali stayed at the door and kept watch until Bella finished her business. Then the dog came inside, leaped gracefully back up onto the bed, and curled into a small ball in her designated spot in the middle of the foot of their bed.

"I thought you'd be interested," Stu said, "because, for one thing, it's from right here in Arizona."

"Where in Arizona?"

"Bisbee."

"What exactly are we talking about?"

"It's a column called Bisbee Buzzings from the local newspaper, the *Bisbee Bee*, written by someone named Marliss Shackleford. It reads more like a blog than an actual article, but it posted just a few minutes ago at 6:45. The electronic version evidently comes out before the paper version."

"What does it say?" B. asked with a hint of impatience leaking into his voice.

Stu cleared his throat and began reading aloud.

Early this morning the Cochise County Sheriff's Office was investigating a fatality motor vehicle incident at the point where Highway 92 crosses the San Pedro River. Although Sheriff Joanna Brady refused to make any comments, this reporter was able to ascertain that the case involves a delivery truck that slammed through the guardrail into the riverbed. The damaged truck was clearly visible, but my understanding is that the investigation is being conducted as a possible homicide.

An anonymous source close to the investigation, speaking without permission, claimed that the truck was transporting a load of LEGO sets when it crashed in the early morning hours. There were indications that automatic weapons fire was involved.

So what's really going on here? Is this a situation where bad guys with guns targeted some poor truck driver who was minding his own business and was gunned down for simply doing his job? If that's the case, every resident of Cochise County is in danger and needs to be on high alert.

What I'm asking is this: When will someone from Sheriff Brady's department come forward and speak candidly about what's really going on? In the meantime, I can assure you that, as more information becomes available, your intrepid reporter will be on the job.

B. couldn't help but be pleased that the automated media surveillance network he and Stu had created had managed to pick up on that one-word mention from a tiny electronic newspaper article in an out-of-the-way corner of Arizona. But he also knew why Stu was calling him. LEGO sets were essentially limited editions. Once a popular model was no longer available through regular retail channels, the prices of those sets skyrocketed, creating a lucrative black market trade. The LEGO company, based in Denmark, had hired High Noon as an outside source to address that black market and to search out the source of inventory that was obviously going astray.

The sets were manufactured at several overseas locations. B. had recommended placing GPS locator chips inside the boxes of some of the higher-priced models, concealed inside the gel-packs used for moisture protection. That idea had been dismissed out of hand as being "unworkable and too expensive."

Having a chip inside even one of the sets from the wreck would have been a huge help about now. The regular radio-frequency identification chips, RFIDs, on the outsides of the packages would provide some information, however, including where they had been manufactured and where they were going. B. assumed that legitimate freight haulers would be using eighteen-wheelers and traveling on interstate highways. They wouldn't be utilizing midsize box trucks on back roads in the middle of the night. If there were LEGO sets involved in the incident, B. was confident that, one way or the other, they were stolen goods.

"That's all?" B. asked. "Just that one-word mention?"

"So far."

"Nothing more on local television feeds?"

"The place where the wreck happened is a good seventy-five miles outside Tucson," Stu replied. "A motor vehicle accident, even a fatality MVA, in Cochise County generally wouldn't garner any attention from the Tucson news outlets. If the incident ends up being classified as a homicide, however, the Tucson stations will be all over it."

"We need to be all over it before they are," B. declared. "I want someone with a chip reader on the scene as soon as possible. Can you find out where and when the latest LEGO shipments have come ashore? Since we have an ending point, if we can pin down a beginning point, we may be able to track down who's responsible."

"I'll get Cami started on the shipping situation the moment she comes in," Stu said. "We have a chip reader here, but getting it to Cochise County in a hurry is a problem. I checked. We're talking a five-hour trip. As for obtaining permission to scan the boxes, good luck with that."

Cami Lee was a recent computer sciences graduate whom B. had snagged to be Stu's assistant. She was a dynamite five-foot-nothing package, bright and talented.

She was also totally capable when it came to doing her job, which included dealing with Stuart Ramey's gruff style and less-than-easygoing personality.

"Ali and I will be on our way to Cottonwood in a matter of minutes," B. said. "Try to find out any additional details you can about that wreck."

"If you're going to Bisbee, wouldn't it make more sense for you to leave directly from home?" Stu suggested.

"No," B. said firmly. "We're coming there first."

Seated at the foot of the bed, petting Bella, Ali was caught off guard by B.'s use of the plural pronoun "we."

Taking the hint, Ali dashed into the bathroom. When she emerged minutes later, showered but still in her robe, B. was back on the phone with someone else. "Right," he was saying. "The R66 will be just fine. What's the pilot's name again?" There was a pause while he made a note in his iPad.

Ali knew that the R66 was a Robinson helicopter, which meant B. was on the phone with Heli-Pros, a helicopter charter outfit out of Scottsdale that B. used on occasion.

"Okay, Chuck," B. continued. "Landing at the Sierra Vista airport sounds about right: That should be closer than anywhere else. Can you have a rental car there? . . . Good . . . Yes, there will be two passengers. The lead passenger will be my wife, Ali Reynolds. She should be listed on my customer profile. The second one will be Stuart Ramey."

B. paused again and then turned to Ali. "How much do you weigh?"

"Are we even having this conversation?" she demanded, hands on her hips, but she knew why he was asking. In order to calculate the range, the charter outfit needed to know the weight of the passengers. "One thirty-three," she added.

B. repeated the information into the phone then turned to Ali again. "Any idea how much Stu weighs?"

"You think you're going to talk Stu Ramey into going for a ride in a helicopter?" Ali asked. "Are you nuts? And why aren't you going?"

"How much?" B. insisted, ignoring her query.

"Two forty or maybe two fifty," Ali said with a shrug, "but that's just a guess."

B. passed along that information as well. "Right," he said. "The usual place. I know Chuck isn't our customary pilot. Let him know that we've got an approved helipad painted on the far northeastern corner of the High Noon parking lot."

Ali waited until he was off the phone. "You still haven't answered my question."

"Because I'm going to be spending my whole day dealing with corporate guys from every corner of the planet. I can't afford to be out of reach for as long as it takes to get back and forth to Bisbee. Stu would be lost on his own, and Cami's not experienced enough."

Shaking her head, Ali collected Bella and took her to the kitchen. Leland Brooks, their majordomo, was already on hand with a freshly brewed pot of coffee. "Will you and Mr. Simpson be wanting breakfast?"

"Sounds like breakfast of any kind is off the list for this morning," she told him as he busied himself dishing out Bella's food. "B. and I have to head out for Cottonwood as soon as we're both decent. There's some kind of crisis afoot, so whatever you were planning for dinner should probably be put on hold. I'm being deputized to a crime scene in Cochise County. I don't know where B. will end up, and I have no idea when we'll be back."

"In other words, business as usual," Leland said with a smile. "I take it you won't be going into the office in Flagstaff today."

Weeks earlier, Ali and B. both had been involved in the take-down of a polygamous group called The Family located in northern Arizona. The group's leader, Richard Lowell, knowing he was about to be brought to justice for human trafficking, had gunned down most of the men in the cult, leaving the affected women and children to fend for themselves.

Some of the women had left The Family's compound willingly. Others who tried to stay on ended up being evicted when the state discovered that most of the dwellings in the community weren't built up to code and needed to be leveled. Most of the displaced homemakers had few job skills, and the kids were years behind students of the same age as far as scholastic achievement was concerned. Working as a volunteer three days a week out of an office shoehorned into the Flagstaff YWCA, Ali's job was to smooth out some of the bumps and difficulties The Family's women and children struggled with as they tried to find their way in a world entirely foreign to them.

"This is a priority right now," Ali told Leland. "I'll call the Y and let them know I'm traveling and won't be in. Since I'm a volunteer, obviously they can't fire me."

When Ali returned to the bedroom with two cups of coffee in hand, she found that B., fully dressed, was back on the phone, speaking urgently and fluently in a language Ali suspected to be Danish. It was a lengthy conversation. By the time it ended, Ali was dressed and both of their coffee cups were empty. On their way to the garage, they found that Leland had freshly loaded travel mugs waiting for them on the kitchen counter.

"I'm telling you, you're never going to be able to talk Stu Ramey into a helicopter," Ali insisted again, once they were in B.'s car and belted into their seats. "He's scared to death of flying."

"He flew to Vegas for the wedding," B. countered. "He flew to Paris last winter."

"Yes, he did," Ali conceded, "but it was under protest, and those trips were on board airplanes. Big difference. Planes are one thing; helicopters are another. He won't go."

"He will if you ask him," B. said. "After all, aren't you the smooth talker who persuaded him to take both those trips?"

"But why does Stu need to go in the first place?" Ali objected. "I'm not exactly tech savvy, but I'm pretty sure I'm smart enough to operate an RFID chip reader and relay the information back to you."

"I'm sure you are, too," B. replied. "But think about this: Supposing a crook of some kind has been tasked with driving a truckload of stolen merchandise from one place to another. How's he going to figure out how to get there?"

"If he hasn't been there before, he'd probably need a GPS device of some kind," Ali answered.

"Right. And who do you suppose is one of the most qualified people on earth when it comes to extracting information out of whatever device Mr. Bad Guy may have been using? Not you and not me, either. Stu can do it with his eyes closed, but he has to be there—boots on the ground—to do the work. It's just like a haircut: You can't get a haircut over the phone."

Ali's phone rang. When she saw Cami's name on the display, Ali put the call on speaker so B. could hear as well.

"Hi, Cami," Ali said. "I'm here and so is B."

"Good morning, guys," Cami said cheerfully. "Here's what I've got for you so far. The most recent shipment from LEGO arrived in Long Beach by way of the manufacturing plant in Monterrey, Mexico, yesterday morning. It consisted of twenty-five shipping containers devoted solely to LEGO. The last of that shipment was off-loaded yesterday by approximately three P.M. According to the GPS chips on the pallets, most of those containers are now en route to their final destinations with the exception of ones that have already been delivered at various West Coast distribution centers between San Diego and San Francisco."

Adding GPS locator beacons to all the pallets had been done at B.'s suggestion. Each chip listed the individual pallet's weight as well as its final destination.

"We know from the readings on the pallet tracking system that the designated weight on each pallet remains unchanged from what it was when it left the plant in Mexico."

"All the pallets may still weigh the same amount," B. said darkly, "but I'm betting some of them aren't carrying their original payloads or maybe the boxes in the wrecked truck are from a pallet that was never chipped in the first place."

"As in 'no chip, no pallet'?" Ali asked.

B. nodded. "Which would mean there are people working this scam at both ends of the food chain, and we need to find out who they are."

Cami waited quietly on the phone, listening, until B. and Ali finished their own discussion. "Is that all you need me to do, then?" she asked.

"Not exactly," Ali said. "What's Stu's favorite Subway sandwich?"

"The club," Cami answered without hesitation. "With mayo, lettuce, tomato, and Jack cheese. Why?"

"Go get two of them," Ali said, "one for him and one for me. It turns out he and I about to take a little trip, and we'll need some sustenance along the way."

"What kind of trip?" Cami asked.

"Never mind. We'll tell you when we get there."

By the time B. pulled into High Noon's lot, Ali had finished letting the YWCA know that she would be a no-show for that day at least and maybe longer. Cami arrived at the same time they did. She was just exiting her car with a pair of sandwich bags in hand, when the shadow of a landing helicopter passed over her head and then swooped down for a landing in the far corner of the lot.

Cami looked at it and then back at Ali and B. "Surely you don't think Stu's going to ride in that."

"He'll have to," B. said. "This is an important client, and we need a quick turnaround."

Cami shook her head. "Good luck with that," she said, and stalked inside with B. and Ali right behind her.

"Hey," the unsuspecting Stu said when he saw them. "Marliss Shackleford just updated her blog."

"What's new?"

"Come look."

B. and Ali walked over to Stu's bank of computers and read over his shoulder.

At a hastily called press briefing this morning, Chief Deputy Tom Hadlock, media spokesman for the Cochise County Sheriff's Office, has just confirmed what I had reported earlier. The fatality truck accident that occurred earlier today on Highway 92 east of Palominas is now being investigated as a homicide.

According to Chief Deputy Hadlock, the vehicle, carrying a load of possibly stolen goods, was attacked with a barrage of automatic gunfire just west of the San Pedro bridge. The driver of the vehicle, still unidentified, was found dead at the scene. An autopsy is scheduled later this morning with the Cochise County Medical Examiner.

Chief Deputy Hadlock is urging anyone who might have been traveling on Highway 92 between the hours of midnight and three A.M. to contact the sheriff's office, especially if they happened to spot anything out of the ordinary.

In the briefing, Chief Deputy Hadlock said the truck was carrying "contraband" of some kind and declined to discuss the nature of said goods. But that's just him. He may still be playing the old "refuse to confirm nor deny" game, but I'm convinced that the stolen goods in question are LEGO sets.

Stay tuned and keep in mind that you heard it here first.

"I suspect Ms. Shackleford here most likely isn't one of the local sheriff's favorite people," Ali observed when she finished reading the blog post. "There's some obvious animosity here, and someone who publishes unsubstantiated rumors is liable to be blackballed from the room."

"Which means you should probably have a little chat with Ms. Shackleford when you're down there," B. said. "After all, I'm not the kind of person who turns up my nose at unsubstantiated rumors."

"You're going there?" Stu asked. "To Bisbee?"

"No," B. said. "You are—you and Ali. There's likely to be a tech component to all this. If so, I'm hoping you can glean as much information from that as possible."

"But I already told you," Stu said. "It's more than a five-hour drive from here."

"We won't be driving," Ali said. "B. called Heli-Pros. Our aircraft is already out in the parking lot, ready to go."

"A chartered helicopter?" Stu said, sounding alarmed. "You expect me to get on a helicopter? I don't do helicopters. I weigh too much, and I know too much about gravity."

"Stu, we need you to do this," B. reasoned. "LEGO is an important client, and we need to do whatever's necessary to learn what we can about what's happened."

"Not if it means I have to ride in a helicopter," Stu said determinedly, shaking his head. "I won't go."

"Please," Ali begged. "We need you on the ground to sort things out."

"Send Cami," Stu said. "She can do everything I can do . . . well, almost everything. And if something turns up that stumps her, as long as she has my tool kit and a video camera, I can walk her through whatever needs to be done"

Stu reached under his desk and pulled out a worn leather bag that TV's Marcus Welby, MD, might have dragged along with him on house calls back in the sixties.

"Trust me," he said, handing the bag over to Cami. "Most everything you need is in there, except for the RFID reader itself. My cloner's in there, too, by the way."

"Really?" Cami said, brightening. "You're going to turn me loose with your cloner?"

Ali knew the cloner to be a piece of specialized cell phone duplicating equipment that Stu had never before allowed out of his personal possession.

"I'm pretty sure you're trustworthy," Stu said. "In fact, I'm sure of it."

After Stu's ringing endorsement of Cami's capabilities, Ali realized that both she and B. had been overruled and outmaneuvered.

"So much for not being able to give a haircut over the phone," she said with a grin in B.'s direction. "I guess they're possible these days after all. All right, Cami," she added, turning to the young woman. "I guess that other club sandwich belongs to you. Wheels up in five."

Right around five thirty, with the horizon slowly brightening in the east, Dave Hollicker sought out Joanna and shook an evidence bag in front of her face. "Hey, boss," he said gleefully, "we've got some."

"Some what?" Joanna echoed. "Bullets, I hope."

"Yup. Five so far, and we'll probably find more."

"What kind of bullets?"

"They're 7.62 NATO rounds," Dave answered. "That means we're most likely looking for an AK-47."

"That news doesn't exactly make me feel warm and fuzzy," Joanna told him.

"Me neither."

"Anything else?"

"A broken Garmin GPS, a cell phone that's smashed to pieces and dead as a doornail, a crack pipe, a wallet with fifteen hundred dollars in it in cash. There's also a California driver's license belonging to one Fredrico Arturo Gomez with an address in Bakersfield, California."

"So we have a pretty good idea of who our victim is, then?" Joanna asked.

"No such luck," Dave replied. "When I ran the license, it turned out to be phony and so was the address."

"So either he's an illegal, a crook, or both?"

"That's about the size of it. Once the ME collects his prints, we may get a hit on one of those. With the crack pipe in play, most likely this isn't his first rodeo, and his prints will be in the system."

The radio on the shoulder of Joanna's uniform squawked awake. "Sheriff Brady," Armando Ruiz barked in her ear. "The SCRs are here asking what you want them to do."

Joanna's watch said six A.M. sharp as she started back up the steep embankment. George Winfield and his band of eight eager-beaver reservists stood at the ready. Gathered around a nine-passenger minivan, they were busy examining the metal detectors they had just been issued.

"We're ready to go to work," George told her. "What do you want us to do?"

"This is a shooting that was not random. We're operating on the assumption that the victim was deliberately targeted. We're looking for shell casings, folks, a whole bunch of shell casings. We've had vehicles driving back and forth all morning, and no one has spotted anything on the pavement. That suggests that the shooter was off the roadway somewhere, maybe hiding in the brush, and waiting for our victim to pass by. I want you to start from where the truck went through the guardrail and then, using the metal detectors, work your way back, searching both sides of the highway both visually and with the detectors.

"I'm asking for a systematic, inch-by-inch scan from the edge of the pavement out to the fence line and back again. If you find casings, do not touch them or move them. Call George immediately so he can notify one of my CSIs to come take charge of the evidence. And if you see any recent shoe prints or tire prints near the casings—or anywhere else, for that matter—please avoid obliterating them if at all possible."

As the SCRs set off to do her bidding, Joanna stood between the torn pieces of guardrail and stared down at the scene, convinced that she'd made the right call. With the number of holes in the truck—in both the cab and the bed—there had to be dozens of casings out there somewhere. The fact that Agent Cannon had been on the scene summoning assistance such a short time after the crash meant the shooter wouldn't have had time to hang around collecting his brass. Information gleaned from that might well lead back to both the weapon in question as well as the shooter.

Even without additional evidence, it was clear to Joanna that this had to have been an ambush with the shooter lying in wait until the truck reached a certain point in the road. Had the shooter merely intended to disable the truck and lift the cargo, the shots would have been aimed at the engine block or the tires. The shots into the truck's cab had all been kill shots, so who was the target here? Just the driver, or was it someone behind the driver—maybe whoever might well have forked over $1,500 to have the load transported? Either way, the first order of business was establishing the driver's identity.

Ten minutes after the SCRs were deployed, George called her. "Okay," he said. "We found your casings—a whole flock of 'em—inside a mesquite grove on the left side of the road just west of the parking lot for the Saddle Up Steakhouse. Couldn't see any tire tracks at all. The restaurant's parking lot is paved, so the shooter may have parked on that and walked from there. With all the grass on the shoulder of the road, I doubt you'll find footprints."

"Probably not," Joanna agreed.

"But as close as this is to Hereford," George continued, "I'm surprised no one heard anything."

"Tell your guys I said 'Thanks and good work,'" Joanna told him. "Make that 'great work.' I'll send the CSI team down to bag and tag the casings. I'll also get someone on the horn to the owners of the steakhouse to see if they have any security cameras."

"Wait a minute," George said. "Are you telling me I dragged everybody out of bed for something that only lasted ten minutes and now I'm supposed to say, 'Go home and go back to bed'?"

Joanna thought about that for a second. "No," she said finally. "Don't do that. Once the CSI's finish processing the scene down on the river, we'll need someone to go around collecting LEGO sets—hundreds of them—and load them onto another truck."

"How much time before they'll be ready for us?" George asked. "Enough for us to head back to the café in Palominas for some breakfast?"

"That should work out fine," Joanna assured him.

By seven thirty the SCRs, now sporting latex gloves, were down in the riverbed gathering scattered LEGO sets and packing them one by one into the U-Haul truck that Deputy Stock had parked on the bank nearest the highway. Joanna felt guilty watching people she regarded as "old codgers" hoofing it through the sand, but the truth was she needed the help and they seemed to be having a ball. Besides, if she'd called in her deputies to do the job, there would have been no one left out on patrol.

As the boxes were gathered and loaded, it soon became apparent that a second U-Haul would not be required. The same could not be said of the totaled box truck. That one for sure required two flatbed tow trucks: one for the cab and one for the body, which had literally split into two pieces. The tow truck guys were in the process of finishing loading the cab onto the second flatbed, when Joanna's phone rang. Her secretary, Kristin Gregovich, was on the line.

"I know you've got your hands full out there today, Sheriff Brady," Kristin said, "but I just had a call from Dr. Baldwin. Jaime's already up at the morgue, waiting. Dr. Baldwin wants to know if you're still coming or should she do the autopsy without you?"

Glancing at her watch, Joanna was astonished to discover that it was almost eight thirty. She had been at the crime scene for the better part of five hours, and she was now almost half an hour late for the autopsy.

"Tell Dr. Baldwin I'm sorry to have kept her waiting," Joanna said, sprinting back up the embankment to where her Yukon was still parked. "I'm on my way right now. I'm probably another half hour out at most."

The trip to the morgue wasn't one that merited lights and sirens, but Joanna drove well over the posted limits to get there. When she arrived in the parking lot, Jaime was climbing out of his car to go back inside.

"What's up," she asked, hurrying to intercept him.

"Dr. Baldwin took the victim's prints and I just finished running them," he reported. "Turns out Mr. Fredrico Gomez is actually a small-time crook out of Santa Ana, California—one Alberto Ricardo 'Taquito' Mendoza." He simulated quotation marks in the air with his index fingers when saying the word "Taquito."

"His nickname is Taquito?" Joanna asked. "Really?"

"That's what it says on his rap sheet."

"What else does it say?"

"Small-time drug violations, mostly: possession with intent to sell, everything from crack to meth. He's been out on probation for three months. I'm sure this little out-of-state venture would have sent him straight back to the slammer. Now that he's dead, that's a moot point."

Jaime was already properly dressed for the occasion. All he needed to do was slip a new pair of paper booties on over his shoes. It took a moment longer for Joanna to dress herself in the paper gown and booties that constituted proper autopsy-viewing attire. When she finally entered the room, Dr. Baldwin stood over the naked body with a scalpel in hand and a frown on her face.

"It's about time," she said.

"Sorry, sorry, sorry," Joanna murmured in return. "It was crazy out there."

The pallid body had been stripped of its clothing and washed. There were at least four entrance wounds visible, but those weren't easy to see among hundreds of jagged lacerations that covered the entire left side of the body. A broken piece of the truck's steering wheel still protruded from the chest wall. The part of the body that should have been a face was totally unrecognizable.

"He went through the windshield," the ME explained as Joanna took her place at the table.

"How?" Joanna asked. "I saw deployed airbags."

"They deployed, all right, but by the time the truck slammed into the tree, they had already deflated. Some of the lacerations and the broken steering wheel are from that. Most of them, though, were caused by the bullets propelling shrapnel from the outside of the truck into the cab."

Using the scalpel as a pointer, Dr. Baldwin indicated the various entry wounds, which Joanna had already noticed. "We have bullet wounds here, here, here, and here—four of them in all. These two are nothing more than flesh wounds and would not have been fatal. The other two bullets entered his chest cavity. Presumably those remain lodged inside, since there are no exit wounds. I'm assuming I'll be able to retrieve them."

Joanna kept trying to pay attention as Kendra droned on in an emotionless voice; she might have used it to discuss the weather.

"From the debris we found on the clothing, I suspect that at least one of the chest wound shots entered the cab through the driver's-side window. The nonfatal wounds came in through the door itself. From here it looks as though either the bullets killed him or else the broken steering wheel. The only way we'll be able to sort that out is to get on with it, so let's get started."

Joanna steeled herself for that first cut. Dr. Baldwin was still speaking as her scalpel sliced into the pale chest and she found that the ME's voice, strangely muffled, had somehow drifted into the background. For a time she seemed to be speaking from very far away. Then suddenly her voice was much closer at hand and much sharper. "Hey. Are you all right? For God's sake, Jaime, catch her!"

The next thing Joanna knew, Jaime had grabbed her under the arms. Holding her upright, he manhandled her across the room and held her up in front of a large stainless steel sink in time for her to be very sick. Embarrassed beyond bearing, she shrugged her way out of Jaime's grasp, cleaned off her face, and dried it with a paper towel.

"Hey," Kendra Baldwin said when Joanna gathered herself and turned back toward the examining table. "I thought you were an old hand at this."

In truth Joanna really was an old hand. She'd been through countless autopsies through the years and never once with this kind of humiliating result.

"Sorry," she said. "It must have been something I ate."

"No harm, no foul," the Dr. Baldwin said lightly. "It happens to the best of us, but you still look a little green. If you want to take a rain check . . ."

"No," Joanna said firmly. "I'll be fine."

And she was. It took a lot of grit, but she managed to hang in there through the remainder of the procedure. When the autopsy finally ended with Dr. Baldwin's declaration of "death by homicidal violence," Joanna didn't hang around for any chitchat. Once out in the mercifully fresh air, she waited for Detective Carbajal to emerge as well. The nausea that had plagued her earlier had passed. Having long since missed breakfast, she was starving.

"It's almost eleven," she said, glancing at her watch. "Want to go grab a bite?"

Jaime shook his head. "Delcia packed me a lunch," he said. "Besides, I need to get back to the department and give Deb a hand with the paperwork." Jaime started to walk away, then he stopped and turned back to her. "What happened inside there, boss, is between us," he told her. "It's nobody else's business."

Both embarrassed and gratified, Joanna took a moment before answering. "Thank you," she said. "Thanks a lot."

Still humiliated and nursing a headache, Joanna headed for Daisy's Café in Bisbee. The restaurant's new owner, Liza Machett, greeted her at the door. "It's eleven," she said, "so you can have your choice: breakfast or lunch."

Liza had turned up in Bisbee months earlier. She had come to town on the run from a band of murderous thugs who were on the trail of her long-estranged brother. Unfortunately, her brother—the ME who had made Joanna's life miserable—had already fallen victim to the same bad guys. As Guy Machett's half sister and as his only surviving heir, she inherited both his house on the Vista and a fair amount of cash—enough to purchase the café when the previous owners decided to retire. Much to the relief of most of the townsfolk, once Liza took over, she made precious few changes to the menu, although she did occasionally offer a breakfast special of apple-filled Dutch pancakes.

"Breakfast," Joanna answered. "Eggs over easy, crisp bacon, whole wheat toast, refried beans instead of hash browns. And some coffee," she added, remembering the still-full cup of coffee sitting cold and almost untouched in her parked Yukon. "I've had a very long morning."

The coffee arrived first, of course. Joanna's very first taste of it was enough to make her want to race for the nearest restroom. She pushed the cup away and then sat there staring at it, because she remembered all too well the other two times in her life when she hadn't been able to tolerate coffee.

Once the helicopter landed in Sierra Vista, naturally there was a hang-up with the rental car. The delay in getting the car meant that Ali and Cami were also late in arriving at the crime scene. By the time they reached the bridge over the San Pedro, only a strip of yellow crime scene tape stretching between two crumpled segments of guardrail served as evidence that anything out of the ordinary had occurred earlier in the day.

"What now?" Cami asked.

"I guess we head for the sheriff's office."

With Ali at the wheel, Cami keyed the address of the Cochise County Sheriff's Office into the GPS. Cami Lee was California born and bred. When she hired on with High Noon, she had driven over on I-40, dropped down I-17 to Sedona and Cottonwood, and stayed there.

This was her first venture out into the wilds of southern Arizona.

"I don't think I ever realized Arizona was this big," she said.

"You need to spend some time touring around and learning about your new home," Ali told her. "There's a lot to see."

They drove into Bisbee by what seemed like a back way. The Justice Center was located on a tract of land that was well outside the town itself. They pulled into the parking lot right at eleven. Inside, Cami lingered in the background, clutching Stu's tool kit, while Ali approached the counter in the lobby, business card in hand.

"My name is Ali Reynolds. I'm an investigator with a firm called High Noon Security. Ms. Lee here is my associate. We'd like to see Sheriff Brady," she said.

"Is this about the next press briefing?" the clerk asked. "That's scheduled for noon."

"It has nothing to do with the press briefing," Ali said. "We're here about that truckload of LEGO sets that came to grief in the San Pedro riverbed early this morning."

That statement was enough to provoke a raised eyebrow from the young woman behind the counter. "One moment," she said.

Except it wasn't just one moment. For the next ten minutes, Ali and Cami cooled their heels in the lobby. One whole wall was devoted to a glass display case featuring photos of previous sheriffs of Cochise. The ones dating from the late 1800s and the early 1900s were all dour-faced men with handlebar mustaches, some photographed on horseback. The more recent sheriffs, mostly without facial hair, looked like standard chiefs of police, businesslike and serious. The newest one featured a young girl in a Brownie uniform, grinning from ear to ear and dragging a wagonload of Girl Scout cookies.

Ali realized that the photo's stark contrast from the others carried an important message. Joanna Brady was the first and only female sheriff in this part of the world. In that case, Ali figured that was either very good or very bad. Trailblazers were generally one of two types. Confident women were comfortable in their own skins and able to work with others with little difficulty. Ones lacking that confidence were generally a pain in the butt. Since this sheriff had gone against the grain enough to post this particular photo, Ali dared hope Sheriff Joanna Brady was one of the former.

Soon an inner door opened and another young woman walked into the room. "I'm Kristin Gregovich, Sheriff Brady's secretary," she said. "The sheriff is out of the office at the moment, but she should be back in a few minutes. Would you care to wait inside?"

Kristin led them through a locked security door, down a long hallway, and into a secondary lobby that was much smaller than the first.

"Can I get you some coffee?"

When Ali and Cami both nodded, Kristin went to fetch it. Returning with the coffee, Kristin took a seat at the desk and busied herself on the computer while another ten minutes dragged by. Ali was almost ready to give up when the door behind Kristin's desk opened and a uniformed thirty-something young woman marched into the room. She had bright red hair, a sheriff's badge pinned to her chest, and ten or so pounds of armament and equipment belted to her hip. Since the woman hadn't come in through the lobby entrance, she'd either been in the office the whole time or else had come in the back way.

"I'm Sheriff Brady," she announced. "You wanted to see me?"

Ali and Cami both stood up. Ali, at five ten, felt as though she had wandered into the land of the Lilliputians. The sheriff couldn't have been more than five four or so, but she towered over the diminutive Cami.

"It's about what happened this morning," Ali said. "The truck wreck on Highway 92."

Sheriff Brady crossed her arms. "What about it?"

In answer, Ali produced a copy of a letter that B. had faxed to her in care of the fixed-base operator at the Sierra Vista Municipal Airport. It was a copy of a handwritten document on what appeared to be corporate stationery. She waited quietly while Sheriff Brady read it through.

> *To whom it may concern:*
> *This letter will serve to introduce Alison Reynolds and Camille Lee, two investigators for a security firm called High Noon Enterprises. They are assisting us with an investigation into missing merchandise that disappeared from a shipment that arrived in the U.S. via Long Beach late last week, some of which may have been on board a truck that crashed in your jurisdiction earlier today.*

When she finished reading, Sheriff Brady handed the paper back to Ali. "You expect me to believe that this guy is top dog in the world of LEGO?" she asked.

"You're welcome to Google him," Ali replied.

"The press briefing we had earlier made no mention of LEGO, and the next one isn't due to start for twenty minutes. Do you mind telling me how someone in Denmark already knows there were LEGO sets in our wrecked truck?"

"We read about it online," Ali answered "in an article posted by someone from right here in Bisbee. What was her name again?"

"Marliss," Cami replied instantly. "Marliss Shackleford."

Sheriff Brady shook her head and rolled her eyes. "Spare me," she said. "That woman's going to be the death of me, but I guess you need to come on in."

They followed the sheriff past the secretary's desk and into what turned out to be a private office. Behind a desk piled high with an untidy collection of paperwork was a wall of windows that looked out at a line of forbidding gray hills topped with limestone cliffs. Between the back parking lot and the mountains was an expanse of wilderness dotted with ocotillo, prickly pear, bear grass, and yucca. It had rained recently enough that the spindly branches of the ocotillo were covered with bright green leaves.

Sheriff Brady motioned them into guest chairs and then sat down on the far side of the desk. "I'm not sure why you're here," she said. "You're both welcome to attend the press briefing, but I'm sure you understand that I can't and won't comment on an ongoing investigation."

"We're not interested in the briefing," Ali said at once. "Would it be possible for us to examine one of the LEGO sets?"

"Please." Joanna shook her head. "Those sets are part

of the evidence in what appears to be a sophisticated criminal enterprise. You can't expect—"

Ali interrupted her: "How many LEGO sets were inside that wrecked truck?"

"Five thousand two hundred and seventy," Sheriff Brady answered at once. The SCRs had given her a complete inventory.

Cami pulled out an iPad, keyed in some numbers, and then consulted whatever showed on her screen. "According to the shipping manifest, there were four pallets coming from Monterrey, Mexico, containing that number of individual sets," she said quietly.

The sheriff shot Cami a questioning glance. "You know how many sets were on each pallet?"

"Yes," Ali said. "If you would allow us to examine one of the boxes with our RFID chip reader, we'll be able to tell you where and when the box was manufactured and where it was going."

For a moment, the sheriff said nothing. Then, making up her mind, she rose to her feet. "All right," she said. "This way."

Sheriff Brady led the way back down the hall and past the door through which they had entered, a series of interview rooms, and a break room before using a keypad to unlock the security door on what turned out to be what appeared to be a well-equipped laboratory. Two people, a young man and a young woman, were working there. They looked up questioningly as Joanna led Ali and Cami inside.

"These ladies, Ms. Reynolds and Ms. Lee, are doing some investigation into the LEGO connection to what happened out along the San Pedro this morning," Sheriff

Brady explained. To Ali and Cami she said, "This is my CSI team, Casey Ledford and Dave Hollicker."

Casey and Dave stepped forward to shake hands.

"They process whatever evidence that doesn't require being forwarded to the state patrol crime lab in Tucson," Sheriff Brady continued. "Casey's specialty is latent fingerprints, but we're a small department and they both have to be jacks-of-all-trades."

"You're looking into the LEGO connection?" Casey asked. "Over on my table I've got three dozen shell casings and a slew of bullets from what was probably an AK-47. I always thought LEGO sets were just toys. Since when are they worth going to war with automatic weapons?"

"These sets are manufactured in what amounts to limited editions," Ali explained. "When one set sells out in regular retail channels, there's a backstreet demand that can cause the prices of those unavailable sets to escalate into the stratosphere. Serious collectors are willing to pay the going rate, whatever that might be. Diverting part of a major shipment away from retailers this early in the sales cycle will create a shortage of that particular item from the get-go. My company, High Noon Enterprises, is charged with tracking down whoever is behind the diversion of these goods."

"And our job is tracking down a killer," Joanna countered. "That's a higher priority than chasing after stolen goods."

"Have you identified your victim?" Ali asked, hoping that her and Cami's inside knowledge of the LEGO situation might make Joanna a little more amenable to sharing information.

Joanna considered for a moment before she nodded and replied, "His name is Alberto Ricardo Mendoza, sometimes called Taquito. His prints were in the system. He has a rap sheet with mostly drug violations but no violent crimes. We've reached out to the California state prison system for next-of-kin information and were told his mother lives in Mazatlán. He was carrying a fake driver's license at the time of the wreck. As for the truck he was driving, it's an off-brand rental from Anaheim, rented in the name of Gomez, paid for in cash."

"Cash?" Ali asked. "Who in their right mind would rent a truck to someone for cash?"

Joanna sighed. "Someone who didn't want to know who was using the truck or what it was hauling."

"Knowing where the shipment originated would help us," Cami interjected quietly, speaking for the first time. "And it might help you as well. It could give you a point of origin for the truck. If we could just check one of the boxes with the RFID reader . . ."

"Where are they?" Joanna asked, looking in Dave's direction.

He shrugged. "There wasn't enough room to bring all the boxes in here. We asked the jail commander if we could commandeer one of his cells. He's got nobody in solitary at the moment, so he was glad to oblige."

"All right, then," Joanna said. "How about if you take Ms. Lee over to the jail and let her do whatever it is she needs to do. With gloves, however," she cautioned. "We're still looking for fingerprints wherever possible."

"And that includes looking for prints on my shell casings," Casey added. "If you don't mind, I'd like to get back to them. I've got an ATF agent due to arrive here any minute. I want to finish dusting for prints before he shows up to take charge."

Dave led Cami out of the room, and Casey returned to her examining table, leaving Joanna and Ali on their own.

"I noticed your certificate from APA in your office," Ali said. "Tough course."

She had deliberately used cop jargon in her reference to the Arizona Police Academy, and she was rewarded by a visible double take from Sheriff Brady. "You've heard about it?"

"Been there," Ali explained. "I used to be a television newscaster, but the shelf life of female news anchors is amazingly short. When mine ran out, I thought for a time I'd end up in law enforcement. Sheriff Gordon up in Yavapai County sent me to the police academy in Peoria. I made it through all right, even at what some of my classmates regarded as my 'very advanced age.' Then the economy took a nosedive, and the offer to work for Yavapai County went away. Besides," she added with a shrug, "I'm better off doing what I do now."

"Which is?"

"Doing PR and the occasional bit of investigative work for my husband's firm."

Joanna nodded thoughtfully. "Yavapai County. I actually know Sheriff Gordon," she added with a small grin. "I've played poker with him on occasion—and cleaned his clock, too."

With that small exchange, the whole tenor of the visit seemed to change. By the time Cami and Dave returned from their visit to the jail, Ali and Joanna were standing side by side at a lab table laden with some of the bagged and tagged evidence that had been collected from the crime scene earlier in the morning while Joanna explained that most of it would be picked up later in the afternoon and driven to the crime lab in Tucson for further examination.

Ali glanced up and caught Cami's eye as she and Dave entered. "Find anything?"

"The boxes are definitely from the most recent Monterrey shipment," Cami answered. "If we could have the license information and description of that truck, I could ask Stu to start checking on traffic cameras going backwards from here. If the trip here originated in California, the driver would have had to pass through at least one Border Patrol checkpoint and more likely multiple ones, to say nothing of state-run truck inspection stations. That should give us a trail of bread crumbs to follow."

"Wait," Ali said, focusing suddenly on that one word: "bread crumbs."

"What about this?" she asked, pointing at an evidence bag containing the mangled remains of what had once been a dashboard-mounted GPS. "Don't these leave bread crumbs, too, so you can find your way back the way you came?"

"A lot of them do," Cami agreed. "If I could take a look at this one, I might be able to find out."

"It's broken," Joanna said. "What good will looking at it do for us?"

"The screen may be broken, but most likely the chip inside is just fine," Cami pointed out. "May I?"

Joanna shrugged. "I don't suppose it would hurt," she said without enthusiasm. "Go ahead and help yourself, but again, wear gloves."

Dave passed Cami a new pair of gloves from an open box on the next table over. Moments later she began carefully removing broken pieces of the device from the bag and laying them out in an orderly fashion on the lab table. The studied concentration with which she arranged them somehow took Ali back to her high school biology class when they'd had to dissect a frog.

"It's an ordinary Garmin and the bread crumbs should be there," Cami remarked as she worked. "Fortunately, I've already got a plug-in app for that." She paused long enough to take a photo of the model number on the back of the GPS. A moment later, Ali heard the sound of a departing e-mail. "I sent it to Stu," Cami explained. "With the serial and model number, he'll be able to start tracking the point of purchase."

With that, Cami turned her attention back to the broken machine. "That's what I needed," she said, "a micro-USB port. If I can turn thing on, I should be able to download the history."

To Joanna's way of thinking, Cami Lee looked more like a seventh grader than a college graduate. The very idea of having the young woman messing with evidence from one of her homicides made Joanna squirm in her chair.

Why on earth did I let these women into my lab? she asked herself. *What the hell was I thinking? I should have tossed them out on their ear when I had the chance.*

The problem was she hadn't done so. Now, having given her tacit permission for them to be there, she couldn't very well pull the plug. It was too late to go down that road. On the other hand, Joanna knew that there were always built-in delays in sending evidence to the crime lab in Tucson, where cases from smaller jurisdictions always took a backseat to whatever was going on in Pima or Maricopa Counties. If by some miracle Cami was able to extract some usable information from that broken GPS this very afternoon . . .

After having been momentarily lost in thought, Joanna returned to the conversation and to Cami's running commentary. For a split second Joanna was back in Dr. Baldwin's morgue and hearing her narration of the driver's autopsy. The very thought of it made Joanna's stomach clench. Joanna definitely didn't want to go there. Absolutely not.

Refocusing on Cami's progress, Joanna noticed that the power cord to the GPS had been sliced in half. It lay on the table before Cami in two pieces. "If the power cord is wrecked, how are you going to hook it up?" she asked.

"No problem," Cami said confidently. "All it takes is the mini-USB connection, and I'm pretty sure Stu has one of those in his tool kit."

She opened a battered black leather case and pulled out a fistful of power cords held together by plastic tie-wraps. She plugged one end of the cord into an opening on the broken frame of the GPS and plugged the other end into the port on her iPad. "Here goes," she said, punching what was left of the on/off switch. "Let's see if there's any life in this old contraption."

A moment later, the screen on her iPad lit up. "Bingo," she said triumphantly, turning the iPad so both Joanna and Ali both could see the screen.

"It looks just like a GPS," Joanna said in amazement.

"That's because it *is* a GPS," Cami assured her. "This

GPS," she added, pointing to the damaged remains of the device that were now connected to hers. "Now, if you'll give me a minute, I'll download everything here into a micro-SD card and we'll be good to go."

It was clear to Joanna that at this point Cami was simply having fun. What followed was a long, silent pause while the download process took place. Once the download was complete, even more time passed before the newly reconstituted GPS was able to get its bearings. Finally it did.

"Okay," Cami said. "What do you want to know? How about if we take a look at Recently Found?"

Joanna waited, holding her breath, while the GPS hourglass tipped back and forth. "Yay," Cami said finally. "There it is. Starting location is an address in Long Beach which . . . Give me a minute," she added, switching over to another program, ". . . just happens to be a shipping terminal at the Port of Long Beach. And now let's hear it for that checkered flag. Does any of this look familiar?"

She passed the iPad over to Joanna. It took a moment for Joanna to realize what she was seeing. Squeezing her fingers together on the screen, the focus on the map narrowed, revealing far greater detail.

"That's Holzmann Road," she said at last. "It leads to Helmer Holzmann's place, a ranch located at the base of the Mule Mountains. Helmer's wife, Greta, died a few years back. The old man lives out there all by himself. Why on earth would someone be taking a load of LEGO sets there?"

Then, only a moment later, Joanna answered her own question. "Oh, no." she said. I had forgotten all about them, but I wonder if they're connected."

"If what is connected?" Ali asked.

"The shipping containers."

"What shipping containers?"

"As sheriff, I'm required to attend the board of supervisors meetings. A few months ago, Helmer appeared before the board on his son's behalf, asking for a variance so his son could build a retirement home out of a collection of shipping containers. The containers had evidently already been hauled onto his property, but the board wouldn't give him the variance. What if those shipping containers have nothing to do with building a house? What if they're being used to store stolen LEGO sets?"

"You said Mr. Holzmann's son wanted to build a retirement home on the ranch. Do you have any idea what he'd be retiring from?"

"I'm pretty sure he works for U.S. Customs," Joanna said. "Somewhere in California."

"That may be our connection, then," Ali said. "If you're running a smuggling operation, what could be handier than having an inside guy? His last name is Holzmann?"

Joanna nodded.

"What's his first name?"

"He's quite a bit older than I am. We weren't in school together, but Ernie might know," Joanna said, picking up the phone.

"Who's Ernie?"

"One of my detectives." She waited a moment until someone must have picked up. "Hey, Ernie. What's Helmer Holzmann's son's name?" She paused. "Thanks," she added a moment later. "I should have remembered that."

She turned back to Ali. "His first name is Hans. Why?"

Ali was already on her phone, with Stu's line ringing in the background.

"Wait," Joanna objected. "Who are you calling? I didn't give you permission to share details about this case with just anybody."

Ali held up her hand. "Stu Ramey isn't just anybody," she said. "He's High Noon's information guru. Let me give him a first and last name and see what he can come up with."

"What kind of information guru?" Joanna asked.

But Ali was already back on the line. "Yes, first name is Hans. Last name is spelled H-O-L-Z-M-A-N-N. He may work for U.S. Customs and Border Protection."

There was another long pause when the only sound in the room was the ticking of the clock. While they waited, Joanna went back to fuming in silence.

"I'm sure that's the one," Ali said at last, turning to Joanna with a smile lighting up her face. "Hans Dieter Holzmann—that is the son's full name, isn't it?"

"I'm sure it is, but how did you do that?" Joanna wanted to know.

"Our resident magician just accessed the U.S. Customs employee database. Turns out, there's only one employee named Holzmann on their list: Hans Dieter Holzmann. And guess where he works? The cargo ship terminal in Long Beach where that LEGO shipment just happened to come ashore late last week."

Ali returned to the phone. "Yes, Stu. Do some data mining and send us everything you can find on Mr. Holzmann, including whether or not he's at work today. If he's involved in this operation and has somehow learned that his shipment has gone horribly awry, he may be trying to do some troubleshooting from his end."

"Before you hang up," Cami said, "may I talk to Stu for a minute?"

"Sure," Ali said, giving her the phone.

"Stu, I just sent you the coordinates of where the truck was going: the intersection of Holzmann Road and U.S. Highway 92. The ranch belongs to Hans Holzmann's father. Now might be a good time to check out our new time-share access to satellite imagery."

Ali silently nodded her agreement. Months earlier, during a serious crisis when High Noon had needed real-time satellite imagery, Stu had managed to come up with a work-around. They had since joined a private consortium that gave them access on an as-needed basis. The initial sign-up fee had been jaw-droppingly expensive. After that, however, the charges were on a pay-as-you-go basis with the attendant fees billed back to the client.

"That's right," Cami said into the phone. "If you can, take a look at everything that's there: house, outbuildings, whatever. We've also just learned there may be several metal shipping containers on the property. Try taking a look at those as well."

"Wait a minute," Joanna said. "You think your magician guy, wherever he is, will actually be able to see the containers?"

"You'd be surprised what he can see," Cami said, pointing to another evidence bag. "Do you mind if I take a look at that phone?"

Kristin popped her head in the door. "It's time for the press briefing, Sheriff Brady. Tom Hadlock would like to have you on hand for that."

Sighing, Joanna looked first at Cami, then at the phone, and finally at Dave Hollicker. "If we end up needing that phone in court, it's your job to maintain the chain of evidence."

"Yes, ma'am," Dave said. "Will do."

As Sheriff Brady left the lab, Ali's phone rang with B.'s caller ID showing on the screen.

"Stu just told me about the situation on the ranch," B. told her. "I've got a call in to corporate right now. Using satellite imagery will cost a ton of money, but if we can break this operation wide open, I'm betting they'll cough up the fee."

"Good," Ali said. "What if what we're dealing with are the kind of unclipped ghost pallets you mentioned earlier? Supposing whoever's in Monterrey loads unchipped pallets into one or more shipping containers. The inside guy who works for customs tags those for special attention, and during those 'special inspections' said pallets simply disappear. That might not be too difficult, since—as far as anybody but the crooks are concerned—they never existed in the first place."

"Sounds feasible," B. said before adding, "Oops, getting a call back. Bye."

By the time Ali was off the phone, Cami was already returning the damaged cell phone to the evidence bag. "It's a burner," she said in answer to Ali's unasked question. "I sent Stu the model info so he can start looking for point of purchase, but given the circumstances I'm not going to attempt to get inside it without better equipment and a search warrant."

Ali nodded. "Right," she said.

After all, High Noon's responsibility was to their client. Sheriff Brady had a homicide to solve. In order for the information on the phone to be usable in court, it had to be legally obtained with a properly filed search warrant.

Cami's iPad and Ali's phone both began pinging with incoming messages as Stu's data-mining efforts yielded results. Glancing through them, Ali saw Hans Holzmann's home address for two separate residences, several phone numbers and e-mail addresses, as well as the license information on four different vehicles, one of which Ali recognized as a very pricey Mercedes, along with an equally pricey Range Rover.

Ali glanced at Cami. "U.S. Customs must be paying their employees very well these days."

Cami nodded. "Look at these property tax records. There are two separate houses, one in Palm Desert and another in Rolling Hills, California. The taxes on either one of those are more than I make in a year. How big do you suppose the mortgages are?"

"More than Mr. Holzmann could handle with his government salary alone," Ali suggested. "And if he already has a 'retirement' home in Palm Desert, why would he want to use shipping containers to construct another one on his father's property here in Arizona?"

"Good question," Cami said.

Stu's information continued to pour in at breathtaking speed. Hans Holzmann had been arrested once for DUI in his early twenties. His transcripts from Cochise College and Arizona State University showed up, as did his discharge papers from the U.S. Army, in which he had served with honor during Desert Storm. He was married with two children, one of whom had graduated from college, and the other was currently enrolled as an honors student at UCLA.

"What we have here is a crook who is evidently a decent husband and father," Ali observed. "Go figure."

Sheriff Brady returned to the room. "What's happening?" she asked.

"We're getting a ton of information on Hans Holzmann, but so far nothing particularly useful."

"And the phone?"

"Cami looked at it but didn't try to get inside. You'll need a warrant," Ali answered.

"We'll have one," Joanna answered. "Did you hear anything back on the satellite—"

Sheriff Brady's question was interrupted by the ringing of Ali's phone. Ali listened for a moment. "Okay," she said. "Send it to me and to Cami, but let me get Sheriff Brady's e-mail address for you so she can have it, too."

Joanna reeled off her e-mail address and then hurried over to the oversized computer monitor on Dave Hollicker's desktop. By the time Ali's e-mail account alerted her to a new message, Joanna had opened a mail screen on Dave's computer. Moments later the same image appeared on the screens of all three devices: Ali's phone, Cami's iPad, and Dave's desktop. At first only a grid pattern was visible, but gradually pieces of brownish desert landscape appeared in an out-of-focus haze before changing into something more understandable. Once the image finished resolving itself, the clarity was amazing. Ali saw a house with what appeared to be a tin roof. Nearby were two more structures. One looked like a barn with a corral out back. The other appeared to be a tin-roofed two-car garage.

"Stu says we need to scroll over north and east from the house," Cami said, "closer to the base of the mountains."

Joanna found the shipping containers first. "Holy crap!" she exclaimed. "Not only are the shipping containers there, look at those trucks!"

Working on a smaller screen, Ali took longer to locate that part of the image. When she did, she saw that the shipping containers—five of them in all—were lined up end to end along a dirt track. Parked perpendicularly to each container, about where the door opening should have been, was a bright yellow box truck very much like the one that had come to grief in the bed of the San Pedro River early that morning.

"How long ago was this taken?" Sheriff Brady demanded. Ali had to move away from the image in order to call B., pass along the sheriff's question, and then relay the answer.

"This one was taken a little over an hour ago."

As Ali delivered B.'s message, a little red-haired dynamo sprang into action. Joanna made for the door and dashed down the hall, barking orders into her shoulder-mounted radio as she went.

"Dispatch, I want all westbound traffic on Highway 92 stopped at Melody Lane and all eastbound traffic stopped at that new steakhouse in Palominas ASAP. Call out the tactical operations team. Any of members of the TAC team currently on the far side of the San Pedro should assemble in the parking lot at the restaurant, where Deputy Stock will be the incident commander. Everyone else should proceed to the intersection of Highway 92 and Melody Lane. Lights but no sirens. No telling how far sound travels over the desert, and we don't want them to know that we're coming. Once officers arrive at their designated locations, they're to set up roadblocks and deploy as many spike strips as they have available. We need to shut these guys down."

The conversation was briefly out of Ali's earshot as Joanna ducked into her office. "Yes," she was saying when Ali followed her inside. "If this is related to the earlier incident, we may be dealing with automatic weapons. We need to stop these guys, but we also need to be safe. That means that nobody is to show up at either roadblock without a Kevlar vest. We believe the suspects will be driving a convoy of yellow box trucks loaded with contraband."

Inside the office, Joanna paused long enough to don her own vest.

"If the image is from an hour and a half ago, will we be in time?" Ali asked.

"'We'?" Joanna repeated. "Did you hear what I just said? I want my TAC team, my emergency response guys out there. No civilians. Period!"

Cami appeared in the doorway to Joanna's office, iPad in hand. "Excuse me, Sheriff Brady, but I think you're going to need us. Mr. Simpson has asked the pilot of our chartered helicopter to do a single fly-over of the site and relay what he sees back to me, including—with any luck—some video footage. He's on his way there now. As the crow flies, he's probably less than ten minutes out."

"He's sending video footage to you?"

Cami nodded. "That's the plan."

Joanna looked first at Cami, then at Ali. Finally, with a

sigh of defeat, she relented. "All right, then," she agreed. "The two of you can ride along, but both of you are to stay in the car, well back from the roadblock. Understand?"

Ali wanted to object but didn't. Instead, she climbed into the front passenger seat of Joanna's Yukon without a word. For one thing, the sheriff was right. Ali had her trusty Glock along, right there in her small-of-back holster, but in a matchup against an AK-47 or something of a similar caliber, the handgun would have all the firepower of a slingshot. As for going into a firefight without wearing Kevlar vests? That would be downright stupid.

The Yukon left the back parking lot of the Justice Center leading a parade of five or six other vehicles, all of them traveling fast with lights flashing but no blaring sirens. Cami sat in the backseat staring at her iPad and seemingly willing something to show up on the screen. Ali watched warily as the Yukon's speedometer headed for the stratosphere, making her wish Joanna would pay more attention to her driving and less to her radio.

"Is Deputy Stock on the scene in Palominas?"

"He's about five minutes out," the dispatcher said. Ali thought the dispatcher's name was Larry, but she couldn't be sure.

"Can you patch me through to him?"

"Hang on."

Moments later a different voice came through the radio. "Deputy Stock here."

"When you set up your roadblock, I want it to go from fence line to fence line," she said. "Don't deploy the spike strips until you're sure all oncoming traffic has been stopped. Try to lay them out as far to the west of the roadblock as possible, out of sight of it if possible. It'll be better if they hit the spikes before they see you."

"You want strips laid out on the shoulders, too?"

"Absolutely, but only if you have enough," Joanna answered. "Otherwise they might try driving around. We need these guys stuck on rims before they hit either of the roadblocks."

By then Ali noticed they were speeding along beside what was evidently a huge mine tailings dump. Up ahead, Ali could see buildings on either side of the highway. Ali and Cami had come this route earlier on their way to the Justice Center. Knowing they were fast approaching the town itself as well as a complicated roundabout, Ali was more than ready for Sheriff Brady to lift her lead foot off the damned gas pedal . . . which she did, but only at the last moment. When they swung into the traffic circle, Joanna was still driving way faster than Ali would have liked, but she was relieved to see that uniformed municipal cops had cleared the way for them by shutting down all adjoining intersections.

"Pulling up at the scene now, Sheriff Brady," Deputy Stock said. "Over and out."

Larry's voice immediately came back on the line. "Anything else?"

"Yes. Call Frank Montoya in Sierra Vista. Tell him what's up and let him know we're asking for mutual aid. I have way more people on the roadblock on the Bisbee side than I have on his side. Ask him if he can send backup."

"Will do."

Ali watched out the window as the town flew past, starting with a few residential neighborhoods on either side. Beyond that, the road was mostly empty desert. When they came to another area of businesses and housing, the houses seemed to be set back from the highway, while the various businesses were not. Ali knew that if the bad guys somehow made it past the roadblock, the people in those businesses—a taco stand, a gas station, a grocery store, an insurance agency—would all be at risk, customers and proprietors alike. She wanted to shout "Take cover!" out the window to warn them, but she didn't. It wasn't her place. Sheriff Brady was calling the shots here, not Ali Reynolds.

They came to what seemed to be the edge of town. Joanna slowed abruptly just short of a growing traffic jam. After pausing for a moment at the back of the line, Joanna veered off the pavement and onto the shoulder, dodging around the stopped vehicles and going to the front of the line, where four other cop cars were already parked across the roadway. With only one try, Joanna deftly pulled the Yukon into the single remaining open space, a spot so tight that her back bumper was almost on top of the front bumper of the car just behind hers, while her front bumper was nosed up against a barbed-wire fence.

"As I said," she cautioned as she opened the door and started to climb out, "you're both to stay here."

Just then Cami's phone rang.

"Okay, Stu," Cami said when she answered. "Put him through when you can."

Joanna climbed back inside, shut the door, and waited. An oversized heavy-duty Sprinter with the sheriff's office logo on the door and the identifying letters *TT* painted on the side was parked in front, parallel to the four blocking cars.

TT, Ali told herself. *Tactical Team.*

An officer in full battle dress emerged from the Sprinter. As he hurried up to Joanna's Yukon, she buzzed the window open.

"Is everybody here, Deputy Ruiz?" she asked.

"Not yet. We're still short two, including Detective Carbajal," he told her. "In the meantime, we're collecting spike strips. You got any with you?"

She nodded. "In the back," she said, clicking open the rear lift gate.

He reappeared a moment later holding an armload of strips. "Turns out Deputy Stock is short in the spike strip department," Ruiz reported. "Once we deploy ours, we'll need to see if there's enough to reinforce his supply."

"Which may leave your guys in the middle when all hell breaks loose," Joanna objected.

"Yes," he agreed, "but we're in better shape to deal with that than you are. We're armor plated. You're not."

"Yes, Chuck," Cami's voice said from the backseat. "I can hear you."

"Wait, Deputy Ruiz," Sheriff Brady said. "Let's see if there's an update."

Cami delivered the pilot's words in the rapid-fire fashion of a trained interpreter. "Just flew over. They seem to be forming up in a convoy. Four of the trucks are already in line."

"Crap," Joanna muttered, turning to Deputy Ruiz. "We don't have much time, so don't wait around for Jaime any longer. Whoever doesn't show up doesn't show up. Those trucks have three miles of dirt road to travel. Even if they leave right now, they won't be going fast. You should be able to get your strips down and be past Holzmann Road with additional ones for Jeremy before they hit the highway. Go now. It's going to be a squeaker."

Ruiz was off in a flash. "Okay, Chuck," Cami was saying. "Thanks so much."

"Wait," Ali said. "Don't hang up. Ask him if he can do us a favor and come get us."

"Come get us?" Joanna demanded. "Are you kidding?"

"If this is war and you're the general," Ali said, "wouldn't we all be better off if you're somewhere that will allow you to see all the action as you direct your troops?"

Joanna turned to Cami. "Ask the pilot if he can keep us out of range of automatic weapons fire."

Cami asked the question and came back with another. "He wants to know what the bad guys are carrying?"

"At least one AK-47 and maybe more."

There was another brief pause. "Chuck says that he flew over AK-47s in the Middle East, and unless they have grenade launchers handy, his bird will be just fine."

"Then I guess we're going airborne," Joanna said. "Tell him to land on the highway just in front of the roadblock. Come on." She clambered out of the driver's seat.

Stunned by Joanna's sudden change of heart, Ali started after her, just as her phone began to ring. Ali knew who was calling: B. If she answered and told him what was happening, she also knew exactly what he'd say, too: *Don't go.* Instead of answering, she let the call go to voice mail. By the time Ali was on the ground, Joanna had opened the autolocking back door so Cami could step out of the Yukon.

"Wait," Cami said, not moving. "Does this mean I'm coming, too?"

"Everybody's coming," Joanna said, "but only if you want to. Can you handle a weapon?"

"No," Cami stammered.

"Doesn't matter. You're our dedicated com girl for the day, in charge of keeping us in touch with the mother ship. What about you, Ali?" Joanna asked. "Is that weapon in your small-of-back holster just for decoration, or do you know how to use it?"

"I can use it," Ali said. "But I'd rather not need to."

Joanna gave her an appraising look. "That makes two of us," she said.

On the one hand, Joanna Brady knew she had no business involving civilians in what was bound to be a dangerous operation, but without Cami's and Ali's capable help they wouldn't be here right now. The GPS evidence that had brought the Holzmann Road destination to Joanna's attention would still be waiting to be transported to the crime lab in Tucson. By the time the lab got around to processing it, the trucks would be long gone.

In other words, she owed Ali and Cami big-time. They would be involved in the firefight without having signed one of those legalese CYA forms civilians always had to sign before doing a ride-along. The board of supervisors would be appalled. To make matters worse, Joanna was bringing a multimillion-dollar helicopter into the mix. If this went south, Joanna figured she'd probably be better off dead than caught up in the middle of a liability lawsuit hurricane.

"Come on, ladies," she said with as much confidence as she could muster. "Time to saddle up."

Walking around the Yukon, she had to climb up on

the front bumper of the patrol car parked behind hers to reach into the cargo space. Her hand emerged holding not one but two Kevlar vests. She handed the smaller one to Cami and the larger to Ali.

"Put these on," she told them. "They won't fit exactly, but they'll do."

When Joanna had been pregnant with Dennis, her added girth required that she move up to a larger-size vest. After Denny was born, she went back to her original one, but she kept the other in reserve. Cami pulled it on. The petite young woman seemed to swim in the thing, but Joanna deemed it better than nothing.

As for the one she handed Ali, it had once belonged to Deputy Dan Sloan, her department's only fallen officer in the course of Joanna's seven years in office. Dan was wearing the vest the night he was gunned down, shot in the abdomen where there was no Kevlar protection. After Dan's funeral, his widow brought the vest back to the sheriff's office in the hope that someone else could use it. Joanna accepted it even though she had understood even then that, out of respect for Dan, none of her other officers would ever agree to wear it. Not only did Joanna accept the vest, she kept it, too, more as a reminder than out of any expectation that it would ever again be used. Once Ali slipped it on, Joanna was gratified to see she was tall enough for the vest to fit fairly well. And since Ali didn't know the vest's backstory, Joanna thought it better not to pass it along.

Another battle-dressed guy showed up just then. "Why'd the van leave without me?" he demanded. "I told them I was coming."

"Good of you to join us, Detective Carbajal. The TAC team left without you because there wasn't time to wait around any longer," Joanna said. "I needed them to deliver spike strips to the other roadblock. That had to happen sooner than later, but as long as you're here, you're now in charge."

"Where are you going to be?"

Jaime's question was drowned out by the noisy clatter of an arriving helicopter. "In that, apparently," she said with a nod toward the chopper, which was hovering for a landing.

"Sheriff Brady!" a woman's shrill voice called over the noisy racket from the helicopter. "Sheriff Brady! They won't let me through!"

Joanna glanced over her shoulder in time to see Marliss Shackleford twist away from the young deputy who was trying to restrain her and come striding forward.

"Can I have a few words?" Marliss asked. "Please?"

"Your first duty as incident commander," Joanna hissed in Jaime Carbajal's ear, "is to get that woman out of here." Then she turned to face Marliss herself.

"Sorry," Joanna told the determined reporter. "I'm afraid this isn't a good time. Get out of here. Now!" Then she turned back to Cami. "What's the pilot's name again?"

"Chuck," Cami answered. "His name is Chuck."

It took some doing for the three women to climb on board. The steps were taller than either Cami or Joanna could manage on their own. Fortunately Jaime was right there to give them a needed boost.

"Earphones," Chuck said as they settled in. Joanna inserted her radio's earbud before putting on the aircraft's padded earphones. Ali made no attempt at introductions until after they were all seated and strapped in with their earphones properly in place.

"I'm Chuck," the pilot said with a half salute in Joanna's direction. "At your service, Sheriff Brady. What can I do for you today?"

"Take us back to where you saw those trucks, and keep us out of range."

"Will do," he said agreeably. "As for staying out of range, I don't want a hard landing any more than you do."

They took off then. The aircraft wheeled into the air and set off toward the northwest. Joanna didn't watch the altimeter. Her eyes remained focused on the horizon. A minute or so later she spotted what she was looking for: plumes of dust rising skyward.

She pointed. "That's got to be our guys. Follow the highway but stay a long way above it. Once they hit that, we need to know which way they turn."

Chuck took a position and held steady, hovering far above the spot where Holzmann Road intersected with the highway. The slow caravan came up to the intersection and stopped. Then, to Joanna's dismay, they turned neither right nor left. Instead, they continued straight on, crossing the paved highway and continuing southward on a narrow dirt track that was far less traveled than the portion of the road north of the highway.

"Why are they going there?" Joanna demanded. "That part of road goes nowhere. The ranch at the end of it was abandoned years ago."

Chuck turned the aircraft ninety degrees. From that vantage point it was easy to see that the road came to an end all right, stopping in front of some kind of metal structure large enough to be a pole barn.

Joanna went back on the air. "All units, continue to man the roadblocks on Highway 92. We still have the possibility of an active shooting situation here. TAC Team, suspects are continuing to travel south on Holzmann Road on the south side of Highway 92. Gather up some of those spike strips, come back here, and establish a third roadblock on Holzmann somewhere south of the highway. The suspects are either making a run for the border or they may be headed for a large structure of some kind that's located a mile or so north of the border. And, Dispatch? Contact Leo Guzman, the local Border Patrol commander. Tell him we've located a possible smuggling operation here. See if he can have some of his agents respond, approaching the scene from the south. There's no road there, but that's why the Feds buy all those green and white SUVs."

Below the aircraft, the moving caravan slowed to a crawl as the road went down into a steep gully. On the far side of that, the road was reduced to little more than a cow path.

"TAC Team, a mile and a half or so in from the highway, the road seems to be a lot worse. Yes, the van is four-wheel drive with good ground clearance, but I'm not sure it'll negotiate both the gully and the sharp turn right after it. Set up north of the gully. We want that Sprinter ready to rock and roll if we need it."

"Do you think they know we're onto them?" Ali asked.

"If they've seen us up here, maybe," Chuck replied. "But that road looks pretty challenging. I have a feeling they're too busy driving to be watching the sky."

As the moving trucks continued creeping southward, Larry Kendrick's voice came through the radio. "Border Patrol has been notified. Officers are en route. TAC team is traveling south on Holzmann Road and will let us know once they've established their position."

By now it was clear that the metal-roofed building it-self was most likely the trucks' intended destination. "Pull back up before they get there," Joanna warned Chuck. "If they get out to open the door, they'll hear us. On the off chance they don't know we're here, let's try to keep it that way."

Chuck immediately complied, taking the chopper a fair distance to the west, away from both the moving trucks and the barn, before hovering again. "This should put us out of earshot," he said. "There's a pair of binocu-lars stowed back there. They might be strong enough to give you a view of what's happening on the ground."

A moment later Ali tapped Joanna on the shoulder and passed the binoculars forward. It took a moment for Joanna to adjust them to the size of her face. After that, it took even longer for change the focus and eventually lo-cate the barn. She found it just as the first truck reached the barn and rolled right inside without pausing and with-out needing someone to get out and open the door. The other trucks followed.

"Whatever that building is, it has an automatic door of some kind," Joanna informed the others. "They're all inside."

The helicopter hung motionless in the air while Jo-anna continued to peer through the binoculars. Finally Chuck spoke. "Maintain position or . . ."

Joanna held up her hand. "Wait," she said. "They're coming back out."

"The trucks?" Ali asked.

"No, some other vehicle—one vehicle only. TAC Team, heads up. Bad guys are coming your way. Are you in position?"

"Roger that," Deputy Ruiz replied.

"There's another bird in the air," Chuck said, nodding toward the east, where a dot on the horizon gradually resolved itself into an approaching helicopter.

"That'll be Border Patrol," Joanna said.

On occasions like this, it was beyond frustrating that ongoing differences in radio frequencies made it impossible for Joanna to communicate with Border Patrol radios directly, but she was glad reinforcements were arriving on the scene. Even though she wouldn't be down on the ground with her TAC team where she felt she should have been, she could, thanks to Ali Reynolds, be her guys' eye in the sky.

"Let's move in a little closer," Joanna told Chuck. "Okay, TAC Team, the vehicle appears to be a black Hummer. Looks like it has one occupant. Repeat, one occupant only."

"There were five trucks and five drivers," Ali said. "What happened to the others?"

"I hate to think," Joanna answered.

Deputy Ruiz was still talking spike strips. "Those strips of ours aren't going to help much with a Hummer. The guy will hit the gas, go off road, and drive around them."

"If that happens," Joanna said, "then somebody had better figure out another way to take out his tires. Four-wheel drive is fine. On rims? Not so much."

"We're on it."

"Jaime, are you there?"

"Here, boss. What do you need?

"What's the situation where you are?"

"City of Bisbee has officers on-site to man the roadblock. I can take two deputies and go serve as backup for the TAC team."

"Do that, but have somebody take my Yukon out of the roadblock, bring it along, and fill that spot with another vehicle. I left the keys inside. Once I get out of this helicopter, I'm going to want to have my own wheels."

Chuck had moved the helicopter closer to the action. They were high enough to see the moving Hummer on one side of the curve and gully and, half a mile or so beyond it, the TAC team's Sprinter parked with the front of the vehicle pointing back the way they had come. That way, if they needed to leave in a hurry, they wouldn't have to turn around first.

"Okay, TAC Team, he's incoming," Joanna announced. "He just ducked into the gully. When he tops the rise, you should have visual contact, but so will he."

With the binoculars still pressed to her face, Joanna felt her heartbeat accelerate. Her officers' lives were on the line down there. A guy she suspected of being a stone-cold killer, someone who was armed and dangerous, was headed in their direction. She had put her people there, but she was not. As far as Joanna Brady was concerned, she should have stayed on the ground with them, but at this point all she could do was watch from the sidelines.

The Hummer topped the rise and ground to a sudden stop. Joanna was sure shots were being exchanged, but over the noise of the helicopter there was no way to tell for sure. A moment later the Hummer's driver bailed. Joanna could see that the guy was holding his weapon pointed at the Sprinter. She couldn't see the bullets flying from the barrel, but her soul registered every one.

Then the guy took off running, dodging away from the Hummer and trying to disappear into the desert.

"Shots fired!" Ruiz shouted into his mic. "Runner!"

"Stay on him," Joanna told Chuck. "On him but out of range."

"Roger that."

It wasn't until the aircraft flew closer that the suspect seemed to notice its presence. He stopped and looked up. Then he raised his weapon, pointed it in their direction, and tried to fire again.

"He should have studied geometry or physics," Chuck observed with a laugh. "No way can he reach us up here with that thing. Every time he pulls the trigger, he has that much less ammo. Bad for him. Good for us."

Joanna knew Chuck was trying to lighten her load, but her whole being still locked on the drama unfolding below, and she was in no mood for joking around. She watched as the TAC team spread out in pursuit of the gunman. Her heart was in her throat, knowing that every step they took carried her officers closer to the shooter and put them in even greater danger.

Then, as quickly as it began, it ended. Joanna saw the guy start in alarm and look back over his shoulder just as a black-and-brown streak crashed into him.

"Spike's got him!" she shouted into her own mic, recognizing the canine member of her department's K-9 unit. "Suspect is on the ground!"

Within moments the officers converged on the scene. Takedowns were always the most dangerous part of any pursuit. She continued to hold her breath until Armando Ruiz's elated voice came through her radio.

"Suspect in custody!"

"Great job, guys!" Joanna said. "Great job!" There were tears of gratitude in her eyes. She had to wipe them away before she spoke again. "Somebody needs to go check out the barn. I have a feeling the other four guys who drove inside won't be walking out. Chuck, how about we go find my Yukon. I can see where it's parked from here. Since there won't be any traffic, you can put this thing down right there on the highway to let us out. I want to go see what, if anything, this creep has to say for himself."

Knowing how much was at stake, Ali had stayed quiet and motioned Cami to do the same during most of the firefight. After all, Joanna's officers were caught up in a life-and-death struggle, and Sheriff Brady didn't need comments from the peanut gallery while those lives were on the line. Ali kept her phone on silent, but she knew from the constant buzzing that there had been a flurry of missed calls. When she checked, she saw they were all from B.

Chuck landed in the middle of the pavement. "I'm assuming you're not ready to bail right now," he said as Ali rose to exit. "How about if I go back to the airport and be on standby. Give me a call half an hour before you're ready to leave for Sedona."

"Thank you," she said. "We will."

Once she was back on solid ground, Ali called B. "Sorry to leave you hanging like that," she said, "but it's over now. The TAC team caught the guy. They probably wouldn't have managed it without having Chuck and his helicopter at our disposal."

Just then a marked patrol vehicle, a Tahoe with a

woman at the wheel, pulled up. "Sheriff Brady," she called through the passenger window. "TAC team is calling for you. Four gunshot victims in the barn down the road. No survivors."

Ali watched as the horror of those words flitted briefly across Sheriff Brady's face, then she straightened her shoulders. "Okay," she said. "If it's all right with you, Deb, I'll ride with you." She turned to Ali. "How about if you and Cami wait here? I'll have someone come pick you up and take you back to the department for your car."

"Of course," Ali said. "That'll be fine." She tried to be gracious, but it was clear she had no other choice.

Cami, on the other hand, was totally engrossed with her iPad. "Thanks for the info, Stu," she said.

"I'm trying to tell you the same thing Stu is," B. said impatiently when Ali returned the phone to her ear. "He's spent the whole time working his magic. Hans Holzmann didn't show up at work today. His wife reported him missing earlier this afternoon. She said he left home in the middle of the night—told her that there was some kind of emergency at work, except he didn't go to work. Stu also managed to pick up on a trail of Holzmann's credit card transactions: He bought gas and a sandwich in Blythe, California; stopped at a McDonald's in Gila Bend; bought another tank of gas in Sierra Vista at ten thirty this morning. And guess what? That extra vehicle parked out in front of the house belonging to Mr. Holzmann the elder turns out to be a Range Rover."

"And Hans Dieter Holzmann just happens to drive a Range Rover," Ali supplied.

"Bingo."

"From what we've been able to learn, the shooting that started this whole mess was first called in around two A.M. The satellite shot was time stamped eleven A.M. It takes eight and a half hours minimum to drive from Rolling Hills, California, to Holzmann Road in Cochise County."

"So Hans Holzmann knew something had gone haywire with the shipment at almost the same time the cops did. He immediately hopped in his car and came straight here."

"Right," B. agreed. "Which makes me wonder, what if he was lured here? What if this was nothing but an elaborate trap?"

"So far the body count here on the ground is up to five," Ali told him. "Based on that, I'm thinking things are looking pretty grim for Mr. Holzmann—maybe for both Mr. Holzmanns."

An unmarked patrol car showed up, this one an aging but well-preserved Crown Victoria. The man at the wheel was older than the other people Ali had seen in Joanna's department. "I'm Detective Ernie Carpenter," he said. "I've been assigned to take you two ladies back to the Justice Center."

"Before you do that," Ali told him, "I think there may be another problem."

When she finished explaining the situation, Carpenter got on the horn to request additional assistance. Ali heard the weariness in Joanna's voice as she replied. "All right, Ernie. Take one of the deputies and go check it out. In the meantime, give Ali the keys to my Tahoe. She can drive herself back to the department, but tell her to watch out for spike strips."

"All right, ladies," Ernie said when she finished. "Help yourselves."

Yet another departmental SUV, a Tahoe again, appeared on the scene. Ali wondered how many of those were part of Sheriff Brady's collection of rolling stock. As the SUV followed the Crown Vic up Holzmann Road, Ali turned to Cami. "In other words, here's our hat, what's our hurry, and don't let the door slam on our butts on the way out?" she grumbled. "How about a little gratitude?"

They climbed into Joanna's Yukon. The seat was set so far forward that Ali could barely get her legs under the steering wheel. Once she finished adjusting the seat and the mirrors, she turned to Cami. "You know what? This sucks. We're the whole reason the Cochise County Sheriff's Office is on top of this right now. If it weren't for us, they wouldn't know about the trucks, wouldn't know about the bodies in the barn or whatever it is, and wouldn't have caught the shooter. I'm a little tired of being told to sit down and shut up, aren't you?"

Cami nodded. "Right," she said. "It's like we're suddenly invisible or something."

"The shooter is in custody. So what say we go check out what's happening with Helmer and Hans Holzmann?"

"Sounds good to me."

Ali turned the key in the ignition, put the Yukon in gear, executed a U-turn, and followed the other two vehicles north from Highway 92. Even there, the road was in bad enough shape that she was glad they had a high-clearance vehicle complete with four-wheel drive. The road ended abruptly at a closed gate with a row of newly leafed cottonwoods on either side. Beyond the gate was a house, barn, corral, and outbuildings—the same ones Ali remembered seeing on the satellite image earlier. The Ranger Rover was where they had seen it, too. The Crown Vic and the Tahoe were parked directly behind it, but neither driver was anywhere in sight.

Ali pulled up to the gate and stopped. Cami rolled down her window. "Should we go in or wait here?" Cami asked.

There was something about this whole situation that was bothering Ali—something that wasn't right. "No," she said. "We should just turn around and go back."

As Ali put the car in reverse and turned to see where she was going, a giant of a man materialized from behind one of the nearby trees. He reached in through the open window and grabbed Cami. Using only one hand, he managed to wrestle her out of her seat belt and drag her, screaming and struggling, out through the open window. The window control buttons were right there on Ali's armrest, but by the time Ali realized that, Cami was half in and half out of the car, and she couldn't touch them. A hard clap on the head silenced Cami. As she slumped in the man's arms, Ali saw the gun in his left hand.

"Who are you?" Ali demanded.

"Who I am doesn't matter," he snarled. "What matters is this: You give me a ride and we go where I say. Now, unlock the back door here. The girl and I will ride in back. If you try anything—anything at all—she dies. Got it?"

Ali hesitated, but only for a moment. Cami was in mortal danger at that moment. And who had put her there? Ali Reynolds had. Ali glanced at the house to see if one of the officers had heard Cami's scream. No one appeared at a door or peered out a window, so apparently they hadn't. If Cami Lee was going to be saved, Ali Reynolds would have to be the one to do it.

"Got it," she said.

"Well?" he demanded impatiently. "Are you going to unlock the door or not?"

"Just a minute," Ali said. "It's not my car. I need to find the right button."

She made a show of pushing buttons, raising random windows up and down. By the time she finally unlocked the door, Cami had come to enough that she was the one who opened it. Her captor gripped the terrified girl with one hand while holding a handgun that looked like a .38 to Cami's head. Her eyes were open wide with fear and pleading for help. She was obviously terrified.

Once the door opened, the man lifted Cami off the ground and shoved her into the vehicle. He had to push her bodily across the bench seat before closing the door behind him. In the split second he was preoccupied with that, Ali managed to extract the Glock from her small-of-back holster. Once she had the weapon out, she slipped it under her thigh where it was out of sight but still close at hand.

"All right," the man said. "We're in. Now turn around and get going."

Ali listened for the distinctive sound of seat belts locking, but none came. The man with the gun wasn't belted in, but then, neither was Cami.

Ali took her time and made several tries before finally executing the U-turn, hoping all the while that either Detective Carpenter or the deputy would emerge from the house and see what was happening. No one did.

"Where to?" Ali asked once they started back down Holzmann Road.

"Away from here," he said. "The place is crawling with cops, and leaving in a cop car seems like a good idea to me."

There was indistinct radio chatter on the radio. Nothing Ali heard told her that the roadblocks had been dismantled. She hoped they hadn't been, but in an attempt to distract the man from what was being said over the air, Ali turned herself into a regular chatty Cathy.

"They caught your buddy," she said conversationally. "You know, the guy in the Hummer?"

"They caught Julio? So what?" he said. "He's got connections around here. He'll get out."

"I don't think so," Ali said. "He killed the four drivers," Ali said.

A quick check in the rearview mirror told her that hearing about the dead drivers had blindsided the guy. "Julio killed them?"

"Yup," Ali said. "Gunned them down right there in the warehouse. Your friend Julio sounds like the kind of guy who wouldn't want to leave any witnesses behind," she added. "Once he had all those LEGO boxes, maybe he was going to take you out, too."

"He wouldn't."

"Are you sure?"

"He said he'd come get me once the trucks were taken care of. All I needed was time to finish what I'd started. The thing is it took longer than I expected to get the old man to tell me where Hans was hiding."

"You killed both of them?" Ali asked.

"Of course I did. Hans was a cheating son of a bitch," he said. "That's the whole reason I came here—to teach him a lesson."

With his every casual admission, Ali slipped deeper

into despair. If their captor was this forthcoming, it probably meant that the other two officers—both Detective Carpenter and the deputy—were dead as well. This guy was spilling out all the details because he had no intention of leaving Ali and Cami alive to tell the tale. Still, right at that moment, Ali knew her best option was to keep him talking.

"Cheating you out of stolen LEGO sets?" Ali asked.

"Look, me and Hans were supposedly partners," he said. "It turns out he's been robbing me blind the whole time, and I only just now found out. Those old sets he had stowed away here—ones I knew nothing about—are worth a fortune. Who would do something like that?"

"My father told me once there's no honor among thieves," Ali said. "Maybe you didn't get the memo."

"Shut up," he said.

So Ali shut up. By then they were nearing the end of Holzmann Road and approaching Highway 92. Creeping up to the stop sign, she paused and looked both ways. There wasn't a single vehicle in sight in either direction. That probably meant that the roadblocks were still in place.

"Which way?" Ali asked. "Right or left?"

"Suit yourself."

It suited Ali to turn left and head back toward Bisbee. She knew exactly where that roadblock was located, and she also knew a little about the lay of the land. She suspected the one near Bisbee was closer to Holzmann Road than the one near the river. Ali expected that as soon as the guy saw the roadblock, he'd go ballistic. At least, she hoped that was what would happen. With his attention focused elsewhere, maybe she'd have a chance—her one and only chance—to use the gun.

"So you like to play with LEGOs, then?" she asked, ignoring the fact that he had told her to shut up. "You must."

"I don't give a rat's ass about LEGO sets," he growled. "I was in it for the money, and that jackass Hans was scamming me out of some of my share and probably other people out of theirs, too."

That's when Ali realized this was more than just a one- or two-guy conspiracy. There were lots of people involved.

"So you showed him," she said.

"I sure as hell did. Taquito had hauled stuff for us before. The first time I saw him down on the docks, picking up something I knew nothing about, I worried that something was up. After that, I kept an eye on him. This time around I kept track of the ghost pallets, and it's a good thing I did. Turns out there were a couple of extras that Hans had hidden away. Everybody knew about the extra pallets, but Hans was the only one who knew about those *extra* extra pallets. This time, when Taquito showed up down on the docks when there wasn't a shipment scheduled for us, I knew it was time to pull the trigger."

"Are you saying you shot him yourself?" Ali asked.

The guy laughed at that. "I mean I pulled the trigger in a manner of speaking. You meet a lot of useful people in a job like mine—you know, people who can get stuff done or who know people who can get stuff done. Years ago, one of them put me in touch with Julio, who happens to be a very useful guy from Naco, Sonora. He also happens to have all kinds of connections. When I told him what was up, he told me he knew of a place close to Hans's dad's place—an empty warehouse—where we could store the stuff temporarily once we laid hands on it. He found the drivers, located the trucks, handled the whole thing."

"Including shooting Taquito?"

"Sure. I put a GPS tracker on the bumper of his truck and knew his every move. By the time he came through Palominas, Julio was ready and waiting."

They were nearing town. Ali saw, to her relief, that the roadblock was still in place. With the risky maneuver she had in mind, she needed to have all other vehicles safely off the road. The man in the backseat spotted the roadblock almost as soon as she did. He leaned forward in his seat, peering warily out the windshield. "What the hell? Turn around," he ordered. "Go the other way."

"But they'll see us," Ali warned. "They'll come after us."

"I don't care. Go the other way. Now."

Ali slowed and put the car into a careful U-turn. She briefly considered ramming an abutment on a nearby bridge crossing a dry wash, but she chose not to. With Cami in the back and not wearing a seat belt, she was afraid to try it. Moments later, with the Yukon back on the pavement and westbound once more, Ali checked in the rearview mirror, hoping one of the cops at the roadblock had noticed the turning vehicle and come after them, but so far no one had. As her mother, Edie Larson, liked to say, "God helps those who help themselves." This time around, the only help available was Ali herself.

Ali's mother also despised liars in the worst way, but desperate times called for desperate measures, and lie she would—to the very best of her ability.

Ali felt the Glock pressing painfully against the back

of her leg, but she wasn't ready to bring it out into the open. She had already calculated what her next moves would be, and she couldn't afford to have her only weapon get away from her and go clattering around on the floorboard of the front seat. No, when the time came, she needed to have that gun in her hand and nowhere else.

She made a show of peering into the rearview mirror. "Oops," she said aloud after a long moment. "Here they come."

As the man behind her leaned forward again, peering into the rearview mirror to check for himself, Ali slammed on the brakes. The sudden change in momentum threw him forward against the back of the front seat. Cami, too, was propelled forward. Praying that the man's .38 had been knocked from his grip, Ali used both hands to pull the Yukon out of a 360-degree spin and bring it to an abrupt stop.

"You bitch!" he screamed behind her. "I'll kill you both."

Feeling a sudden pressure against the back of her seat, Ali knew for sure that her wild zigzagging had done the job. The man had crawled behind her seat and was reaching for his fallen weapon. That meant he was now on Cami's side of the SUV. Without a moment's hesitation, Ali pulled the sweat-covered Glock out from under her leg, raised it, and pulled the trigger, sending a bullet cleanly through the safety screen. The shot, fired at very close range, plugged him in the shoulder. Ali knew at once that it wasn't a fatal wound—she hadn't intended for it to be fatal—but the shot had succeeded in taking that damned .38 out of play on a permanent basis.

With the man bleeding, writhing, and howling in pain, Ali opened the back door. The .38 had come to rest against the doorjamb. Ali immediately grabbed it and flung it into the underbrush. Then, with a strength she didn't know she possessed, she took Cami by the arm and dragged her from the vehicle. Once Cami was safely on the ground, Ali slammed the door shut. The Tahoe was a cop car after all. Anybody who was imprisoned inside the back passenger seat behind the safety divider and with the doors locked wouldn't be going anywhere until someone on the outside opened the door.

Cami simply sank down on the pavement as though she didn't trust her legs to support her.

"Are you hurt?" Ali asked.

"You shot him!" Cami exclaimed breathlessly. "How did you do that?"

"First off, you have to have a gun," Ali said. "And if you're going to keep working on this job, you're not only going to have one, you're going to learn to use it. Now, call 911. Tell them we're about two miles east of the Bisbee roadblock with a gunshot victim in the back of Sheriff Brady's Tahoe. In the meantime, I'd better call B. I have a feeling all of this is going to take time, and I don't think we'll want to have that helicopter on standby while everything is being sorted out."

"Hey," B. said cheerfully when he answered. "I was worried about you and I'm glad to hear your voice. Are you on your way?"

"Not exactly," Ali said. "Cami and I may need some help getting back home."

"Why?" B. asked, sounding suddenly worried. "Did

something go haywire with the helicopter? Did you wreck the rental car?"

"No to both," Ali said. "You'll be happy to know that we seem to have solved at least part of your missing-LEGO problem, and I just shot one of the responsible parties."

"You did what?" B. demanded.

"You heard me," Ali said. "I shot the guy. He's not dead. He'll be fine eventually. Cami just called 911, and the cops are coming this way even as we speak. I'll have to tell you the rest of it later. Just get in the car and come get us. Please."

Joanna dragged her weary body into the house a full twenty hours after leaving it. Butch was already sound asleep. She'd called him earlier to tell him what was going on. Now, with him snoring softly beside her, Joanna lay on the bed and tried to force the day's ugly images out of her head.

What had started out as a single dead truck driver the day before had turned into the wholesale slaughter of eight people. The first victim, Alberto "Taquito" Mendoza, a small-time hood who regularly hauled stolen goods for Hans Holzmann and some of his coconspirators, had been shot to pieces gangster-style on the far side of the San Pedro.

Then there were the four truck drivers gunned down together in what was probably a single volley of bullets from an AK-47. It would be a long time before Joanna would be able to wipe that bloody carnage from her memory bank. They'd been slaughtered, mostly likely with the same weapon a Naco, Sonora, gangster wannabe had been carrying when Spike knocked him to the ground and chewed a hole in his wrist.

So far Joanna's people had managed to identify only one of the slain drivers. Undocumented immigrants, they had been recruited from the day-laborer pool at a Home Depot store in Tucson. None of them had been carrying driver's licenses at the time, so three of their names were still a mystery. The one they had identified was "known to law enforcement" due to three separate DUIs. He had been identified through fingerprint records.

Next came Helmer and Hans Holzmann, father and son. As far as Joanna knew, Helmer was a good man who had raised a wretch for a son. Ernie Carpenter and a relatively new member of the department, Deputy Jim Rider, had found the bodies of both Helmer and Hans Holzmann in the barn behind the house. Helmer's body exhibited clear signs of torture. Both men had been bound, gagged, and then shot to death execution-style.

And who was the mastermind behind all this? A lowlife named Lester Kraft who turned out to be pissed-off longshoreman from Long Beach who supplemented his "meager" $100,000-a-year salary by joining forces with group led by a corrupt U.S. Customs guy to smuggle contraband LEGO sets into the country. The fact that Hans Holzmann had been caught cheating on one of his erstwhile partners-in-crime was what had set this whole ugly killing spree in motion. Lester had hired a thug from Naco, Sonora, Julio Archuleta, to do the job, and he had evidently been responsible for most of the wet work—with the exception of Helmer and Hans. Archuleta was someone who had long been a person of interest in any number of criminal enterprises in southeastern Arizona, but this was the first time anyone had been able to catch him red-handed. Thank you, Spike.

Joanna still thought the whole idea of people being killed over LEGO sets was utterly preposterous, but those eight bodies lined up in Kendra Baldwin's morgue, awaiting autopsies, were all too real.

At last Joanna's brain shut down. She fell into a deep, dreamless sleep. Her eyes blinked open in the morning to see the sun shining in through her window high enough for her to understand that she was already late for work. When Butch opened the bedroom door, she knew exactly what he was doing—something he often did: bringing her that first morning cup of coffee. But this morning the very smell of it sent her racing into the bathroom, retching repeatedly into the toilet bowl.

Once she flushed the toilet and cleaned her face, she opened the door to find him standing there, still holding the coffee, his face awash in worry. "What's wrong? Are you sick?" he asked. "What can I do?"

"Get rid of the coffee," she said. "I can't stand the smell of it."

"But you love coffee."

"Not right now I don't."

He turned on his heel and took the coffee away. When he came back, he was grinning from ear to ear. "Are you really?" he asked, taking her in his arms and holding her close.

"I think so," Joanna groaned into his chest. "But when you go to the store later, pick up a pregnancy test. We need to know for sure."

"What's your reelection committee going to think?"

"It's none of their business. What do *you* think?"

"I'm delighted," Butch said. "And do you know what I want?"

"What?"

"A little girl with bright red hair and green eyes," Butch said, "just like her mother's."

Turn the page to read
the next gripping Ali Reynolds novel

CLAWBACK

Available in Spring 2016

Prologue

After years of running Sedona's Sugarloaf Café, Bob Larson was enjoying the fruits of his labors and one of the most enjoyable benefits of retirement—the opportunity to sit at the kitchen counter, linger over a second cup of coffee, and watch the morning news. Short-order cooks in diners never see the news at that time of day. They're always too busy dealing with the morning rush.

His attention had drifted momentarily to an Anna's hummingbird delicately sipping nectar from the blooming paloverde just outside the living room window, but the words "Ocotillo Fund Management" penetrated his consciousness and drew his attention back to the screen. Realizing he'd missed the first part of the story, he grabbed for the remote and ran the footage back to the beginning of the segment, so the sweet-faced, blond-haired news anchor could take another crack at it.

"Yesterday, employees at the Phoenix-based Ocotillo Fund Management arrived at work to find the doors chained shut. Late yesterday afternoon, the Securities and Exchange Commission announced that they are launching a full investigation into allegations that monies have gone missing. An unnamed company source and former employee said the move came as a complete surprise to all concerned. This morning, we've left several messages for the company's founder and CEO, Jason McKinzie. So far those messages have gone unanswered."

Ocotillo Fund Management? The company Bob and his wife, Edie, had chosen to manage their retirement funds? How could that be? With his heart hammering in his chest and both hands shaking, Bob set down his coffee mug and pulled his cell phone out of his pocket. Then he scrolled through his contacts list until he found Dan Frazier's number—numbers, actually—work, home in Sedona, home in Paradise Valley, and cell. He tried the cell as well as both home numbers. Those calls all went to voice mail. The last one—to the work number—didn't go through at all. Instead, there was a tuneless three-toned signal followed by the standard notification.

"The number you have reached is not in service at this time. If you feel you have reached this message in error, please check the number and try again."

Bob Larson did not try again. He ended the call and slipped the phone into the pocket of his worn khaki shirt. That was only to be expected. If the office's doors were locked, the phones would have been turned off as well. So it was hardly a surprise that there was no answer—no answer on the phones and no answers to his questions, either. Not to his questions so much as to his fears—the clutch of fear that grabbed his gut and twisted it, turning that last cup of morning coffee into acid.

Leaving both the remote and his coffee cup on the kitchen counter, he staggered over to one of the pair of comfortable easy chairs he and Edie had bought new when it came time to furnish their two-bedroom unit at Sedona Shadows. He was grateful Edie wasn't there and hadn't seen the news. She had been off at her morning water aerobics session. She was still down at the pool, doing whatever it was the ladies did for an hour or so every morning. Blissfully unaware, she had no idea of the financial calamity that had just befallen them, but Bob did. He understood it completely.

Their nest egg was gone. Wiped out. The safety net they had carefully put aside for a rainy day had evaporated. Much as Bob wanted to un-know the extent of what had just happened, he couldn't. He also knew it was his fault. Not his alone, of course—damn Dan Frazier, anyway. That was the thing that caused a white-hot knot of anger to form in Bob's gut. He and Dan were friends— friends first and clients later.

They'd known each other since their early twenties. When Dan's dream of becoming a CPA had come to grief, he'd gone to work in his father's property and casualty insurance agency there in town, where Bob and Edie Larson had been among his first customers. They'd stuck with him through the years as Dan's insurance business grew and prospered. Over time he had added an alphabet soup of official designations behind his name, enough incomprehensible letters to choke a horse, Chartered this and Certified that.

Somewhere along the way, Dan had hit the big time, partnering with Jason McKinzie, a young hotshot financial wizard who had taken central Arizona by storm. Jason had invited Dan to join Ocotillo Fund Management, and where Dan went, Bob and Edie inevitably followed.

Once on board the OFM juggernaut, Dan had continued to maintain his Sedona office, running the insurance part of the business with underlings, while he spent most of his time operating out of the corporate office in Phoenix—the very one where the doors had been locked and the phones were no longer in service.

Dan had been a regular at the Sugarloaf, back when Bob and Edie still owned it. He and Dan had worked several community service projects over the years, and when Dan was able to go to a Barrett-Jackson auction and come away with a fully restored 1966 Mustang convertible, he had come to Bob looking for advice on the care and feeding of it.

Through the years, Bob and Edie had salted away money for retirement, stashing it in Ocotillo-managed accounts that Dan had recommended. When Bob reached age seventy-and-a-half and had to start taking annual distributions from his retirement account, they'd still been running the restaurant and hadn't needed the money, so they had plugged those funds back into non-tax-deferred accounts with Ocotillo as well. When they had finally decided to sell the diner, Dan had used his connections to help locate the business broker who had effected the transaction. Since their unit in Sedona Shadows was essentially a rental, they'd had to pay a deposit, but they hadn't needed either a down payment or a mortgage. That's when they decided to put the proceeds from the sale of the restaurant into an Ocotillo account as well.

"Are you sure about that?" the always-practical Edie had asked. "Isn't that a lot like putting all our eggs in one basket?"

"Dan's a good friend," Bob had replied. "He wouldn't steer us wrong, would he?"

The problem was, he had steered them wrong. Bob remembered everything about their discussion that day, after the sale of the restaurant—every single word, and now all their retirement eggs were lost beyond repair. The news reporter had mentioned that the SEC was now involved, and Bob had no idea what that meant or what would happen next. Bankruptcy? Lawyers? All of that was above his pay grade, but Bob did understand that if lawyers got their grubby paws on the process, whatever happened next was bound to be expensive. If he and Edie were lucky—very lucky—they'd maybe get pennies back on the dollar from an amount that, with the sale of the diner as well as the accompanying living quarters, had risen to a total of over a million bucks.

When they sold the Sugarloaf, they had splurged on a new Buick for Edie—her toes-up Buick, as she called it—and on some new furniture for their unit at Sedona Shadows, but the rest of the money had been carefully salted away—with none other than Ocotillo Fund Management!

When Dan had first urged them to move their IRAs and defined benefit accounts over to Ocotillo, he had brought them a shiny, full-color prospectus.

"How can Jason McKinzie do this?" Edie had asked, after reading it through. "How is it possible for him to beat everyone else's earnings by two to four points?"

"By being smarter than the average bear," Dan had replied with an engaging grin. "He's bright enough to spot market corrections coming in advance. That way he unloads underachieving properties before things go south, and he has cash to reinvest while prices are still low. That's what you have to do in this business—be ahead of the curve."

In the end, though, having voiced her opinion, Edie had left it up to Bob to make the final decision. "I'm the one who knows everything there is to know about flour and yeast," she told him. "You're the one with the head for business."

Armed with Edie's somewhat grudging agreement, Bob had gone along with his old friend, Dan, and signed on the dotted line. Ocotillo had three separate funds for him to choose from, and Bob had opted for the most conservative of the three. Two points above the market was one thing. Four points or six? That sounded like too much of a good thing, so he had settled on the lowest of the three.

But now it was gone—all of it. Ocotillo was out of business. The office was locked, the phones were off. As for Jason McKinzie? He was most likely in the wind, but what about Dan Frazier—Bob's good friend, his old pal? What was he doing right about now? Did he have the good grace to at least feel guilty about what had happened? Was he ashamed of himself for not warning people in advance?

That was the thing Bob could hardly stomach. Dan must have known this was coming. The "unnamed source" the newscaster referred to, the one who said all this came as a "complete surprise," was maybe low enough on the totem pole that he had no idea about what was happening, but Dan was another story. He had been part of upper management in the firm—at least that was what he had always implied to Bob and Edie. If the venture was about to implode, he must have had some inkling in advance that something was wrong.

And yet, a few weeks earlier, when Bob and Edie had run into Dan and Millie Frazier at the annual Kiwanis Mother's Day Pancake Feed at the high school, Dan had been his jolly old self, glad-handing everyone who came within reach and giving the ladies, Edie included, discreet pecks on the cheek. It irked Bob now to realize that, the entire time, he had to have been putting on a show and pretending that everything was A-OK. He hadn't said a word to Bob that day that implied there was anything amiss. There hadn't been even the smallest hint that the firm was in trouble or that disaster was on its way.

Dan had been a businessman in town for decades, so it stood to reason that he was well known in the community, but today Bob couldn't help wondering how many other folks at that pancake breakfast had been duped out of their life savings in the same way he and Edie had. How many poor rubes had the snake-in-the-grass jerk greeted that morning with his firm handshake and misleading smile? Remembering that breakfast, Bob blinked back to the memory of introducing him to Betsy Peterson, one of Sedona Shadows's most recent arrivals and the grandmother of his grandson's wife, Athena.

Betsy was in the process of selling her properties in Minnesota, and Bob had intended to introduce her to Dan as well with the suggestion that she might consider putting her funds under Dan's management. She had said, "Thanks, but no thanks," as far as Dan was concerned. *Thank God for that!* Bob told himself. At least he had dodged that bullet.

Glancing at his watch, Bob realized that Edie and

Betsy would be finishing up with water aerobics any minute. To everyone's surprise, after arriving at Sedona Shadows, eighty-something Betsy had taken to Edie Larson and to water aerobics like nobody's business. The two women's daily joint sessions in the pool along with a shared interest in a set of mutual great-grandkids had helped Betsy and Edie form a fast friendship.

Right that moment, Bob wasn't ready to face either one of them and admit to either his wife or to her friend exactly what had happened. What he really wanted to do was track down Dan Frazier and punch the guy in the nose—or at least give the jerk a piece of his mind.

Bob stood up, grabbed his keys off the table by the door, and headed for the vintage '72 Bronco that—due to his skill as a mechanic—still ran like a top. Bob's aging Bronco and Dan Frazier's recently purchased Mustang were only six years apart in terms of model years, but no one would mistake Bob's workhorse vehicle for a showpiece. The Mustang was a low-mileage, highly polished, spoiled brat of a car, best used in fair-weather conditions only. The Bronco, on the other hand, dented but dependable, was a one-owner beast that had gotten Bob out of more than one tricky off-road situation. If the odometer—the one thing that didn't work—had still been functioning, Bob estimated it would have turned over for the fourth time well before this.

Not wanting to encounter the women on their way into the building, Bob double-timed it outside to his assigned covered parking spot. As he drove the three miles and many roundabouts on his way to Dan's place on the far side of town, Bob realized this was probably a fool's errand. Jason McKinzie had most likely run for the hills well in advance of the raid, and Dan Frazier might have pulled a similar stunt. Still, going to Dan's place gave Bob an excuse for not facing Edie right then and having to give her the bad news.

Dan Frazier's Sedona residence on Elberta Drive was modest in terms of Sedona's current real estate market, which tended toward the McMansion end of the housing spectrum. The house dated from an earlier time in his career, from when Dan had just started working for his father's insurance agency. The in-town location meant it was long on convenience and had reasonably good views. Still, this one was little more than humble pie when compared to the spectacular hillside residence Millie and Dan occupied in Paradise Valley. That one came complete with a four-car garage. The one in Sedona was only a two-car.

Once he turned off onto Elberta Drive, Bob stopped two houses short of the recently installed rolling gate at the bottom of Dan's driveway. For a time—a period of several minutes—Bob simply sat there with the car windows open and the engine running, trying to consider what the hell he was going to say to this man who had once been his friend: How could you do this? How dare you do this? What the hell kind of friend are you? None of those seemed adequate to the task.

At last, when Bob finally put the Bronco in gear to move forward, he was surprised to see that Dan's rolling gate stood wide open. It was one of those that could be set to open automatically for incoming traffic during the day and then locked down over night. Installed after the purchase of that prized Mustang, Bob never remembered seeing it left open before.

As soon as Bob turned into the Fraziers' driveway, one of the two garage doors began to rise. Once it was wide open, Bob could see that two cars were parked inside—Dan's Mustang and Millie's Volvo SUV. He more than half expected that one or the other of the vehicles would slam into gear and come speeding out of the garage. If the driver did so without looking, they'd probably crash straight into him. For sure, a collision like that would be harder on either of Dan's upscale vehicles than it would be on Bob's aging Bronco. Expecting the blow, Bob put the Bronco in park and waited, but nothing happened.

Neither of the cars moved. The backup lights didn't come on. There was no sign of life inside the garage. Tiring of waiting, Bob gave up, shut off the engine, and exited his own vehicle. Entering the garage, he heard the rumbling of the Mustang's V-8 engine, but no driver was visible behind the wheel.

"Hey, Dan," Bob called. "Are you in there?"

For a time, nothing happened. Then, over the hum of the engine, he heard a faint call. "Help me. Please."

Bob sprinted forward. When he was even with the driver's door and could see inside the open window, he realized Dan was in the vehicle after all—slumped over against the passenger seat so his head wasn't visible over the seat back. What was visible was blood—way too much blood—from what looked like either a bullet or stab wound to the gut.

Bob had served as a corpsman in Vietnam. He knew his way around bloody wounds, and he knew what needed to be done. He pulled his phone out of his pocket and dialed 911. "We need help," he barked into the phone. "Man down and seriously wounded. Can't tell if it's a gunshot wound or a knife wound."

"Knife," Dan managed. "He had a knife."

"Make that a knife wound," Bob corrected.

With his phone still on speaker, Bob gave the emergency dispatch operator Dan's address. Then, with the call still active, he slipped the device into his shirt pocket, freeing both hands so he could reach inside, hoping to apply pressure on the wound even though he already suspected that the damage was too severe. The wound was bleeding profusely. Even at first glance, Bob doubted it was survivable.

"Tried to go for help," Dan mumbled weakly, batting away Bob's suddenly bloodied hand. "Go check on Millie," he urged. "Please!"

"Millie?" Bob asked. "Where is she?"

"House. She's in the house."

"Help is coming," Bob assured him, drawing away. "I'll go check."

After first switching off the Mustang's engine, Bob raced into the house through a door that opened into the laundry room. There were bloodied footprints staggering from side to side and leading from the kitchen into the garage. Most likely Dan had come this way, in an attempt either to escape the carnage or to summon help. Bob registered the stains on the floor and reflexively tried to dodge them, but he was too focused on moving fast to avoid the bloodied footprints entirely.

Once through the laundry room, he came to an abrupt halt and stood unmoving in the kitchen doorway. Millie Frazier lay facedown in the center of the room in a rapidly expanding pool of blood. What looked to be a butcher knife was buried to the hilt between her shoulder blades.

Horrorstruck, Bob didn't know what to do. Should he try to check for a pulse that most likely wasn't there or simply retreat the way he had come? Then, in the sudden silence, a tiny voice spoke to him from his pocket. "Sir, are you still there? Emergency units are on the way."

"There are two victims," he said. "Two stabbing victims—one in the garage and one in the house. It looks like one of them is dead."

That was the moment when Millie Frazier shuddered. Up to that moment, he had been sure she was dead. Darting across the room to where she lay, he slipped in pooled blood and fell forward. When he came to rest, he was lying facedown on the injured woman's back only inches from the hilt of the knife. Sheer luck had kept him from landing on it full force. It took a moment for him to heave himself off her and scoot to a spot where his face was near hers, close enough so she could see him. Her eyes blinked open, but they were dazed and out of focus.

"It's me, Millie," he said. "Bob Larson. I've called 911. Help is on the way. They'll be here soon. Who did this to you?"

For a moment her eyes seemed to register recognition. "Bob?" she mumbled. "But where's Dan?"

"He's out in the garage," Bob answered. "He's still alive."

"He's a good man," she whispered. "Tell him I love him. Be sure to tell him that."

The focus faded from her eyes. Her impossibly shallow breathing became even more so.

"Stay with me," Bob pleaded, taking her hand and

holding it in hopes of comforting her. "Someone will be here soon."

But it was too late. After a moment, eyes that had blinked open at the sound of his voice stared emptily into space. Bob checked again for a pulse. This time it wasn't there. Scrambling to his feet, he slipped and fell to his knees. He had to grab hold of the countertop to pull himself back upright. Back on his feet, he dashed out of the room the same way he had entered.

Back in the garage, he leaned into the car and then stepped away once more. The wail of oncoming sirens cut through the silence, but Bob knew the EMTs would be too late twice over. Millie Frazier was gone, and so was her husband. The tiny voice of the emergency operator still spoke to him from his pocket, demanding an update. Reaching for the phone, he simply ended the call, paying no attention to the bloody prints he left on the face of his phone.

With sickening clarity, Bob Larson understood that once the cops arrived, they would find three bloodied people at the residence. Only one of them would be alive—the guy who had called it in—and he was most likely the one who would become their prime suspect.

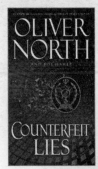